W9-CND-316

THE RELUCTANT CONSTABLE

Recent Titles by Sara Fraser from Severn House

A BITTER LEGACY
THE TROOPER'S WIFE
THE WORKHOUSE DOCTOR

THE RELUCTANT CONSTABLE

Sara Fraser

severn House

This first world edition published in Great Britain 2007 by
SEVERN HOUSE PUBLISHERS LTD of
9–15 High Street, Sutton, Surrey SM1 1DF.
This first world edition published in the USA 2007 by
SEVERN HOUSE PUBLISHERS INC of
595 Madison Avenue, New York, N.Y. 10022.

British Library Cataloguing in Publication Data

Fraser, Sara
  The reluctant constable
  1. Police - England - Worcestershire - Fiction 2. Great
  Britain - History - George IV, 1820-1830 - Fiction
  3. Detective and mystery stories
  I. Title
  823.9'14[F]

ISBN-13: 978-0-7278-6525-0   (cased)

All Severn House titles are printed on acid-free paper.

Typeset by Palimpsest Book Production Ltd.,
Grangemouth, Stirlingshire, Scotland.
Printed and bound in Great Britain by
MPG Books Ltd., Bodmin, Cornwall.

One

Redditch Township, Parish of Tardebigge, Worcestershire
March 31st, 1826

It was five o'clock and in the darkness of early morning the half-timbered house was only a black shadowy bulk to the eyes of the man watching from his hiding place in the clump of woodland. The bitterly cold wind was gusting, rattling leafless branches, rustling dry gorse shrubs, penetrating the watcher's clothing to enfold his clammy skin in its icy embrace. Yet he was impervious to any physical discomfort. The demons in his mind were all powerful, all dominant, relentlessly driving him onwards to assuage the lusts of his body.

A faint glow suddenly appeared in one of the ground-floor windows, and the watcher's breathing quickened. Breaking from cover he moved stealthily towards the glimmering light, his boots crunching on the hard-frosted ground. He reached the window and carefully positioning himself at the side peered through the lowest of the bulbous-glassed panes, inwardly cursing the misshapen glass for distorting the image that he saw.

Inside the room the girl was standing in her nightshift staring at herself in the large cracked mirror that hung on the wall beside the curtainless leaded window, while her three younger sisters were still asleep in the large bed that she shared with them. She pulled the nightshift over her head and cast it aside, then studied her naked reflection, turning and twisting her shapely, high-breasted body so that the gentle light of the candle shimmered upon her white flesh.

The watcher's breath rasped in his throat, and as his excitement intensified guttural moans dribbled through his slack wet lips. His right hand moved beneath his greatcoat, pushing down into his breeches to fondle and knead his throbbing manhood. His left hand pulled the sharp-bladed knife from his pocket and stabbed it again and again and again into the timbers of the wall.

The room door opened and an older woman bustled in, scolding.

'Will you get on and get yourself dressed, our Amy, and give over gawping at yourself in that glass.'

She suddenly looked across at the window, and moved quickly to it, cupping her hands to her eyes to shield them from the candlelight as she peered through the bulbous panes.

'What's up?' the girl asked curiously.

'I thought I saw something move outside,' the woman told her, then shrugged her shoulders dismissively. 'Well, there aren't nothing there that I can see. Now get yourself dressed right this minute, or you won't have time to eat your breakfast, because then you'll be late for work; and Tommy Fowkes has already give you a warning about coming late, aren't he.'

Amy Danks grinned cheekily. 'And I've already give Tommy Fowkes a warning about letting his hands wander too free. I told him, I'm a respectable girl from the Mount Pleasant, not some loose-living drab from Silver Street. So you keep your hands to yourself, Tommy Fowkes, or else my dad'll be paying you a visit, and it won't be a friendly visit neither.'

Her mother tried to frown disapprovingly at her eldest daughter, but could not restrain a giggle.

'I don't know where you gets your sauce from, my wench; it aren't from me, and that's a fact . . . Now get dressed, 'ull you, afore your dad gets up. He won't stand for your nonsense like I does.'

Outside, lying flat and pressed close against the wall beneath the window, the man waited until the muffled voices ceased and the candlelight disappeared, then as stealthily as he had come he disappeared back into the sheltering woodland. But the lusts raging through his body had not been assuaged, the demonic voices in his mind were still all powerful, all dominant, and he obeyed their commands, and went in search of other consummation.

Beneath the wayside hedge the old tramp woman awoke from restless sleep, shivering uncontrollably, her body aching from the cold. Groaning with the pain of her stiffened joints, she clambered to her feet, and stood for some moments trying to decide which way to go. She was weak with hunger, sick and feverish, and knew that she must find food and shelter very quickly, or die from want and exposure.

'I've got to get straight to the poorhouse. This fuckin' weather'll be the death o' me else.'

She hobbled slowly and painfully along the narrow lane wishing that the dawn would come so that at least she could determine her whereabouts.

The sounds of approaching hoof-beats came to her ears. She halted, peering short-sightedly up and down the twisting lane, and when the horseman came around the bend before her called hoarsely, 'Can you help me, Master. I needs to get to the poorhouse.'

The horseman reined in, and asked, 'Are there more of you around?'

'No. I'm by meself.'

'Well then, you're in luck. I'm heading in that direction. I'll show you the shortcut through the woods. It's not far.'

'Bless you, Master! Bless you! You're a bloody godsend, so you are.'

The horseman led the way along the lane and the old woman hobbled behind, gasping for breath even though the horse was only travelling at a slow walk.

The lane entered dense woodland and the horseman swung off onto a narrower track which led deep into the trees.

'Do it now!' urged the voices in his head. 'Do it now!'

In a small clearing surrounding a brick-and-timber shanty he reined to a halt and dismounted, tethering the horse to a low hanging branch.

'We'm not there yet, am we? There's no fuckin' house here?' The old woman peered about her, fearful suspicion rapidly burgeoning. 'There's just a shed here! It aren't no poorhouse! What's you stopping for? I aren't got nothing to rob! I aren't got nothing!'

'Oh yes, you've got something all right,' the horseman hissed breathily, and the sharp blade in his hand rammed through the tramp's layers of rags, burying itself deep in the sagging flesh.

The old woman screamed in shock and terror as she

staggered backwards, and the horseman followed, stabbing again and again and again.

The screaming woman collided with the horse. Frightened, the beast reared and bolted, breaking the slender branch as it tore the reins free and went crashing through the thick undergrowth.

The tramp crumpled to the ground, her screams choking on her own blood. Dribbling guttural moans through his slack wet lips the horseman sank down onto his knees, kneading his groin with both bloodstained hands, watching his victim jerking spasmodically, choking on blood, until the final shudder of death. Only then did the he achieve his gasping, orgasmic satisfaction; and still panting heavily rose and moved away to go in search of his bolted horse.

Two

The Fox and Goose Inn standing on the southern side of the wide triangular central green of Redditch Town was the favoured meeting place for the men who considered themselves to be the ruling class of the parish of Tardebigge. Now at ten o'clock on this bitterly cold final morning of the month of March 1826, certain of these rulers, all influential members of the select vestry, were gathering at the inn, each man obsequiously greeted at the door by the huge-bellied innkeeper, Tommy Fowkes, his florid features sheened with sweat despite the frosty air, audibly grunting with the effort of bowing low.

'It's an honour to receive you, Mr Hemming, sir.

'It's an honour to receive you, Mr Milward, sir.

'Mr Smallwood, sir! What an unexpected honour. I do hope that you're fully recovered from your unfortunate accident, sir?

'It's an honour to receive you, Parson Clayton.' The Reverend John Clayton was a unusually ugly young man who possessed an exceptionally muscular physique.

Fowkes shepherded each newcomer into the best bar parlour

where, before a roaring fire, comfortable chairs and a table of food and drink, attended by a pert young serving girl, had been set out for their pleasure. Tommy Fowkes himself took their cloaks, top hats and gloves and hung them on the wall hooks, before bowing out of their presence.

All the newcomers accepted glasses of wine from the serving girl, who was then dismissed from the room by John Clayton.

'This matter is best kept to ourselves, I believe, gentlemen.' He smiled at his companions, who stared frowningly back at his rugged features.

'Then let us get on with the business, if you please, Parson,' William Hemming snapped tersely. 'Time means money to we masters, and I for one don't wish to waste hours on this matter. We three have more pressing affairs to be dealing with, unlike yourself, Parson.'

'Hear hear.' His two fellow men of business supported him.

Despite the instant resentment that flared within him at the other man's belittling tone, John Clayton kept the smile on his lips. As a lowly, virtually penniless curate he could not risk antagonizing these rich and powerful needle masters; they were the dominant force in this district, which was the world-wide centre of the needle industry.

'The matter in question is that of the appointment of the new parish constable, gentlemen. Not one of the men listed is willing to serve in that capacity. They are all voicing the very strongest of objections.'

'None of them ever wants to be constable.' Hemming's thin lips twisted in a grim smile. 'But the thought of having to pay ten sovereigns' penalty for refusing to do their lawful duty always changes their minds for them, don't it.'

'Of course it does,' Samuel Smallwood interjected irritably, 'so just take any name from the list and tell the bugger that he's the new parish constable, and if he don't like it, he must lump it!' He reached out his hand. 'Here, give me the list, Parson, and we'll settle this matter in a jiffy.'

Clayton gave the sheet of paper into the other man's grasp.

Smallwood took a small magnifying glass from his inner pocket and quickly scanned the names, muttering them aloud. 'Clement, Abbot, Andrews, Huins, Robinson, Potts?' He frowned. 'Who's this bugger? I can't recall his name. Thomas Potts? Who's he when he's about?'

'Never mind who he might be, he's now the new constable,' William Hemming growled. 'Are we all agreed, gentlemen.'

He paused, they nodded and he declared, 'That's settled then, Parson. You can send the crier to tell this Potts chap that he's to attend here in this room tomorrow morning at ten o'clock sharp to be sworn in by the magistrates.'

Outside the closed door of the bar parlour, Amy Danks, the young serving girl, had her ear firmly pressed against the keyhole. She held her hand over her mouth in shocked concern.

'Tom Potts to be the constable? Oh my lord. Oh my lord! Poor Tom ! Just wait till the pointer lads gets hold of him. He'll get bloody slaughtered if he tries to put one of them in the lock-up after they've had a skinful of drink.'

Three

Elderly, stoop-shouldered Jimmy Grier, resplendent in the uniform of plumed tricorne hat, scarlet waistcoat and green tailcoat of the town crier of Redditch and its southerly satellite villages of Headless Cross and Crabbs Cross, was cursing the cold weather.

'Damn and blast you for bringing my rheumatics back on to me! Damn and blast you!'

For two hours he had shuffled painfully up and down the hilly streets of the town, halting at intervals to ring his brass bell, and bawl hoarsely, 'Oyez Oyez. . . . Butcher Vincent has freshly killed beef in store . . . Grocer Groby begs to inform his patrons that a new package of China tea has arrived . . . . The funeral of the Widow Powell is this coming Friday morn. All mourners to be at St Stephen's chapel at nine o'clock sharp . . . And the select vestry have this day appointed Master Thomas Potts to be parish constable . . . God save the King!'

When Grier reached the wide triangular plateau of the green he took shelter from the biting north-east wind in the doorway of the small Chapel of St Stephen, which stood on the green facing west across the broad roadway to the row of shops and houses on the opposite side.

As he rubbed his sore joints he peered through watery eyes at the huddled group of ragged-shawled women and small barefoot children who were standing outside Charles Scambler's bakery, begging departing customers for bread.

Another elderly man joined him in the doorway.

'There'll be big troubles in this town afore long, Jimmy. You mark my words if there won't. I've seen it all afore. There's too many poor buggers nigh on starving to death. There'll be bread riots here again if things don't alter. You mark my words if there won't.'

Grier nodded sadly. 'I reckon you'm right. But it's the same trouble all over the bloody country, aren't it. All the trade's gone flat, and it'll get worse afore it gets better, you can be sure o' that.' He grimaced and complained, 'But I've got enough of me own troubles, 'aven't I. I've got to go all the bloody way up Mount Pleasant to tell Master Thomas Potts he's the new constable, and me rheumatics is playing me up something cruel.'

'Thomas Potts? Who's he when he's about? What's his trade?'

'I can't say.' Green shrugged his shoulders. 'There was a surgeon o' that name hereabouts when I was still a young nipper, but the family left the district years ago and went off abroad somewhere. Some said that they'd been left a lot of money and a big estate by some relation who'd died. Anyway, all I knows is that this Potts come here to live a couple o' years since, and because he's got a rateable tenement then he can be made to be constable. But judging by the amount o' rate he's paying, he aren't living rich, I shouldn't think.'

'Well, sooner him than me be made constable.' The other man chuckled grimly. 'There's too many wrong 'uns in this town for any Christian soul to keep in order.'

'You'm right there.' Grier sighed heavily and slowly trudged away.

The isolated, tumbledown, two-storeyed cottage was almost a mile distant from St Stephen's Chapel. It stood back from the rutted track which topped the long ridgeway running southwards and upwards from the flat central plateau of Redditch town to link with the hamlets of Headless Cross and Crabbs Cross.

Dusk was falling when Jimmy Grier hammered on the weathered front door, his mood made foul by his badly aching joints.

A very tall, gangly bodied, dark-haired man who looked to be in his early thirties, and was dressed in a plain rustic smock and knee breeches, answered the summons.

'You'll be Master Potts? Thomas Potts?' Grier demanded gruffly.

'I am.' Tom Potts nodded.

'I been sent here on official business, to tell you that you've been appointed as the new constable of the parish o' Tardebigge.'

'Me? Appointed as constable?' Tom Potts' dark eyes and long lean features mirrored his shocked dismay. 'On whose authority?'

'On the authority of the gentlemen o' the select vestry of the parish o' Tardebigge, Master Potts. And you'm to come down to the Fox and Goose by ten o'clock sharp tomorrow morn, to be sworn in by Lord Aston, and the Reverend Timmins, them being the lawful magistrates of this here parish and county. I'll say goodnight to you.'

Tom Potts stood watching the departing crier until the man was lost to sight in the deepening dusk. Then a woman's voice shouted querulously from within the cottage, 'Thomas! Thomas! Will you shut that door! You're letting all the heat out! You great lummox, you! And the lamp needs lighting! It's pitch-black in here! My God! If ever in Creation's time any poor woman was cursed with such a useless great lummox of a son as I've been, then I'd like to know who it was, and I'd weep over the poor soul's grave for pity of her sufferings.'

Tom sighed resignedly, and closed the door.

Four

The Right Honourable and Reverend Walter Hutchinson, Lord Aston, considered that his secular position as justice of the peace for the county of Worcestershire, and his spiritual position as the vicar of Tardebigge parish, were scant rewards for a man of his immense abilities and attainments. In the privacy of his own thoughts he constantly reproached God for His cruelty in not rewarding His faithful servant, Walter Hutchinson, with more elevated and powerful spiritual and secular posts, and a greater portion of worldly wealth. His bitter discontent with his own station in life caused him to regard all those about him with either resentful envy or utter contempt, attitudes reflected by the constant sour expression on his heavy sallow features and his manner of address to those whom he looked upon as beneath him, which was virtually everyone of lower rank than an earl or a bishop.

His solace in life was gluttony, a comfort to which his bulky body and bulging jowls bore ample testimony. But even this pleasure took its toll, and he was a martyr to frequent attacks of chronic indigestion, a bodily affliction for which he also reproached his long-suffering God.

It was unfortunate for the malefactors at this morning's special sessions, held in the bar parlour of the Fox and Goose, that Hutchinson had breakfasted upon a huge plateful of broiled beefsteaks and onions and a bottle of port wine, a combination which invariably brought on an attack of indigestion, which in its turn ensured that the several offenders would receive the very maximum punishments that could be awarded by the law.

Tom Potts, top hat in hand, was standing in the empty tap room waiting to be summoned before the bench. He felt tense and nervous, and his fingers were fidgety upon the worn nap of his shabby hat.

'Hello, Master Tom.' Amy Danks smiled as she came into the room, and pointed to the low ceiling beams. 'You'll not be able put your hat on in here, will you, without walking on your knees. You'm too tall by far for this roof.'

'So I am, Amy,' Tom agreed readily. He was very fond of this pertly pretty young girl, one of the numerous offspring of his nearest neighbour, Josiah Danks, a gamekeeper in the service of the Earl of Plymouth, who owned vast tracts of land in Tardebigge and the neighbouring parishes.

'You'm looking very fine, Master Tom.' She stared admiringly at his dark broadcloth coat, plum-coloured waistcoat, pantaloons, high collar and silken cravat. 'You looks like a real gentleman.'

'Why thank you, Amy.' Tom was touched by the open admiration in her expression, but was ruefully conscious of the holes in the soles of his highly polished boots, and the advanced age of the clothing he wore. 'But truth to tell, if you were to look more closely you'd see that what I'm wearing has been much worn and is starting to fray badly.'

'That don't matter to me. I still reckon that you looks like a real gentleman,' she asserted warmly, and her eyes shone with something much warmer than mere admiration. She seemed about to say something more, but a man entered the room.

'Draw me a glass o' cider, Amy, I'm parched.'

'Yes, Master Cashmore.' She moved behind the narrow-topped bar counter.

Tom recognized the stockily built man as Joseph Cashmore, the incumbent parish constable, and greeted him politely.

'Good morning, Master Cashmore. My name is Thomas Potts. I'm waiting to be sworn in as your replacement.'

Cashmore regarded him levelly. 'I've heard your name, Master Potts, but haven't ever spoke with you afore to my recollection.'

'And a very good name it is too, Master Cashmore. There's none of the Potts family ever been in your lock-up.' Amy grinned cheekily and placed the pewter tankard of cider on the bar.

'Well, I've heard nothing bad of it, I do say,' Cashmore acknowledged. 'Will you take a drink with me, Master Potts?'

'At any other time I'd be honoured to drink with you, Master Cashmore. But I think that it's best I don't take any drink until after I've seen the magistrates.' Tom smiled. 'But could I trouble you to give me advice on how best to act as a constable?'

The other man grimaced and pointed to a scar on his brow. 'Gladly, Master Potts. Just take care to duck and dodge when the pointer lads are on the randy.' Then he added with a frown, 'I'll tell you truly that I'm bloody glad my year is over and done with. Being constable is a rotten job. There's no pay for it. You have to turn your own neighbours in, and sometimes even haul your own kith and kin afore the beaks . . . And you get no thanks from anybody, even when you're doing the right and lawful thing. And what's more, the way matters are going in this country, and in this parish, things'll be a bloody sight worse afore they gets better for any o' them who are unlucky enough to be constables.

'Anyway, I'm done with it now because I've just handed my staff back to the bench, and I'm no longer the constable o' this parish . . . Thank the Lord!'

He lifted the tankard from the counter, drained it empty in a series of long noisy gulps, then slammed it down on to the counter.

'Put that one on my tab, Amy, and I'll settle it come Saturday. I'm off to move my stuff back into my own house.' Without another word he turned on his heel and walked out through the door.

Trepidation invaded Tom, in company with a fast burgeoning sense of depression.

Amy noted his sombre expression and tried to cheer him up.

'You don't want to pay heed to what Cashmore says, Master Tom. I've heard a few things while working here, I can tell you. I've heard that Cashmore made a good thing out of being constable. He was up to all the dodges and made good money, and that's the Gospel truth that is. And it wasn't any pointer what give him that scar. It was some showmen off the fair because he'd cheated 'em out of some money. He deserved what they give him, and more besides.'

Tom forced a wan smile. 'It doesn't signify who left him with a mark, Amy. The truth is that I'm no good at fisticuffs, and never have been. I don't believe that I'm able to over-power any man and arrest him, and that is what constables need to be capable of doing, isn't it.' He shook his head and muttered despondently, 'I fear that I'm a weakly, cowardly sort of fellow, Amy.'

'I don't believe so,' she contradicted forcefully. 'Not for a moment!'

Tom's nervous tension created a physical response, and he was abruptly assailed by an overwhelming need to relieve himself.

'I must use the privy, Amy. Where is it?'

'Go along the passage out to the back and then go down towards the bottom of the yard. The stink'll guide you to it once you'm that far.

*   *   *

'Thomas Potts? Thomas Potts? Present yourself before the bench!'

The loud shouts echoed and re-echoed throughout the inn.

'Thomas Potts? Present yourself before the bench!'

The repeated summons sounded faintly in Tom's ears where he sat upon the rough wooden boarding of the stench-filled privy, his trousers and drawers around his ankles.

He frantically scrabbled at his clothing as he rushed from the privy and back towards the inn.

'Devil take you, Potts! How dare you have the insolence to keep me waiting?' Walter Hutchinson roared in fury. 'How dare you? How dare you? I'll make you sorry for it, damn you! I'll make you sorry!'

Momentarily taken aback by this unexpected onslaught, Tom could only stare bewilderedly at the scene before him. The two magistrates were seated in armchairs facing the door: a third man, Joseph Blackwell, the clerk to the magistrates, was seated to one side of them at a table strewn with papers, ledgers, inkwells, quill pens and a large Bible.

The magistrates were clad alike in the black full-skirted coats, breeches and stockings of their calling, both with white, short-queued tie-wigs perched upon their heads. There the similarity ended, because Reverend Timmins was as woefully pasty-faced and meagre-bodied as the Lord Aston was purple-faced and fat.

'Well, man? Well? Well?' Hutchinson bellowed.

Tom gathered his senses, and sought to mollify the other man. He bowed respectfully 'I do most humbly apologize, my lord. I was forced to answer a most pressing call of nature.'

'Nature? Call of nature?' Hutchinson's bloodshot eyes bulged in disbelief that he could have heard such an excuse. 'You dare to say this to me. Let me tell you something, whatever your name is. There can be no call of nature that takes precedence over the summons to appear before me! Remember that fact in future, or it will go very hard with you. And that is a true fact of nature!'

The small-statured, pedantic-mannered Joseph Blackwell Esquire, now smoothly intervened.

'If you will forgive the intrusion, my lord, might I respectfully remind you that the Earl is expecting your arrival at your

earliest convenience; and that since this is now the only business left to be dealt with, it can be very quickly completed
to your lordship's satisfaction. The Earl is most eager for the
pleasure of your company, my lord.'

'Humpphh!' Hutchinson grunted, and taking this for his
compliance Blackwell beckoned Tom to his desk.

'Can you read and write, Master Potts?'

'I can.'

'Very well, take the Bible in your right hand, this paper in
your left hand, and repeat in a clear voice what is written
thereon.'

Tom cleared his throat, and read aloud. 'I, Thomas Potts,
of Redditch in the parish of Tardebigge, do swear that I will
well and truly serve our sovereign lord, the King, in the office
of constable for the Parish of Tardebigge, for the year now
next following—'

'Stop reading!' Hutchinson roared, and swung to order
Blackwell. 'He must take the other oath, as a corrective for
his insolent tardiness in appearing before this bench.'

'Very well, my lord,' Blackwell answered submissively, and
with a warning frown to Tom took back the first paper and
replaced it with another. 'Be well advised, Master Potts, that
Lord Aston is empowered by law to command this alternative form of oath to be taken by you. Now read on.'

'I, Thomas Potts . . . do swear that I will well and truly
serve our sovereign lord, the King, in the office of constable
for the Parish of Tardebigge until another constable shall be
sworn in my stead, according to the best of my skill and
knowledge. So help me God.'

'You can instruct this fellow in his duties, Blackwell. I must
go immediately to wait upon the Earl.' Hutchinson laboriously
pushed himself up from the chair and waddled ponderously
out of the room, with the Reverend Timmins tiptoeing close
behind him.

The full realization of what he had just sworn to do caused
Tom to indignantly confront Joseph Blackwell.

'This is not fair, sir! You've tricked me into swearing to
serve as a constable for God only knows how long.'

The smaller man was unabashed. 'No, Master Potts, I did
not trick you into anything. But let this be a salutary warning
to you. If you anger Lord Aston again, then he will most

certainly give you cause to regret doing so. He is a bad man to cross.'

From among the heap of papers on the table Blackwell lifted a small leather-bound book and a thin sheaf of printed pages, and pressed both into Tom's hands. 'Take these and study them well. The book contains all the laws now in force relating to parish business, and the duties and obligations of all parish officers, including your own as constable. These papers contain the details and the tables for any expenses and fees you are entitled to lay claim to when fulfilling your official duties. If you have any questions concerning those duties and obligations then you may call upon me at my office, which is situated at the top of the Fish Hill.'

Blackwell bent and lifted from under his chair a wooden crown-topped blue, red and gold painted truncheon nearly three feet in length and placed it on the table.

'And here is your badge of office, Master Potts.' The hint of a smile played around his lips. 'You will discover that it is a more formidable weapon than it first appears. The top six inches are filled with lead. So take care that you don't cave in any skulls when you wield it . . . Master Cashmore will deliver the keys of the lock-up over to you tomorrow, and now I bid you good day.'

He gathered the ledgers, papers, inkwells, quill pens and Bible in his arms and left Tom staring disconsolately at the truncheon.

Amy Danks reappeared, and frowned with concern. 'You looks as if you've lost a pound and found a penny, Master Tom.'

He shrugged and smiled ruefully. 'It's April the first, isn't it, Amy, All Fools' Day; and I can't help feeling that I've just been made a fool of. I could well end up serving as constable for years.'

'Will you be moving your things today?'

'Moving? Moving my things? Why would I do that?'

'Well, you'll be living in the lock-up now that you'm constable, won't you. Cashmore had to live there, and he didn't half used to moan about it, as well. He used to say why should he have to live in that bloody hole when he had a perfectly good house of his own to live in . . . But it made no odds. Lord Aston said that he'd got to live there, like it or lump it, because the constable has to be in the middle o' the town where people can easily find him. And when there's prisoners in the lock-up then the constable has to be there to stop them breaking free.'

Tom shook his head in dismay. 'My God! It just gets better and better, doesn't it! I shudder to think what my mother will have to say about being taken to live in the lock-up. She rants at me continually now because we live in a rented cottage, instead of a mansion of our own.'

The girl's blue eyes sparkled with mischievous amusement, and she giggled. 'Never mind, Master Tom. At least you'll be living rent-free, won't you, so you can put the money you'll be saving towards buying a mansion of your own.'

Her cheeky high spirits were infectious, and Tom could not help but chuckle with her.

'Indeed I shall, Amy. I'll go now and tell my mother the good news. I'm sure that it will cheer her immensely.'

The trio of young men lounging against the railings of St Stephen's burial yard on the corner of the central crossroads were dressed alike. On their shaggy-haired heads they wore square hats fashioned from brown paper. Their waistcoats were leather, their shirts red. Around their throats they sported garishly coloured neckerchiefs. All wore knee breeches, thick woollen stockings and wooden-soled clogs.

The occasional passers-by, seeing their rig-outs, the virtual uniform favoured by the town's needle-pointers, gave them a wide berth, just in case even at this early hour they might be already drunk and spoiling for trouble.

Tom came out of the Fox and Goose and walked towards the crossroads some forty yards distant, self-consciously carrying his constable's staff. He saw the trio, and gulped nervously. 'I hope they're not looking for trouble. That's the last thing that I need today.'

The needle-pointers of Redditch Town were a notorious breed of men. Their work was the dry-grinding of needle points. Sitting on a wooden saddle bending close over whirling grindstones, the rows of needles between his flattened palms jetting out showers of sparks as he ground the points, a pointer could earn anything up to four or five pounds a week, compared to the average earnings of other needle workers of eight to ten shillings. The simple reason the pointers were so well paid was that their work killed them within seven or eight years. The fine steel and stone dust thrown up by the whirling grindstones entered their lungs and mercilessly lacerated the cells until the tissues filled with blood and literally drowned them. There would at any given time be between a hundred and twenty and a hundred and fifty pointers working throughout the needle district. None would be under twenty years of age, and only a mere handful aged more than twenty-eight.

It was only the wildest and most reckless men who would become pointers. Men who deliberately chose a short and merry life with ample money to spend on drink and women in preference to the longer life of drudgery and comparative poverty of their fellow workers. Knowing that they faced almost certain early and agonizing deaths, the pointers were uncaring of any consequences of their drunken debaucheries. They showed little or no respect for the morals and mores of civilized society, and they brawled with the savagery of wild beasts – attributes which had caused them to become feared throughout the needle district and farther regions.

As Tom drew nearer to the trio he deliberately kept his gaze directly forwards so as not to make any eye contact with them.

Sandy-haired, scar-faced, Ritchie Bint, the biggest and oldest of the trio, noticed Tom's approach, and he grinned when he saw the gaudily painted staff in the tall man's hand.

'Well now, lads, just take a gander at that long streak o' piss across the road theer. I reckon he'll be our new constable. Him that was being cried around town yesterday, of the name of Thomas Potts.'

Tommy Chance and John Hancox stared closely.

'Bloody hell! I's seen more meat on a fuckin' drumstick!' Chance's broken, yellowed teeth bared in a contemptuous snarl. 'What's his trade? He don't look to have the bloody muscle to be able to do more than a bit o' sewing and knitting.'

John Hancox, short and broad-shouldered, had been a pointer for only two months, and his twenty-year-old features were still fresh and rosy, not yet displaying the ravages of excessive drinking, murderous toil and ferocious brawling that marked the faces of his companions. He was itching to prove himself to be as wild and reckless as they were, and suddenly recognized that here was the ideal opportunity.

The tall gangly figure of the new constable was some fifteen yards distant across the road, passing them with his gaze set stiffly forwards.

Hancox snatched up a stone from the dirt roadway and hurled it with all his force to impact upon the passing man's top hat and knock it flying from his head.

Tom was momentarily stunned with surprise at feeling his hat thumped from his head. He halted in bewilderment, staring blankly down at the hat lying on the gravel. At the crossroads a bevy of shawled and bonneted housewives out shopping had stopped to exchange gossip, and the one of them who had seen the stone thrown, excitedly told her friends what had happened. All turned in unison to gaze with avid interest at the victim and his assailant, while a passing horseman reined in his mount to watch.

Ritchie Bint and Tommy Chance roared with jeering laughter, and young Hancox puffed out his chest and preened in pride.

Tom turned his gaze towards the jeering men, desperately trying to marshal his thoughts. To make sense of what had happened.

Ritchie Bint pointed at the top hat and shouted, 'Aye, mate, is that your hat? You'd best pick it up afore it gets trod on.'

Tom was being torn by mixed emotions. Fear of physical confrontation, growing anger and above all else, confusion. He just did not know what he should do. How should he react?

'What's you looking at us like that for, mate?' Tommy Chance snarled aggressively. 'We aren't done nothing to you.' He pointed eastwards towards the Fox and Goose. 'The kid who chucked that stone at you run into that entryway next to the pub theer.'

'And he'll be miles away afore you can lay hands on him, if you keeps on standing there like a bloody mawkin. So if I was you I'd pick me hat up and get after him,' Ritchie Bint advised with a jeering grin, and jerked his head at his friends. 'Come on, lads, we got time for a couple o' pints afore we goes to work.'

The trio swaggered away, passing across the front of the chapel, heading towards the Crown Inn on the top of the long

Fish Hill, which fell steeply northwards into the valley of the River Arrow.

While the pointers had been baiting Tom Potts, curious eyes had come to doorways and windows to stare at the scene, and more passers-by had halted to watch and listen.

Standing watching the trio swaggering away, Tom became aware of the sounds of talking and sniggering, and his heart sank as he looked around to see that a now sizeable crowd had witnessed what he could only regard as his own cowardly impotence. Face flushed with embarrassment, he picked his hat up from the gravel and hurried away, retracing his own steps to avoid having to pass through the gathering at the crossroads. Burning with shame, he heard the raucous laughter burst out from the spectators of his hurried retreat.

At the crossroads the solitary horseman who had witnessed the entire incident smiled inwardly with satisfaction.

'It looks like they've appointed a stupid, cowardly oaf as constable. So I've nothing to fear from that quarter.'

Five

It was close to midnight and Tom Potts was sitting at the table reading the dog-eared pages of the *New Universal Parish Officer* by the weak glimmering light of the small candle-lamp at his elbow. The guttering snores of his sleeping mother sounded through the warped ill-fitting floorboards above his head.

A repeated tapping on the outer door broke Tom's concentration and he rose and went to open it.

'You're up burning midnight oil again, I see, Master Potts,' the caller greeted him, 'so I hope you'll forgive me disturbing you at such an hour.'

'Of course, Master Danks.' Tom smiled. 'Will you come in? I was just about to smoke a pipe, so perhaps you'll share it with me.'

'Gladly.' Josiah Danks removed his broad-brimmed billy-cock hat as he stepped into the room, burly-bodied, ruddy-featured, radiating strength and confidence. Tom could well understand why this man, his nearest neighbour, was widely considered to be the finest gamekeeper in the entire needle district, and was both respected and feared by the poaching fraternity.

Danks sat down on the wooden chair facing Tom's across the table, and carefully laid his long-barrelled Tower musket on the floor beside him, while Tom brought out two short-stemmed clay pipes and a pouch of tobacco from the wall cupboard and placed them on the table between them.

'I see that you've chosen your old Brown Bess for tonight's patrol, Master Danks.'

'Indeed I have. There's nothing matches a well-aimed musket ball to put the fear o' Christ up them Brummagem poachers. A blunderbuss is all very well when you're close up, but it takes too much time to reload it. Now with my musket I can reload and fire up to four or five times a minute. Ten years' service in the Royal Marines taught me how to do that. We was always a damn sight sharper at musketry than the army, and that's a fact.' There was no trace of boasting in the game-keeper's voice, merely a statement of firm conviction.

Nothing more was said until both had filled, tamped and lit their pipes and were puffing out the first clouds of fragrant smoke.

'Now what was it you wanted to see me about, Master Danks?' Tom broke the silence.

'Well, me and Mrs Danks have been talking a lot about this lately, and so I've come here tonight to tell you what it is that me and Mrs Danks'd like to happen. So with your permission I'll tell you straight out.'

'Please do,' Tom invited him, and Danks' next words caused him to bite down so hard in shock that his teeth almost broke the slender clay pipestem.

'We wants you to marry our Amy.'

'To marry Amy?' Tom gasped.

'To marry our Amy,' Danks confirmed firmly. 'She's coming up to eighteen years old, and it's far above time she was wed. Mrs Danks was fourteen when I wed her, and our Amy ought to be wed by now.'

Tom was so completely nonplussed, he could think of no words of reply.

The other man grinned and nodded. 'Oh, I can see that this has took you by surprise, Master Potts. But surely you knows that our Amy has been more than a bit sweet on you ever since you come to live here. Truth to tell, it's herself that has asked me to come and speak to you about it . . . And I can't refuse our Amy anything that she asks me to do.'

Struggling to gather his thoughts, Tom could only protest weakly, 'But I'm nearly twice Amy's age, Master Danks . . . And I've no position in life, or any money or possessions to offer a wife. It's almost more than I can manage to support my mother and myself.'

He gestured around the bleak, meagre room and its few sticks of cheap wooden furniture. 'Apart from the bedding and beds upstairs, some pots and pans and a few books and other oddments, this is all I have in the world, Master Danks. I couldn't consider marrying anyone . . . I've nothing to offer anyone. Least of all a sweet, pretty young girl like Amy.'

'But you was sworn in as constable this morning,' the other man reminded him, 'and that's a start in bettering your fortunes, aren't it.' He winked knowingly. 'Joe Cashmore might have moaned and groaned about being constable, but I knows for a fact that he made a pretty penny out of it. The only reason that he aren't still the constable is that he upset some of them that he shouldn't have done. If he had his way, he'd stay as constable for life, so he would . . . And that's a certain sure fact, that is. Because he's said exactly that to me more than once or twice.'

Playing for time to think, Tom drew deeply on his pipe exhaling clouds of smoke around his head. He had no wish to offend this man, whom he liked and respected, nor to hurt young Amy's feelings in any way whatsoever. He was truly and deeply fond of the girl and considered her to be very pretty indeed. Naturally at times the fanciful thoughts of there someday being a romantic attachment had entered his mind, but he had always firmly suppressed such fancies, having long accepted that marriage was out of the question for a man in his impoverished state, and with no foreseeable prospects of ever bettering that condition.

From the room above a loud snorting and coughing suddenly

erupted, followed by a sustained wailing outcry, and Tom thankfully seized upon this opportunity to escape.

'It's my mother, Master Danks. You'll have to excuse me. I must go and care for her . . . She's been most unwell lately . . . Perhaps we could discuss this matter at some later date.'

'Very well, Master Potts.' The gamekeeper rose to his feet and took up his musket, then winked knowingly. 'But I shouldn't let a chance like this slip away from you. There's a lot o' the young bloods hereabouts are setting their caps at our Amy, and more than a few o' the older ones as well. You needs to strike while the iron's hot, if you get my meaning.'

'I do, Master Danks. And many thanks for calling . . . I'm coming directly, Mother.' Tom escaped up the narrow stairway.

Six

Tom had hoped to move his mother, goods and chattels into the lock-up during the evening hours of darkness, but George Jolly the carrier was adamant that his horse and four-wheeled flat-cart were only available during the daylight hours.

'If the good Lord had intended for me to work in the dark, then He'd have give me cat's eyes, and that's what He aren't done. So it's daytime, or no time, and you can take it or leave it as you please,' he stated sullenly.

'I can't think what the good Lord was doing to give you the name of Jolly,' Tom thought with ironic amusement, but aloud he reluctantly accepted. 'Very well, Master Jolly. Daytime it shall be.'

At dawn next day George Jolly arrived at the isolated cottage, and with Tom's help the work of loading commenced. The few pieces of furniture and the meagre collection of domestic implements and personal possessions were very quickly and easily stowed upon the cart. Then it was the turn of the Widow

Potts, who had remained out of sight in the rear of the cottage, to take her place upon it.

'Bugger me!' Jolly scowled, when he set eyes on her, and asked Tom, 'How the bloody hell does she get up and down them narrow stairs? It must be a bloody tight squeeze!'

The Widow Potts was as short and fat as her son was tall and lean. Clad in unrelieved black mourning, her disagreeable, purple-pink face filling the wide wings of her poke-bonnet, she shuffled ponderously towards the cart, leaning heavily upon two stout walking sticks, grunting and wheezing, panting out ceaseless querulous complaints.

The carrier mentally computed her weight, and frowning, shook his head in emphatic denial. 'Unless you'm four times stronger than you looks to be, Master Potts, there's no way that you and me are going to lift her onto the cart by ourselves. And I aren't going to risk putting me back out by trying neither.'

'But she'll have to ride on the cart,' Tom protested, 'she's not able to walk more than a few paces.'

'Then you'll have to find some more men to help lift her onto it. Because I'm not going to damage meself by trying with just the two on us.' Jolly was adamant.

'You saucy devil!' Widow Potts scowled at him, and turned on Tom, hissing virulently. 'If you were a man, instead of a useless great nancy, you'd horsewhip this piece of rubbish for insulting your mother.'

'Don't you go calling me rubbish, missus,' Jolly bridled instantly, 'or I'll chuck this lot off my wagon and leave you to it!'

'Be quiet, Mother, for pity's sake!' Tom beseeched her. 'Master Jolly here is our only hope of making this move this week.'

'Making this move?' she demanded furiously. 'And whose fault is it that we are making this move? And whose fault is it that we don't have our own carriage and pair? And whose fault is it that we are brought so low and degraded in this life that we have to be dependent on low, ignorant creatures such as this one to move anywhere?'

'Please, Master Jolly, pay no heed to her. She's not in health,' Tom pleaded desperately. 'I'll go and find some help for us.'

The carrier made a show of peering around the wooded

hilly landscape, and sneered. 'Well, me eyes aren't as good as they once was, but I'm buggered if I can see anybody close hereabouts.'

'I've a neighbour, just behind that copse of trees there.' Tom pointed in the direction of the Danks' house. 'I'll run and fetch him. He's a very strong man indeed, Master Jolly. He'll be able to quite easily lift my mother onto the cart by himself, I've no doubt on that score.'

'You be quick about it then, Master Potts. Because I've no more time to waste here. I've other jobs to be seeing to. So if you aren't back real quick, then I'm off-loading me wagon. I've a good mind to do that anyway, because I don't stand for women becalling me like your mam's a-doing.'

'Please bear with me, Master Jolly. And Mother, for pity's sake hold your tongue while I'm gone.'

Tom ran as fast as he was able to the Danks' house and Mrs Danks answered the door to his frantic hammerings.

'No, me man aren't here, Master Potts. He's sent word that he won't be back until late this afternoon.'

Tom's heart sank, and then he caught sight of the huge wheelbarrow. His thoughts raced, and after a moment or two he asked, 'Might I borrow your wheelbarrow for an hour or so, Mrs Danks?'

'All right.' She smiled and closed the door.

'What's you brought that back for?' Jolly frowned suspiciously. 'Am you intending to carry your furniture on it, instead of my wagon?'

'No, Master Jolly.' Tom smiled reassuringly. 'Not my furniture, but my mother. It will serve very well, I assure you.'

He placed the barrow behind the rear of the cart, and used rope to lash its handles securely to the cart's tailgate.

'My mother can sit like this.' Tom seated himself on the barrow, with his long legs stretching out each side of its single wheel. 'You see the advantages, don't you, Master Jolly. We merely have to lower my mother into it, and then pull her out of it when we reach our destination. There is no danger at all of either of us straining our backs.'

The other man pondered for a moment, and then shrugged and accepted. 'Ahr! All right, then.'

Widow Potts was not so amenable, however, and furiously

berated her son. 'You great fool, you! Have you lost what few
wits you had? You'll not put me into that contraption! Do you
think that I'm a pile of horseshit to be carried in that stinking
thing? I'll not sit in it, and that's final! You cursed great blockhead, you!'

Grunting with effort she raised one of her sticks and struck
viciously at Tom's head. Her wild swing took her off balance
and she began to totter.

Tom recognized his chance, and darting forwards he grasped
her arms and steered her helpless staggering so that the backs
of her legs collided with the front of the barrow, and she
sagged down into its capacious body, the reception of her
huge heavy buttocks causing its stoutly fashioned iron-braced
woodwork to strain and groan in protest.

He tried fruitlessly to soothe her. 'I'm sorry, Mother, but
I've no choice. Try to calm yourself, do. We shall soon be at
our new lodgings.'

She attempted to lever herself up from the barrow, but her
weight defeated all her efforts. 'Damn you! I wish you were
in your grave! Damn you!' she raged, and kept trying to hit
him with both sticks.

Sighing resignedly, Tom joined Jolly at the horse's head.
'Right, Master Jolly. Let us get on the road.'

Any transhipment of household goods and chattels always
attracted curious attention throughout the needle district.
People took great interest in seeing what their old or new
neighbours possessed in the way of furnishings, domestic
implements and other articles. This morning the curious stares
quickly metamorphosed into howls of laughter and loud shouts
for all and sundry to come and see the fat woman in the wheelbarrow.

Even before the cart had reached the junction of the Mount
Pleasant and the town's Front Hill and Back Hill it had attracted
a small crowd of noisy followers. Tom was red-faced with
embarrassment, and his mother was purple with rage, striking
out with her sticks and shrieking abuse at the mocking,
laughing followers. Tom fell back to walk directly behind his
mother in a fruitless attempt to shield her from the crowd,
and was driven by guilt to apologize repeatedly, but his words
only caused her to direct her abuse and blows at him.

Where Mount Pleasant forked to become the steeper Front and Back Hills of Redditch there were two taverns, the Black Horse and the Duke of York, both of which attracted men and women to take a livening drink before commencing their long, weary hours of drudgery. Drawn by the noisy onset of the cart the drinkers swarmed out from the two taverns, swelling the crowd of followers into a tumultuous procession.

'It's Jack Spratt and his missus come to Redditch,' a wag bellowed, and the crowd instantly took up the gibe, chanting in unison at the tops of their voices:

> *Oh Jack Spratt could eat no fat,*
> *And his wife could eat no lean,*
> *But between the pair of them,*
> *They licked the platter clean.*
> *Oh Jack Spratt could eat no fat,*
> *And his wife could eat no lean . . .*

George Jolly laughed and joined in the chanting as the procession passed down the Front Hill to the flat central plateau and travelled on along the main street towards the crossroads, and all the time the crowds were increasing. Men, women and children came hurrying from the needle mills and the small needle workshops that operated in almost every street, court and alley of the town, until it seemed that the entire population of Redditch had come to join the seething, chanting, laughing, jeering mass of humanity.

The cacophony reached the ears of the two men standing chatting in St Stephen's Chapel's burial yard.

'That sounds ominous.' The Reverend John Clayton chuckled wryly. 'It would seem that our good townsfolk are on the randy again.'

'Then we'd best stay well clear until it's all over, John.' Dr Hugh Laylor grinned. 'Because if they follow their usual inclinations we shall both have our work cut out. You to pray God for forgiveness for their sins, and I to patch up the casualties.'

In age, height and exceptionally fine physique, the pair were doubles. But in looks and clothing they were opposites. Hugh Laylor was dressed in expensively tailored hunting dress of gilt-buttoned red coat, blue stock, white breeches, black top hat and black riding boots glistening like polished glass. His handsome face, framed by immaculately barbered dark brown hair and side whiskers, impelled even the most primly staid of women to risk a lingering look.

John Clayton's features, when compared to his present companion's, could at best only be described as not too repulsively ugly, and his rusty black clerical garb was woefully threadbare, darned and patched.

The tumultuous uproar drew quickly nearer and as it did so the repetitive chanting could be clearly distinguished.

Hugh Laylor lifted his hand in astonishment. 'Just listen to that! "Jack Spratt could eat no fat, and his wife could eat no lean!" Why in Heaven's name are they yelling that old rhyme?'

The vanguard of the crowd spilled into and filled the crossroads, and John Clayton stepped upon the raised kerb of a tombstone so that he could see above their heads. He frowned in puzzlement. 'It's George Jolly they appear to be mobbing. But why? He's one of their own, isn't he?'

Then he sighted Tom Potts' top-hatted head following close behind the cart, which by now was turning eastwards to travel down past the Fox and Goose towards the lock-up. At the change of direction the crowd swirled, momentarily creating a gap through which Clayton glimpsed for an instant the grotesque spectacle of the hugely fat Widow Potts sitting in the wheelbarrow, and he realized.

'Oh dear Lord! That's why they're chanting. It's the new constable they're mobbing! It has to be stopped!' He ran out from the chapel yard and into the crowd, buffeting aside those who got in his way and shouting furiously, 'Stop this! Stop this now!'

The sudden eruption into their midst of this formidable figure shocked those nearest to the cart into abrupt silence, although on the further edges the raucous chanting and jeering continued.

Clayton grabbed the horse's lead rein and by sheer brute strength dragged it to a halt. Then he clambered up onto the rear of the cart and roared at the dense mass of upturned staring faces.

'You should be ashamed of yourselves for mobbing a helpless old woman in this manner.' He pointed at one man. 'Harry Chambers, I helped you bury your mother last week, what would she say if she could see you tormenting this poor old soul?'

Widow Potts knuckled her eyes and wailed piteously, and some in the crowd began to look shame-faced.

Born and bred in Redditch, John Clayton understood his townspeople very well. He knew that if he continued to berate them, a sizeable number would react aggressively, and with their propensity for violence there would certainly be blood-shed. So he spoke more softly, and appealed to them.

'Good people, just look at this poor old soul. She is badly frightened and much distressed. I beg you all, go away from here and leave her in peace.'

The appeal to their better natures had its desired effect and after a few moments the crowd began to disperse.

'Thank you very much, sir.' Tom Potts lifted his hat and bowed slightly. 'I'm greatly indebted to you. I must confess that I was becoming fearful for my mother and myself.'

'I'm happy to have been of service, Master Potts.' John Clayton's interest was sparked by Tom's gentlemanly tone of voice. He got down from the cart, and found that most unusually his own six foot height was topped by several inches.

'You're an exceptionally tall fellow, Master Potts,' he couldn't help but remark, 'which should be advantageous in your new position. Your height alone will overawe some of our wild lads, I don't doubt.'

Tom shook his head and smiled ruefully. 'I fear that my lack of muscular strength and pugilistic talent cancels out my advantage in height, sir.'

Looking at the lean features and dark eyes and hearing the pleasantly mellow-toned voice, John Clayton experienced a warmth of feeling towards this new constable. 'I'll accompany you the rest of your way. My presence will perhaps deter any fresh-comers from tormenting you and this lady.'

Widow Potts had ceased her noisy wailing, and now told their rescuer, 'It was God's mercy that brought you to save me, sir. You have my eternal gratitude.'

Clayton bowed. 'It is an honour to have been of assistance to you.' He noted that her small piglike eyes held no trace of tears, and thought to himself, 'Why now, I don't believe that she was as distressed as she made out to be.'

'I wasn't always in my present lowly position in life, sir.'

She scowled petulantly towards Tom. 'And if my son here was anything other than totally useless, I would still be riding in my own carriage. He has always been a burden to me, and will be until my dying day. And that, sir, is a day that I will welcome because it will free me from all my sufferings.'

The cart lurched forwards, jerking her violently, and she shouted angrily at George Jolly, 'You stupid oaf! You're shaking me half to death! If I were a man I'd give you a good thrashing!'

Tom felt embarrassed by her, but stayed silent.

The two men walked side by side, and Clayton asked, 'Do you have a profession, Master Potts?'

'No.' There was regret in Tom's dark eyes. 'I was intended for medicine, but after my father died there were not sufficient funds for me to continue my studies.'

The clergyman found himself becoming increasingly curious about his companion. 'Forgive my prying further into your private affairs, Master Potts, but might I ask where you lived before you came to Redditch?'

'As a youngster I lived in several countries, sir. My father was a military surgeon, you see. He was born here in Redditch, and told me much about this town, which he loved dearly. So I always had a strong desire to come here.'

'And what do you think of Redditch now that you are here?'

'I like it very much.' Tom smiled. 'And shall be very content to spend the rest of my days here.'

The lock-up stood on the forked junction where the Market Place met the Red Lion and Alcester streets some forty yards eastwards beyond the Fox and Goose. Built two years previously and paid for by a public subscription, it resembled a small keep of a medieval castle. Rectangular in shape, two storeys high, stone fronted and with castellated battlements, its arched front entrance was a massive iron-studded door, flanked by two arrow slits. Two yards to the right-hand side of the door the stocks and whipping post had been erected.

When the cart halted in front of the lock-up, Joseph Cashmore was standing in its open doorway, impatiently twirling a ring of large keys. He grinned with scarcely veiled contempt. 'That warn't a good start for you as constable, was it, Master Potts? Everybody calling you Jack Spratt. It don't seem that they've got any respect for you, does it?'

Tom displayed no resentment, and merely agreed mildly. 'I fear that you're right in what you say, Master Cashmore.'

'Here, take these.' Cashmore pressed the ring of keys into Tom's hand. 'There's two prisoners in the cells. I took them both up for vagrancy three days since. Lord Aston's give 'em a month at hard labour apiece, so you'll need to shift 'em to Worcester Gaol as soon as you can. Take care that you don't let 'em escape.'

With that parting admonition he walked away.

John Clayton was unlashing the ropes that secured the wheelbarrow. George Jolly began to unload the cart and lifting a heavy wooden chest let it drop with a crash onto the ground.

'Take care, you stupid oaf,' Widow Potts remonstrated angrily. 'If you damage any of my things I'll make you sorry for it! Now pick that chest up and move it inside.'

'Move it yourself, you miserable old cow!' Jolly growled. 'I've had my belly-full o' you.'

'Now now, Master Jolly. Show some respect for age,' John Clayton reprimanded him.

'It's her that needs to show some respect, Parson.' The carrier was unabashed. 'Speaking to honest folk as if they were dogs. This is the last time I'll be shifting anything of hers, and that's certain sure, that is.' Displaying great muscular strength, Clayton lifted the old woman bodily from the wheelbarrow and carried her in his arms into the building.

Tom helped the carrier to unload the furniture and other articles and stack them against the wall then paid him.

'You'm a nice enough chap, Master Potts.' Jolly pocketed his fee. 'And I've naught against you personally. But I'll shift nothing else for you until that old besom learns to mind her manners and speak civil to honest folk.'

Tom made no reply, and when the cart had creaked away, entered his new home for the first time.

The stench was thick and vile, a compound of excreta, urine, stale sweat, unwashed flesh and dank walls and floors.

The ground floor was a wide passage between two rows of cell doors. At the far end of the passage was another smaller iron-studded door, with an arrow slit each side of it, and to one side of the door a flight of steep steps led up to the floor above, from where his mother's loud complaining was resounding. When the doors were closed the only daylight in the passage came from the arrow slits at front and rear.

Tom walked slowly along the passage, opening the small observation hatches in the cell doors and peering curiously through the narrow gaps.

The cells were uniformly dark, dirty and cramped, with a small iron grille high on the outside wall to admit air, beneath which was a low wooden pallet which served as a bed. The two prisoners were also uniform in their ragged filth.

Tom was appalled by their wretched appearance, and at that moment could think of nothing to say to either of them.

He unlocked the rear door and found it opened onto a narrow stone-flagged yard surrounded by a high wall surmounted by close-set rusty iron spikes. A doorless, rancid-smelling privy was built against the wall to his left, and a long-handled water pump stood against the right-hand wall.

John Clayton's boots echoed on the wooden stairs, and he grinned sympathetically as he joined Tom in the yard.

'It's not exactly a luxurious dwelling, is it, Master Potts? But at least you've a pump to hand; and a good scrubbing will lessen the stink somewhat, I'm sure. Come, I'll help you to get your goods upstairs.'

Tom was relieved to find that the upstairs quarters consisted of two separate large rooms and a smaller one, all three with casement windows and fire grates incorporating ovens and pot hangers. The rooms were clean, the walls and ceilings lime-washed, and the stench of the ground floor much less notice-able.

'I'm sure that we shall be very comfortable here, Mother.' He interrupted her barrage of querulous complaints, and helped her to sit down on the chair he had carried upstairs. 'You rest now, while we finish bringing the stuff up, and then I'll get you something to eat and drink.

'Eat and drink! Eat and drink! The stink of this rotten hole is sickening me to my stomach! It will stop me from eating or drinking ever again! Was there ever another poor woman who has suffered as I've suffered? Was there ever another poor woman who was ever cursed with such a cruel and unnatural son?'

Tom could only sigh in resignation and carry on with moving the furniture.

The last article was the heavy wooden chest that the carrier had dropped. Tom and Clayton carried it up between them and when they put it down Tom opened it with a frisson of anxiety. He lifted and examined a large brass and mahogany microscope, and exhaled a thankful sigh of relief to find it undamaged.

John Clayton stared admiringly. 'That's a very fine piece of craftsmanship you have there, Master Potts.'

Tom smiled with gratification. 'Yes, it's a new pattern, and amazingly powerful. I bought it last year.'

'And spent good money that we could ill-afford,' Widow Potts complained bitterly. 'And now he wastes hours and hours sitting staring into it. Hours when he should be doing things for me, or trying to find work and earn money. And when he's not staring into that useless contraption he's got his head stuck in some mouldy old book or other, or he's spending hours messing about with bits of rotten meat and suchlike. Is it any wonder that I'm always so frazzled and worn down with grief and worry, when I have such a wasteful, idle creature for a son. If it were not for the small annuity my husband bequeathed, I'd have starved to death long since.'

'But, ma'am, there are countless wonders to be seen through the lenses of a microscope, and all the world's knowledge to be discovered in books. Surely it's better that your son should occupy his time with such self-improving interests, rather than waste it roistering in the alehouses as all too many of our townsfolk do?' Clayton defended Tom warmly.

When the cleric left Tom accompanied him to the front door, where John Clayton proffered his hand.

Tom shook it firmly. 'Many thanks for you kindness, sir. It has been much appreciated by both my mother and me.'

The cleric made a gesture of dismissal. 'It was nothing. I do believe, however, that you and I are going to become very good friends indeed. So from this moment on let us dispense with formalities. I shall be John, to you, and you shall be Tom to me.'

'I'd like that very much,' Tom agreed happily.

'It's settled, then. I must now bid you good day, Tom.'

'Good day, John, and thank you again.'

As Tom closed the door, the foul stench enveloped him instantly, and he ruefully accepted that his next job must be to scrub and cleanse every single inch of the walls, floors and ceilings on the ground floor.

'What will the people next call me if they see me doing this?' he thought with wry amusement. 'Will it be Dolly Scrub-Mop, I wonder?'

Seven

It was the jarringly loud jangling of the upper- and ground-floor bells which roused Tom to fuddled consciousness in the early dawn. He sat up in his narrow bed, blinking hard at these unfamiliar surroundings. Still in his nightshirt and tasselled nightcap, he reluctantly dragged himself to open the casement window and look down to see who was tugging so violently at the front entrance bell rope.

Amy Danks beamed rosily up at him, and lifted high the small basket in her hands. 'I've brought the prisoners' grub, Master Tom. Tommy Fowkes has got the parish contract to feed any pauper prisoners in the lock-up.' She winked knowingly. 'Him and Cashmore made a few bob from it this last year, I can tell you.'

'I'll be down directly, Amy,' Tom said.

'Well, I hope you're wearing your breeches under that nightshirt, or folks'll be saying that you and me are getting up to high jinks.' She giggled.

As always he found her high spirits infectious, and chuckling he replied, 'There's no need for concern, Amy. I shall guard both our reputations by putting all my clothes on immediately.'

She assumed an exaggerated expression of disappointment. 'Oh! What a pity that would be, Master Tom!'

'You behave yourself, my girl!' he mock-scolded.

As he dressed he was uncomfortably aware of sore muscles and stiff joints engendered by the long hard toil of moving furniture, scrubbing and cleaning which he had only completed some two hours past midnight.

'I really must strengthen my body,' he told himself with a sense of shame. 'Physically I'm nothing less than a pathetic weakling.'

'Thomas! Thomas, where are you?' Widow Potts' harsh corncrake complaint echoed through the building. 'Why must you wake me up with all this noise of bells? Why must you destroy any fleeting sleep I manage to have? You wicked, unnatural wretch!'

Tom grimaced resignedly and called, 'Try to go back to sleep, Mother. The bells have stopped now.'

As he passed down the lower passageway one of the prisoners bellowed irately, 'That better be me breakfast come. I'm near clemmed to bleedin' death, I be!'

The hinges squealed in protest as Tom dragged the heavy door ajar, and he was met with Amy's demand. 'Well, Master Tom? What's your answer?'

'Answer?' He stared blankly. 'Answer to what question, Amy?'

'The one you was asked the other day.'

Tom still didn't comprehend, and could only repeat, 'The answer to what question?'

Her soft pink lips pursed in exasperation. 'You know very well what question, Master Tom! Are you agreeable to us getting wed? Me and you?'

She bent to place the basket on the ground, then straightened to run her hands down her shapely body, smiling coquettishly.

'You just look at me, Master Tom, and tell me if there's any prettier girl in this town. You knows that there aren't, don't you. We could be happily wedded, as soon as the banns are called. And I'd be a very good and obedient wife to you, in all things.'

For some moments Tom could only stand in silence as he battled with a troubling melange of emotions. He had in full measure all of the natural human longings for a family of his own; and with each passing year was becoming increasingly conscious that he was facing a bleak future with the onset of a barren old age bereft of wife or children of his own flesh and blood.

Marriage to Amy Danks was a very pleasurable prospect to contemplate, knowing as he did her kind heart and spirited, happy nature. These attributes, coupled with her pretty face and nubile body, made marriage to her a temptation that even a saint would find extremely difficult to resist. And at this moment Tom did not want to resist that temptation. He wanted with all his heart to say yes to her offer of marriage. Yet he knew that marriage would only result in Amy suffering both his financial hardships and the onerous burden of caring for his mother. His own decency of character kept him from entrapping this young woman into sharing his present bleak existence.

'Well?' she pressed anxiously, her white teeth gleaming between her lusciously tempting lips. 'Has the cat got your tongue, Master Tom? Tell me if we're going to get wed or not!'

Tormented by long years of self-enforced celibacy, he was fighting desperately the overwhelming hunger to take her in his arms, to crush his mouth upon her inviting lips, to caress her full firm breasts and rounded curves.

He shook his head, desperately trying to control the rampaging, tormenting desires coursing through his mind and body, so that he could explain to her just why he could not at this time agree to marry her, no matter how much he wanted to do so.

Amy's own inner nervous tension caused her to totally misunderstand his shaken head, which she immediately interpreted as a rejection. Angry pique flared through her.

'Sod you, then!' she spat out furiously. 'There's plenty more men hereabouts who'll be begging to give their eye teeth to have me for their bride! I wouldn't marry you now, not if you was the last man left alive on this earth!'

She kicked the basket at him and ran back towards the Fox and Goose, her long skirt and apron flying up around her slender ankles and shapely calves.

'Amy? Amy, wait! Please let me explain!' he shouted after her in dismay, and on impulse started in pursuit, but tripped over the basket and fell headlong, flat on his face. The impact punched the air from his lungs, and he rolled over onto his back, fighting to draw breath.

'Were you attempting to take that young woman into custody, Constable Potts? Or was she making her escape from this prison?'

Tom opened his screwed tight eyes to see the deep-lined features of Joseph Blackwell Esquire staring quizzically down at him. His own features twisted in dismay. Dragging in sufficient breath to reply, he gasped a denial.

'No, sir. Neither of those things were taking place.'

'Then will you please do me the favour of rising from this undignified position, Potts? I have matters of official business to impart to you,' Blackwell requested with acidic politeness.

'Of course, sir.' Still badly flustered, Tom scrambled to his feet, explaining lamely, 'It was merely an unfortunate mishap. I accidentally tripped over the basket.'

Blackwell clucked his tongue, and in scathing tones told Tom, 'From what I've heard, and now have witnessed with my own eyes, it appears to me that you have a definite propensity to encounter unfortunate mishaps. You were assaulted by three roughnecks, whom you allowed to go unpunished for their gross insult towards the office of constable. You have been publicly mobbed and ridiculed for carrying your mother here in what was a most grotesquely undignified mode of transport, and now I witness you making a complete fool of yourself in front of this very lock-up.

'I tell you frankly, Potts, that in my opinion you have made a most unsatisfactory beginning in the post of constable of this parish, and that you are already in danger of becoming a laughing-stock throughout the entire needle district. What have you to say about all this?'

Engulfed by mortification, Tom bowed his head, momentarily unable to meet the other man's eyes.

'Well, man? Have you anything to say to me?' Blackwell goaded harshly. 'Or do you remain dumb because you know there is nothing that can be said which will excuse pitifully inept behaviour?'

Tom drew in a series of long deep breaths, and as he did so he experienced deep within his being the birthing of a determination to win this other man's respect. He forced himself to meet full on the scorn and contempt in the shorter man's gaze.

'I won't attempt to dispute what you have said to me, sir,' he stated quietly. 'I am all too well aware of my own deficiencies of character and courage. However, what I will say to you, is that despite those deficiencies, I fully intend to do

my lawful duty as the constable of this parish, no matter what
consequence that may entail for me.'

Joseph Blackwell Esquire was a shrewd, hard-bitten man
with a lifetime's experience of the vagaries of human nature.
He stared long and searchingly into the dark brown eyes now
unflinchingly meeting his own, and what he recognized in
their lucent depths was the quality of absolute sincerity.

Finally he nodded in acceptance. 'Yes, Master Potts. I
do believe that you mean what you say. So let us put this
unfortunate beginning behind us, and start afresh. Are we
in agreement?'

He held out his hand, and Tom shook it gratefully. 'Indeed
we are, sir.'

'Good!' Blackwell became brisk and businesslike. 'You will
escort your two prisoners to Worcester Gaol today. Richard
Humphries' coach will be the mode of transport. Make sure
that they are securely shackled together, and remember to
bring the shackles and padlocks back with you. We don't want
the expense of replacing them.

'To share the costs of transport other prisoners and escorts
will be picked up en route, at Bromsgrove and Droitwich.
Might I advise that you make immediate preparations for your
departure, because the coach will be here shortly. Good day
to you, Constable.'

Alone again, Tom had a brief respite in which to examine
his own emotions, and found them curiously mixed. Distress
at upsetting Amy so. Relief that he and Blackwell had, for
the time being at least, a cordial relationship. A rapidly
strengthening determination to make a success of his term of
office as constable. A determination also to try and heal the
rift with Amy. All of these succeeded each other in repeated
progressions, intermingled with a sense of anticipatory excitement that he was about to embark upon his first official duty
as the Constable of Tardebigge Parish.

A shout from inside broke into his train of thought. 'Where's
me grub? I'm bleedin' starving, I am!'

The rough treatment that the basket had received from both
Amy and Tom had scattered its contents across a roadway
still wet and muddy from the previous night's rain showers.
Those contents consisted of a few crusts of half mouldy bread
and some cheese rinds.

'No wonder Tommy Fowkes and Cashmore made a profit from the pauper prisoners' rations,' Tom thought wryly.

He left the scraps where they lay, and used some of his own limited domestic store of bread and cheese to feed the two vagrants. But when his largesse was received with vociferous, foul-mouthed complaints about its quantity and quality, he began to wish that he had picked up the spillage from the basket and fed the two men with that.

Eight

It was the penultimate Sunday morning in April and the prevailing winds had swung and changed their direction so that now they carried the warmer airs of springtime up from the southwards to loosen the chill northern grip of winter upon the land.

The two young women, freed for the Sabbath day from their work in the needle mills, left their respective homes in Silver Street and headed for the extensive woodlands bordering the low-lying fields immediately west of the town. Both were clad alike in torn old gowns, grimy mob-caps and wooden-soled clogs; and both had small rope-slung wooden kegs hanging from their shoulders.

As they passed the Fox and Goose an upstairs window opened and Amy Danks thrust her head out.

'Hello, Nance, hello, Sal. Are you going leeching?'

'Where else'd we be going, dressed in these bloody rags.' Nance Harper, the elder of the women grinned, displaying her decayed, broken teeth. 'And it'll do Sal good to get a bit o' peace and quiet in the woods.'

Amy looked at Sal Payne and frowned with concern. The woman's face was badly discoloured by old and fresh bruises, and her left eye was swollen shut and weeping bloody tears.

'I see your husband has been up to his tricks again, Sal,' she declared angrily. 'You ought to leave the rotten bugger.

He'll put you in your grave one of these fine days.'

'You're wasting your breath talking to this silly sarft cow, Amy,' Nance spat out disgustedly. 'She thinks the sun shines out of his arsehole. She tells him that she loves him even while he's knocking seven bells out of her!'

'It's not his fault.' Sal Payne defended him in tear-jerky gasps. 'It's only when I upsets him and drives him to lose his temper that he hits me. He's very nice to me most days.'

'Oh yes, so he is. He's always nice to you on them days that all the pigs goes flying about the sky.' Nance's voice dripped sarcasm.

Sal rounded angrily on her companion. 'If you're going to keep on becalling my Alfie all day, then I'm not coming another step with you!'

Nance was unperturbed by this threat, and rejoined calmly, 'Oh, you'll come with me all right, my duck. Because your lovely Alfie'll most probably be back tonight from wherever he's been gallivanting this last week; and he'll certain sure have no money, 'ull he. And none of the pubs in this town'll give him any tick, will they. So the only way he's going to have any money tonight to put across the Red Lion's bar is by you selling some leeches to Dr Laylor, aren't it! Oh yes, my duck, you'll be coming every step o' the way with me, and that's as sure as God made little apples, that is.'

She grinned up at Amy and waved her arm. 'Ta-ta, Amy my love. Remember now, if you ever gets wed, then let it be to a tiny weak man who you can give a good hiding to whenever you fancies. That's the way to wedded bliss, that is. As for this sarft cow? She's made her bed, and she must lie in it. That's the way the world is. Ta-ta, again.'

Amy waved back and watched the two women walk on towards the crossroads, then looked in the opposite direction at the castellated lock-up. A by now familiar confusion of simultaneous anger, chagrin and yearning assailed her. The chagrin was engendered by the memory of how she had asked Tom Potts to marry her. The anger was fired by the way he had reacted to that offer. The yearning was for a resumption of their close relationship.

Up to this point the anger had been the dominant force, and on the several occasions that Tom had tried to speak with her she had rudely rebuffed him by turning her back and running away, refusing even to listen. As the days passed, however, she experienced ever more frequent and increasingly poignant yearnings to hear his voice and share his company. She knew from the conversations of the inn's customers that Tom had made a poor first impression as constable, and she found herself fiercely resenting the mocking gibes some of them made about him.

'I do still love him. Even though he don't want to wed me,' she was reluctantly forced to admit to herself in the deepest depths of her mind.

Now, staring at the lock-up, she was assailed by an intensely powerful impulse to see and speak with him. 'But how can I approach him, after the way I've treated him when he's tried to speak to me?'

An idea suddenly came to her, and slamming shut the window she hurried out of the room and down the stairs.

'This porridge is lumpy, and you've put too much salt in it again. And the cheese is too hard for me to chew. Haven't I told you time and time again to soften the cheese afore you cuts it up into my porridge? You useless great fool!' Noisily smacking her lips and champing her toothless gums, Widow Potts kept up a continuous tirade of complaint as she greedily slurped down her breakfast.

The jangling of the bells enabled Tom to escape further abuse. 'I'll have to leave you for now, Mother.' He sighed with relief, and rushed to answer the summons. When he pulled open the front door he exclaimed in delighted surprise.

'Amy! I'm so pleased to see you!'

She was also pleased at his evident delight, but could not resist the spiteful impulse to punish him further for rejecting her offer of marriage, and told him sharply, 'You needn't grin like a Cheshire cat, Master Potts. This aren't a social call. I'm only here on business.'

'Oh!' He looked instantly crestfallen, and she could not suppress a fleeting hint of a satisfied smile, as she went on, 'I want to ask you about something. Something concerning a friend of mine.'

'I'm at your service, Amy. Would you care to step inside?'

From the cupola of St Stephen's Chapel the bell began to toll out the call to morning service, and Amy did not want to be subjected to the curious stares of the worshippers obeying that call.

She stepped across the doorway, and could not help but remark, 'This place don't stink half as bad as it did. And it looks a lot cleaner as well.'

'I'm pleased that you say that.' Tom felt quite inordinately gratified that his long arduous hours of scrubbing and cleaning had earned some recognition. 'Of course, there hasn't been anyone locked up since I took the tramps to Worcester. I've had a very quiet time of it.' He smiled warmly at her. 'In fact this is the first time that anyone has come to me on business since the day I took those two to the gaol.'

Together with him in close proximity once more, realizing how glad he was to be speaking with her, seeing the tenderness in his gaze, Amy could feel herself softening towards him. But then she resolved, 'No, I'll not fully forgive him yet. It's too soon for that. He must suffer a while longer.'

'Now how can I be of service to you, Amy?' Tom wanted with all his heart to tell her just how much he wished that he was in the position to offer her marriage and a home and family of her own. But could not summon sufficient courage to risk her scornful reaction.

'It's not me who needs your service,' she rejoined tartly. 'It's a friend of mine. Sal Payne. From Silver Street. Her husband, Alfie Payne, keeps on battering her black and blue. If he's not stopped, he'll end up killing the poor girl.'

As he listened Tom felt his heart sinking. Silver Street! The most notorious slum in the entire needle district. The lair of some of the most savage and degraded men and women in the community. It was an extended fetid alleyway which at its far end debouched into an enclosed square. Its main entrance was through a narrow archway built onto the side of the Red Lion, the favoured haunt of the notoriously violent needle-pointers.

Amy waited expectantly for his reply.

'What exactly is it that you want me to do?' Tom queried hesitantly.

'Dear God! I want you to stop him ill-treating her, o' course!' she exclaimed, as if incredulous that he could have asked her such a stupid question.

He coughed nervously, before explaining, 'I have read many

books of law, Amy. Unfortunately, it is perfectly legal for a husband to chastise his wife, or children, just so long as the stick he uses to beat them is no thicker than his thumb.'

'I'm not a fool!' she protested angrily. 'I know very well that husbands can beat their wives and kids, rotten beasts and cowards that them who do so are! But Alfie Payne don't just knock Sal about a bit, he half-kills the poor girl!'

'Is your friend prepared to lay charges against her husband?' Tom asked.

Amy shrugged uncertainly. 'Well, I can't say for sure, but I reckon it's a bit unlikely that she would. Because when I tell her to leave him, all she does is to tell me that it's all her own fault that he beats her. That she deserves it!' She shook her head in mystified wonder. 'She says she loves him with all her heart! I can only think that he's knocked any bit o' good sense out of her!'

'Is there anyone else who would bring charges against him on her behalf? Preferably a close relative.'

'You must be joking!' Amy scoffed. 'Alfie Payne's one of the hard cases of this town. He's a really nasty piece of work when he gets riled. He'd stick a knife in you as soon as look at you. Who's going to risk crossing him for the sake of a poor trod-down soul like Sal, who hasn't got a farthing, and all her kinfolk long dead and buried? I'm too frightened of him to do it myself, and I'll admit to that without any shame at all.'

Then she smiled sweetly at him. 'It will have to be you that stops him ill-using her, Tom. There's no one else in this town who's willing or able to do it. So it will have to be you.'

Tom swallowed hard. He was beginning to wish that this visit had never happened, despite her smiling so sweetly at him, and using his diminutive name for the first time in their acquaintance without the prefix of 'Master'.

He coughed several times to ease the nervous tension constricting his throat, and with a strained smile assured her, 'I shall do my best, Amy. I promise you.'

'I know that you will, Tom.' She nodded, and raising on tiptoe reached up, cupped his face with her hands, drew his head down low and planted a resounding kiss upon the tip of his nose. Then she turned and ran through the door giggling with mischievous delight, leaving Tom staring after her in bemusement.

Nine

The ancient trackways that threaded through the myriads of trees and lush green glades of the Pitcheroak Wood had for long centuries been traversed by humans and animals. Prehistoric clans, Celtic tribes, Roman legions, Saxons, Normans, hunters, outlaws, swineherds, drovers, tinkers, gypsies, tramps; all had sought shelter beneath the great branches of oak and ash and elm.

The man crouching by the side of the half-strangled, half-dead rabbit loosed the snare from its neck. He lifted the animal's warm and quivering body, smiling with satisfaction at how young and succulent its flesh felt; and grunting with pleasure, slowly crushed its windpipe between his strong hands until its body gave a last spasmodic jerk and it was finally dead.

Carefully he re-set the noose of the snare, and rose to his feet. Then he abruptly stiffened and remained absolutely motionless as he heard the faint echoes of voices carried on the breeze. After some moments he turned his head slowly from side to side, using his keen hearing to pinpoint the direction and distance the sounds were coming from. Then he moved toward them as swiftly and stealthily as a predatory animal moves toward its prey.

'Bloody hell, Sal! Can't you walk a bit faster? We won't get to the pool before bloody nightfall else.' Nance Harper halted at the top of the steeply rising pathway to shout at her friend who was lagging behind.

Sal's breathing was laboured, her body wet with sweat, and she was wincing with every step. She came to a standstill and pressing both hands against her lower ribs, panted, 'Me ribs are hurting something cruel. I reckon I might have bust a couple of 'em, they're so sore.'

'If your ribs are busted, then it aren't you who did the busting, you sarft cow. It was that evil bastard you'm wed to. And it serves you right for staying with the rotten bugger.' Nance growled unsympathetically, but went back down the steep rise and took her friend's arm. 'Come on, lean your weight on me. Once we gets over this bit, then it's all downhill. You can sit and rest at the pool.'

The pair struggled slowly up and over the crest of the rise, and Nance gently squeezed her friend's arm, encouraging her. 'There now, my duck. That's the worst done. It's all easy passage from here. Bloody hell! What's this? Bloody hell!'

The man who suddenly stepped out from the bushes to startle her grinned, and challenged them. 'What's you pair doing here? Thinking of doing a bit o' poaching, are you?'

'Bloody Josiah Danks!' Nance Harper was half indignant, half laughing. 'You nearly scared me out o' me wits, you daft bugger! For two pins I'd take that bloody gun o' yours and shove it up your arse!'

'Oh, would you now?' Danks chuckled, and winked lewdly. 'And then I'd be shoving something up your arse, and it wouldn't be me gun. Don't you be forgetting that I was one of His Majesty's Royal Marines for a good many years, and arsehole rules the navy.'

'Then surely it'll be me husband you'll be preferring to me, won't it, Josiah? I'd best run back home and tell him to get bent over ready for you,' Nance riposted instantly, and both women cackled with screeching laughter.

Danks laughed with them, then indicated the small wooden kegs. 'Going leeching, are you? I reckon you'd do best to try the upper end of the pool, because with last night's rain the bottom end has got to be over chest high by now.' He leered at Nance's well-filled bodice. 'And you don't want any leeches sucking on those pair o' beauties, do you, Nance?'

She winked saucily. 'Oh, I dunno about that! It might make a nice change from me husband slobbering on 'em like the pig he is.'

Danks' tongue flicked across his lips. 'Well, Nance, I reckon that any man would make a pig of himself over you. You'm a very tasty dish indeed.'

Nance preened at the compliment. 'You'm full o' sweet

talk, aren't you? Anyway, we got to get on, so I'll say ta-ta to you, Josiah.'

Danks stepped aside to let the women pass and after a last lustful leer at their well-curved rears disappeared once more into the dense undergrowth.

The big pool was secluded deep in the woods, imprisoned for most of its circumference by high, thickly bushed banks. Its dark opaque waters mottled with the floating fronds and broad leaves of weeds and water plants.

'Bloody hell!' Nance cursed disgruntledly when she saw the depth of water measured by the long branch she wielded. 'We'll be up to our tits in it!'

'If it's that deep, we could get drownded,' Sal Payne suggested nervously. 'Perhaps we shouldn't go into the water today?'

'Don't talk so bloody sarft!' Nance rounded on her sharply. 'I said up to our tits, not over our bloody heads!' She hurled the branch into the water, and began to unlace her bodice.

Sal stared in surprise. 'What are you doing?'

'I'm taking me clothes off! What else does it look like I'm doing, you silly, sarft cow?' Nance exclaimed with exaggerated mock-wonderment at her friend's stupidity. 'And I'm taking me clothes off because I don't want to get them sopping wet. And if you don't want to get your clothes sopping wet, then I suggest that you oughter take yours off as well.'

'Oh, I dunno about that.' Sal shook her head doubtfully. 'Suppose somebody was to see us, all naked like? My Alfie'd kill me if he ever found out that some other bloke had seen me naked.'

Nance showed no sympathy. 'Well, you can suit yourself. But I knows one thing for sure. I aren't going to go into that water by meself, and get all wet and perished with cold, and then share my leeches with you. And I knows another thing for sure, as well!'

'What's that?'

'That your lovely Alfie'll bloody well kill you if you don't bring him back some money for his booze tonight.'

Sal sighed wearily, and began to unlace her bodice.

Once naked, Nance gingerly lowered herself into the cold dark water.

'Bloody hell!' she gasped. 'Bloody hell, it's freezing!'

As she slowly waded further out the water laved over her full firm breasts, while behind her gasping shrieks announced that Sal had followed her into the pool.

Crouching in hiding on the far bank of the pool the watcher's excitement mounted uncontrollably as the two women stripped to disclose their white bodies to his avid gaze. He unbuttoned his breeches and began to stroke and fondle his genitals. Then angry frustration struck through him as first one then the other entered the water, shielding their rounded thighs and full breasts from his sight.

'You whores!' he hissed through clenched teeth. 'You filthy whores! You're trying to cheat me! I'll teach you, filthy whores! I'll have both birds wi' one stone this time.'

His left hand drew the sharp-bladed knife from his coat pocket, and lying flat to the ground he moved snakelike along the top of the bank, inching ever closer towards where the women's clothes lay discarded.

Nance levered herself out of the pool and stood up on the bank. She grinned with satisfaction when she saw the small slimy-black worm-like leeches that had bitten onto her legs.

'I've got some, Sal,' she shouted happily, and then began to carefully detach them from her soft white skin and drop their wriggling bodies into the wooden keg.

Within seconds Sal had joined her, and shivering and gasping began to detach her own catch of leeches.

The watcher's breath moaned from his slack wet mouth as he snaked closer and closer, a predatory beast readying himself to spring.

'Come on out o' there, you dirty bugger! I see'd you coming a bloody mile off.' Nance Harper shrieked with laughter as she snatched up her gown to shield her naked body.

Sal Payne squealed and crouched down, covering her breasts with her hands.

Josiah Danks roared with laughter and stepped out from concealment behind some bushes.

'You knowed I been here all along, Nance. That's why you took your clothes off. Just to tease me.'

'That's right! Just to let you see a bit of what you'm never going to get.' Nance Harper was not at all perturbed that he had seen her naked body. Like so many slum-born, slum-bred women raised in tiny mean hovels crammed with people of all ages, bereft of any degree of privacy or delicacy of manner, she had witnessed and experienced sexual intimacies virtually from birth.

Sal Payne was disturbed, however, and she angrily threatened the gamekeeper. 'If I tells my husband about you peeping-tomming me, he'll knock your bloody head off your shoulders, Josiah Danks!'

The gamekeeper chuckled unafraid. 'It'll take a better man than Alfie Payne to knock my head off, me duck. I warn't ten years in the Royal Marines for nothing, you know.'

'Well then just bugger off, 'ull you, and leave us in peace,' she retorted.

'All right, me duck. I was only having a bit o' fun. There's no need for you to be so mad at me. I'm going. But I won't be far away, so if you needs me just give a shout.'

While the three of them were talking, the watcher snaked back to his original hiding place. Racked with frustration, moans dribbled from his slack wet mouth. He rose onto his knees, staring across the wide expanse of water. Frantically masturbating with his right hand, his left hand viciously stabbed the knife blade again and again and again into the limp body of the dead rabbit on the ground beside him. He climaxed orgasmically, crying out as the semen spurted, and then he sagged onto the ground, his body a foetal curl, his wet mouth sucking the blood of the ripped and torn animal from his fingers.

Josiah Danks was now walking away from the pool.

'Did you hear that, Josiah?' Nance shouted after him.

He stopped and turned. 'Hear what?'

'It sounded like somebody crying out.' Nance stood listening hard.

'I didn't hear nothing.' Sal plucked the last leech from her flesh. ' 'Ull you sod off, Danksie. I wants to get this leeching over and done with. I'm perished with the cold.'

'Ahr, all right, I'm going.' The gamekeeper grinned and told Nance, 'It'll have been a rabbit took by a stoat most likely.'

'Must have been,' Nance agreed, and led the way back into the pool. 'Come on then, Sal. Let's get done here.'

The women were still slowly wading around their circuits as the watcher stealthily crawled away, leaving the small bloody heap of ripped flesh and fur where it lay.

Ten

It was late in the afternoon, and during the hours since Amy had called on him Tom's nervous tension had gradually mounted. He was dreading the prospect of a violent confrontation with Alfie Payne. He had tried to immerse himself in his books and microscopic studies, but like a nagging toothache the fear of potential violence constantly intruded into his thoughts, making it impossible for him to concentrate on anything else.

He continually paced up and down his room until his mother shrieked that he was disturbing her.

'Will you stop clumping around in those great clod-hopper boots! You're making more noise than a herd of elephants! I can't get a moment's peace and quiet! Poor wretched soul that I am, I pray for the Good Lord to take me up into His Paradise! And the sooner the better!'

Tom moved downstairs to pace up and down the passage between the cells.

'You pathetic coward!' he berated himself disgustedly. 'Why can't you be brave like other men? John Clayton wouldn't hesitate to tackle Alfie Payne. Why am I such a weakly cowering dolly-mop? My father would be ashamed to own me for his son. He'd have taken a horsewhip to Payne and given him a damn good thrashing for ill-using his wife so cruelly.'

The loud jangling of the bells came as a welcome distraction, and he creaked open the front door to find Joseph Blackwell's pale, lined features staring sombrely at him.

'I trust that you will forgive my intruding upon your Sabbath, Master Potts.'

'Of course, sir. Will you step inside?'

'No thank you. I'll only detain you for a very few moments. Tell me, how well do you know this district and its environs?

For example, do you know the exact delineation of the parish boundaries?'

'No, sir, I don't.'

'Might you possess the Military Survey Number 54 map of this area?'

Tom was again forced to answer in the negative.

'No matter.' Blackwell proffered a sheet of folded vellum. 'This is the map in question. Keep it and study it well, Master Potts. I would strongly advise you to explore thoroughly the parish and its environs and become familiar with the settlements and terrain. Make acquaintance with as many of the people as you can, and find out all that is possible about their characters and antecedents. The more that you discover and come to know well, then the more effective you will be as our constable: and the lighter the burden that you carry upon your shoulders as our constable.'

A wintry smile briefly curved Blackwell's thin lips. 'I wish you well, Master Potts, and I hope that you will accept this advice in the spirit that I offer it?'

Tom was greatly touched by this totally unexpected act of kindness. 'Indeed I do accept your kind advice, sir; and I thank you most heartily for it.' On impulse he asked tentatively. 'May I impose upon your kindness even further, and ask your advice on a matter which is troubling me?'

Without waiting for reply, he quickly related all that Amy had told him about Alfie and Sal Payne, and finished by requesting. 'What do you advise me to do, sir? I really have little or no idea of how best to proceed in this matter.'

Blackwell pursed his lips and briefly pondered the question before replying. 'Sadly, Master Potts, wife-beaters are all too common in this world. They live in palaces and they live in hovels. They are to be found within the highest society in the land, and the lowest.

'Alfred Payne has been summoned before the bench several times to answer for various misdemeanours. I consider him to be a worthless reprobate. But unless the woman brings charges against him on her own account, I fear that the law provides her with scant defence against his cruelty.

'However, I do know that Alfred Payne is not a popular figure among his neighbours, and many of them would greatly enjoy seeing him brought to heel. I very much doubt that any

of his fellow reprobates would intervene to aid him, should
he be seen receiving a just measure of punishment in repay-
ment for his own brutality. In fact, I am certain that anyone
who succeeded in giving Payne a good hiding would be warmly
applauded throughout this town. That individual would also
gain a reputation as someone to be treated with all due respect
and consideration.'

The wintry smile fleetingly curved the thin lips once more.

'So my advice to you is to follow the dictates of your
conscience. But remember, you will be acting in your private
capacity as a man, and not officially as a parish constable. I
bid you good day, Master Potts.'

Tom closed the door and resumed his restless pacing up
and down the passage. Almost an hour passed before he finally
steeled himself to face the ordeal which lay ahead. He returned
to his room, put on his coat and top hat, and picked up the
constable's staff of office. Then, remembering what Joseph
Blackwell had said, he laid it down.

He could hear loud snoring from his mother's room, and
was relieved that he wouldn't have to face her prying
questions about the reason for his going out. He left quietly,
locking the big front door behind him, and walked with a
slowness engendered by his dire forebodings of what he was
heading for.

'What?' Alfred Payne's dirty, unshaven face glowered threateningly. 'What do you mean, the doctor warn't in? You'm
bloody lying! I knows for a fact that he's in his house,
because I saw him go into it with me own eyes, not an hour
since.'

'No, Alfie, I'm not lying. You can ask Nance,' Sal protested
fearfully. 'We went to his house, and his housekeeper told us
that he'd gone out, and that she didn't expect him back until
really late tonight. Honest, Alfie, that's what she told us. You
can ask Nance.'

'If that's so, then where am the leeches?' he challenged.

'We left'm with the housekeeper. She said that we was to
come back for the money in the morning.'

'In the morning?' he roared, and rose from the low stool he
had been sitting on in front of the rusty, fireless grate. 'What good
is that to me? I needs some money now, you bloody useless bitch!'

'I'm sorry, Alfie, I'm sorry.' She was pallid with fear, her voice shaking as she pleaded desperately. 'I'll go first thing tomorrow and get the money off him for the leeches. Honest I will, Alfie. Honest! I swears it!'

'"Honest, Alfie! Honest! I swears it!"' he jeered in a mocking falsetto, and came at her in a sudden rush.

Sal screamed in terror and pain as his fists slammed into her face.

Tom's pace slowed even more as he reached the Red Lion and saw the two men lounging against the arched entrance to Silver Street.

'Well now, just look at who's come to visit us, Tommy.' Ritchie Bint took off his brown-paper hat and bowed with a flourish. 'We're honoured to have you call on us, Constable Potts.'

Tommy Chance bared his broken yellow teeth in a menacing snarl. 'What brings you here, Potts? Has somebody made a complaint about us?'

For a moment Tom's tight-screwed nerves threatened to fail him, but he fought down the urge to turn and retreat.

'No, my coming here has nothing to do with either of you.' He reached the archway and went to pass between the pair, but Ritchie Bint moved to block his way.

'Why have you come, then? It can't be a social visit you'd be making.' He grinned savagely. 'No bloody constable ever comes to our lovely street for a social visit. Come to think on it, precious few others ever comes to make a social visit, unless they's been born and bred here.'

Tom's heart pounded, and he quailed momentarily, but perversely his angry self-disgust for his own fear served to steel him. 'I'm come to speak with Alfie Payne. Can you please tell me which is his house?'

'Come to speak with Alfie Payne, has you.' Ritchie Bint's interest was immediately roused. 'What's he been up to this time?'

'That is no business of yours. It's a private matter between him and me.' Tom was astounded at his own temerity as he heard himself rebuffing this formidable brawler. 'Now can you please direct me to his house?'

As he spoke, Tom heard the anguished shrieking coming

from one of the tumbledown terraced hovels that lined both sides of the long narrow rancid-stenched alleyway.

Ritchie Bint's grin broadened, and he jerked his head towards the terraces. 'That's Alfie Payne's pigsty. The one where that wench is scrawkin'. Alfie's giving his missus her regular Sunday treat by the sound of it.'

'Thank you.' Tom stepped around the other man and walked steadily onwards, uncomfortably conscious of his boots instantly becoming fouled with the human and animal excreta, rotten vegetable waste and puddled muddied urine that smothered the cobbles.

The advent of this stranger created an instant stir of curiosity. Frowsty heads poked from broken casement windows, ragged urchins came running, front doors opened and people came to peer at him as he passed. He could hear their eager questions but kept his gaze stiffly forwards, not meeting any of their stares, or replying.

When he reached the door of Payne's hovel the anguished shrieks had metamorphosed into a sobbing moaning. The dread of what might now ensue threatened to overwhelm him, but he swallowed hard and forced his fist to hammer on the cracked panels.

The door was flung open and squat, shaven-headed, flat-snouted Alfie Payne appeared bellowing belligerently.

'Why the fuck are you trying to kick my door in, you long streak o' piss?'

Tom looked over the much shorter man's head and saw the woman slumped on hands and knees in a crumpled sobbing, moaning heap, blood from her smashed nose dripping down to pool upon the floor. The sight of her pitiable condition shocked and appalled Tom.

'You did this to her?' he demanded, pointing at the woman.

'O' course I did. Who else is in here?' Payne appeared to be surprised by Tom's words. 'And if you don't fuck off real sharpish, I'll be doing the same to you.'

Although fear was shivering through him, Tom forced himself to stand his ground. 'I should warn you that I'm the new constable of this parish.' He struggled to keep his voice firm. 'And if you continue to ill-treat your wife in this manner, then I'll arrest you.'

'You'll arrest me?' Alfie Payne reacted incredulously. 'Arrest me? You can't arrest me for giving me own missus a bit of a slapping!'

'Oh yes I can arrest you,' Tom reiterated.

Payne hawked and spat contemptuously onto Tom's boot. 'Oh no you can't. My missus is my lawful property, and I can do whatever I wants with her. Now fuck off!' He slammed the door shut in Tom's face.

By now a sizeable crowd of interested onlookers had gathered, pressing closely around Tom, the combined smells of their unwashed flesh and foul breaths creating a fetid miasma.

He turned to stare at their faces, expecting to see jeering contempt, but to his surprise most displayed only avid interest, and some were even indicating sympathetic support.

'It's good o' you to try and help Sal,' one blowsy harridan nodded. 'You'm the first law man that ever has. Bloody Alfie Payne deserves to get took to jail for the way he serves poor Sal.'

Several mutters of approbation greeted her words.

'Alfie Payne's right in what he says, though. He can do what he likes to his own woman, and it's nobody's business but his,' a grizzled old man grunted sourly, and other voices growled agreement.

As if to emphasize that Payne was doing exactly what he liked with his wife, another wailing shriek of pain came from inside the hovel, and a sobbing, choking, pleading.

'No, Alfie. Please! No more! I'm sorry! I'm sorry!'

'That's your fault, Potts, that she's getting an extra kicking.' Ritchie Bint shouted accusingly at Tom from the rear of the crowd. 'Alfie would have left off hammering her after a bit. But because o' you coming and sticking your nose in, he'll lay into her for bloody hours now just for badness.'

Another shuddering shriek of agony filled Tom's hearing, and suddenly a terrible anger such as he had never experienced before in his entire life surged through him, driving all fear before it, filling him with a desperate resolve to put a stop to Sal Payne's purgatory.

He lifted his boot and drove it with all his strength against the flimsy door, smashing it wide open.

The next instant Alfie Payne's squat powerful body hurtled from the hovel, cannoning into Tom, sending him stumbling backwards, colliding with onlookers who pushed him back towards Payne. Who met him with a flurry of punches, the heavy impacts jolting and jarring Tom's head from side to side, sending his top hat flying.

The crowd erupted in roaring excitement, became a swirling mass of bodies, jostling, pushing, struggling with each other to gain vantage points.

Dazed and disorientated by the storm of blows Tom again stumbled backwards, and Payne came after him like a savage beast, giving the taller man no chance to gather his senses, or even try to defend himself. A crushing punch on Tom's jaw dropped him to his knees. A vicious kick into the side of his head sent him crashing onto the filthy cobbles, his temple bludgeoning with sickening force upon them. The roaring of the crowd came fainter and fainter in his ears, then ceased entirely, and he was only aware of the sensation of falling helplessly downwards through a swirling maelstrom of flashing lights. Down, down, down until at last he was enveloped within a pitch-black, bottomless pit.

Eleven

It was the painful throbbing in his head which roused Tom to full consciousness, and with that arousal came the jumbled recollections of the brawl.

'Oh dear God! What have I done? What madness possessed me?' He was in his own narrow bed, clad only in his night-shirt. 'How did I get here? Who undressed me?' He fruitlessly racked his brain for any remembrance, but none came.

Sunlight was streaming through the windowpanes.

'What time is it, I wonder?'

His fingers explored the swollen cuts upon his face and the bandage around his skull, and he winced involuntarily as he cautiously probed the soreness of his wounds.

Pushing aside his bed coverings he gingerly pushed himself upright into a sitting position and swung his feet to the floor, groaning as the movement sharply intensified the painful throbbing in his head. He waited for the sickening throbbing to lessen and ease, before standing up. A wave of giddiness caused him to sway violently and he grabbed the headboard to steady himself. Battling the urge to lie back down on the bed in surrender.

His mouth was uncomfortably dry and metallic tasting, and as soon as the giddiness passed he went to the small washstand by the window and greedily drank from the jug of water set on it. The cool, musty tasting liquid soothed the discomfort of his parched mouth and throat, and he immediately began to feel much better. An examination of his facial lumps and cuts in the small wall mirror invoked the rueful reaction, 'Oh well, I was never a handsome fellow, was I. These won't impair my looks to any degree.'

The door of his room opened slightly, and the pretty face of Amy Danks peeped around its edge. 'I thought I heard you moving about, Tom.'

He was surprised to see her. 'What are you doing here, Amy?'

'I've been waiting for you to wake up.' She frowned. 'Am you feeling well enough to be up out of bed?'

'Yes, I'm fine. But what time is it? And how did I get back here? Who undressed me? Who bandaged my head?'

She raised her hands as a shield against the barrage of questions. 'How can I tell you anything, if you won't let me get a word in edgeways?'

'Sorry.' He smiled apologetically.

'It's nigh on noontime. You've been out for the count since yesterday afternoon. Ritchie Bint and his mates carried you back here, and it was Reverend Clayton and Dr Laylor between them who undressed you and cleaned and bandaged you and put you to bed. I told Tommy Fowkes that he must let me stay here for a while to see to your mam's needs, just until you was up and about again. I've been here since last night. I slept in the big chair in your mam's room.'

She paused, her face mirroring her troubled thoughts, then apologized haltingly. 'I'm ever so sorry that I got you into this mess, it's all my fault for egging you on so. I should have known that you'd be no match for Alfie Payne. If Ritchie Bint and his mates hadn't stopped him in time, the evil bugger would have kicked you to death. I'm sorry for what I did. Truly I am.'

Tears shimmered in her blue eyes, and she pressed a large clean piece of rag to her face.

'No, no, you mustn't blame yourself.' Tom hastened to reassure her, gently patting her shoulder. 'It's not your fault in any way. The only blame in this affair is Alfie Payne's, for being the vile brute that he is.' He grimaced wryly. 'I'm a poor excuse for St George, am I not. The first time I try to slay a dragon and rescue a damsel, the brute all but slays me instead.'

'Don't blame yourself for that, Tom,' Amy rejoined, her voice muffled by the voluminous rag. 'You just forgot to put your armour on, and take your spear with you. If you had of done, then you would have beat him for sure.'

Her quick wit evoked his delighted laughter, and she lowered the rag and giggled with him.

He stared fondly down into her shining eyes, struggling to control the impulse to bend and press his mouth to her luscious lips. Fighting against what he conceived to be his own selfish and unfair desire, which was to ask her to wait for what might be many years, until he had gained enough material security to marry her. Because the thought of marrying her at this present time, of entrapping her into sharing his present parlous financial situation, was still anathema to him. He had witnessed all too many times the terrible sufferings that poverty and hardship inflicted upon women and children.

'Thomas? Thomas? Is that you, you great useless fool? Come here to me, right now! I've got a bone to pick with you!'

His mother's harsh grating voice came as a paradoxical relief. 'I'd best go to her before she bursts a blood vessel with shouting at me.' He smiled at Amy, and shouted, 'I'm coming directly, Mother!'

'I've washed your clothes, and hung them in the yard to dry, and cleaned your top hat as best I could,' Amy informed him. 'They was all filthy dirty from rolling about in the muck. So you'll have to find something else to wear until they've dried out.'

'Thank you very much.' He was greatly moved by this further confirmation of her essentially sweet nature.

'Thomas?' Widow Potts shrieked furiously. 'Will you get in here right this second?'

'You'd best go to your mam, afore she blows up. And I'll have to get back real quick now to the Fox, or else Tommy Fowkes'll be blowing up.' Amy giggled, and then became suddenly serious. 'And don't go getting yourself into any more trouble on my account. Promise me!'

He nodded, and assured her, 'I solemnly promise you that I'll get into no further trouble on your account.'

Relieved and satisfied by that assurance she left smiling happily.

Tom smiled grimly to himself. 'Whatever further troubles I get into will be all on my own account, Amy, my love.'

In self-wonderment, he was discovering that the brutally ignominious defeat suffered at the hands of Alfie Payne had, by some mysterious alchemy, aroused in the depths of his being a rapidly burgeoning sense of resolute determination.

'I may always continue to be a weakly, cowardly sort of fellow. But I swear that I shall never again shirk or turn away from any confrontation with the likes of Alfie Payne. I shall try always to do what is right, no matter how hard I'm shivering in my boots, and I'll force myself to face up to any dangers that I must. I swear it to the memory of my father. I swear it!'

'Thomas? Damn you, where are you, you useless great fool?' Widow Potts shrieked hoarsely.

Tom chuckled ruefully. 'But perhaps I'll allow my cowardice to rule me, if on occasion it will save me from facing up to my mother.'

Later in the day, Tom was sweeping the raised front paving of the lock-up when an elegantly dressed horseman reined in his mount to introduce himself.

'My name is Hugh Laylor, Master Potts. I'm the doctor who was called here by the Reverend Clayton to treat your wounds yesterday; but of course you were in no condition to have any recollection of our meeting. I'm pleased to find you up and active. How's your head feeling?' Laylor's pleasant manner was as prepossessing as his physical appearance.

'Only a trifle tender to the touch, sir. I'm most grateful to you for treating me, and I thank you for doing so.' Tom quite naturally assumed that the doctor had come for payment for his services. He rapidly computed how much money he possessed at this moment, and found the amount to be virtually nil; and the next instalment of the minute annuity income was not due until nearly the middle of next month. He and his mother would be forced to survive on credit until then. Deeply embarrassed, he requested, 'Would it be convenient for me to settle the bill for your services on this day next fortnight, sir?'

His embarrassment metamorphosed into mortified shame when the other man roared with laughter and waved his hand in denial.

'I'm not come here for any payment, Master Potts. I rendered my services at the request of the overseer to the poor, so the parish will pay my fee. Indeed I would have treated your wounds for free if necessary. It is wonderful that we have at last discovered a constable who is brave enough to go single-handedly into Silver Street and beard one of its most fearsome pugilists in his own den.'

'I do apologize most sincerely,' Tom stuttered. 'I meant no offence. I truly didn't mean to—'

'Enough, Master Potts! I beg you! You have nothing to apologize for. The subject of any payment is closed, and I don't wish to discuss it further!' Laylor admonished sternly.

'But . . . Well, I feel . . . I am most . . .' Tom stuttered into silence.

'That's better.' Laylor nodded with satisfaction, then asked him eagerly, 'Now will you please satisfy my burning curiosity, Master Potts, and tell me why you didn't summon the other constables to aid you in tackling such a notorious bruiser?'

'Other constables?' Tom could only stare blankly.

Seeing this reaction, his questioner slapped his thigh resoundingly and roared with laughter again.

Tom's brows furrowed in baffled incomprehension.

Laylor managed to control his mirth sufficiently to explain. 'Forgive my unseemly outburst, Master Potts. But I recognize a Machiavellian hand in this. The hand of that sly old fellow, Joseph Blackwell Esquire!'

'Forgive me, sir, but I really don't understand. Could you explain more fully why the parish is paying my bill?' Tom asked.

'No, Master Potts. You must go to Blackwell and obtain
the explanation from his own lips.' Laylor smilingly saluted
in farewell, and cantered away.

'What's going on? Why has the parish paid for me? Why
wasn't I told that there were other constables?' A torrent of
questions filled Tom's thoughts. 'What's Blackwell's part in
all of this? Is he setting out to make me look even more of
a clown that I already do in the eyes of the people hereabouts?'

Indignant anger suddenly flared, and without stopping to
think further he strode purposefully across the green towards
Blackwell's office premises on the brow of Fish Hill.

It was Joseph Blackwell himself who came in answer to the
furious rapping of the brass lion's-head door knocker.

'Have you turned warlock, Master Potts? Man-witch?' There
was a hint of twinkling amusement in his rheumy eyes, as he
pointed his extended forefinger at the broom that Tom was
carrying. 'Is this now your chosen mode of transport? Or
perhaps you have supplanted Old Spragge in his post of market
sweeper?'

Tom's anger overrode any discomfiture caused by the
sarcastic gibes, and he gritted out, 'I think that you owe me
some explanations, Mr Blackwell.'

Blackwell's thin lips curved in the wintry smile. 'Step inside
my office, Master Potts, and you shall hear those explanations.'

He led Tom along a gloomy passage into a large room, the
walls of which were lined with shelves filled with books,
rolled parchments and ribbon-tied sheaves of documents.

'Pray be seated.' He indicated a chair facing his own across
the huge leather-topped desk. 'Can I offer you a glass of wine?
Or something a little stronger, perhaps?'

'No thank you,' Tom refused stiffly and sat down.

Blackwell took his own seat and leaning back in it, steepled
his forefingers before his mouth, his rheumy eyes shrewdly
evaluating the man before him.

The silence lasted for what seemed to Tom an inordinate
length of time, and at last he was driven to demand impatiently, 'Well, Mr Blackwell? Am I to hear any explanations?'

'Of course you are.' Blackwell became brisk and businesslike. 'Firstly let me explain my own status here in this
parish. I am clerk to the magistrates. I am also the parish

clerk, the select vestry clerk, the senior overseer to the poor and one of the chapel wardens of St Stephen's. Holding these several posts burdens me with many responsibilities, and means of course that I am a very busy man.'

He paused to await Tom's reaction.

'Yes. Obviously you must be,' Tom answered brusquely. 'But surely, despite your multitude of responsibilities, you could still have spared me the very few seconds needed to tell me who the other constables are? I also am eager to know why you have had my doctor's bill paid by the parish, as if I were a pauper? And why Dr Laylor should have referred to your "Machiavellian hand"?'

Blackwell chuckled dryly in amusement. 'Did he now!'

'Yes, he did.' Tom's indignant anger was still smouldering. 'I will tell you frankly, sir, that I feel you have somehow been using me to further some hidden agenda of your own!'

'No, I've not been using you to further any hidden agenda, Master Potts,' the other man denied firmly. 'But instead, testing your mettle!' He held up his hand to enjoin Tom's silence. 'Hear me out, I beg you! I freely admit to having deliberately encouraged you to tackle Alfred Payne. I wanted to test your physical courage. To my satisfaction, you passed that test. I have made discreet enquiries as to your moral character. Again, I was fully satisfied with what I discovered. I also know that you are highly intelligent, of good education and considerable erudition.'

The wintry smile briefly curved the thin lips. 'Albeit a little too resentful of having your medical treatment paid for as if you were a pauper! Which, to speak bluntly, Master Potts, knowing as I do your present straitened financial circumstances, to all intents and purpose is the condition of life to which you are very near.'

'I am not ashamed of being poor!' Tom counter-attacked. 'But I would be truly ashamed to be in possession of wealth gained by grinding down and exploiting those beneath me, as all too many of the rich and powerful do in this parish.'

'Those sentiments do you credit, Master Potts,' Blackwell congratulated him sincerely. 'However, praiseworthy sentiments by themselves do not put food on a man's table. So I shall ensure that as constable you will gain sufficient income to enable you to live in reasonable comfort.'

He noted the instant wariness in Tom's demeanour, and hastened to assure him, 'That income will not accrue from any sort of corrupt or dishonest practice, Master Potts. I do not countenance such, as Cashmore has found out to his cost.'

Tom found that his indignation-fuelled anger was rapidly ebbing away, to be superseded by an equally rapidly increasing curiosity as to what was to come. He could sense that this man was speaking with absolute sincerity, and was impelled to ask, 'Why have you gone to such lengths to test me, and to discover so much about me? What is it exactly that you want from me?'

'That is very simply explained, Master Potts. I want you to help me to ensure that this parish is a safe place for decent, law-abiding people to dwell in. There is a deal too much criminality here. Criminality which for the most part goes undetected and unpunished until its damage has been done. Our system of policing is woefully inadequate for this modern age. We appoint as constables men who have not the slightest idea of how to investigate a crime or to detect the perpetrators, and added to this, they are also local men with local family connections, who cannot really act impartially when that is what is of paramount importance.

'My greatest wish, and firmest intention, is to establish a body of parish police who have enquiring minds, a degree of erudition, the ability to be impartial and the qualities of courage, fortitude and initiative. Men such as yourself, Master Potts.'

'I'm honoured that you attribute such qualities to me, sir, but I truly don't feel that I possess any of them in any considerable measure,' Tom felt impelled to disclaim. Another niggling thought, that this man before him was laying claims to a degree of authority and power that he did not possess, intruded so strongly that it forced Tom to query uncomfortably.

'Please forgive my asking. I don't wish to appear rude . . . But isn't it true that the county magistrates are responsible for enforcing the law and appointing the police in this or any other parish of this country, and that it is only the select vestrymen who can recommend potential constables?'

'Of course it is!' Blackwell readily confirmed. 'But I believe that I can state without fear of contradiction that the Earl of

Plymouth, Lord Aston and the other justices of the peace rely almost completely upon my advice in these matters. Also, by virtue of the other posts that I hold, I am in close and constant contact with those other men who wield power and influence in this parish, and flatter myself that I am held in some considerable degree of respect by them. So much so, that they also rely greatly upon my advice.'

He chuckled and added. 'You must forgive the vanity of an old man, Master Potts, but I often picture myself, fancifully of course, as being in the position of the spider in the centre of its web.'

Tom found himself appreciating the other man's dry sense of humour, and couldn't help but smile. 'Indeed, sir. I confess that at this moment I find myself thinking that your fanciful picture is in fact a concrete reality.'

'Indeed, sir, so it is,' Blackwell agreed complacently. Then he asked, 'Well? Are you ready to join with me? To become my ally in the fight against the criminals and wrongdoers of this parish, and to bring them to justice no matter how low or high their rank in life? And think well before you give me your answer.'

'Am I ready to join with him? Do I want to become my brother's keeper?' Tom asked himself. 'Do I want to help Blackwell enforce laws which I myself regard as being unjust and oppressive? And why should I risk life and limb defending the property of the rich and powerful? Or trying to arrest violent men? Or wasting my time in fruitless investigations and enquiries?'

Then penetrating through all his doubts a voice whispered from the depths of his mind, 'But it will be exciting and interesting, will it not? And your life these last years has begun to seem increasingly dull and pointless. This is the chance to discover how much of a man you really are. So take it! Take it!'

He drew a deep breath and nodded. 'Yes, sir. I will join you.'

'I never doubted for one moment that you would.' Blackwell exuded satisfaction, and handed a small piece of paper across the desk. 'Here are the names and addresses of your fellow constables. One is Charles Bromley, whose shop stands near to baker Scambler's. The other is John Hollis. You will find his cottage at Webheath. I suggest that you make yourself known to them. I have my own opinions as to their individual worth, but you of course will make your own judgements.'

Tom briefly scanned the names. 'I shall call upon them as soon as possible.'

Blackwell handed across a thin sheaf of larger sheets. 'Now the information contained in these papers must remain absolutely confidential between you and me, Master Potts. They are copies of my own private records concerning the proven local rogues and vagabonds, and certain other individuals whom I strongly suspect of being wrongdoers. Study them until you know them by heart, but keep them securely locked away from any others' eyes, and never divulge their contents to anyone.'

'I shall do as you say, sir.' Tom was already experiencing a burning curiosity to learn what secrets these papers contained.

'Good!' Blackwell rose from his chair, and now his voice and manner were brusque. 'I will not detain you further, Master Potts. Remember, I shall always be available to you for any advice you may find yourself in need of. But it is much preferable that whenever and wherever possible you act upon your own initiative. Good day to you.'

Eager to meet his new colleagues, Tom decided to go immediately to Charles Bromley's shop.

It was a small, twin bow-fronted house with a wooden board over its door proclaiming in ornate gilt letters 'Bromley's Stationery Emporium for All Articles of Stationery. Rare and Ancient Books and New Literature'.

Tom carefully leaned his besom-broom against the outside doorpost before entering to the accompanying tinkling of the doorbell, and to his surprise found himself in an empty room.

With a clumping of clogs a dour-featured mob-capped, apron-swathed woman appeared framed in the interior doorway, and eyeing Tom's bandaged head, suspiciously challenged him.

'What's you come for? Because I'll tell you now, if it's money you wants, Bromley's got none! His creditors come and stripped out the last bit o' stock, and the last ha'penny yesterday morn! They'll be coming back tomorrow to take the walls and roof, I shouldn't wonder!'

'No, ma'am, I've not come here for money.' Tom hastily went on to explain the purpose of his visit.

'Well, Bromley aren't here. He's gone to Brummagem, and he might be gone for a month or for good! So it's a waste o' time you coming back here again. Shut the door soft on your way out. I can't a-bear any slammings!'

Disconcerted by his reception, Tom silently obeyed. Outside he retrieved his broom.

'What my reception by John Hollis might turn out to be like, God only knows.' He smiled in wry amusement. 'So I don't think I'll risk meeting him today.'

Twelve

Late April, 1826

The sixty-year-old man, still raw-boned and powerfully built, was sitting at the head of the long table, surreptitiously studying his dinner guests eating, drinking and talking animatedly to each other. Joseph Turner was a satisfied man. This gathering of some of the most important and influential people in the parish signified that he had at last put his lowly beginnings completely behind him, that after long years of gruelling toil and hardship, he had achieved his life-long goal. He had become a successful 'master'; and the proof of this were these people, with names such as Millward, Boulton, Holyoake, who were enjoying his hospitality tonight in his fine house on the eastern outskirts of Redditch.

Most of Turner's guests were past the first flush of youth. The clean-shaven men were dressed in plain, country-tailored clothes: their womenfolk inclined to plumpness, tightly corseted breasts bulging from low-cut gowns. Some women wore large turbans on their heads, others the huge floppy 'evening berets' adorned with flowers and feathers. All present were sweating heavily from the effects of the stuffy heat created by the myriad candles, the flaming logs in the hearth and their own gluttony.

The meal had started with turtle soup, followed by roasted capons, roasted leverets, sirloin of beef with Yorkshire puddings, ox tongues, hams, marrow puddings, mince pies, walnuts, filberts, dried fruits and dishes of preserved ginger, washed down with wine, ale, cider, perry.

As dish followed dish and bottle followed bottle, eyes began to glisten and lose focus. Voices slurred. Carefully practised enunciation of speech and correct mode of polite address metamorphosed into louder, rougher accents and cruder phrases. Laughter was no longer modulated but rang out raucously, and related anecdotes became noticeably more boastful, more salacious. Both men and women were displaying their lowly origins. They were what the aristocracy contemptuously termed the nouveau riches. They had not been born into wealth, political power and privilege. Whatever wealth they possessed had been accrued by hard work, shrewd business sense and ruthless acumen. They were members of that newly emergent, thrusting middle class of manufacturers, traders and entrepreneurs who were now demanding to share the political power and privilege of the aristocracy.

The youngest man present, however, sitting halfway down from the head of the table, was betraying nothing of his origins. He only toyed with his food, eating little, drinking less, and remaining aloof from the conversations around him. Compared to the other males present he was an exotic dandy in his London-fashion coat with its padded chest and shoulders, gaudy silk waistcoat and cravat, barber-curled hair, and fringed side whiskers and beard meeting beneath his chin to frame his thickly rouged, round face.

Joseph Turner's gaze frequently rested upon this flabby bodied young man, his stepson, and each time a scowl furrowed his brows, as he asked himself bitterly, 'Why am I saddled with a bloody useless foppish bugger like him there? There's no bloody justice in this world!'

Then inevitably, Turner's gaze would shift to the far end of the table, where his beautiful wife was seated as hostess, and he would tell himself resignedly, 'Ah well, he's the price I must pay to have her in my bed.'

At thirty-five years of age Eleri Turner was in the full bloom of her womanhood, with black hair, green eyes, lush body, white teeth and lilting voice. There were many men who lusted after her, and envied the husband who could take his pleasure at will with such a desirable bed-mate.

Although Eleri Turner appeared to be engrossed in conversation with the men on either side of her, she was well aware of her husband glowering at her son, Gareth.

'Pig! Rotten, miserable pig!' she cursed Turner mentally, while smiling radiantly at Hugh Laylor seated to her right hand, and John Clayton to her left.

The last course had been served and demolished, and it was time for the ladies to withdraw and leave the gentlemen to their cigars and masculine talk.

'Mrs Turner!' Her husband gave the signal, and Eleri led the ladies into the drawing room.

The two maidservants brought in boxes of cigars, and bottles of port and brandy, and the men changed their seats to move closer to their host.

Glasses were refilled, the lighting candle passed from hand to hand, and clouds of fragrant smoke wreathed the air.

Joseph Turner glowered at his stepson. 'I doubt that you'll find our talk of any interest, boy.'

Gareth's features showed no emotion. He rose, bowed to the company and left the room without speaking.

'How old is he?' Jason Holyoake, short, fat, red-faced and sweaty, wanted to know.

'Eighteen years, and not done a tap o' work on any day of them, lazy useless bugger that he is!' Turner exclaimed disgustedly. 'If it wasn't for his mam, I'd chuck him out into the bloody street this very night.'

'Well, Joseph, if you'll chuck your missus out together with him, I'll gladly take both of 'em in. I'll make room in me own bed for one of 'em, at least.' Holyoake leered, and the laughter that greeted his sally persisted despite the other man's angry glare.

'Come now, Joseph, don't take offence. I was only kidding you on,' Holyoake placated him, 'so let's get down to business, and waste no more time.'

He addressed the rest of the gathering. 'Are we all agreed, gentlemen. Do we cut the rates?'

There was a general chorus of assent.

'We have to.'

'We've no other choice.'

'You've never spoke a truer word than that!'

'So be it!' Joseph Turner smiled grimly. 'We announce the cuts tomorrow.'

'Gentlemen, may I speak?' John Clayton rose to his feet.

'Bloody hell, Parson! I don't reckon we needs any prayers or hymn-singing tonight! All we needs is a few more bottles o' this fine brandy,' Holyoake protested jovially, to general laughter.

John Clayton didn't join in the merriment. His expression was grave and troubled. 'Your decision to cut the rates of pay of your workers can only result in much increased hardship and suffering throughout this parish. There are already too many of our people enduring terrible deprivations. This cut could provoke a violent reaction from them.'

'That's as maybe, Parson, but their present deprivations are no fault of ours. Trade is sadly depressed throughout the entire country. If we are to survive and maintain our businesses, then we are forced to take harsh measures,' aquiline-profiled Charles Millward pointed out quietly. 'You talk of violent reaction . . . Well, we are already living in very violent times. There have been serious riots in Lancashire, and reports of civil unrest from many other areas. For which I lay much of the blame upon those who hold power over all of us. We are ruled by a monarchy, an aristocracy and a political establishment which can only be described as tyrannical and totally corrupt!'

He paused and smiled at Clayton's shocked expression. 'I see that I surprise you with my radical views, Parson. Well, I formed those views when I was still only a boy. My parents were paupers, and I became a parish orphan at an early age. Only a stroke of amazing good fortune and a great deal of hard toil enabled me to gain an education and rise from my lowly beginnings.

'I tell you these things about my past so that you will understand that I do not take my decision to cut the rates of pay from any motive of self-gain. I and these other gentlemen really do not have any other course of action open to us if we are to survive in business. Surely it is better for the workers to endure this temporary reduction in their rates of pay than to have their masters driven out of business, resulting in those same workers receiving no wages at all?'

Faced with such a quietly stated and reasonable explanation, John Clayton felt somewhat deflated. From personal experience he knew Charles Millward, in sharp contrast to some of his fellow masters, was an honourable man, and a benevolent employer. Clayton now felt that were he to continue to argue against the wage cuts, then he would be behaving unjustly towards him.

He bowed to the other man. 'Of course I fully accept what you have told me, sir. And I shall say no more on this subject.'

'That's it, Parson, you just stick to your praying and sermonizing and leave matters of business to them who knows what they'm talking about. Which you has just plainly showed us that you most definitely don't,' Jason Holyoake admonished him petulantly, and lifted his glass of brandy above his head. 'Let me propose a couple of toasts, gentlemen. Firstly a toast to our most respected and revered townsman, Mr Charles Millward, for talking such good sense; and secondly, a toast to wish damnation on them who pokes their noses into matters they knows nothing about, and which are none of their bloody business anyway!'

The gathering applauded uproariously, cheering, hammering their fists on the table and stamping their feet in a thunderous accompaniment.

John Clayton sat with head bowed, smarting under his humiliation, miserably wishing with all his heart that he had kept his mouth shut.

In a paddock a field's distance behind Joseph Turner's large house a flock of ewes were penned for lambing. Against the paddock hedge their elderly shepherd, Ebenezer Tolley, had constructed a small hut of hurdles lined with straw to shelter those ewes that he judged might give birth during the cold night hours. The noise of the applause from the house carried clearly through the thick fogged air as he sat on the ground inside the chill darkness of the hurdle hut, chewing painfully with his few remaining decayed teeth on hard dry bread and harder drier cheese.

'Hark to them lucky buggers, Kippy.' He prodded the dog awake with his iron-shod boot. 'They'm having great sport by the sound of it. I'll bet they'm chompin' on a sight better grub than we's got here.' He yawned widely and stretched his arms. 'I'll be bloody glad when tonight's over and done with, and I can get a few winks o' sleep. I'm fair bloody knackered, and that's no lie. I'm getting too old for this game, Kippy. Just like you'm too old, you bugger.'

The aged dog grunted as if in agreement, and lowered its head to the ground once more in slumber.

The man prowling in the black shadows on the other side of the hedge heard the shepherd's gruff tones, and taken by surprise halted. Listening hard, he remained completely motionless for long minutes.

Inside the hut Ebenezer Tolley's head drooped in sleep and he began to snore. The motionless man waited until it became a continuous repetition, and then moved on and noiselessly climbed over the paddock gate.

The nearest ewe bleated as the black figure loomed over it, and bolted, panicking the rest of the flock. Bleating in loud concert they swirled frantically around the paddock. One ewe remained lying on the ground unable to run with the flock because it was giving birth to its lamb. Paralysed with terror it made no sound as the sharp blade of the knife plunged into its throat.

In the hut the dog lifted its head, roused by the flock's terrified rampage, and began to bark, waking Tolley. Half stupefied with sleep the old man stumbled from the hut. His first instinct was to hurry to the gate to ensure that it was still closed. In the foggy darkness he didn't see the black figure of the intruder, who was also running towards the gate, until they collided. The impact slammed Tolley to the ground, and by the time he had recovered sufficiently to clamber to his feet the intruder had disappeared into the night.

'Bastard dog! Bastard dog! I hadn't finished! I hadn't finished! Bastard dog!' The curses dribbled from the intruder's slack wet lips as he slowed his pace and halted, listening hard for any sound of pursuit. He drew the back of his hand across his mouth, tasting the salty blood, and the tormenting demons in his mind jeered relentlessly.

'You bloody fool! That's no use to you! It's not some dumb beast that you really need, is it! You need a woman! You need to use a woman! It's got to be a woman next time! It's got to be another woman!'

He rocked his upper body backwards and forwards, his breath rasping in his throat. 'Yes! You're right! Yes! I must use a woman! Use a woman! Next time it must be another woman!'

Thirteen

'**D**on't you try telling me that a bloody fox or a dog did this. I'm telling you it was human hands. I knocked into the bugger and he sent me sprawling arse over tit, so he did. That's why I come to you, Master Potts. I wants you to catch the bugger who did this.'

Tom stood side by side with the old man, staring down at the mutilated bodies of the ewe and lamb.

'Me master's trying to blame me for it. He says I were drunk or asleep and that it's foxes or dogs. So I said to him, how many times has he seen a bloody fox or dog cut a sheep's bloody throat? He hadn't got any answer to that. Come down wi' me, I said to him, and see for yourself if I aren't telling the truth. But he says he's too busy, and that it was me who could have slashed the sheep's throat to cover up me own drunken slackness.'

'Who is your master?' Tom asked.

'Joe Turner.'

'Turner the needle master?'

'The very same. The sheep am a bit of a hobby for him.'

Tom knelt to examine the dead animals more closely. The ewe's throat had been slashed so deeply that its head was all but separated from its body, which had been ripped wide open and the half-born lamb torn out from the gaping wound and decapitated.

'Whoever did this must be a madman.' Tom was appalled at such ferocity inflicted on helpless animals.

'I'll give the bugger madman if I gets me hands on him!' The old man vowed angrily. ''Ull you do something for me, Master Potts? 'Ull you go up to the house and tell Joe Turner that it was human hands that did this, and not any dog or fox. He'll believe it when it comes from you.'

'Yes, I'll do that.' Tom agreed absently. He was thinking hard, covertly examining his companion's muddied smock, leggings and boots. The hands of the perpetrator of this butchery would have been blood-soaked, his clothing and footwear heavily and freshly bloodstained. There were no such fresh stains on Tolley's boots or clothing, and his hands were thick with weeks old dirt.

'You say that this man knocked you over and then climbed over the gate?'

'I do say.'

'Let me see the bottoms of your boots.'

'What for?' Tolley demanded suspiciously.

'Whoever did this might have left a trail of footprints, and I need to be able to eliminate your own.'

The soles of Tolley's boots were distinctive, cross-barred with thick iron strips.

'Right, Master Tolley, I'll see what I can find.'

Tom moved slowly towards the gate, closely scanning the short newly growing, still dew-wet grass, but apart from his and Tolley's freshly made tracks could not discern any clear trail of other footprints. The frantic swirling of the flock had obliterated any other previous tracks.

On the gate he found fresh bloody smears where the man's hands must have gripped the bars as he climbed over.

Very close to the other side of the gate Tom's intent scrutiny detected two footprints which appeared to be freshly made in the rain-softened ground. They were widely set and running parallel to the gate bars. He knelt and carefully began to feel around and across the depths, floors and outlines of the two imprints with his fingertips.

'They're a man's judging by their size, and they're not mine or Tolley's, because there's no feel of either my pattern of boot studs or Tolley's cross-bars. So in all probability these are the intruder's,' he decided. 'And they're deep enough to have been caused by a heavy man.' He pondered for a few moments, and suddenly wondered, 'But why are they parallel to the gate, and why spaced so? Surely they should be pointing towards or away from it? Unless . . . ?'

Again he turned his scrutiny onto the gate bars, looking for fresh mud or scrapes on their upper edges, but discovered none.

He was abruptly certain. 'He didn't clamber over the gate! He vaulted over it! These prints were more likely made by a medium-sized man, who was vaulting sideways over the gate and landing heavily. Tolley said that the man he was knocked down by was running very fast. He has to be young, fit and athletic to be able to run so fast and to vault a gate of this height.'

Tom experienced an exhilarating sensation of excitement and told himself elatedly, 'I do believe that I've a talent for this investigation lark!'

His elation heightened when he discovered a trail of similarly shaped footprints leading westwards across the field in the direction of the town and Joseph Turner's fine house. But that elation was dampened when the footprint trail reached a hard stony cart track and disappeared.

For more than an hour Tom searched along the track's verges trying to discover if the trail picked up again, but found no traces. Finally he reluctantly accepted that there was nothing to be gained by continuing the search, but vowed determinedly that this setback would only be temporary.

'I'm not giving up the search for him. I'll lay him by the heels eventually. No matter how long it takes. But now I'd best call on the Turners and tell them that I am totally confident that Ebenezer Tolley is telling the truth.'

'Me master's not in, but me mistress says that she'll speak to you.' The maidservant glared at Tom's muddied boots. 'And you'd best not dare put a foot over this doorstep, because me mistress won't take kindly to you tramping muck into the house; and nor will I neither.'

Tom nodded in wry acceptance, and not for the first time in his life marvelled at the arrogance displayed by domestic servants when encountering those whom they considered to be their inferiors in social status.

'So, Master Potts, my maid informs me that you are our parish constable.' Eleri Turner's perfumed fragrance filled Tom's nostrils. 'And what brings you to call on me?'

'The dead sheep, ma'am.' Tom was impressed with her exotic beauty. 'Your shepherd asked me to speak with your husband and confirm that it was not foxes or dogs that killed the sheep, but human hands.'

'Human hands?' Her black eyes displayed a momentary unease.

'That is my opinion also, ma'am; and I believe that Ebenezer Tolley is truthful when he tells of encountering the man who did it.' Tom had noted her momentary unease and tried to reassure her. 'I have read of similar outrages, ma'am, and I'm confident that the perpetrator presents no threat to you or anyone else in this household. The men who commit these types of crime are usually found to be considered harmless and inoffensive by their neighbours.'

'So we are to accept that we can all sleep safely in our beds, Mother; because we have it on the authority of a bumpkin constable?' Gareth Jenkins, engulfed in a voluminous dressing gown, had been listening to the conversation unnoticed.

She turned on him angrily. 'For pity's sake, Gareth, can you not make your presence known like any normal person? Why must you always sneak around and creep up on people so?'

'Because I choose to do so, Mother. That's how I come to learn so many things about other people.' The young man's manner was so unpleasantly supercilious that Tom found himself disliking him instantly.

He came forwards to face Tom, and sneered. 'My God! You're taller than a steeple! Tell me now, is it cold up there?'

Long accustomed to such gibes, Tom refused to let this young man bait him, and merely replied equably. 'I believe the temperature is no lower than that on your own level, sir.'

He bowed to Eleri Turner. 'Rest assured, ma'am, that I shall do my utmost to discover the man responsible for this outrage.'

She smiled seductively. 'I'm sure that you will, Master Potts, and please do not hesitate to call upon me for any help that I can give you.'

Tom experienced a frisson of sexual desire, and could not help but wonder how such a beautiful woman could have given birth to such an unprepossessing son. 'Now now, Thomas!' he warned himself. 'Don't let yourself become distracted from what you're about just because a gorgeous woman smiles at you.'

He took his leave and walked away; and conscious that her

black eyes were still watching him found that he was keeping his back straight and chin high. 'You soft-headed fool, you!' He grinned wryly at his own susceptibility to Eleri Turner's physical charms.

Putting all thoughts of her out of his mind, he decided that it might be helpful to his investigations if he introduced himself to his other fellow constable, John Hollis. He would perhaps know if there had been other similar instances of such savage butchery in the past few years, which might serve to yield some clues concerning the perpetrator.

Fourteen

The hamlet of Webheath was a mile and a half west of Redditch and the shortest route to it was through the Pitcheroak Woods. The day was fine and sunny and Tom enjoyed the leisurely stroll along the ancient main footpath beneath the wide spreading branches. Although it was a working day he met with many passers-by, some of them with bundles of faggots on their backs which they had collected from the broken branches of storm-toppled trees and dead shrubs, and he exchanged pleasant greetings. One encounter brought him to an abrupt standstill, however, and caused his heartbeat to quicken in fearful shock.

'Well now, fancy meeting you here.' Alfie Payne's brutal face grinned. 'Am you spying on me by any chance? Trying to catch me poaching?'

'No, I'm not!' Tom shook his head, fighting to master his fear of this formidable brawler.

Payne lifted up the sack he was carrying in his right hand and swung it from side to side. 'But I'll bet you'm wondering what it is I got in this bag?'

Although dreading physical confrontation, Tom was determined not to let this man humiliate him, and he steeled himself to reply as firmly as he could.

'Since you ask, Master Payne, and there is poaching going on in these woods, then yes, I am now wondering what you've got in there. So perhaps you'd be good enough to show me?'

'And if I won't? Then what'll you do?' There was open challenge in Payne's tone.

Suddenly Tom experienced an inner sense of wonderment, as his determined resolution to gain the mastery of his physical fear became dominant, and he said firmly, 'You see this staff that I'm carrying, Payne. This means that I am presently on duty, and empowered to act in the King's name. And in the King's name, I'm now ordering you to show me the contents of that sack.'

'Or what?' Payne spat out.

'Or I'll arrest you for obstructing me in my duty.'

'I can break you in half as easy as snapping a twig, you long streak o' piss!' Payne snarled ferociously. 'And I reckon that's just what I'm going to do, right this second!'

For a moment Tom felt himself quailing inside. Then movement caught his eye, and relief flooded.

'Look behind you.' He pointed his staff. 'We have a witness. And I don't believe that you'll take the risk of trying to break him like a twig. Not when you see what he has with him.'

The man in the distance coming down the long pathway towards them, his features concealed by the broad-brimmed hat drawn low over his brow, had a pair of what looked to be white-coated Old English bulldogs on leashes.

'I can call on that man and his dogs to aid me in arresting you,' Tom claimed confidently. 'And he must obey me. That is the law. So make your choice now. Will you show me what is in your sack?'

For a brief instant Payne looked as if he was going to spring at Tom. But then, mouthing furious obscenities, he opened the mouth of the sack to disclose its contents – animal bones, stinking of the rotten scraps of flesh still attached to them.

'Thank you for your cooperation, Master Payne.' Tom could not help but feel a triumphant satisfaction. 'You may go about your business now.'

Snarling and muttering, Payne hurried away.

Tom looked towards the oncoming man and dogs, and as they came nearer received a further shock of surprise when he recognized the newcomer.

Ritchie Bint grinned when he reached Tom, and hauled his snapping, slavering dogs to a halt. 'Come to heel, damn you! This man aren't any feast o' meat for you pair o' bastards! It's our new constable.' He peered keenly at Tom's features. 'You'm still bandaged I see, but the rest o' your kisser is nigh on healed up, Master Potts. It's a mercy that you warn't hurt worse on that day.'

'I believe it's you that I have to thank for that mercy, Master Bint.' Tom gratitude was heartfelt, as was his guilt for not having searched this man out and thanking him sooner. 'I'm told that if it wasn't for your intervention I might have been crippled for life. I'm truly grateful to you. I can only apologize for not seeking you out to give you my thanks. It's a poor excuse for ill manners, I know, but to tell you the truth I was nervous of entering Silver Street again, as well as being very uncertain of how I would be received there.'

'Most likely with a handful o' shit chucked at you.' Bint grinned. 'I got more than a few moans from some o' me neighbours for helping a constable, I can tell you. But I liked the way that you had a go at helping Sal Payne. It showed that you'm not a bad chap at heart, even though you'm on the side of them rich buggers who lords it over the likes o' me.'

'I'm truly sorry if your neighbours are criticizing you for helping me,' Tom assured him sincerely. 'And I don't feel that I'm on any other side to you. We are both human beings and born equal in the sight of God, as are all men.'

'All men born equal in the sight o' God?' Bint scoffed good-naturedly. 'Well, if you believes that, you'll believe anything! But I can't stop here talking wi' you any longer. I've got to first-blood these pair o' savages, and time's getting short.'

'First-blood them?' The images of the dead ewe and its lamb instantly came into Tom's mind, coupled with momentary suspicion.

'That's right.' Bint looked fondly at the two slavering animals. 'I'm matching 'em against a couple of Ikey Reed's young 'uns within the hour. I reckon these two'll win easy. Their dad was a real champion. Best scrapper I ever owned. And when it comes to scrapping, then breeding shows, don't it.'

'Oh, I see. They're going to fight.' Understanding came to Tom. Personally he took no pleasure from, and had scant interest in, the sport of dog-fighting. Nor of fox-hunting, cock-fighting, badger-drawing, bull-baiting, rat-killing, or any other blood-sport. But he was a man of his time, and from birth had been raised in a world which believed all other species to be soulless entities created by God solely for the use, consumption and pleasure of human beings. So, as a consequence of his upbringing and indoctrination, he regarded blood sports as being among the normal and acceptable pastimes of his fellow-men.

'Well, I wish you and them luck, Master Bint.'

'Luck don't come into it.' Bint grinned. 'It's breeding that counts, and they's got that in spades. So long, now.'

The two men parted amicably.

The half-timbered cottage of John Hollis was set back from the road, fronted by a broad belt of greensward, its rear close against the woodland boundary stream.

Tom stopped a carter to enquire its whereabouts, and the man jerked his thumb over his shoulder and chuckled.

'You wants John Hollis, does you? You just keep on along down there a bit, and you can't miss him. The daft bugger's performing again, so you'll hear him afore you sees him.'

Tom walked on, and soon heard a distant voice. He quickened his pace; the voice became louder and he could clearly distinguish its sonorously toned utterances.

'The first Monday in August begins Redditch Fair
And people flock thither for to sell their ware,
When the farmer folk all gather here
To sell their beasts and buy their beer . . .'

Tom reached the broad belt of greensward and halted, staring disbelievingly at the man before him. He was standing on top of a large upturned barrel in the middle of the open space jerkily waving his arms and declaiming:

'The Bromsgrove butchers they come to buy
And will have fat ware tho' the price is high.
They buy them all up and drive them away,
If the price is too high why the people must pay . . .'

He saw Tom and scowlingly demanded,

'And who the devil might you be,
Who stands there gaping wide at me?

Are you a man who means me well,
Or an evil demon sent from hell?'
Tom was struggling to keep from bursting into laughter.

John Hollis presented an unusual spectacle. He was tall and
of skeletal build with an exceptionally long hooked nose and
chin, thickly rouged cheeks, his shoulder-length hair hennaed
to a bright orange hue, and wearing only a canvas smock,
with bare legs and feet. He was bizarre in both appearance,
and mannerisms of speech and movement.

Tom controlled his mirth and bowed politely.

'If you are Master John Hollis, then I am your fellow
constable, Thomas Potts.'

'Are you, by God! Well, I am most certainly John Hollis,
the bard of Redditch, and the high constable of Tardebigge
parish.'

Hollis leapt high from the barrel, turned a complete somer-
sault in the air, and landed lightly on the ground in a display
of acrobatic agility that caused Tom's jaw to drop momentarily in astonishment.

'Did you hear my recitation, Master Potts? And do you
note my simple rustic garb?' Hollis gestured theatrically at
his clothing. 'I don it in homage to the greatest man who ever
lived. The immortal William Shakespeare. Our very own
"sweet Swan of Avon". With whom I pride myself on sharing
not only a quite remarkable physical resemblance, but also a
quite remarkable bardic gift.'

Once again Tom was struggling to keep a straight face.

'I am a very gifted poet, Master Potts,' John Hollis declared,
and striking an histrionic pose declaimed in sonorous tones:
'The poem entitled "Defiance to Boney". Created by John
Hollis, Esquire in the year eighteen hundred and six by this
same John Hollis, Esquire when he was still only a stripling
of tender years . . .

> Mr Boney, your heart is stony.
> If England you invade,
> With your ragged crew,
> We'll run you through,
> And put you to bed with a spade.
> We think it right with you to fight
> For our liberty and laws;

The God we serve will us preserve
All in so good a cause.

He gusted a sigh of absolute satisfaction. 'There now, Master
Potts, is that not a truly sublime piece of verse? Am I not a
truly gifted poet?'

'It is indeed sublime, and you are undoubtedly gifted, Master
Hollis.' Tom was forced to grit the words out from between
hard-clenched teeth so desperately was he fighting back his
laughter.

John Hollis preened, basking in this praise, then in a
blatantly false show of self-deprecation shook his head and
waved his hands. 'You are too kind, Master Potts. Far too
kind. It is but a poor thing.'

'Can I ask for how long you've been a constable?' Tom
enquired.

'For eleven years, four months, six days and two hours,
come this noontime,' Hollis recited proudly.

'My God!' Tom uttered in shock. 'Why have you served
for so long?'

'Because he's as daft as a brush!' the man who had come
from the cottage to join them grunted, and introduced himself.
'I'm John's twin, James; and I knows you to be Thomas Potts
because I saw you down the town the other day and asked
about you.'

In build and facial features James Hollis was the almost
exact double of his twin, but his close-cropped hair was a
natural brown, his weather-beaten cheeks rouge-free, and his
clothing the rough-cut coat, breeches and boots of a labouring
man.

He rested his extremely large calloused hands on his
brother's shoulders and told him, 'Your grub's on the table,
our John. Go and ate it afore it gets cold. Go on now!' He
pushed his brother gently towards the house.

John Hollis hulloed in delight. 'Pottage! Sweet-savoured
pottage! I shall hie me to my mess of pottage!' He ran swiftly
to the house, hulloeing continuously and every few steps
springing high into the air.

James Hollis' expression was sombre as he watched his
sibling's eccentric progress and explained quietly, 'You's
caught him on one of his bad days, Master Potts. He has these

turns every now and again. But in between times he can be as sensible as any man. I'm well used to folks making mock of him, but I don't take kindly to it; and I've given a good hiding to more than a few of them who takes pleasure in tormenting him.'

He turned his head to peer searchingly into Tom's face for long moments, then nodded as if satisfied with what he discerned there. 'But I don't reckon there was nastiness in your mind when you was near to busting out laughing at him, so there's no reason why you and me need fall out.'

'I'm happy to hear you say that, Master Hollis.' Tom was relieved to hear that this sinewy-bodied, huge-handed man was not to be his enemy.

'Is there anything you wants to ask me?' Hollis asked.

'Well, yes, there is something that I want to ask you; and I mean no offence, I assure you. But I can't help but wonder why your brother has been made to be a constable for so many years, in view of his . . . his . . . well, in view of his . . .'

'His lunatic fits!' James Hollis bluntly finished the sentence, and grinned mirthlessly as he explained. 'He's been kept as constable as a personal favour to me from Joseph Blackwell. I'm a mason by trade, and me work takes me away from home quite a bit. Having the staff gives our John the protection o' the law, and a chance to earn a couple o' shillings now and again. And like I said afore, when he aren't having one of his turns, he's sensible as any other man. O' course I don't like to go anywhere too far away to work when he's like he is now.'

'It does you great credit that you care for your brother so deeply,' Tom complimented sincerely, 'and Joseph Blackwell also for favouring you as he does.'

'Yes, Blackwell's a good honest man. Mind you, when he's in his right senses our John does his duty well. He's fit and strong and afraid of nothing nor nobody. You'll find him a good man to have at your side when you're having trouble with the roughnecks.'

'I'm sure I'll be more than pleased to have him by me at such times, Master Hollis, because I'm not much use as a fighting man myself,' Tom admitted ruefully.

James Hollis made no immediate reply, but only peered searchingly once more at Tom's face for some seconds. Then he proffered his hand.

'I likes your style, Master Potts. So we'll shake hands and part with good feelings. I'll send word to you as soon as our John is back to his rightful senses again.'

On his way back to the lock-up, Tom couldn't stop himself chuckling with wry amusement.

'So much for Joseph Blackwell's vision of a parish police with enquiring minds, courage, fortitude and the rest. Instead he has a runaway debtor, a periodic lunatic poet and a weakly, cowardly article like me. God help us all!'

Fifteen

Mid-May, 1826

It was early morning of the Wednesday following the Monday petty sessions, and sitting at his desk Joseph Blackwell checked the entry he had just made in the big leather-bound ledger, sprinkled blotting powder from its shaker onto the wet ink, blew off the surplus and closed the ledger with a resounding thump. From his desk drawer he took three folded and wax-sealed sheets of paper and handed them to Tom.

'Here's work for you to do. Summonses against butcher Vincent for failure to removed a stinking nuisance at his slaughter shed, and against widow Clark for non-payment of tithes. This other one is a removal order for a pauper woman, Ann Washwood, and her children from our poorhouse to Kings Norton parish. You will escort her and hand her over to the poor overseers there. The children are very young so you may hire a horse and cart to transport them. We'll claim back the cost from the Kings Norton vestry in due course. She needs to be removed at the earliest opportunity. This very day if that is at all possible, and failing that, tomorrow at first light. Good day to you, Master Potts.'

'Very well, sir.' Tom accepted the documents and stowed

them away in his shoulder-slung canvas haversack, but instead of leaving, stood his ground and asked, 'The woman, Ann Washwood, what if she resists being removed?'

'Then you must do your duty, Master Potts, and use whatever force is needed to remove her,' Blackwell replied.

'Use force, against a poor defenceless woman?' Tom questioned uncomfortably.

'If necessary. Because let me make it very clear to you, if you fail to do your duty then Lord Aston will most certainly make your life extremely unpleasant.' Blackwell gusted a snort of exasperation. 'We live in a harsh and wicked world, Master Potts, and all that we have to protect ourselves against those who would prey on us is the law. And the law can only be effective if it is executed to its very letter. Now I have work to do, so let me bid you a good day.'

Tom walked out feeling very doubtful about whether he could bring himself to use force to transport Ann Washwood and her children.

'What's the matter wi' folk these days? Be they all too kettle-stomached to stand a bit of honest stink, or what? Whose been moaning about my offal now?' Henry Vincent, slaughterer and butcher, as red-skinned and solid-fleshed as any of the sides of beef he trimmed and purveyed, received the summons with very bad grace. 'There's nothing of a nuisance about my shop! Just take a look at me. Don't I look hale and hearty, and I'm here every day that God sends!'

'Indeed you do, Master Vincent. You're the very picture of health,' Tom agreed hastily, feeling nervous about the way the butcher was threateningly brandishing his huge bloodstained cleaver. 'But the summons does not concern your shop. Some time ago a relative of one of the Tardebigge churchwardens went personally to Lord Aston to complain about the terrible stench emanating from your slaughter shed in Red Lane, but Lord Aston only brought it to the attention of Master Blackwell a few days since. I don't know the name of the complainant. I'm merely the messenger in this instance.'

'But I aren't killed any beast there for months.' Vincent shook his head in puzzlement. 'I aren't been near the place. I've been doing me slaughtering out back because it's handier since I've had the new outhouse built. And another thing, my shed in Red Lane was scrubbed out afore being barred and padlocked up, so there's nothing in there to make a stink. So some bugger's trying to make trouble for me for no reason that I knows of, and when I finds out who it is then I'll be teaching 'em a lesson that they won't forget in a hurry, you mark my words,' he growled.

'I'm sure that you will, Master Vincent. Good day to you.' Tom beat a hasty retreat from the butcher's shop, and with each rapid step he took to widen the distance from it, felt a corresponding relief.

The next call he made was on the widow Clark, who lived on the Unicorn Hill close to the town crossroads.

The motherly looking, benevolently smiling woman who answered the door to his knocking instantly metamorphosed into a foul-mouthed, strident harridan when he told her the purpose of his visit.

Once more Tom was forced to beat a hasty retreat, and she hurled the summons after him, shrieking furiously, 'You can wipe your bloody arse on this, you long streak o' piss!'

He decided he would go and have a quiet smoke of his pipe back at the lock-up before he tackled the journey to the poor-house and the task he was dreading of removing the pauper woman and her baby.

The Tardebigge parish poorhouse was an isolated decayed farmhouse and its ramshackle outbuildings, set on the northern edges of a flat expanse of fields to the south-east of Webheath hamlet. From its windows the distant blue-grey ranges of the Malvern Hills and the Broadway Hill could be seen on clear days, and two miles to its south-west the graceful slender spire of the Tardebigge parish church shimmered in the sunlight on its high ridge above the Worcester and Birmingham Canal.

Tom drove the horse and cart up the deeply rutted lane and reined in before the large farmhouse. He got down from the cart seat and looked at the two separate front doors. 'Which one should I knock at?' he wondered.

His unspoken question was answered for him when the nearer door opened and a short stocky woman wearing a shabby black dress and a man's wide-brimmed, soft-crowned hat, stood framed in the doorway.

She glowered at his crowned staff and snapped. 'I've been expecting you . . . It's a sin and a shame, so it is!'

'I'm Thomas Potts, constable of Tardebigge parish.' Tom was disconcerted by the hostility radiating from her. 'May I ask who you are, ma'am?'

'I'm Mrs Lewis. Wife to Edwin Lewis, the master of this poorhouse.'

'Then I'd like to speak to your husband please, Mrs Lewis.'

'He aren't here, so you'll have to make do with me.'

'Very well. I've come for Ann Washwood and her children. The vestry has ordered their removal to Kings Norton. Here is the official notification.' He took out the removal order and held it towards her, and she gathered a mouthful of saliva and spat on it.

'That's what I thinks of that bloody order,' she hissed venomously. 'And of the bloody Tardebigge vestry as well! It's a sin and a shame, so it is, forcing her to be shifted! Not that you'll care a bugger for that, will you.'

'How can you say that when you know nothing about me?' Tom protested, his discomfiture increasing with every second. 'I'm only doing my duty.'

'Duty? Duty? You're doing your duty?' she sneered contemptuously. 'My man was a soldier. He fought at Salamanca, and Vitoria and Toulouse and Waterloo, and I was there with him through all them long years in Portugal and Spain and then in France and Belgium. That what I calls doing duty, Mr Constable of Tardebigge Parish. Not dragging some poor wench and her kids back to bloody Kings Norton!'

She suddenly stepped from the doorway, causing Tom to take an involuntarily step backwards.

'Come on along wi' me, Mr Tardebigge Constable, I wants to show you summat!' She stamped around to the rear of the house, and Tom nervously followed, wondering if this irate woman was leading him into an ambush.

She led him into a low-roofed, brick-built shed which contained two huge leaden troughs in which animal carcasses were salted down to be cured and preserved.

There was a tiny rag-covered mound on the centre of one trough, and the woman beckoned him to it. 'Take a look at this, Mr Tardebigge Constable, and then tell me again about you'm only doing your duty.'

She whipped back the rag covering, and Tom gasped.

A small dead child was lying on its back, its little arms folded across its chest, a peeled onion crammed into its open mouth.

'This is one of Ann Washwood's babbies.' Mrs Lewis' fingers tenderly stroked the small head. 'And the bloody rotten Tardebigge vestry won't pay to give it a decent Christian burial. The poor wench has got to carry this poor little cratur back to Kings Norton with her, and try to get it buried decent there.'

She carefully replaced the rag, gently arranging its folds, and there were tears glinting in her eyes when she turned to look at Tom, and this time spoke less heatedly, but still with anger throbbing in her voice. 'Ann's got no right of settlement in this parish because she warn't born here. She come to work at Erasmus Dolton's farm just under a year since, and the dirty bugger put her in the family way, then threw her out.'

'You're telling me that Ann Washwood is pregnant?' Tom felt concerned and shocked.

'O' course she is! Why else do you think that the vestry am chucking her out of the parish?' The woman reacted as if she couldn't credit his ignorance. 'They don't want the kid born a bastard here and entitled to parish relief, does they. They reckons they've got too many parish bastards on relief as it is.'

'And you believe that Erasmus Dolton is responsible for her present pregnancy?' Tom had come across Dolton several times since coming to live in Redditch, and considered him to be coarse and brutish.

'O' course it's him! Ann swears to that before God hisself! And I knows the poor wench well enough to know when she's speaking the truth,' Mrs Lewis affirmed heatedly, and her words carried the ring of truth. 'He's well known for making free with his women servants, and for knocking them about as well.'

Now an intense pity for Ann Washwood and her dead and living children, coupled with contempt and anger for Erasmus Dolton, flooded through Tom. 'And I'll swear before God that I'll have no part in removing Ann Washwood from this parish,' he promised. 'And what's more, if you can persuade her to lay a charge against Erasmus Dolton as being the father of her unborn, then I'll do all that I can to help her to make an application for a bastardy order. He should be made to pay for what he's done.'

'He never will be,' the woman declared with absolute certainty in her voice. 'He's got one of the biggest farms in the parish, and he's rolling in money. And his dad was a vestryman and churchwarden right up to the day of his death. You mark my words, that Erasmus Dolton knows all there is to know about what the bloody vestrymen gets up to, to line their own pockets. So there's nobody who's anybody is ever going to risk going against him.'

'Maybe if I spoke to Ann Washwood and offered her my help, she might bring a charge against him?' Tom offered.

The woman regretfully shook her head. 'She aren't here just now. She went out first thing this morning to go to Dolton's farm to ask him to take some pity on her, and help her. Not that that'll do any good. He's nothing but a cruel, evil pig! I shouldn't think she'll get back here afore nightfall.'

'Very well.' Tom didn't argue the point. 'At any rate, I shan't report that I haven't removed her for as long as I can avoid doing so. So at least she'll have a few more days' grace.'

'You're a good-hearted man, Master Potts.' She reached out and patted his shoulder. 'And may God bless you for being so.'

Embarrassed by her praise, Tom flustered. 'I must go, Mrs Lewis.'

She walked with him back to the front of the house, and stood waving as the horse and cart lurched back down the lane until out of sight.

Tom could not shake off the disturbing mental image of the rag-shrouded dead child, its delicate features so grotesquely distorted by the onion crammed into its mouth.

'Why in this modern age do people still believe that forcing an onion into the mouth of a corpse delays the rot and stench of death? Why do such superstitions still exert so much power even over those who are otherwise intelligent people?'

Then he grimaced ruefully. 'And why do I not walk under ladders, and throw spilled salt over my left shoulder to blind the Devil's eyes?'

The prospect of what Lord Aston might do to him for failing

in his duty to remove Ann Washwood from the parish was causing Tom some considerable apprehension, but he mentally steeled himself.

'Be damned to Aston! I'll not let him force me to do it, no matter what punishment he threatens me with.'

While passing back through Webheath hamlet Tom realized that he was only about a mile distant from the Red Lane where butcher Vincent's old slaughter shed was situated, and decided that he would make the necessary detour to discover the reason for the complaint.

The sun was high and warm, with only a few small fluffy clouds dappling the blue skies. Birds were singing and the scents of pastures and woodlands filled Tom's nostrils. His mood, darkened by the visit to the poorhouse, began to lighten once more, and he pursed his lips to whistle a lilting tune.

At the junction of the main road and the Red Lane he met with a horse and cart toiling up the steep incline of the lane, and hailed the cart driver.

'How do I find butcher Vincent's shambles?'

The man and jerked his thumb back over his shoulder. 'Go down there a bit and there's a cobbled track leading off to your right. Vincent's shed is just a few yards up there.'

The warm still air was heavy with the noisome cloying odour of rotting flesh as Tom halted the cart in the small gravelled clearing which surrounded the large wooden shed. Since childhood his military surgeon father, keen for his son to follow in his footsteps, had encouraged Tom to watch the treatments of living patients, and examinations of the dead. Long accustomed to the unpleasant spectacle and smell of diseased, dead and decaying flesh, Tom was not perturbed by the rancid air that assailed his nostrils and sat studying what was around him.

To one side was a large heap of whitening animal bones, many of which had been scattered across the gravel by marauding animals, but Tom could see no dead animals to account for the stomach sickening stench with its peculiar hint of sweetness.

He noticed that the double doors of the shed were slightly ajar and frowned thoughtfully. 'I'm sure Vincent said that he'd left this shed barred and padlocked.' Getting down from the cart he went to look inside the building.

The rusted iron hinges squealed as he pulled the heavy door further open and peered into the shadowed interior. The cloying stench enveloped him with its full force and buzzing fly wings swarmed about his head, brushing against his face as he moved closer to the massive wooden chopping block that dominated the centre of the floor so that he could see clearly what it was that lay on its surface.

'Dear God, who or what did this?' he uttered aloud, as he stared in horrified recognition at the rotting, black-green, liquefying flesh and bone that had once been a human being.

Sixteen

'A headless human corpse? A headless naked human corpse?' Joseph Blackwell exclaimed incredulously. 'You are telling me that you have discovered a headless human corpse in Henry Vincent's old slaughter shed?'

'Yes indeed, Master Blackwell, and I want you to authorize me to place a guard upon the site and allow no one entrance until I have completed my own inspections there. Perhaps then one of our local medical men could carry out a post-mortem.'

The older man sat pondering silently for some time, then nodded. 'Very well. You have full authority to act as you see fit. Any expenses that you incur will be met from the parish chest. Now tell me, what are your thoughts concerning this cadaver?'

'Well, I've only had a somewhat cursory look at it and the maggots and rats et cetera have feasted upon the remains, but I am confident that they are of an elderly woman. There are portions of her breasts and vagina surviving and the pubic hairs are grey. The condition of the flesh leads me to believe that death occurred several weeks past.'

'The loss of the head? Could it have been caused by animals or birds feeding on the corpse?'

'I think not.' Tom shook his head. 'But as I've said, I've

only had a cursory look. The most pressing need is to secure
the site against intrusion, which is why I've come to you in
such haste. I've also got to make a thorough search of the
shed and its environs to find her clothes or other belongings.
I didn't see any, but there's a deal of places where they could
be.'

'Yes, of course, Master Potts, and I shall not detain you a
moment longer. But report back here to me as soon as possible.'

'I will, sir.'

As Tom was leaving the room Blackwell asked a final question. 'Do you think that there is any likelihood at all that this
death could possibly be from natural causes? That this could
be the work of body-snatchers?'

'No, sir, I do not.' Tom answered with conviction. 'I think
that the woman was murdered.'

From Blackwell's office he went directly to the livery stables
of Richard Humphries and extended the hire of the horse and
cart, then set off to look in on his mother at the lock-up.

When he neared the lock-up, however, and saw the tall
skeletal man who was waiting outside the arched entrance his
heart sank.

'Oh no! The last thing I want at this moment is to have to
listen to the ranting of a lunatic poet.'

He started to turn his horse. But as he did so John Hollis
came running after him, shouting, 'Master Potts, I need to
speak to you! Master Potts?'

Tom reluctantly reined to a halt.

John Hollis reached him and immediately said, 'My most
profound apologies to you, Master Potts, for the unfortunate
circumstance of our last meeting. Thanks be to God, I'm once
again perfectly compos mentis, and would much appreciate
your giving me the time to prove that is so.'

Hollis was neatly dressed in coat and breeches; his long
orange-hued hair was now cropped short, and hidden beneath
a peaked cap.

Tom studied the other man closely. Hollis' eyes were clear
and steady, his mode of speech modulated and precise. His
bodily movements were smooth and controlled instead of
erratic and jerky.

'I'm very happy to see you fully recovered, Master Hollis.'

'Alas, I fear that I shall never be fully recovered, Master

Potts.' Hollis shook his head sadly. 'My lunatic fits will undoubtedly re-occur for varying periods throughout my life. But on the evidence so far, I can now anticipate several months of sanity before the next attack.'

'I sincerely hope that it will be for a much longer period, Master Hollis.' Tom smiled, and on impulse said, 'Would you care to share a jug of ale with me? I'm intending to take a brief break before going about my duties.'

'I would indeed,' Hollis accepted gratefully, and the two of them went side by side towards the lock-up, where Tom got down from the cart and tethered the horse to the pillory post.

When they entered the building Tom could hear the loud-snorting snoring of his mother and sighed with relief. 'My mother's asleep, Master Hollis, so if you don't object we'll go to the Horse and Jockey for our ale, and avoid the risk of disturbing her.'

'Gladly!' Hollis agreed readily.

In the tavern bar parlour they settled themselves comfortably at a corner table and with their long churchwarden pipes drawing well, and pewter tankards of ale before them, they began to talk.

At first they talked of general subjects and Tom found himself quickly warming towards his companion, who was proving to be an erudite man with a pleasing personality and a wry sense of humour.

As time passed and they grew easier in each other's company, their conversation became more personal, and they exchanged many details of their past lives; and their opinions of various people that they knew of in the town and its environs. It pleased both of them that they found in many instances that those opinions coincided almost exactly.

When Tom told him of his discovery at the slaughter shed, and of his own conviction that the woman had been murdered, Hollis was greatly interested and immediately offered his assistance. Tom immediately accepted.

'I'm very grateful for your help. Will you go up there now to stand guard? I'll follow when I've dealt with a couple of things here. It might be for the best if you didn't go into the clearing but stayed at the entrance until my arrival.'

'Very well.' John Hollis smiled happily. 'Do you know,

Master Potts, I'm certain that between us we shall solve this mystery, and there's my hand on it.'

They shook hands and parted with the shared conviction that they had found a new friend.

When Tom returned to the clearing he had a large wooden box on the cart.

'Is that for the poor woman's remains?' John Hollis enquired.

'Yes, the only coffin Harry Bates has in stock is required for a funeral tomorrow, so he's loaned me this box as a temporary alternative.' Tom smiled wryly. 'Mind you, I can't see our vestry paying for a new coffin for the woman, so no doubt we'll bury her in it, if she can't be identified. Will you stay here on guard, please. Don't let anyone come into the yard.'

Leaving the horse and cart with Hollis, Tom slung his knapsack over his shoulder and went to the shed. He opened the double doors to their fullest extent to admit as much daylight into the gloomy interior as possible, then stood and carefully scrutinized what was before him.

Apart from the huge central chopping block with its macabre occupant, the shed was bare. He studied the flag-stoned floor as he moved around its edges, keeping close to the walls, and then circuited ever closer to the chopping-block. He frowned in puzzlement. The dusty flagstones were littered with small animal droppings, dead flies, maggots and pupal cases, but he could find no pools of dried blood. If the woman had been killed and beheaded here, then there would certainly be lavish traces of blood. 'But if she was killed and beheaded elsewhere, why would her killer bother to bring the remains here?' Tom asked himself.

Crouching low, using a large magnifying glass he closely examined the floor between the doors and the chopping block, gently moving the dust with a small soft brush. Eventually he found what he sought: a line of small dark stains which could have been made by drops of blood falling from the corpse as it was carried to the chopping block.

He moved to take a closer look at the corpse. Even though it was badly decomposed and disfigured it was still apparent that the belly had been ripped open from the pubic bone to the sternum and Tom doubted that rats or maggots had done that by themselves.

Going outside he made a slow circuit and careful scrutiny of the clearing, stopping many times to closely examine the gravel through his magnifying glass, searching for signs of a violent struggle, but knowing that any bloodstains would have been washed away by the frequent rain showers of the previous weeks. It was almost an hour before he found a dense spatter of minute papery fly-pupal cases between the small pebbles, and very carefully transferred them into a small snuffbox. Then he examined the undergrowth next to them, and his excitement mounted when he saw crushed-down shrubs, and the dangling slender broken tree branch from which many of the buds had been stripped. He beckoned to John Hollis to join him.

'It's possible that this is the spot where the woman was attacked and beheaded, John, and bled onto the gravel. Blowflies lay their eggs on their food sources, such as blood.' He displayed the pupal cases in the snuffbox. 'These look to be fly-pupal cases, which encase the maggots when they begin their transmutation into flies. And look at those broken shrubs, it would take a very heavy weight or impact to crush them down so.'

He fell silent, staring hard at the dangling partially stripped broken branch as his mind raced. 'What might break and simultaneously strip that branch?' he mused aloud.

'Could someone have tried to stop themselves from falling and grabbed the branch with their hands?' Hollis suggested.

'It's possible,' Tom conceded, and moved into the undergrowth to discover that there were further trampled small shrubs in a narrow line. He stamped his heavy boots down on other neighbouring shrubs, and found that it took a repeated heavy stamping to crush them to the ground.

'I suppose this might have been done by people struggling with each other.'

'It could,' John Hollis agreed. 'But might not it also have been done by an animal?'

Inspiration exploded in Tom's mind. 'Of course! It could have been done by a bolting horse. That branch might have been its tether, and when it bolted the reins broke the branch and stripped the buds from it.'

'And it could have been people fighting that caused the horse to bolt?' John Hollis offered excitedly.

'So our killer or killers came here on horseback.' Tom was becoming elated.

'Or perhaps the dead woman did, and was killed for her horse?' John Hollis' eyes were shining with his own elation.

'That also seems likely,' Tom readily conceded. 'And the killer hid the head and clothes so that the victim couldn't be identified. But why did he take her into the shed and place her on top of the chopping block?'

'Well, to hide her so that he would have time to escape before she was discovered.'

'But if he merely wanted to hide her in the shed, why not just pitch her onto the floor inside it and close the doors? Why did he go to the trouble to place her carefully on the chopping block?' Tom frowned in concentration, considering the killer's motivations for doing what he had. Ideas coursing through his mind were considered, disregarded, accepted as possibilities in rapid succession.

A further troubling thought struck him and he voiced it aloud. 'The ewe's belly was ripped open, wasn't it; and the lamb was decapitated.'

'The lamb?'

'Yes, the lamb.' Tom told of the slaughtered ewe and its lamb, and John Hollis mulled over this story for some considerable time before recounting:

'Many years past my grandfather was repairing the masonry of a church in a village in Dorset. A similar happening occurred while he was there. At first people considered it to be the action of someone with a grudge against the beast's owner, who was unpopular locally. But during the next months several other sheep, and a horse, were likewise cruelly slaughtered, and they belonged to different people. Then one night a local man was discovered in the act of murdering his wife. He had used a knife to stab and slash her to death. Before he was hanged he confessed to the previous killings of the animals. He claimed that voices in his head drove him to do these terrible things.'

Hollis paused and stared keenly at Tom, before asking quietly, 'Tell me, Tom, are you perhaps wondering if the person who killed the ewe and lamb might also be implicated in this killing?'

Tom nodded thoughtfully. 'I am, John. I am indeed.'

Seventeen

A month had passed since the discovery of the dead woman, and the sensation created by it throughout the needle district had abated.

Despite all enquiries throughout Tardebigge and its adjoining parishes she remained unidentified. What had been established, however, after Hugh Laylor had performed a painstaking post-mortem, was that she had suffered multiple stab wounds. Now she was lying in a pauper's grave, buried in the large box because as Tom Potts had rightly surmised the select vestry would not go to the expense of buying a coffin for her.

During a dark and rainy night in mid-June, Timmy and Maria Docherty and their swarm of children pitched their tent and tethered their two donkeys on a piece of wasteland bordering the road between the Crabbs and Headless Crosses. Soon after dawn Timmy Docherty shouldered his pack of tools and set out to tramp the two hamlets, bellowing hoarsely at every tenement he came to, 'Pots and pans? Do you have any pots and pans needs mending? Pots and pans? Pots and pans to mend?'

Back at the tent heavily pregnant Maria Docherty roused her three eldest girls, aged fifteen, twelve and eleven, and instructed the two youngest.

'Now you, Eileen, head straight into the centre o' the town. Maura, you go with her. Split up once you're there and work different streets. Don't forget now that the old biddies are the likeliest marks, so make sure that you shed plenty o' tears when you front them, and remember to keep a sharp eye out for any constables. Get off wi' you now.'

The barefoot, raggedly clad, painfully thin and undersized girls scampered away. The remaining girl, lissom-bodied

Siobhan, was combing her long red hair and Maria Docherty praised her.

'That's it, honey. Making yourself look pretty is the way to do it.'

The girl clucked her tongue in petulant impatience. 'Don't I know that already, Mammy. Why do you have to keep on telling me what I already know so well?'

'Don't you be giving me any of your lip, or you'll be feeling the back o' me hand, so you will,' her mother warned sharply.

Siobhan was unafraid of the threat. 'You belt me, and I'll be telling me da about that gold sovereign you got hid away up your arse.'

'Oh, will you now? Well, you tell him about me bit o' money, and I'll slit your fuckin' throat, so I will!' the woman spat out.

The girl threw back her head and pealed with laughter. 'And then I'll be dead, and you'll be hung, and me da will be spending the whole sovereign on getting pissed, won't he. And he'll not give a bugger for what's happened to either of us.'

Maria Docherty's anger dispelled as quickly as it had arisen, and she joined in her daughter's laughter. 'You're right there, me darlint. The bastard never gives a fuckin' thought to me nor you when he gets the drink in him.'

The tent and donkeys had been noted by people passing along the road and while most only went on their way without comment, there were others who exchanged frowns and made disparaging comments.

'Thomas? Thomas, will you come and help me? If ever another poor woman suffered such cruel treatment from her own flesh and blood, then I'd like to meet her, and we could weep together!' Widow Potts' voice rose to an ear-rending screech. 'Thomaassss? Thomaassss?'

Tom had just finished painstakingly preparing some specimen slides for his microscope and was relishing the prospect of examining their wonders.

'Dear God!' he sighed heavily, and reluctantly went into his mother's room.

She was lying in bed, her fat face encased in a frilled

nightcap, the whiteness of which highlighted her purpled complexion.

'What do you need, Mother?'

'I need you to empty my commode.'

'But I've already emptied it once this morning.'

'And I've already used it again, haven't I, you great fool! Can't you smell the stink?'

Tom sniffed the air, and could only detect the scents of the bunches of dried herbs hanging on the walls, the stale dried sweat of his mother's body and the other normal strong-smelling odours of everyday life. He didn't want to waste time and breath in further argument, however, so he raised the wooden cover, lifted out the large lidded chamber pot and carried it downstairs to empty its contents into the yard privy.

Back upstairs his mother's tirade of abuse and maudlin self-pity went on and on, and knowing that he would get no peace to study his specimen slides for perhaps hours, Tom put on his coat and hat, took up his staff and the Military Survey Map and went out.

During the weeks that he had been constable, Tom had acted upon Joseph Blackwell's advice to familiarize himself with the parish, its environs and inhabitants, and he had found the military map an invaluable aid.

A peculiarity of the physical layout of Redditch, and its satellite villages, the Headless and Crabbs Crosses, was their being divided on their eastern and southern extremities into the separate parishes of Tardebigge, Ipsley and Studley. This was because the ancient shire boundary of Worcestershire and Warwickshire ran south to north through the district, joining the boundary of Tardebigge parish at Crabbs Cross, where three of the needle district's parish boundaries junctioned, Tardebigge, Ipsley and Studley. The county boundary then passed down the main road linking to Headless Cross, and continued down the Mount Pleasant and the Back Hill and the long stretch of the road called Ipsley Street, until it reached the farthest eastern edge of Redditch, a close-huddled collection of houses and factories known locally as Brecon. Here the boundary curved and fell sharply eastwards down the sunken road called the Holloway to cross the broad fecund valley of the River Arrow before swinging northwards once more.

This administrative partition of the town and villages greatly handicapped those trying to enforce the law, as Tom had already discovered for himself, because as Tardebigge constable he had no official powers in Ipsley, and someone could flout the law only yards from him across the parish boundary, and he could do nothing in his official capacity to stop them.

He left the lock-up and walked slowly eastwards along Red Lion Street to where at its far end it joined Ipsley Street. It was at this junction that the Big Pool lay, a broad, deep, rounded expanse of stinking, stagnant water in which dead cats and dogs floated, and the refuse and sewage of the surrounding tenements and workshops were emptied.

The eastern half of the Big Pool lay in Ipsley parish, the western half in Tardebigge parish. It was considered by many in Redditch that the fetid condition of the water was the cause of much of the fevers and maladies which afflicted those unfortunate enough to live in its close vicinity, and several medical men had tried to have it drained. But the respective vestries of the two parishes could not reach agreement on who should pay what for the draining and filling in the pestilential hole; and so it continued to fester for year after year after year, inflicting suffering and death.

Now, as always when he reached the Big Pool, Tom could not help but feel angry that the men who possessed the power to rectify this sorry state of affairs instead served their own selfish interests rather than act for the general good. He was standing counting the numbers of dead animals floating on the thick-scummed surface when he was hailed by George Jolly coming down from the direction of the Back Hill with his horse and cart.

'I was just coming to find you, Master Potts. There's some Paddy tinkers camping by the road between the Crosses. You needs to run 'em off a bit sharpish before there's trouble.'

'Are they doing any harm to anyone?' Tom felt the familiar sense of apprehension tightening his chest. So far in his tenure of office the only violent confrontation he had experienced had been the incident with Alfie Payne. To his own pleasant surprise the town had been unusually quiet and peaceful and his official duties had consisted solely of serving various warrants and summonses, checking pedlars', hawkers' and hucksters' licences to trade and carrying out some errands and message-bearing for Joseph Blackwell. Because of the sensational discovery and the need in these last weeks for him to devote himself to making enquiries about the dead woman, he was sure that the failure to remove Ann Washwood and her children to Kings Norton had not yet been noted by Blackwell.

'Not yet they aren't. But you knows what tinkers are like. They always causes trouble, thievin' bastards that they all are!' George Jolly asserted dogmatically.

'Well, if they're not causing trouble at present there's little or nothing that I can do, Master Jolly. Everyone is entitled to stop to rest for a while by the roadside.'

'By the roadside, yes. But not on private land. And most of all not on land that I rents!' Jolly's face was reddening with anger. 'And it's my bit o' grazing land that the buggers am on, and their bloody donkeys am eating my grass. That's stealing, that is!'

'Have you told them that they're on your rental, and they must go?' Tom queried.

'O' course not! They'm likely to knock me bloody head off! Old Johnny Styler got nigh on murdered by bloody tinkers when he told 'em to shift off his land. It's your job to shift the buggers. That's what you'm made a constable for.'

Tom reluctantly accepted that he must do something about this complaint. 'All right, Master Jolly. I'll come with you now and talk to these tinkers.'

'I aren't got time to traipse all the way back up there. I've got work to do,' Jolly objected indignantly. 'You'll have to go by yourself. Just go through Headless past the White Hart, and you'll see the camp halfway towards Crabbs Cross. I wants the buggers shifted sharpish, Master Potts. If they'm still there tonight, then I'll be laying a complaint against you before Lord Aston.'

With that parting threat the carter lashed his horse into movement.

'Now let's have a look at you, me darlint. Jasus, but you're the pretty cratur and no mistake.' Inside the tent Maria Docherty regarded her eldest daughter with loving pride.

Siobhan was clad in a neat dark-grey gown and plain black bonnet. Stout boots were on her dainty feet, and when she lifted her skirt she displayed a glimpse of white petticoat and black woollen stockings.

'Now you have the letter safe, don't you, darlint?'

'Of course I do! It's in me bag! Don't fuss so, Mammy. I know well what I'm about, don't I. I've been doing it long enough, God only knows!' Siobhan scolded her.

She stepped out of the tent and halted. 'Mammy, there's a man coming.'

Her mother peered out from the tent flap and exclaimed, 'Jasus! He looks like a bloody beanpole!'

'He's carrying a crown staff, Mammy, I reckon he's a constable.'

Seeing the two females, Tom had no wish to alarm them and called as he neared them, 'There's no need for you to be frightened. I'm the constable of this parish and I just want to have a few words with you.'

Maria Docherty stepped out from the tent, pulling her shabby gown tightly around her swollen body to emphasize her pregnancy. As she did so her brood of small children came swarming to cluster about her, and trained by their parents since birth how to react to any possibly hostile stranger coming to their camp, they immediately vented wails and whimpers of distress.

'Oh, your honour, we're doing no harm,' Maria whimpered pitifully. 'I'm that sick and weary from carrying this babby in me womb, we just had to stop here and rest for a wee while, or it could have been the death o' me.'

Disconcerted by the wailings of the small children and the woman's distress, Tom hesitated.

He was also puzzled by the glaring contrast between the neatly dressed, fresh clean appearance of the pretty young red-haired girl, and the rags and grimy skins of the woman and children.

'We're hard-working, honest people, your honour.' The woman spread her arms in appeal. 'Me man is out this very minute looking for work, trying to earn a few pennies to feed these little ones. And me eldest girl here, is just on her way back to her own place of service, your honour. She's a maid-servant to a fine respectable family up in Birmingham. We just need to rest here for a wee while, your honour, and then we'll be on our way.'

'Please, ma'am, let me speak.' Tom's sympathies were roused, and he held his hand up to silence her. 'I've no wish to cause you any trouble or distress, but there's been a complaint made against you. This is private land, and the owner wants you off it.'

'Ohhh Jasus!' Maria Docherty's features twisted in dismay. 'We thought it was just a bit o' waste, your honour. If we'd known it was private, then we'd not have put a foot on it, I swear to you on me children's lives, your honour. Ohhh Jasus! What's going to become of us? What's going to happen to us?'

The small children's wailing and whimpering erupted into a heart-rending outpouring of fear and distress, which acted upon Tom, causing him to experience a shamed guilt. In desperation he promised, 'I'll help you to find somewhere else to camp, ma'am. I give you my word on that.'

'Ohhh, you've the heart of gold, and I bless you for it from the bottom of me own heart, your honour. But how can I move me tent, in the state I'm in? Me eldest has to go now, this very minute, to get back to her place of service, and me man might not be back till long after dark, him having to tramp so far to look for work, your honour. If I was to try and shift this tent in my condition, I could end up losing this babby inside me, and losing me own life as well. In fact, I'm feeling so weak and badly and sick right this minute that I'm ready to collapse and die!'

On receipt of this signal the small children's outcries rose in a crescendo of terror and grief.

'Now calm down! Calm down, all of you!' Tom pleaded. 'I'll move the tent for you myself, and re-erect it.'

Siobhan hugged her mother, and tears fell down her fresh face. 'I'll have to go right now, Mammy, or I'll get the sack from me service, and then what will happen to us all? And how is me daddy going to find you when the tent's been moved?'

'Ohhh Jasus! Ohhh Jasus!' Maria Docherty shrieked in abject misery, burying her face in her hands and rocking her whole body backwards and forwards, backwards and forwards.

Tom was frantically racking his brains for a solution which would bring all this pandemonium to a quick end. He sighed with heartfelt relief as the answer suddenly occurred to him.

Pulling his map out he quickly studied it, before smilingly declaring, 'I have it! I have the solution to this problem! There's no cause to distress yourselves further, ladies. I only need to move your tent onto that piece of land down there across the road. It's less than forty yards, so your man will find it very easily on his return.'

Maria Docherty slyly peeked through her fingers, and covertly nudged Siobhan, who then asked Tom, 'Tell me, sir, what's the difference? It looks just like this piece of land.'

'The difference is, that this land is in Tardebigge parish, and that land down there is in Ipsley parish,' Tom explained with satisfaction. 'I have no jurisdiction in Ipsley, and consequently cannot be made to move you off that piece of land.'

'But the Ipsley constable can move us,' Siobhan objected.

'But he won't,' Tom assured her. 'His name is Terence Jones, and he's presently at home lying in his coffin waiting for burial. He died two nights ago of an apoplexy, and the Ipsley vestry haven't yet nominated his replacement. So you should be able to stay there for perhaps a week without anyone coming to move you on.'

Mother and daughter showered him with profuse thanks and declarations of gratitude, and Tom set to work moving the camp.

As Siobhan took her leave, her mother winked and whispered, 'You'll be able to work the Ipsley parish real easy now, darlint, what with there being no fuckin' constable to watch out for.'

The girl returned the wink and whispered back, 'I reckon I'll be able to work the Tardebigge parish real easy as well, Mammy, if this soft idjit is the best that they can do by way of a constable.'

Tom laboured hard for the next two hours, and left the new campsite with the grateful plaudits of Maria Docherty ringing in his ears: the glow of virtuous satisfaction for having acted as the Good Samaritan warmed him for many hours afterwards.

Eighteen

The Horse and Jockey stood on the Ipsley parish side of the Big Pool and was a favourite haunt and gathering place for the young men and girls of the town. During the summer evenings, when the weather was warm and dry, fiddlers and drummers would play and the young people dance on a broad stretch of flat greensward at the side of the tavern. These evenings of dancing and music drew spectators from all gradations of local society, joining together clapping and singing in concert with the mass-performed jigs, reels and country dances, appreciatively applauding the solo performances by the most agile, accomplished and graceful among the male and female dancers.

Twenty yards to the tavern's rear was a small pasture enclosed by tall thick hawthorn hedgerows, its sole entrance a narrow gap barred by a high close-barred padlocked gate. The pasture was a natural amphitheatre sloping sharply down from the hedgerows towards a flat circular central space some ten yards in diameter. This was the arena where bloody combats were staged between men, between animals, sometimes between women; and sometimes between human and beast.

Ex-prizefighter Billy Middleton, landlord of the Horse and Jockey, was the owner, promoter and master of ceremonies of this arena. He decided who should be allowed admittance. He was the matchmaker. He was the widely preferred purse- and stake-holder, and the final arbiter of disputed wagers. In the context of the needle-district sporting world, Billy Middleton was mentor and confidant of high and low society alike.

Late on this Saturday afternoon in the backyard of his tavern, Billy Middleton was acting in his role as mentor, and advising Gareth Jenkins and Eleri Turner.

'Alfie Payne will train and handle your dogs well enough,

I've had him to train dogs of my own and he's always done a good job of it for me. But if I was you I'd be betting a bundle on Ritchie Bint's beast today. I watched him first-blood it a few weeks since, and it's a little cracker.'

'But surely Dr Laylor's animal is unbeatable, Master Middleton, it's won every fight it's ever had,' Eleri Turner argued.

'And it must be more than double the weight of Bint's dog, and a hell of a lot taller and stronger.' Gareth Jenkins supported his mother.

'That's very true, but what you got to remember is that sometimes it aren't the size of the dog in the fight that counts as much as the size of the fight in the dog. Dr Laylor's beast has been a worthy champion, but now it's had too many fights. You should remember the story about the pitcher and the well.'

'Dear God! Please spare us from any more of your aphorisms, Master Middleton!' Gareth Jenkins snapped petulantly. 'I've yet to see any bull-mastiff outmatched by an Old English bulldog.'

'And I've yet to meet any fool who couldn't be easy parted from his money, Master Jenkins.' A hard edge entered Middleton's tone, and for a brief instant his battered, heavily scar-thickened features displayed menace. 'So if you'd like to make a wager with me, then my money is on Ritchie Bint's beast. I'm betting on the Staffordshire beating the bull-mastiff this time.'

Eleri Turner recognized the hazardous situation that her son was getting himself into, and smoothly intervened. 'Master Middleton, I'm going to follow your advice.' She smiled seductively and stroked his massive shoulder with her gloved fingers. 'When you lay your wager on Ritchie Bint's dog, will you also lay ten sovereigns down for me? I'd be more than grateful if you would do me this kind service.'

Like the vast majority of his townsmen, Billy Middleton was very susceptible to Eleri Turner's charms, and he instantly agreed. 'O' course I will, Missus Turner. You knows that I'm more than willing to do any service for you that I can.'

Her gloved fingers tightened momentarily into a strong pressure, and her dark eyes glowed lucently as she gazed deeply into Middleton's, and murmured, 'I know that very well, Master Middleton. That is why I value your friendship so highly.'

Then she dropped her hand, and pretending to be embarrassed at displaying her feelings, pleaded as if flustered, 'Please, Master Middleton, may my son and I wait inside your house until the time of the match? Only my husband does not much approve of my attending such events, and I've no wish for too many people to see me and bear tales to him.'

'O' course you can, Missus Turner! You shall have my best parlour all to yourselves, and no one shall enter unless you calls for 'em to.'

'Many thanks, Master Middleton.' She smiled radiantly, and directing a covert warning glance at her son, she allowed Billy Middleton to take her arm and lead her into the tavern.

While Eleri Turner waited in the best parlour of the Horse and Jockey, Siobhan Docherty came walking up the sloping sunken track of the Holloway. She was hungry, thirsty and more than a little disgruntled. For two full days she had trudged the lanes of Ipsley parish calling at promising-looking houses, and had so far met with nothing but doors slammed in her face, at times coupled with threats to put the dogs on her if she didn't leave.

The sun was still hot and the lack of any breeze made the heat oppressive. A grassy bank shaded by overhanging trees presented a tempting resting place, and Siobhan sat down and slipping off her shoes began to rub her aching feet.

The pedlar was also travelling up the track towards Redditch Town when he saw the pretty young girl, and he came to stand before her.

At first Siobhan deliberately ignored the man, and he grinned and told her, 'I'm only going to offer you some fine silk ribbons at a dirt-cheap price, my pretty, so there's no call for you to keep from looking at me and pretending I'm not here. I'm not going to bite you.'

She looked up at him, and couldn't help but think that he was a very attractive-looking young man, with his curly black hair, sun-tanned features and fine white teeth.

He slipped the large pack from his broad shoulders and, placing it on the ground, opened its flap and took out a handful of brightly coloured ribbons which shimmered as he thrust them into the shaft of sunlight lancing through the leaves above.

'Just look at these, my pretty, aren't they beautiful? Just

think how they'll look when you've got them twined into your lovely red hair, and you're dancing with your sweetheart. Because if there's one thing I'm sure about, it's that you've got a sweetheart. A fine, handsome young fella who's mad wi' love for you. And so he should be, because you're the prettiest girl I've met up with since many a long day.'

Siobhan's roving life brought her into close contact with all sorts of people, and she was well aware that there were many dangerous predatory men. However, she did not sense any physical threat to herself in this man, so she smiled and enjoyed his flattery.

'Will you not give me a word, so that I can hear what a sweet voice you must have?' he cajoled. 'Because such a pretty girl as yourself couldn't have anything other than a musical tone when she speaks.'

'I've the musical tone all right, mister, but I've not a penny piece to bless meself with, so all your sweet talk is not going to be able to sell me a ribbon.'

'Ahhhrrr, you're Irish, are you.' He chuckled with satisfaction that he had finally brought her to speak to him. 'And what's a beautiful Irish colleen like yourself doing in these parts? Do you live local?'

She shook her head. 'Me and me family is only passing through here. And if me da finds me talking to the likes of you, he'll not be best pleased. We're a good Catholic family and very respectable. So you'd best be on your way, because he'll be back here directly.' She jerked her thumb over her shoulder. 'He's just gone into the bushes back there to have a shite.'

'And pray God he's enjoying having it, and may it take him an hour to finish it.' The young man's white teeth glistened as he laughed long and loud, and Siobhan laughed with him.

Their laughter attracted the attention of a group of road-menders who were passing on foot, with their picks and shovels and wheelbarrows. They stared at the good-looking couple with lascivious interest, and exchanged comments and gibes among themselves.

'Look at that lucky bastard. He'll be getting between her legs afore this night's over and done with, I'll wager.'

'If I was him I 'uddent be waiting for bloody nightfall, I'll tell you. I'd have her into them bushes up there afore you could say Jack Robinson.'

'Ahrr, you'd have her into them bushes all right, I don't doubt, Jack. But from what your missus told me the last time I had her, you 'uddent be able to get it up when you got there.'

'Ahrr, she told me that as well, when I left her last night.'

'You can shut your dirty lying mouths, both on you. Because I knows for a fact that my missus only ever has a shag wi' gennulmen, and never wi' scruffy buggers like you two.' They continued on their way in an outburst of ribald laughter.

'My name is Ricardo Pozo. What's your name, my pretty?'

'Ricardo Pozo? What sort of a quare name is that?' Siobhan pulled a face.

'It's a Spanish name.' He smiled. 'My mam and dad are from Spain. But I'm born and bred here in England, so I'm an Englishman.'

'Me da won't care for any of you,' Siobhan asserted. 'He don't like nobody but the Irish. And precious few o' them neither.'

'Well, at least tell me your name,' he coaxed.

'It's Siobhan. Siobhan Docherty.' She was becoming increasingly taken with his good looks and charming manner.

'Siobhan.' He repeated almost caressingly, 'Siobhan ... Your name's as beautiful as you are.' He stared at her intently, and then asked, 'Tell me truly now, do you have a sweetheart?'

Her first impulse was to tease him coquettishly. 'I might have, or I might not. But either way it's none of your business.'

'Tell me,' he pleaded gently. 'Please. I know that we don't know each other, but the moment I set eyes on you, I thought to myself, there sits the most beautiful girl I've ever set my eyes on. And if she isn't spoken for, then I must get to know her. Because she's just the sort of girl that I've always dreamed of having for my very own sweetheart.'

'Phooo!' She tossed her head in ostentatious dismissal. 'And why would I be wanting a low-born pedlar for a sweetheart when I can take my pick of fine high-born gentlemen?'

'Because if you were this low-born pedlar's sweetheart, then he'd treat you like a queen.'

Siobhan would have liked to continue this harmless flirtation with this handsome man, but the vision of her father's angry threatening face rose up in her mind, and she knew that she must earn some money or face a beating. 'Where is it that you're going to now?'

'Up to Mother Readman's lodging house in Silver Street,' he told her. 'Why don't you come with me, and share my supper?'

'Share your bed, you mean?' she accused, and he laughed and shook his head.

'No! I didn't mean that. But if you're willing to share my bed, then you'll be more than welcome to.'

She seized on this opportunity, both to tease him further and to get away from him so that she could try yet another house. 'Don't you dare insult me! I'll not stay here a moment longer!' She jumped to her feet, feigning anger. 'Just keep away from me! If you follow me, then I'll start screaming blue murder.'

She pushed past him, gathered her skirts up around her knees and ran swiftly away.

Ricardo Pozo stood staring after her in shocked bemusement. 'What the hell did I do?' he asked himself over and over again. 'What the hell did I do?'

She stopped some twenty yards distant and shouted back over her shoulder, 'Our camp's up between the Crosses, on the Ipsley side o' the road. But don't you let me da catch you hanging around there, or he'll be having your guts for garters.' Then she giggled and ran on.

He laughed delightedly, and shouted after her, 'So long as I get to see you again, then I don't give a bugger for your da nor another twenty like him.'

Nineteen

The large house was set back from the road and its pink gravelled driveway, painted facade and large, carefully manicured front garden betokened affluence, as did the glossy-coated pony and gleaming trap tethered outside the pillared front portico.

Siobhan tugged on the bell-pull and when a neatly uniformed little maidservant opened the door, said, 'You can tell your master that Miss Charlotte Fitzsimmons is here as arranged.'

Siobhan confidently stepped forwards, psychologically pressuring the maidservant into moving aside and allowing her entrance to the hallway.

Like the outside of the house, the hallway was a testament to wealth, with fine furnishings and tapestried walls.

'I'm sorry, miss, but who was it you said you was?' the very young maid queried nervously.

'Miss Charlotte Fitzsimmons.' Siobhan smiled kindly. 'Your master is at home, I hope?'

'Oh yes, miss. But he's with the doctor at present.'

'No matter.' Siobhan seated herself upon one of the ornate chairs lining the hallway. 'I can wait until he's done with the doctor.'

The maidservant's expression betrayed her uneasiness at having admitted this stranger into the house.

Siobhan flicked her fingers in a gesture of dismissal. 'You can go about your work. I'm perfectly comfortable waiting here for your master.'

Even as she spoke one of the hallway doors opened and an elegantly dressed, exceptionally handsome man came through it in company with an elderly white-haired, frail-bodied man clad in a suit of black mourning clothes.

'It appears we have a visitor, Father.' Hugh Laylor stared curiously at the attractive young stranger. 'Were you expecting anyone?'

'No, I don't think so.' The elderly man shook his head, blinking his eyes and staring vaguely about him, but didn't look in Siobhan's direction, and turned and went back into the room.

'Milly, see to your master,' Hugh Laylor instructed the maid, who bobbed a curtsey and hurried to obey, leaving Siobhan and Laylor alone in the hallway.

Siobhan rose and curtseyed. 'Good afternoon, sir. Please forgive me for coming here like this, but I'm in desperate trouble, and sorely in need of help.' From her small pocket bag she took a folded multi-paged letter and proffered it to

Laylor. 'Would you be so kind as to read this letter, sir. It explains my plight.'

Hugh Laylor studied the contents, frequently glancing up from the pages at Siobhan as he did so.

She stood with downcast head, her hands clasped before her as if she were silently praying.

When he had finished reading, he looked at her with a gleam of amusement in his fine lustrous eyes.

'This is a tragic story, Miss Fitzsimmons. It appears that fate has treated you with uncommon cruelty. To lose both of your parents within such a brief span after nursing them so devotedly for so many years must have broken your heart.'

She lifted her head and he saw the shining tears brimming in her eyes.

'Indeed it was, sir.' Her voice trembled. 'But I take comfort from knowing that our sweet Saviour has them both clasped in his loving arms.'

'And the gentleman who wrote this letter, did he not give you money so that you could return to the convent in Ireland where you intend to enter as a novitiate nun?'

'Indeed he did, sir, on the very day he took ship for America. He gave me ample money for the journey, and more besides. But I was robbed, sir. Robbed in London. The thieves took everything except the clothes I'm standing in.'

Hugh Laylor shook his head as if in sad acceptance. 'There's a deal of wickedness in this world. But how have you managed to reach Redditch?' He gestured towards her clothing. 'You don't look to be unduly travel-worn. Quite the contrary, in fact. You are the very picture of neat cleanliness.'

'God saw my trouble and came to help me, sir.' Siobhan stared at him with wide-eyed guilelessness. 'I've been helped by a poor tinker family from my own country, who took pity on me, even though they're in such sore straits themselves. I've travelled up to here with them, sir, and we're camped on the road between the Crosses. They've treated me as if I were their own flesh and blood from the goodness of their hearts. But now I have to part from them, because they're going back towards London, and I have to press on to Liverpool and try to find a passage back to Ireland.'

'How long have you been here in Redditch?'

'Just a couple of days, sir.'

'And yesterday I believe that you called at the house of the Turner family in the area we call Brecon.'

'I may have done, sir. I've called at several houses in this town, but unfortunately no one has been willing to help me.'

Tears welled from her eyes and fell down her cheeks, and she wiped them away, pleading with Laylor, 'Please, sir, can you help me? Can you please find it in your heart to help me?'

'Indeed I can, girl.' He chuckled grimly. 'Even though I know very well that you are more than capable of helping yourself. As you proved yesterday when you helped yourself to a piece of silver plate from the hall table of the Turner household.'

'I did not! Don't you dare be calling me a thief! I'm a good Catholic girl!'

'You're a light-fingered Paddy trollop, and for two pins I'd haul you before the magistrates myself.' Laylor's handsome face was set and hard.

'I'll not stay here to be insulted!' She turned to leave, but before she could reach the door Laylor grasped her arms in a powerful grip.

'You'll stay here for as long as I choose to keep you here.'

'I never stole nothing!' Knowing that she was no match against his strength, Siobhan utilized a practised tactic, and wailing piteously let her body sag as if near to fainting. 'Nothing, sir! I took nothing!'

'Oh yes you did, girl,' Laylor stated positively. 'And the son of the house gave chase to you, didn't he. But you managed to evade him.'

'That man tried to make free with me, sir! He tried to put his hands on me, and to pull me skirt up. It was only when the woman came that he let go and I was able to escape from the house.'

'Stop lying to me, girl, and listen well. I could have you whipped for stealing, but I know that the rest of your tribal scum would let you be punished rather than they would return any stolen goods. So I've a proposition for you. I'm now going to a tavern called the Horse and Jockey. It's by the Big Pool. Return the piece of silver to me there within the next few hours, and I will reward you with five shillings. If you fail to appear, then I shall have you hunted down and beaten to within an inch of your life. Wait at the side of the tavern for me to come to you, and say nothing to anyone about why you are there.'

'How can I return what I haven't got?' she protested tearfully. 'I never stole nothing!'

'Look lively now, girl.' He pushed her towards the door. 'You've only a few hours to save yourself.'

Twenty

Billy Middleton strode into the centre of the bloodied, trampled grass arena and roared in stentorian tones, 'my lords, ladies, gentlemen and Redditch roughnecks . . .'

'Booo!'

'Booo!'

'Shame on you!'

The crowd of men, women and children massed on the slopes of the pasture heckled him good-naturedly as he roared on.

'The next contest is the one we've all been waiting for. . . .'

'Speak for yourself, Middleton!' a man bellowed from the crowd, and Billy Middleton pointed his hand at the interrupter's face.

'Any more out o' you, Charlie Green, and I'll be re-arranging your snozzle in double quick time.'

Charlie Green swallowed hard, and wisely made no reply.

Middleton sneered contemptuously, and continued his roaring.

'This is the challenge match for the Gold Championship Collar of the needle district between Doctor Laylor's dog, the reigning champion, Saxon . . .'

There came a volley of cheers from Saxon's supporters and backers.

'. . . and the challenger, Master Ritchie Bint's dog, Pepper . . .'

Another volley of cheering from Pepper's supporters and backers.

'Saxon is of the bull-mastiff breed, and weighed in at a

hundred and ten pounds. Pepper is of the bulldog breed, and weighed in at sixty pounds. The referee and only deciding judge is me . . . yours truly, William Augustus Cyril Middleton, Esquire.'

He bowed to all sides, and was treated to another storm of good-natured jeering and heckling.

The two dogs, held on short choke-chains by their respective owners, came down to the centre and were greeted with thunderous applause.

Both men lifted their dogs up in their arms and showed them off to their respective supporters, then Hugh Laylor handed his dog over to Alfie Payne, who was to be its handler for the fight. Ritchie Bint would handle his dog himself.

Wagers were being offered and taken, and now that the two animals were seen in close proximity the majority of the bets were placed on the much bigger, tan-coated Saxon to win.

Hugh Laylor joined Eleri Turner and Gareth Jenkins who were standing in the front row of spectators.

'Where have you been until now?' Eleri Turner queried. 'You've missed some fine fights.' Her face was flushed and her black eyes sparkled with excitement. 'I've won twenty guineas so far. One of Jack Chisholm's beasts let me down, though. The cowardly cur turned tail. I told Jack that he ought to hang the damned thing, and he's promised that he will do just that.'

'And how have you done, Gareth?' Laylor asked.

'Rotten! Haven't picked a winner yet!' The young man's puffy face was petulant. 'I'm relying on Saxon to cover my losses.'

'He will.' Hugh Laylor was supremely confident. 'Bint's dog is too heavily outweighed. It doesn't stand a chance against my beast.'

'Billy Middleton thinks differently.' Eleri Turner smiled. 'He's wagered fifty guineas on Pepper.'

'More fool him.' Laylor smiled. 'I hope that you haven't been foolish enough to follow suit.'

Eleri smiled enigmatically and made no reply.

'By the way, a visitor called at my father's house while I was there. That's one of the reasons for my being delayed,' Laylor told them both. 'It was that same little thief who stole your silver plate.'

'That bitch!' Gareth Jenkins hissed viciously. 'I hope you gave her a damn good thrashing. Because if I get my hands on her I'll smash the thieving bitch's face in. Did you haul her to the lock-up?'

'No, and I didn't give her a thrashing, because doing either wouldn't have got your silver back. But I'm expecting her to come here at some time this evening to return it. I've promised her a small reward when she does so.'

'A reward? You think that the thieving bitch will return our silver? Are you mad, Hugh?'

'No, my boy, I'm not mad,' Laylor replied equably. 'I am however greatly experienced in the ways of this wicked world we live in. She'll come. You'll see.'

'Handlers, blood your dogs,' Billy Middleton roared, and an expectant hush fell upon the crowd.

The two handlers advanced to the centre of the arena, their snapping snarling dogs only kept under control by being half-strangled by the choke-chains.

'Take your bites,' Middleton instructed.

In lightning-quick succession both dogs were allowed a single slash at the other, and the crowd erupted as blood flew from Saxon's ear, and spattered across Pepper's white hide.

'Release!' Middleton shouted.

The choke-chains slipped from the dogs' necks and they charged at each other with the crowd roaring them on.

For the first minutes it seemed that the bigger dog would easily defeat the smaller. Time and time again Saxon's much heavier weight smashed Pepper back and down, and its white coat became covered with its own blood pouring from a dozen torn wounds. But growling, slavering, snarling, Pepper kept coming into the attack, and slowly began to wear down the older dog's strength. Ten minutes passed and now the crowd were venting long-drawn-out bayings as the atavistic blood-lust gripped them. Saxon's flanks were heaving, its short brindle fur smothered in blood as it once more sent Pepper rolling over, but the younger dog rebounded with redoubled fury and viciously clamped its sharp fangs onto Saxon's throat. Blood gushed out. Saxon howled and hurled itself from side to side trying to shake off Pepper, but the smaller dog hung grimly on and gradually the lurches and heaves of Saxon slowed and lost power, and shuddering it fell onto its side. Snarling, snorting on the blood that was gushing from the terrible wound, Pepper began to worry and tear the mouthful of flesh away from Saxon's throat, and the older dog's shuddering intensified, its howling becoming a choking whining.

'Do you accept defeat, Dr Laylor?' Billy Middleton shouted. 'Your beast 'ull be dead else!'

'Let the useless cur die!' Gareth Jenkins exclaimed angrily. 'It's just cost me sixty guineas.'

'And me a hundred, blast its hide!' Laylor grunted disgustedly, but still told Billy Middleton, 'I accept defeat, now try and save my dog.'

'Pepper wins!' Middleton roared in delight. 'Handlers take your beasts! Pepper's the new champion!'

Ritchie Bint slipped the choke-chain around his dog's throat and twisted it tighter and tighter until the strangled Pepper was forced to release its grip on Saxon's throat.

'Pepper! Pepper! Pepper! Pepper! Pepper!' The chant of triumph was bawled in unison from Pepper's backers and supporters, met with counter-howls of derision from the losers.

'Lucky bastards! Lucky bastards! Lucky bastards!'

Like all the other spectators in the front row, Eleri Turner's clothing had been plentifully spattered with the dogs' blood, and there were several smears of it on her face and hands. Flushed and excited by the savage spectacle and its victorious conclusion, she was laughing with pleasure.

'I had ten pounds laid on Pepper. Ten pounds at odds of three to one,' she crowed. 'Now then you two, are you not sorry for ignoring Billy Middleton's advice?'

'I'm not staying here to listen to your bragging, Mama!' Gareth Jenkins stormed furiously up the slope, buffeting those impeding him from his path.

Alfie Payne came to tell Hugh Laylor, 'Your beast's windpipe is sore damaged, Doctor. I don't reckon it can live.'

Laylor sighed and shook his head regretfully. 'I wish now that I hadn't matched the poor devil. Deep down I knew it was getting too old for fighting.' He shook his head again, and muttered, 'You'd best put it out of its misery, Alfie. Then bury it decently. I don't want to see it floating in the Big Pool like your own beasts do.'

'You won't, Doctor.' Alfie Payne grinned and made no effort

to move away until Hugh Laylor handed him some coins, which he bit on before putting them into his pocket.

'Thank you kindly, Doctor. Your money's good, as always. I'll see to the beast directly.'

Laylor saw the blood on Eleri Turner and told her, 'You must come to my house and let me clean the blood away before you go home or Joseph will be angry with you if he sees it, because I don't think for a moment that he knows you're here.'

'Of course he doesn't, because he'd be even more angry, and jealous as well if he knew that I was here with you.' She smiled meaningfully at him and coquettishly stroked his cheek.

'Don't do that here,' he told her sharply. 'Tongues will start wagging!'

'I don't care,' she riposted.

'I do,' he snapped.

With a final regretful glance at his fallen dog, Laylor led Eleri Turner up the slope.

Twenty-One

It was nearly midnight, and the fiddlers, drummers, dancers and dog-fighters were long gone. The last drunk had stumbled from the Horse and Jockey's door and its lights were out. The wind had strengthened and gusts of rain spattered across the stagnant surface of the Big Pool.

Sheltering against the tavern wall, Siobhan Docherty pulled her shawl closer and finally accepted that Hugh Laylor would not be coming to meet her.

'Oh God, he must be intending to send men after me. If they don't kill me, then me da will.'

She was bitterly regretting giving in to temptation and stealing the small silver salver, a crime which her father had always strictly forbidden any of his children to commit. She mentally recalled his constant refrain.

'Begging's fine, because the worst you can get for it is a month in the jug. But if you're caught pinching, you could get transported to Van Diemen's Land for seven long years. So never pinch anything, unless I tell you to. I'll strip the skin off your arses else! And then I'll break your necks!'

She shivered with dread. 'Oh God, I can't tell me da what I've done. He'll tear the arse off me, so he will. He'll kill me, so he will! He'll fuckin' kill me!'

She pulled her shawl over her head and left the shelter of the wall.

On the opposite side of the Big Pool the man hidden in the derelict end cottage of the tumbledown row grunted with satisfaction when he saw the girl move. Driven by the tormenting demonic voices in his head, and the lusts raging through his body, he had been watching her for hours, waiting until it was safe for him to strike. Now he allowed her to put some distance between them, then stealthily followed. His lips were slack and wet, his left hand fondling the handle of the sharp knife in his pocket.

Twenty-Two

It was Monday morning, and the weekly petty sessions were in progress at the Fox and Goose. The tap room was thronged with the sinners and those who were there to bear witness for and against them. In the bar parlour the Reverend Peter Timmins was sitting in solitary judgement upon the malefactors, Lord Aston having been forced to take to his bed in consequence of gorging a large mess of suspect lampreys the previous evening. Joseph Blackwell was in his usual post and Tom Potts was performing in the multiple roles of court usher, prosecuting witness, witness for the defence and escorting officer and gaoler should anyone be unfortunate enough to be sentenced to incarceration in the lock-up.

Peter Timmins was by nature a kindly man, who tried to

live by the tenets of his Christian faith, and when freed from the over-bearing dominance of Lord Aston he was always inclined towards leniency in punishment, particularly for the poor of the parish who in the depths of his soul he feared were more sinned against than sinners. This morning he had admonished, warned, advised and when unable to avoid punitive punishment sentenced the offenders to the very minimum. One after another left the Fox and Goose feeling extremely relieved.

When the proceedings were over Tom also felt relieved that no one had been committed to the lock-up, or sentenced to the stocks or a whipping. This last was a duty that he was dreading having to perform, and he strongly doubted that he was capable of bringing himself to flog any man, woman or child.

He went into the tap room to speak to Amy, who was tending the bar, and found her in conversation with a burly, rough-looking man.

Amy smiled and beckoned to him. 'Come over here, Tom. This man wants words with you.'

'What about?' Tom joined them.

'About me daughter, Siobhan.' The man looked under immense strain. 'She went missing on Saturday, and I can't find hide nor hair of her.'

'Who are you?'

'Me name is Timmy Docherty, and I'm a tinker by trade. Will you be the constable who helped me missus shift our camp?'

'The camp between the Crosses?'

'That's the one. Me missus said that you spoke to me daughter.'

'Is she the pretty young girl with red hair?'

'That's her. Have you seen her around the town anywhere?'

'No, I've not.' Tom's sympathy was aroused by this man's obviously intense anxiety, and he sought to soothe him. 'But young people are sometimes thoughtless, Master Docherty. Perhaps she is staying with friends and hasn't bothered to tell you.'

'She can't be,' the other man denied forcefully. 'We know nobody around these parts. And Siobhan would never go off and stay anywhere without telling me or her ma where she was going.'

'Are you saying that she's never gone missing like this before?'

'Yes, that's what I'm saying. Now will youse help me to look for her or not?' Docherty's voice rose as his anxiety-fuelled impatience flared.

'Of course I'll do whatever I can to help you,' Tom hastened to assure him. 'But I need to know everything that you or your wife can tell me, so as to give me a better idea of where to search for her. Could she have gone on an errand or something similar?'

'She was doing house-calling. Seeing if she could find a bit of work.'

'In which area? What parish?'

Docherty raised his arms and then let them fall as he admitted helplessly. 'I don't know exactly. Round about the district.'

'All right.' Tom nodded. 'Can you describe the clothes she was wearing?'

'She was dressed very dacent and respectable. She had a grey dress and shawl and a black bonnet, and good boots on her feet. She didn't look like a tinker girl at all.'

Tom pondered for a couple of moments, then stated firmly, 'I'm of the opinion that she was working the "distressed tragic orphan" lay, Master Docherty!' Before the tinker could react he went on, 'I've had a report about two very ragged young Irish tinker girls going from house to house begging. Now I'm of the opinion that they're also your girls. I've taken no action to stop them, because they've not been accused of any pilfering or aggressive badgering, and I know that begging is all that they can do to bring in some food. But, as I said before, if I'm to help you find your other daughter, then you must be completely honest and open with me in return.'

'I've been honest wi' you! I'm a God-fearing, honest man!' Docherty blustered, but then his shoulders sagged and he broke down, sobbing brokenly. 'You're right! I have to be straight wi' you. Not knowing where me daughter is or what's happened to her is nigh on killing me and her ma, so it is. And it's my fault. All my fault, so it is.'

'It must be terrible for you and all your family.' Tom patted the other man's shoulder sympathetically. 'Amy, will you please serve this gentleman with a stiff brandy, I'll pay.'

Tom waited patiently until the distressed man had slurped down the drink and regained control of himself, then pressed gently. 'Now, Master Docherty. Let me hear all that you know.'

The tinker drew a long wheezy breath, and began to talk rapidly. 'You have to understand that for us travelling people life can be double hard, and it seems every man's hand is raised against us. There's times that I have to be hard and raise me own hand against me woman and childer just so that we can all survive. My Siobhan was working the orphan lay right enough, but not having a deal of luck with it around here. So the little bitch got desperate and pinched a piece of silver. I know she was risking transportation for doing that, but we're desperate with hunger. She only stole it to feed the kids.'

'What day was this?' Tom asked.

'I don't know for sure. She never told me what she'd done, I only know what her ma told me yesterday. Because Siobhan and her ma and all me kids knows that I won't have them going round pinching. Not unless I tells them to pinch something particular. But I know that Siobhan and her ma hides some of the things they gets up to from me.

'Now on the Saturday I'd the drink taken down at Studley, and I spent the night in a barn there, sleeping it off. When I got back to me camp on the Sunday me missus told me Siobhan had gone missing, and that she'd pinched silver from a big house. I been searching for her ever since. Please, Master Potts, I'm begging youse to help me find my girl. I'm fearful that something bad has happened to her! I'm ready to see her going to prison so long as we can find her safe and well.'

'I'll do my very best to help you,' Tom assured him firmly, and put several more questions to Docherty, the answers to which gave him much to ponder on when the two men finally parted.

Twenty-Three

'**W**hy would you want to offer a reward paid for by the parish for information about a petty thief? An Irish tinker thief, at that? The girl will be many miles from here by now, and undoubtedly safe in the bosom of some other of her tinker brethren . . . What is the value of the piece of silver she's reputedly stolen?'

'I don't know its value,' Tom admitted, 'but Docherty's story had the ring of truth to it. His daughter stole a piece of silver from a large house in this area, on Thursday or Friday last. Someone, who the girl told her mother was a gentleman, knew that the girl was the culprit, and offered her money to return the silver to him. This was on Saturday last. And now she has disappeared.'

'And where was she to meet this gentleman?'

'Outside the Horse and Jockey.'

Joseph Blackwell shook his head in emphatic dismissal. 'Quite frankly, Master Potts, the whole thing sounds like a farrago of nonsense. If any of the owners of our local large houses had been robbed, we would have been the first to know about it. They would be screaming to high Heaven that we hang, draw and quarter the thief in the middle of the Chapel Green, and then gibbet the remains at the crossroad.' He shook his head again. 'No, Master Potts! For some personal reason or other the girl has run away from her family. Runaways are legion, and unless they are involved in some way with the respectable elements of our population, we do not involve ourselves.'

From his desk drawer he took a folded and wax-sealed sheet of paper and frowningly handed it to Tom.

'Here's another copy of the removal order that you deliberately failed to execute when it was issued a month past, and pray don't try telling me that the discovery of that corpse caused you to forget to remove Ann Washwood and her brats. By failing to do so, you have laid yourself open to the charges of wilful disobedience and neglect of your duty as a constable; and you can be sent to prison for it, if Lord Aston is so inclined.'

Tom's heart raced nervously and he drew several sharp intakes of breath, trying to summon his courage.

'With all respect, sir, I would rather go to prison than become the instrument of such cruelty to a poor woman and her helpless children, one of whom was lying dead in a curing trough when I arrived at the poorhouse.'

'Would you indeed choose to go to prison, Master Potts?

Because let me assure you, that can be very quickly arranged for,' Blackwell challenged angrily.

Tom swallowed hard. For a brief instant his nerve wavered, and he asked himself, 'Do I really want to go to prison for the sake of a woman I don't know? What will happen to my mother if I'm jailed? Who'll care for her?'

But driven by an all-powerful impulse, he placed the document on the desk and replied doggedly, 'I am prepared to go to prison for my beliefs, sir. So you can report me to Lord Aston. Because I will never be a party to this cruelty towards that woman and her children.'

For what seemed to be an interminable length of time Joseph Blackwell sat silently scowling, and Tom's heart pounded as he waited to hear what was to befall him, inwardly reiterating to himself, 'I'll not do this cruel thing. I'll not be party to it.'

Then, to Tom's bewilderment, the pale, deep-lined features of the other man smiled grimly. 'I see that you are a man of true principles, Master Potts, and that does you credit. So we'll speak no more of this matter.' He replaced the document in the drawer, and informed him casually, 'The woman has run away from the poorhouse five days since, and abandoned her children to our mercies. She obviously lacks your scruples.'

He took another document from the desk and proffered it to Tom. 'I trust that you'll not object to serving this summons on Erasmus Dolton. He's being charged with failure to maintain one of his bastards. It's not one of Ann Washwood's offspring, by the way, but some other poor girl he's got into trouble.'

'I'll be very happy to do so, sir,' Tom acceded gladly, filled with relief that he had escaped the prospect of being jailed.

He stowed the summons away in his shoulder-slung canvas haversack, but instead of leaving, stood his ground and asked, 'Do you have any objection to my offering a reward at my own expense for information concerning Siobhan Docherty?'

Blackwell blinked several times in surprise. 'At your own expense, Master Potts? Why are you so concerned with this runaway? She's naught but a tinker's brat. If it were down to me I'd have every tinker in this land thrown into the sea for being the villainous, thieving pack of worthless wastrels that they are. They bring nothing but trouble upon decent living folk wherever they go.'

'Nevertheless, sir, I want to investigate further into this girl's disappearance,' Tom persisted stubbornly. 'There is something here that all my instincts are telling me is wrong. That this is not just another case of a runaway girl. It will cost the parish nothing, sir, I will pay the reward.'

'And what about your official duties?' Blackwell challenged huffily. 'How can you be attending to them if you are otherwise engaged upon this wild-goose chase?'

'You may be assured that I shall not neglect my official duties,' Tom stated firmly. 'I give you my solemn word on that score. And with all respect, sir, did you not tell me yourself that you wanted a force of constables who possessed enquiring minds?'

'Oh, very well, do whatever you like!' Blackwell waved his hand in irritable dismissal. 'Go! Leave me in peace! I've work to do.'

'Thank you, sir.' Tom smiled in satisfaction.

He was shutting the door behind him when Blackwell called after him in an ambiguous tone, 'If your instincts prove to be justified, Master Potts, then the parish will fully reimburse you for all your costs, and perhaps a little extra on top, to serve as an acknowledgement of your enquiring mind's extraordinary perceptivity.'

Tom looked back round the edge of the door, but Blackwell's head was bent low over the ledger and he was writing busily.

Shaking his head in wry amusement, Tom left without replying.

As he walked past the chapel burial yard he saw Amy by one of the gravestones, bending over a man seated on the ground. He entered the yard and went to her.

'Amy?'

'Hello, Tom.' She smiled welcomingly. 'I've just brought King William something to eat. The poor soul's had nothing for breakfast.'

Tom regarded the seated man with a degree of pity.

'King William' was the town idiot, a thirty-year-old harelipped deranged simpleton who lived with his aged mother in one of the tumbledown cottages bordering the Big Pool. He spent his days wandering the town and its environs, and most of his nights sleeping rough among the gravestones of the burial yard, or wherever else he might find himself to be when darkness fell. To their credit most of the townspeople treated him with kindness, but there were some who given opportunity would torment him unmercifully, play cruel tricks and badly mistreat him. Looking at the man's bruised face and ripped and soiled clothing, Tom could see that such an encounter had happened very recently.

'What happened to you, William?' he enquired gently. 'Has somebody been nasty to you?'

King William's mouth was crammed too full with the bread and cheese that Amy had brought him to be able to make any intelligible answer. He babbled some mangled gibberish, spraying out a fine rain of chewed food.

'Tell me later, William.' Tom held up his hands to shield his face from the wet spray. 'Eat your breakfast first, then you can tell me.'

'It was Tommy Chance and Simmy Benton who did this to him.' Amy's pretty face flushed with anger. 'They was both as drunk as bob-owlers, but that's no excuse, is it. They'm both evil buggers! Ritchie Bint give them a hell of a hiding when he caught them hurting poor King William here. Fair play to Ritchie Bint, lots of people say that he's a no-good but I think that he's all right, and his heart's in the right place when it comes down to it.'

'I agree with you,' Tom was quick to tell her. 'In my book, Ritchie Bint is a good man.'

'How about the tinker girl? Have you found out anything about her whereabouts yet?'

'No. Truth to tell, Amy, I spent most of yesterday trying to decide how best to go about making my enquiries. I did ask Billy Middleton if he'd seen a girl of that description around his tavern, but he couldn't remember. There were dog-fight matches being held as well as the dancing so there were hundreds of people milling about the area.

'What I've decided is to have her description cried by Jimmy Grier, and to offer a reward for any information that leads to her being traced. Her type of red hair is very distinctive, after all, because there are only a few ginger-top women in this town, and they are mostly sandy, rather than the true Celtic red.'

She smiled mischievously. 'So you've been taking a great

interest in the ginger-snaps, have you, Tom? Is that why you don't want to wed me? You prefer ginger to blonde?'

'You know that's not true,' he flustered.

'I see'd a ginger-top. I see'd a pretty little ginger-top. Down by the Big Pool,' King William rambled to himself. 'But her never see'd me. Oh no. It was dark, it was.' He cackled with laughter. 'I see'd her and the chap, I did. But her never see'd me, 'cos I was hid away, I was. Hid away. Like the chap. I was hid away in the dark a-watching her like him, I was.' He hugged himself, cackling with laughter.

'Did you catch what he said?' Despite King William's harelip-distorted diction, Tom had caught some bits and pieces of the simpleton's ramblings. 'About seeing a pretty ginger-haired girl who was being watched by himself and some other man?'

'Oh, take no notice of what this poor soul says. He comes out with all sorts of nonsense.' Amy patted King William's shoulder soothingly. 'Now be a good boy, William, and go home to your mam. She'll be worrying about you. Go on now.'

The simpleton scurried away, body bowed, head bent low.

'What are you doing today?' Amy asked.

'I've this summons to serve.' Tom frowned unhappily. 'It's a cruel beginning to life for those babies who are born bastards and thrown on the parish. There's little mercy shown to them by the Poor Law.'

Before Amy could reply, her name was called by a passing horseman, who reined in and dismounted at the yard gate.

'Davy? Where did you spring from?' She smiled delightedly and ran to the decently dressed, top-hatted, riding-booted young man, who laughed with pleasure and spread his arms wide in invitation.

Tom experienced uncomfortable stirrings of jealousy as he watched the young couple hug affectionately and kiss each other on the lips.

He hung back until Amy beckoned him.

'Come here, Tom. I want you to meet Davy Rowley. He was my first-ever sweetheart, when we were at dame school. We must have been about four years old, weren't we, Davy.'

'Oh yes, every day of that.' The young man smilingly held out his hand to Tom. 'I'm pleased to meet you, Master . . .'

'Potts! Thomas Potts!' Tom now experienced even stronger stirrings of uneasy jealously, as he felt the strong grip and compared the young man's handsome face and muscular, well-proportioned physique to his own ungainly body and unremarkable looks.

He coughed nervously, unable to think of anything other to say except, 'I trust you are well, Master Rowley.'

'I am indeed, I thank you. I'm in the pink, and as happy as any sand-boy ever was to be back here with Amy once more for a while.'

'Davy is in business on his own account. He's a travelling farrier and horse-doctor, aren't you, Davy? With his own tool-wagon and everything,' Amy said proudly.

'You no longer live locally, then?' Tom enquired, unable to keep himself from hoping that the reply would be negative.

'Oh yes, I've always had a home here. My dad owned the smithy and yard next to Salter's Yard, near the Big Pool there. He died last year, so it's mine now; and I'm going work it, and stop travelling about.' He smiled warmly at Amy. 'I reckon it's time for me to settle down, and maybe have a family of my own.'

Seeing how radiantly Amy was smiling back at this young man, Tom's heart sank, and he was suddenly overcome by an urgent need to get away from them both.

'I'm sorry, but I must leave you now. I've some pressing official business to attend to. Good day to you.'

He marched stiffly away, feeling himself reddening with embarrassment at how gauchely he was behaving.

Twenty-Four

Erasmus Dolton's extensive holdings encompassed the area of dense woodland and bleak wasteland known as Brockhill, a couple of miles north-west of the town. Brockhill Wood had far fewer inviting glades and passable tracks than the more accessible woodlands around Redditch, and its undergrowth was denser and more redolent of decay and death. There were many local legends about it being the haunt of witches, warlocks and evil spirits, and consequently the more superstitious and credulous inhabitants of the district gave it a wide berth. Poachers and scavengers for firewood and kindling were also deterred from entering the wood by Dolton's widely reputed use of a multitude of cunningly concealed trip-wired spring guns and savage-toothed man-traps which could break legs and tear flesh to shreds, plus his own reputation for shooting at intruders without warning.

As Tom trudged along the stony track leading to Brockhill the constantly reccurring mental image of Amy Danks and Davy Rowley hugging and kissing each other was lowering his spirits.

'I've no right to resent that young fellow,' he told himself repeatedly. 'In all truth Amy should marry a fine young man like him, and not tie herself to a useless ageing failure like me.' But no matter how many times he repeated this, the instinctive conviction that Amy was lost to him was a saddening burden to bear.

It was something of a paradoxical relief when he came into view of Dolton's farmstead, and his nervous apprehension about a possible heated confrontation with the man overlaid those troubling mental images.

Some of the fields around him were filled with crops of beans and turnips and corn, while in others cattle and sheep grazed on fecund green pasture. In one field a group of women were toiling hard, hoeing and singling along the drills of turnips, and Tom halted and called to them.

'Do you work for Farmer Dolton?'

'We does, worse luck,' the nearest woman spat out disgruntledly.

'Do you know where I can find him? I'm the constable.'

'He's up in Brockhill Wood. Take care where you puts your feet down in there, Master Constable. It's full o' man-traps and spring guns.'

'Yes, and watch out for him hisself. He'll shoot you dead wi'out a second thought, and give no warning neither.'

'Thank you.' Tom walked on, asking himself nervously, 'Do I really need this? Wouldn't it be better if I just forgot the whole thing and pretended that I couldn't find Dolton?'

Despite the sunshine and warm gentle breeze Brockhill Wood appeared dank and gloomy, and as Tom entered it he experienced a sense of foreboding. When the dense undergrowth and gnarled branches closed around and above him he was struck with the urge to retreat back the way he had come. But gripping his staff tightly with both hands he went further along the narrow muddied path, and deeper into the rank-smelling undergrowth and trees.

Carefully picking his way, eyes searching the ground ahead for any signs of hidden man-traps or tripwires, ears straining for the sounds of humans or animals, Tom gradually became aware of the lack of birdsong. This made him increasingly tense. 'If birds have been frightened away from here, then have they've fled because there is someone or something lying in ambush?'

He fired with anger at his own nervousness. 'Damn you, Potts! Why won't you act as a man should? Why must you shiver and shake like some wretched timid old maid? Act the man for once, can't you!'

Driven by self-disgust, he suddenly shouted at the top of his lungs, 'Halloo? Is there anyone near? Halloo? Halloo?'

Listening intently he continued to move forwards, repeating the shout at short intervals.

The path abruptly widened into a narrow glade, and Tom came to a sudden halt, staring unbelievingly at what was before him.

At the far end of the glade a young man was standing motionless, his face a bloodied mask of terror, and three big aggressive dogs were circling him, displaying long sharp teeth in fierce snarling.

Two other men suddenly burst out of the undergrowth from the side of the glade, and one of them shouted at Tom, 'You'd best keep still and not come any nearer, or the dogs'll turn on you.'

Tom recognized the man who had shouted to be the big-bellied Erasmus Dolton, and after a closer look at the other man knew him also: Gareth Jenkins, the stepson of Joseph Turner.

'Help me, Master Potts! For fuck's sake help me!' the motionless man shrieked.

Tom looked hard at his bloodied features, and recognition dawned. It was the young needle-pointer, John Hancox, all bravado terrified out of him, clothing ripped in a score of places, blood seeping from the bites the dogs had inflicted on his head, arms, legs and body.

'Shut your mouth, you thievin' bastard, or I'll let the dogs have you!' Erasmus Dolton bellowed, and Hancox subsided into muffled whimpering.

His jowly, drink-purpled features radiating menace, Dolton swung to confront Tom. Only inches shorter and huge in bulk, he was a fearsome opponent to face.

'What's you doing trespassing on my land? I don't tolerate trespassers.' He lifted his clenched fist. 'They gets a taste o' this, no matter who or what they might be.'

Tom fought down the impulse to turn and run, and struggling to keep his voice firm replied, 'I'm here in the King's name, to serve a summons on you.'

The big man laughed. ' A summons, is it. What's it for this time?'

'Failing to maintain your bastard daughter. The one that you fathered upon Megan Clint.'

'Oh, that 'un.' Dolton appeared to be unconcerned, and held out his hand. 'Well, give it over, and then sod off.'

Tom passed him the summons, and Dolton grinned at Gareth Jenkins.

'I could paper my parlour with the number o' these I've had served on me these past years. I only has to look at the sluts and they gets a babby in their bellies. I reckon I must be the best stud bull in all England.'

He looked back at Tom and frowned. 'What's you still here for? I've took the summons, so now get your arse off my land.'

Listening to this man, Tom's contempt had burgeoned immeasurably, and this in turn fuelled his determination not to be browbeaten. 'Call off those dogs, Master Dolton. I'm taking that man with me when I leave this wood.'

Dolton stepped closer until his face was only inches from Tom's, his foul breath gusting against Tom's face as he growled, 'What's your name, you bloody beanpole?'

'Potts, Master Dolton. Thomas Potts, constable of Tardebigge parish.' Tom found himself inwardly marvelling at how firm and resonant his voice sounded, in stark contrast to his quaking insides. 'And let me remind you, Master Dolton, that I am here in the King's name. If you attempt to obstruct me and prevent me doing my lawful duty, then you will suffer the consequences.'

Dolton's bloodshot eyes were murderous, but Tom forced himself to meet their malevolent glare without blinking; and it was Dolton who finally blinked and stepped back.

He emitted a short bark of derisive laughter. 'All right, Beanpole. Take this thievin' bugger with you. I want him locked up and charged with poaching.' He took some snare wires from his pocket. 'And here's the proof. We found him setting snares, didn't we, Gareth?'

'Yes. He had a terrier dog with him as well.' Gareth Jenkins was staring at the trembling, whimpering John Hancox, and his puffy features were suffused with pleasure. 'Our dogs tore the mangy cur to pieces. What's left of it is back along the path.'

Tom felt weak with relief, and ready to agree to virtually anything to enable he and John Hancox to get out of this wood. 'Very well, Master Dolton. I'll take him directly to the lock-up, and he'll be brought before the magistrates when the formal charge procedure has been completed. Now will you be kind enough to call off the dogs?'

Gareth Jenkins took a long slender silver whistle from his pocket and placed it between his lips. His cheeks puffed several times, but no sound issued from the whistle.

The dogs immediately stopped circling and snarling, and sat down on their haunches, tongues lolling from the sides of their mouths.

For a moment Tom was startled, but then his memory triggered. Dogs possess an acute sense of hearing, and are able to detect noises well beyond the range of the human ear. This whistle was transmitting signals that no human could hear.

He couldn't help but be impressed, and remarked, 'Those dogs appear to be very well trained.'

'Indeed yes.' Gareth Jenkins smirked with satisfaction. 'They are trained far beyond the comprehension of a bumpkin constable.'

He placed the whistle between his lips and again his cheeks puffed.

The dogs immediately came to him and lay down at his

feet, heads pressed submissively to the ground, bodies and tails absolutely motionless.

'You may take this piece of carrion with you now.' Jenkins smirked.

Tom wasted not a moment. He went to John Hancox, grabbed his arm and quickly hustled him past the dogs and down the narrow path.

The repeated loud rat-tat-tat of the door knocker reverberated through Hugh Laylor's house on the Front Hill, reaching the ears of the man and woman lying in each other's arms in the drowsy aftermath of passionate loving.

'Dammit! I'll have to see who it is.' Hugh Laylor sighed resignedly. 'It could be something serious.'

'Leave it, Cariad. Stay here with me,' Eleri Turner whispered, clasping him close, pressing her lush nakedness against his taut muscularity.

'Believe me, I'll not be gone from you a moment longer than is absolutely necessary, my darling.' He smiled and kissed her, then disengaged himself from her arms and went naked to the window to poke his head out and shout down.

'Who's there, and what do you want?'

'It's Thomas Potts, Doctor. I've a prisoner in the lock-up who is in sore need of your attention. He's been ripped by dogs.'

'Very well, Master Potts. Wait there, I'll be down directly,' Hugh Taylor answered without any hesitation, and closing the window began to dress hurriedly.

Eleri Turner pouted and said petulantly, 'You're in a great hurry to leave me now, aren't you?'

'Of course I'm not! I shall be back as quickly as I can.'

'Why must you go?'

'Because it's my vocation, woman! I'm a doctor. If someone needs my treatment, then I must hasten to give it to them.'

'Well, don't expect me to stay here for hours waiting for you,' she huffed, and pulled away when he bent to kiss her. 'I've other fish that I can fry.'

'Make sure that they're fresh and sweet, then, my darling. Because bad fish can give you a belly-ache, if not something worse.' He chuckled, and left the room, fending off the pillow that she hurled at his head.

* * *

'Oww! Oww! Fuckin' hell!' Crouched naked on the floor of the cell, John Hancox writhed and complained bitterly as the sharp needle drew the waxed threads through his wounded flesh.

'Stop blubbing like a damned infant, and take it like a man,' Hugh Taylor reproved sharply, biting off the threads with his teeth and drawing and knotting the ends tight to close the blood-weeping gashes. 'You're lucky to get off so lightly, you damned rogue!'

'Lucky? Lucky? I been near bit to death by a pack o' wild beasts, and you calls me lucky?' the young pointer protested plaintively. 'I 'uddent call that lucky! I'd call it downright unlucky, I 'ud!'

The lugubrious expression on Hancox's face touched Hugh Laylor's sense of humour and throwing back his head he roared with laughter. Tom Potts could not repress his own chuckle.

'It aren't funny!' Hancox complained. 'Just supposing it had been a little kid them bloody dogs got hold of. They'd ha' torn the little bugger to bits, so they 'ud.'

The thought of this sobered Tom, and he was driven to agree.

'He's right, you know, Doctor. That pack of dogs is very dangerous. They could easily kill a child.'

'But they won't, Master Potts,' Laylor stated confidently. 'Because Mr Jenkins and Farmer Dolton keep them penned, and only take them out under the closest control.'

'But what if the beasts escaped from the pen, and ran free?' Tom questioned.

'What if? What if?' Laylor's handsome face mirrored quick-roused irritation. 'We can't live our lives on the basis of what if, Master Potts. Remember, if it wasn't for damned rogues and thieves like this article here – ' Laylor cuffed Hancox's head with his open palm to give emphasis to his words – 'then honest folk would not have any necessity to keep savage dogs to guard their lives and properties.'

'Well . . . Yes . . . You have justification for what you say,' Tom was forced to acknowledge.

Hugh Laylor bit, tightened and knotted the final thread. 'There! That's it done! You can get dressed now, you damned rogue.'

Muttering and moaning, John Hancox began to put his bloodstained torn clothing back on.

Laylor's eyes gleamed with mischievous humour. 'Listen carefully, Hancox. During the next few months I want you to be watchful for any symptoms of hydrophobia.'

'Hider, what?'

'Phobia, you rogue! Hydrophobia.' Laylor's white teeth glistened wolfishly. 'Be alert for any spasms of the styloglossus, the hyoglossus, thyrohyoid and cricothyroid muscles which may occur at the sight of water.'

'What's them things, them stys and suchlike? And what does you mean, at the sight of water?' Hancox was looking simultaneously baffled and alarmed. 'What's you on about?'

'Rabies, you rogue! One of the dogs that bit you may be rabid, and has consequently infected you also. If that is the case, then the symptoms I've just described can occur at any time during the next hours, days, weeks or even months; and they invariably lead to a hideously painful death.'

'Rabies! Fuckin' Mad Dog Fever!' Hancox emitted a strangled cry of terror, and slumped onto his knees, shaking his head and wrapping his arms around his torso as if to shield himself from harm, moaning over and over again, 'No, no, no, no, no.'

'Oh yes, yes, yes, yes, yes, Master Hancox,' Laylor affirmed pleasantly, and picking up his medical chest left the cell.

Tom looked down at the slumped terrified young man, and his anger flared.

He hurried to catch up with the doctor outside the arched entrance and reproved him heatedly. 'That was a totally unnecessary cruelty to inflict on the poor fellow, Dr Laylor. It was unworthy of you, and you should be ashamed of it.'

'Unworthy of me? Ashamed?' The other man frowned. 'Come now, Master Potts, I merely spoke the truth.'

'That's as maybe, but it was the way in which you did so that I object to.' Tom was not prepared to back down.

Laylor smiled grimly. 'You have only lived in this town for a brief time, Master Potts. I, on the other hand, have been born and bred here. I shall speak to the pointers in whichever way I choose. Because they are little more than brute beasts. When you have seen and treated as many poor unfortunates who have been sorely mistreated and abused by these same pointers, and only then, will you be entitled to criticize my way of speaking to them. A final word of advice, before I leave you . . . Don't make an enemy of me, Master Potts, or you will live to regret doing so. Good day to you.'

The doctor strode away, leaving Tom seething impotently by the arched entrance.

'Well? Was it worth leaving me alone for?' Eleri Turner wanted to know, when Hugh Laylor returned to the bedroom.

'Nothing will ever be worth leaving you for, my darling.' He smiled, and came to kiss her, and this time she returned his embrace with an equal passion.

'Come, we've little time left,' she murmured huskily. 'Let's not waste it.'

He drew back and began to quickly shed his clothes, and as he was doing so, told her, 'Gareth's hunting pack caught a poacher, and it looks as if he made no effort to call them off, because the man has been badly mauled.'

Eleri Turner frowned uneasily, but she made no comment.

'I'm beginning to wonder if Gareth is perhaps becoming too reckless for his own good,' Hugh Laylor offered tentatively, as he got into the bed and drew her towards him.

'Let's not talk of it now,' she breathed, and crushed her lips to his mouth, her hand moving to fondle his erect manhood.

He groaned with pleasure and put all thoughts of Gareth Jenkins from his mind.

Twenty-Five

Following the first two days of Jimmy Grier's crying about Siobhan Docherty there had been several callers at the lock-up claiming that they had information concerning the girl. None of them however could tell Tom where she was now, and their accounts placed her in widely different places at roughly the same times. Coupled with the fact that John Hollis' enquiries so far had also failed to produce any definite lead, Tom was beginning to appreciate the old saw of needles in haystacks.

It was during the third day that one of the parish road-mending gang heard Grier's cry and remembered the pretty red-haired girl in the Holloway. When he finished work that evening he went to the lock-up and told Tom what he had seen.

'Do you know the man she was with?' Tom asked eagerly.

'Not by name. But I've seen him about the town a couple o' times this last year. He's a pedlar, I reckon.'

Tom wrote down the roadman's description and that same hour went to John Hollis' cottage to tell him of this latest lead.

'I don't think he can be a local man,' Hollis decided. 'I don't recognize the description.'

'Then when he's in this area he'll have to lodge somewhere. I'll make enquiries around the town.' Tom smiled. 'I should think that the women will remember the handsome young fellow the roadman described.'

At the end of Silver Street furthest from the Red Lion archway, the alley opened out into a rectangular square surrounded by houses, one of which stood four storeys high. Once the fine home of a prosperous Jacobean landowner, it was now a ramshackle cesspit, a lodging-house licensed for thirty lodgers, but often having nearly double that crammed within its reeking walls. Mother Readman was its proprietress, and ruled its transient and permanent denizens with a rod of iron. Quite literally. As many aggressive lodgers had found out to their cost.

Dour, hatchet-featured, raw-boned, standing six feet tall, Mother Readman feared neither man nor beast. Thirty years old and unmarried, she had inherited the property from her mother, also known as Mother Readman, who in her turn had inherited from her own Mother Readman.

With a huge floppy mobcap on her tight-bunned hair and a man's caped greatcoat over her shabby gown and apron, the incumbent Mother Readman stood facing Tom in the large candle-lit smoke-blackened room where her lodgers spent most of their waking hours, and did their cooking upon the large open range that almost filled one wall. She listened intently to his description of the man he sought, and said nothing until he had finished. Then she stated positively, 'That sounds like the one we calls Pretty Dick. He's a real good-looking lad, and he's a pedlar right enough. He was here a few days since. But he left all of a sudden in the middle o' the Saturday night. I've no idea where he went.'

'Do you know any reason why he would leave at such an hour?'

'No.' She shrugged her broad shoulders. 'They comes and goes as they pleases here. I takes their money in advance, so it don't matter to me if they leaves afore their time's up. They don't get any refunds, that's certain sure.'

'Is this Pretty Dick a violent man? Does he knock women about? Has he got a woman, or family hereabouts? Do you know where he hails from, or what rounds he makes?'

To all of these Mother Readman only shrugged.

At last Tom accepted that he would learn nothing more here, and requested politely, 'Will you please send word to me at the lock-up, if he should come back?'

She nodded, and unexpectedly smiled in a friendly fashion. 'It's that Paddy tinker wench you'm really looking for, aren't it? The one whose feyther has been asking about her all over the town these past days. Is it yourself that's offered the reward?'

After a momentary hesitation, Tom admitted, 'Yes, it is, ma'am.'

'You'm a good soul, Master Potts, there's precious few who'd bother about a missing tinker wench. If I hears anything at all, I'll let you know directly. Truth to tell, Pretty Dick has never struck me as a man who'd harm women. He'll shag 'em right enough, whenever he gets half a chance. But if harm has come to that girl, I think you'd do better looking else-where for who's done it.'

Tom had realized within a brief span of their meeting that he was facing a very shrewd and worldly wise woman. So now he told Mother Readman about the slaughtered sheep, and his belief that the same man was responsible for the murder of the headless woman and could also be involved in the disap-pearance of Siobhan Docherty. He finished by asking, 'Do you have any suspicions about any local man who would be capable of committing such atrocities?'

She grinned mirthlessly. 'There's some hereabouts who'm capable of doing anything, especially when they'm in drink.

'Who in particular do you mean?' Tom pressed.

'Well.' She pursed her lips and considered for some moments, then told him, 'Alfie Payne for one. Then there's one o' them Shrimptons who moved up here from Long Crendon. During the wars wi' Boney, he used to hunt down the French prisoners when they went missing from their billets in Long Crendon. Jacky Shrimpton, his name is . . . And Tommy Chance and Simmy Benton, they'm both evil buggers when they'm in drink.'

She fell silent, but Tom sensed that she wanted to tell him something more, and again he quietly pressed her, 'Is there someone else, who you might be reluctant to tell me of?'

'There might be. But you've got to give me your sworn word that you'll never tell anyone that I've told you their names. Because they carries a lot o' weight in this parish, and could make things very hard for me.'

'I swear by all that I hold sacred that I'll never betray you in such a way,' Tom assured her sincerely.

She stared deeply into his eyes, as if trying to read what they contained, before nodding. 'I trust you, Thomas Potts. Well, the two others I'm thinking of are Erasmus Dolton, and Joe Turner's stepson, Gareth Jenkins. I've heard bad accounts o' what they gets up to wi' the poor wenches who goes to work for Dolton.

'I know for a fact as well that Jenkins tried to make free and throw his weight about wi' the wenches who works at Joe Turner's mill. But fair play to Old Joe. He's a hard, mean bugger, but he won't stand for anybody taking liberties wi' the women and girls who works for him; and he double-quick put a stop to Jenkins' tricks.'

Tom's mind filled with the memory of his own encounter with the pair, and he was about to reply when a group of men, dressed in clay-thick moleskin and corduroy clothing and carrying the picks and shovels of their navvying trade, came noisily into the room.

'You'd best go, Master Potts,' Mother Readman whispered urgently. 'My lodgers don't like to see any parish constables under my roof. It makes 'em uncomfortable.'

'Then I'll say goodbye, ma'am, with many thanks for your help.' Tom made a hasty exit.

The dusk had given way to full nightfall and Silver Street

was in shadowed darkness relieved only here and there by the faint glow of rush lights and tallow candles glimmering behind broken rag-stuffed, dirty window glass.

The air was warm, ragged children played noisily upon the filth-strewn cobbles, men and women sat on doorsteps and lounged against the walls of their wretched tenements talking, laughing, smoking, eating, drinking, creating a tangible atmosphere of easy-going camaraderie.

Not for the first time Tom found himself marvelling at the resilience and humour of these slum-dwellers, whose spirits remained uncrushed despite the bleak hardship and poverty of their lives.

As he walked towards the lock-up he could hear the sounds of voices raised in heated dispute, and, recognizing one of them to be his mother's, he quickened his pace.

'This is a fine time of night to come disturbing me, and you should be ashamed of yourself, you ignorant hound!' Widow Potts was screeching with fury. 'It's wicked to torment a poor weak widow-woman this way. If ever a poor woman suffered as I suffer, then I'd like to have met her! I've told you till I'm blue in the face, my son isn't here, and I don't know where he is, or when he'll be back! Useless, rotten son that he is! So take yourself off, will you, and leave this poor soul in peace!'

'I'm staying right here until your son comes back.' The butcher, Henry Vincent, stubbornly refused to leave. 'So you can like it, or lump it!'

Tom hastened to intervene. 'It's all right, Mother. I'm here now, so you can go back to your room and rest.'

'Rest!' she screeched. 'Rest! The only time I shall be able to rest is when I'm in my grave. And I pray that that happy day comes sooner rather than later. It's terrible the way that I have to live, poor pitiful creature that I am. And it's all your fault, you great useless lazy lump.'

'Very well, Mother,' Tom sighed resignedly. 'Stay here if you prefer.'

'Stay here? Stay here? Yes, you'd like that, wouldn't you? Wicked, unnatural son that you are to me! You'd like me to stay here and catch my death of cold, wouldn't you! Evil beast that you are! Well, you're not going to have the satisfaction of seeing me suffering. I'm going back to my bed.'

She shuffled down the lantern-lit cell passage, loudly calling for all the torments of hell to come down upon Tom's head.

'Well, Master Vincent, what can I do for you?' Tom enquired.

The pale light of the lantern shone on the butcher's worried, tense expression, and he answered in a jerky whisper, 'There's another one up there in Red Lane, Master Potts.'

'Another what, Master Vincent?'

'Another fuckin' dead 'un, a-laying on my chopping block!'

Twenty-Six

'Is it male or female?' Joseph Blackwell questioned.

'I don't rightly know. It's got a covering over it, I just saw its feet sticking out when I lifted me lantern, and didn't stop to look any closer,' Vincent told him. 'I just got out of it as quick as I could, and come to find Master Potts here.'

'Heavens above, man!' Blackwell hissed with exasperation. 'You discover a dead body on your premises, and you don't take a closer look? You're a slaughterman and butcher, for God's sake! Up to your elbows in blood and guts every day!'

'That's as maybe, but for all I knowed, whoever put that dead 'un there could have been hiding watching me, and getting ready to slit my throat.'

Blackwell rose from his desk and pulled the silken bell cord beside the fireplace to summon his servant.

'Saddle my horse and bring it to the front door,' Blackwell instructed him, then turned to Tom. 'You'd best get up to Red Lane and keep watch over the premises, Master Potts. I am going to inform Lord Aston, and then I'll fetch John Hollis to share the watch with you. As for you, Master Vincent, go to your home and say nothing of this to anyone until I tell you otherwise. I don't want to raise any unnecessary alarm among the more timid of our parishioners.'

'I reckon there needs to be the alarm raised.' The butcher's meaty features were sullen. 'There's a bloody murdering maniac running around this parish, and folks ought to be told of it.'

'And they will be.' Blackwell frowned. 'Just as soon as I deem it right and proper that they should be told. Now go home, and say nothing to anyone.'

'All right,' Vincent reluctantly agreed, and left.

Blackwell stared questioningly at Tom. 'Well, Master Potts? What are your thoughts on this?'

'I shall have to wait until daylight enables me to make a thorough inspection of the scene, sir, before I can venture any opinions. But I confess that I'm dreading it might be the missing tinker girl that is lying on that chopping block.'

'And I confess that that very same thought has occurred to me also, Master Potts.' Blackwell frowned grimly. 'There is the possibility that the perpetrator might well be still in the vicinity of the shed. So you'd best take these with you.'

He opened a wall-hung cabinet and took out a brace of holstered pistols and a leather satchel. 'There's balls and powder in the bag. I suggest that you prime and load before going to Red Lane.'

Tom's boots crunched upon the gravel as he walked to the open door of the shed and halted. Body twitching, breath quickening with nervous tension, he raised the loaded pistol in his right hand, and swept the concentrated beam of light from the bulls-eye lantern in his left hand. At a sudden flurry of movement he started violently, almost pulling the trigger as scurrying furry bodies exploded from the top of the chopping block.

'Damn rats. Damn vile beasts!' he cursed, as angry with himself for his frightened reaction as with them for frightening him.

Battling to steady his shaking hand he trained the beam upon the corpse, and saw the bare white feet and ankles protruding from under what looked to be a sheet. He traversed the beam from the feet along the line of the legs, hips, torso, dreading the moment when he would see the head . . . Or an empty space where the head should be.

He caught his breath with thankful relief when the light fell upon a mass of tangled, dirty-blonde hair, long like a woman's.

It was not Siobhan Docherty lying on the chopping block. The face was turned away from him, and Tom was content to take up his post at the shed door, and watch to keep the rats away from the body. 'As soon as it's dawn, I'll begin my inspection. Until then, let the poor woman lie in peace.'

The wind soughed, branches and leaves moved and rustled. An animal screeched from somewhere in the black-shadowed woodland, and Tom's over-stretched nerves were strained to near breaking point as his vivid imagination pictured the killer lurking near, waiting for an opportunity to strike again.

'Hurry up and come here, John Hollis,' he muttered fervently. 'I could do with some friendly company.'

Twenty-Seven

When Joseph Blackwell came to his house the Right Honourable and Reverend Walter Hutchinson, Lord Aston was having his customary pre-bedtime snack, a large pigeon pie washed down with a bottle of claret. Stomach rumbling, belching at intervals, swathed in a huge fur-trimmed dressing gown, with a tasselled sleeping cap on his shaven bullet head, Aston listened in intent silence to what Joseph Blackwell related, then sat carefully considering what he had heard.

Lord Aston was many things, but a fool was not one of them. He had great respect for the hard-headed sagacity of his companion, and now asked, 'Well, Joseph? What do you think is our best course of action?'

'You must go immediately to the Earl and request that he call out our yeomanry troop. I accept that this will bring us no nearer to discovering the maniac, my lord, but we must be seen to be doing something. Yeomanry patrols around the parish will demonstrate to the people that we are doing our best to ensure their safety.' He smiled mirthlessly. 'Of course, you and I know the patrols will do nothing of the sort, but since the introduction of the reduced rates of pay for the needle workers, many of them have been becoming increasingly resentful. The discovery of this second body could be the spark to light the bonfire. Having the yeomanry activated will at least deter many potential trouble-makers from rioting.

'In the meantime, could you also request the Earl to send all his available men to the site in the Red Lane, to assist in keeping it secure? Despite my warning Henry Vincent to say nothing, I am quite confident that the news of this fresh corpse is already spreading fast throughout the parish and beyond. There'll be crowds clamouring there by morning, you may be sure.'

Aston nodded agreement. 'I shall go to the Earl this very hour. Now what is to be done to lay this miscreant by the heels?'

'I believe our best chance of doing that is to allow Thomas Potts to follow his fancies and conduct the investigation, my lord, backed by your full authorization.'

'Potts? Thomas Potts?' Aston barked incredulously. 'That lanky, gangly clown?'

A wintry smile touched Blackwell's thin lips. 'The very same, my lord. I do assure you that I have sound reasons for suggesting such a course of action.'

'Humphh! With my authority? Potts? Humphh!' Aston snorted, waving his hand dismissively. But then he conceded with bad grace, 'Oh very well, Joseph. But on your own head be it. It will be you that will become the laughing-stock for trusting in that gangly fool, not I.'

'Indeed yes, my lord. On my own head be it,' Blackwell accepted equably.

Shortly before dawn Joseph Blackwell arrived at the site in Red Lane, followed closely by Josiah Danks leading a strong contingent of the Earl's labourers, armed with scythes, pitchforks, shovels and flails.

Danks posted his men around the perimeter, and armed with his Brown Bess musket, took his own station at the entrance to the clearing.

Blackwell told Tom that he was now authorized to act as he chose. 'I've every faith in you, Master Potts. Pray do not let me find that my faith has been misplaced.'

'I'll do my very best not to fail you, sir,' Tom promised, even though doubts were racking him as he spoke.

'I'm confident that you will succeed, Master Potts. And now I'll take my leave. I have my other duties to attend to.'

John Hollis came to join Tom at the shed's entrance. 'What would you like me to do, Tom?'

'Pray for me.' Tom smiled ruefully. 'I feel like a man who's just been dropped into the middle of a deep lake, and who can't swim a stroke. And when you've done praying, I want you to go up into the town and bring back bread, cheese and cider for all here, and charge it to the parish. We'll be needing some food and drink before this day is done. I fear it will be a long one.'

It was a bright cloudless dawn, and very soon the daylight was strong enough for Tom to have a clear view of the interior of the shed. He drew a long breath, and steeled himself to begin.

He slung his knapsack over his shoulder and closely scrutinized the flagstones, paying particular attention to the stretch of floor between the doors and the huge chopping block. Seeing nothing that he considered useful he moved slowly towards the block, his gaze fixed on the dead woman. There was no stench of decay cloying the air, and he guessed she had not been dead long.

He circled the block until he could see her face, and grimaced at the livid purple-black mask confronting his eyes. The rats had done some damage but after a long look he considered that she would be recognizable to any who had known her well.

He studied the covering, which was stained and dirty, but could see nothing that resembled large bloodstains. He bent and carefully uncovered the body.

'Dear God!' he gasped in horrified shock. 'What sort of evil beast could do this? Only a demon from hell!'

His stomach heaved and bile filed his mouth. He stumbled from the shed and bent low against its outer wall, retching violently, heaving and straining until his stomach was empty and his throat raw. Straightening, he wiped his streaming eyes, and for the first time became aware of the clamour of excited voices. A sizeable crowd of men, women and children were clustering in the entrance to the clearing, being held back from entering by Josiah Danks and his line of men.

'Hey, Jack Spratt, why can't we have a look at what's in that shed?' a stocky man dressed in the pointer rig shouted, and was instantly supported by the crowd.

'Yeah, we wants to have a look!'

'We wants to see what you's got in there!'

'What's you trying to keep hid from us?'

'Come on, Jack Spratt, what's you so fritted of letting us see?'

'We wants to see! We wants to see! We wants to see! We wants to see!' The chant was instantly taken up by dozens of bawling voices.

The numbers at the entrance were constantly increasing, and Tom could see that soon there would be too many bodies for his line-keepers to hold back if the crowd made a concerted rush at them.

His thoughts raced. The mood of the crowd was not yet threatening, as far as he could judge. But he knew the volatile nature of these people, and how easily they could be roused to anger. If this situation wasn't dealt with quickly then anything could happen, and violence could erupt. Every second that passed increased the likelihood of that happening as their frustration mounted.

'Let us in! Let us in! Let us in! Let us in!' The chant changed, and now there was a more demanding, more menacing timbre in the massed bellowing.

The brace of pistols were on the ground by the door, but Tom let them lie, believing that if he used them as a threat the hot-heads in the crowd would feel driven to display their bravado and challenge him to shoot. He was beginning to experience an overwhelming sense of fearful desperation, and was wishing with all his being that he could disappear from this spot.

'What can I do?' He felt totally helpless. 'What can I do?'

'Cholera!' A voice whispered in his mind. 'The Indian cholera!'

Cholera, that deadly insidious killer; that struck without warning to slay strong healthy people; that left fine healthy bodies reduced to blackened shrivelled corpses within hours.

The next moment, as if some invisible force were impelling him, he found himself walking towards the crowd with arms held high.

The chant died away, and scores of curious eyes stared hard at him.

'Have you just seen me spewing my guts up?' he roared at them. 'Well? Have you?'

Scattered calls and grunts of assent came from among his listeners.

'Well, anyone of you who wants to be spewing their own guts up is welcome to join me in the shed,' he shouted, 'and see what the Indian cholera does to the human body. The shed is full of it, full of the miasma! Full of the cholera! The miasma's floating on the air! The cholera miasma!'

'Cholera!'

'The Indian cholera!'

'He says there's cholera in the shed!'

'He says there's a miasma coming from it!'

The shocked exclamations rippled through the crowd. Faces tensed and paled. Eyes widened in fright. The ravages of the cholera was a favourite horror story told by the local military veterans who had served in the East.

'Come on!' Tom roared challengingly. 'Come on inside with me, and get struck like perhaps I've just been struck! Get struck with the cholera! Come on! What are you waiting for? Come on into the shed with me!'

He strode towards the crowd, arms reaching for them, hands beckoning.

'Come on! Come and catch the cholera with me! Come on! Let's all spew our guts out!'

The stocky-bodied pointer in the forefront of the crowd suddenly panicked. 'I'm getting out from here! Out o' me way, blast you! Gerrout o' me way!' And he began to batter his way back through the dense-packed bodies behind him.

His panic spread like wildfire, and howling, cursing and buffeting each other in their frantic haste to escape, the crowd fled.

Tom halted and stood stock-still. Amazed at what he had done.

Within scant seconds only he and Josiah Danks remained in the clearing.

Danks scowled disgustedly, 'Them bastards I brought here wi' me has all turned tail and run like curs. Just wait till I gets hold of them.'

'And you, Master Danks? Are you not feared of the cholera?' Tom's respect for the gamekeeper's courage was even more firmly rooted now.

'I've seen it afore, Master Potts. When I was out in the East Indies. Cholera either takes you, or it don't, and there's no use trying to run from it. Because if it wants you, it'll come after you. And there aren't a body born yet that can outrun the bugger.'

Tom drew a long breath, and confessed uneasily, 'We don't have to try to outrun it, Master Danks. Because there is no cholera here. That poor woman in the shed didn't die from it, I only said that to try and move those people from here.'

The gamekeeper roared with relieved laughter. 'Well, it's worked, aren't it. You're Jack Artful right enough! So what has killed her, do you reckon?'

'The poor woman was murdered, Master Danks,' Tom told him sombrely. 'And her unborn child murdered with her.'

The smile left the gamekeeper's rugged features. 'This is the second woman to be done in. It looks to me as though there's a bloody lunatic running amok in this parish. There's no woman going to be safe until he's laid by the heels, is there.'

'I fear you're right.'

'Do you recognize her?'

'No.' Tom shook his head, but then added, 'But I have an idea of who she could be. Will you stand on guard, please, Master Danks, while I continue my inspection.'

With his stomach again beginning to churn, Tom reluctantly made his way back into the shed.

More than an hour later he re-emerged, pale-faced and tremble-handed, to find John Hollis had returned with the drink and provisions on a handcart. 'I'm sorry for taking so long, Tom,' Hollis began to apologize, but Tom stopped him.

'It doesn't matter, John. We've no time to waste in eating and drinking. I want you to go to the Webheath poorhouse and bring the master and mistress straight down to the lock-up. If I'm not there when you arrive, then wait for me, for I'll not be long.'

When Hollis had gone Tom asked Josiah Danks, 'Will you give me a hand to load her onto the cart and push her to the lock-up. I'll put her in one of the cells temporarily. Then if you would, I'd like you to return here and thoroughly search the area roundabouts for any pieces of flesh which might be human, such as intestines, kidneys, bladder, womb or pieces of them. If you find any then leave them in situ and come directly to the lock-up.'

He paused, and his features twitched several times with strain, before he added, 'And look also for a tiny baby, minus its head.'

Twenty-Eight

'Judging from the wounds left by ligatures on Ann Washwood's ankles, wrists and arms, and the lividity of her head and shoulders caused by the pooling and coagulation of the blood, I am of the opinion that the killer hung her by her feet while alive, from an overhead hook or beam. Then he eviscerated her and ripped the unborn child from her womb. He then decapitated the child.'

Tom was standing in the ornate, chandelier-lit, opulently furnished salon of Hewell Grange, some two miles to the north-west of Redditch, making his report to a grim-faced audience comprising the Earl of Plymouth, the Right Honourable Other Archer Windsor Clive, whose family seat it was. Lord Aston, Joseph Blackwell. John Clayton. Vestrymen Joseph Turner and Jason Holyoake. Richard Hemming the squire of Bentley, needle master and commander of the Hewell Troop of the Worcestershire Yeomanry; and the mahogany-complexioned Captain John Emmot, a hard-bitten, war-veteran cavalryman, now the Adjutant to the Hewell Troop.

'Are you sure that the woman wath not killed at the Red Lane thite?' the Earl, a florid-faced, plump-bodied young man lisped.

'I am certain of it, my lord,' Tom answered confidently, 'because I can find no trace there of large amounts of blood, or of her lower inner organs and bowels, or the child's body.'

'Inner organth? Bowelth? Child'th body? I do wish you would explain more clearly.'

'I will, my lord. The killer removed all of the lower organs and bowels. It then looks as if he washed the blood away from the mutilations, and left her hanging in that position long enough for the pooling and coagulation of the blood in her head and upper body to take place. When I examined her on the chopping block, I found her lying on her back, with her arms crossed on her breasts, and the head of the child placed in the cavity left by the bowels and lower organs. There was little if any blood on the block or in its vicinity.'

'Devil take you, man!' The Earl's florid cheeks flamed with outrage. 'You're dethtroying my appetite for my thupper with your dethcripthionth. I've heard quite enough for now, thank you . . . Deal with it, gentlemen. You have my full authority to take whatever meathurth you may deem to be nethethary.'

He got to his feet and swayed from the room emanating a heady scent of pomades and unguents.

The men exchanged meaningful glances, and then Joseph Blackwell asked, 'Are you fully confident that the dead woman is indeed the runaway pauper Ann Washwood, Master Potts?'

'I am, sir. I had Mr and Mrs Lewis of the Webheath poorhouse view the body separately, and kept them separated while I sought their opinions, so that they could not confer. Both positively identified her as being Ann Washwood.'

'God dammit! That pauper slut caused us trouble enough when she lived! And now she's causing us a deal more!' Jason Holyoake exclaimed irritably. 'The town's in a damn uproar, and it's all that slut's fault!'

'Shame on you, Mr Holyoake! Show some respect for the dead!' John Clayton reproved angrily. 'The poor woman most certainly did not choose to be so cruelly murdered!'

'No, and I didn't choose to have to pay for all the inconvenience and upset that she is the cause of.'

'Gentlemen! Gentlemen!' Lord Aston sternly imposed his authority. 'Let's have no squabbling amongst ourselves. It will serve no useful purpose.'

The protagonists subsided, glaring at each other.

'And you, Potts?' Lord Aston scowled aggressively at Tom.

'What are you doing to actively track down the villain who did this? Or are you merely sitting on your arse in the lock-up, waiting for him to come to you of his own free will?'

Tom had not slept or eaten for more than forty-eight hours. Bone-weary, hungry and thirsty, he looked at his hectoring questioner's fat, sweaty, drink-purpled face, and was suddenly filled with the murderous impulse to smash it to a bloody pulp with his bare fists.

Joseph Blackwell's keen gaze read the emotion in Tom's eyes, and he instantly reacted, rising to his feet and intervening smoothly. 'Pray forgive my interrupting, my lord, but there is the most pressing matter of the inquest to be organized. We must notify the coroner with all haste, and knowing how lax the present incumbent is in matters of business, I fear that it will need your personal intervention to rouse him to act expeditiously. We also urgently need to settle the payments of costs for the yeomanry patrols."

He looked at Tom and jerked his head. 'Pray wait outside for me, Master Potts, I need to speak with you on another matter.'

Tom waited in the grand entrance hall, passing the time by examining the wall tapestries, pictures, marble busts and furnishings.

He could not help but envy the wealth displayed here, and reflect on the bitter injustices of this life in which the accident of birth gifted so much wealth and power to so few, and condemned so many to such poverty, degradations and sufferings.

'The Earl is a man of exquisite artistic tastes, is he not. He purchased many of these objets d'art during his Grand Tour when he was still little more than a boy.' Joseph Blackwell came to stand beside Tom, who was closely examining a Roman bust.

Tom could not help grimacing a trifle sourly. 'It is easy for a man to cultivate good taste in art if he is born with a golden spoon in his mouth, and freed from any necessity to work for his living.'

The older man's thin lips quirked in a fleeting smile. 'Yes indeed, Master Potts. But we must not allow envy to blind us to the proven fact, that many of these same golden spoons give selfless service for the good of our King and country.'

It was Tom's turn to smile wryly, and admit, 'I plead guilty to the sin of envy, sir; and confess that there are times when I quite enjoy the taste of sour grapes.'

'Your frankness does you credit.' Blackwell clapped his hand on Tom's back. 'Come, let us walk outside. There are things I wish to talk about which I don't want anyone else to hear at this time.'

The night air was warm, the moon shone and only the occasional cloud cast its passing shadow as the two men slowly paced side by side across the designer-landscaped park, with its scenic copses, shrub clumps, ornamental streams and ponds.

'Washwood was reported as a runaway over a week past. How long do you think she has been dead?' Blackwell asked.

'I don't think for that long, sir. There were still slight indications of rigor mortis in her lower extremities; and there were blowfly maggots present which I judged to be still in the first instar stage of development. I would think she has been dead for perhaps two days.'

'Then where has she been for the other days?' Blackwell mused aloud.

'I don't know, but I shall find out,' Tom stated with grim determination.

'Do you have any ideas about where to start seeking?'

'Oh yes, sir.' Tom nodded positively. 'I have ideas in plenty. May I make a request of you?'

'Of course.'

'I need to hire two riding horses, so that John Hollis and I can cover the distances more quickly during the course of our enquiries.'

Blackwell frowned doubtfully. 'Two horses? I don't believe that the vestry will agree to cover the cost of two horses from the parish chest. They'll be complaining about beggars on horseback, I fear.'

'Perhaps you should point out to them that beggars on horseback are much preferable to butchered women,' Tom politely suggested.

'I will, of course, but in the meantime you and John Hollis must go on using Shanks's pony, Master Potts. However, you will have another constable to share the extra duties. Charles Bromley returned from exile yesterday.' Blackwell chuckled dryly. 'It appears he has yet again been able to beg, borrow

or steal sufficient money to pay off his most pressing debts.
Make yourself known to him at the earliest opportunity, Master
Potts. I've already impressed upon him that you are in the
position of headborough of the parish constables, that you
lead this investigation and he must obey your requests in this
matter. Off you go now, and track this murderer down.'

Twenty-Nine

'Tommy Fowkes aren't half moaning about you.' Amy
Danks' bright eyes were dancing with mischievous
amusement. 'He says that since you've been in charge of the
lock-up, he can't hardly make a penny profit from feeding the
prisoners. He says that he's going to give up the contract.'

She placed the basket on the floor and removed its cloth
covering to take out a large crock bowl of savoury-smelling
stew.

'Here's Johnny Hancox's dinner, and Tommy Fowkes says
that I'm to ask you to taste it, and make sure that it's delicate enough fare for the fine gentleman you've got in here as
His Majesty's guest.'

Tom experienced a poignant yearning as he looked at her
pretty rosy-cheeked face. 'We've not had chance to talk much
lately, Amy. I've missed your company.'

'Humph! Missed me, you say!' She tossed her curls, and
scoffed dismissively, 'Well, I've not missed your company,
Tom Potts, because there are plenty of others who take the
trouble to seek my company. Which is what you don't trouble
yourself to do these days.'

'I suppose it's Davy Rowley.' Tom couldn't restrain his flash
of jealousy.

She made no attempt to hide her smile of delight at his reaction, and goaded him further. 'Yes, Davy comes calling on me,
along with others. He's always been sweet on me. Ever since
we were children together. Now that he's beginning to make

his fortune, he's a very good catch for any girl, wouldn't you say? And he's so very attentive to me, and considerate of my feelings. I'm positive he'd make a very good husband.'

'He might well do,' Tom answered stiffly, and despite dreading what her answer might be, was driven to ask, 'And are you considering marrying him?'

'I might be,' she teased. 'And then again, I might not be.'

As if tiring of this game, she abruptly changed the subject, and sniffing the air, queried, 'It smells of raw onions and vinegar in here. Are you plastering them about because she's starting to stink? Where have you got her? Is she in one of the cells? Can I have a look at her?'

'No, you can't! The poor soul isn't a peepshow. And apart from that, she's beginning to decay and is no sight for your eyes.'

'I'm the best judge of what's a sight for my eyes.' She frowned petulantly and stuck out her tongue at him. Then she picked up her basket and flounced out of the lock-up, leaving Tom staring disconsolately after her.

When Tom unlocked the door and entered the cell, John Hancox rose from the wooden palette and gratefully took the bowl of savoury stew from his hands.

'Thank you, Master Potts. Me belly was beginning to think me throat was cut.'

'I'm sorry for the delay, John, but I've been very busy.'

'Have you any idea what's to happen to me?' Hancox questioned with his mouth full of meat and turnip. 'The beaks won't send me to the sessions at Worcester, will they?'

'I shouldn't think so,' Tom reassured him. 'I'll be bringing you before the bench on Monday. Luckily for you, Lord Aston will be in Worcester, so you'll have the Reverend Timmins pass judgement. You'll most likely just get a five-pound fine, because it's your first offence.' He smiled, and added, 'At least, it's the first time you've been caught poaching.'

'Five pounds! That's a bit bloody steep! I hadn't even set a snare when them two bastards set the dogs on me,' the young man grumbled.

'Why did you risk Brockhill Wood, John?' Tom was curious. 'It's got a bad reputation for man-traps and tripwire guns, and

Erasmus Dolton has got the name of being ready to fire at poachers without any warning.'

'It was because of her you've got down the passage there, Annie Washwood.'

'Ann Washwood? How well did you know her?'

The young man leered salaciously. 'I knowed her real well, Master Potts. She was a warm wench, if you gets my meaning, and we lit each other's fire many a time.'

'You had an intimate relationship with her?'

'What's intimate mean?' Hancox's bovine features showed puzzlement.

'Sexual, John. You had a sexual relationship with her.'

'Oh yeah,' Hancox confirmed readily. 'But so did quite a few others in this town. Annie was very partial to a shag, providing she got a drink out of it.'

'How did she connect with you being in Brockhill Wood?'

The pointer hesitated for a few moments, before asking, 'If I tells you, will you keep it to yourself?'

'Yes! No one else will ever know what you tell me,' Tom assured him, and Hancox grinned.

'Yeah, I reckon I can trust you, Master Potts. After all, if it warn't for you getting me away from them two bastards, then God only knows what might have happened to me . . . It was like this, see. Me and Annie had a bargain. She used to shag Dolton when she was working for him, and she used to spy on him as well. She used to watch where he laid his mantraps and set up his spring guns, and take note of 'em. Then she'd show me where they lay; and tell me when he was going to be away at the markets and suchlike. Then I used to go and take pheasants and rabbits from the Brockhill, and I shared the money that I got for 'em with her.'

'Did Dolton come to know about your agreement with Ann Washwood?' Tom's thoughts were racing.

'I don't reckon so.' Hancox shrugged his broad shoulders. 'But if he ever did I 'uddent put it past him to have caved her head in for her. He's well known for using his fists on anybody who crosses him.'

Deep in thought, Tom left Hancox eating the stew, and as he relocked the cell door behind him was surprised by the outer door being suddenly pushed open, and another man entering the building.

'Who are you?' he demanded.

'Charles Bromley. And from the height of you, I take it that you're Master Thomas Potts.'

The newcomer was of middle height and age, pot-bellied, wearing shabby threadbare clothing, a crumpled top hat and bulbous-lensed spectacles which magnified his eyes to an alarming degree.

He removed his hat, revealing a bald pallid pate, with a few strands of greasy grey hair plastered across it, and displayed a row of large, discoloured bone false teeth in a sharklike smile.

'I'm honoured to make your acquaintance, Master Potts.' Bromley's voice was irritatingly mellifluous, his manner overly ingratiating. 'I trust that our personal and professional concord will be of mutual pleasure and benefit.'

In his mind Tom heard again Joseph Blackwell's voice: 'My greatest wish, and firmest intention, is to establish a body of parish police who have enquiring minds, a degree of erudition, the ability to be impartial and the qualities of courage, fortitude and initiative . . .'

'Dear God,' he told himself despairingly. 'At first sight this fellow appears to be even less suited than me to confront desperate criminals and lay them by the heels.'

He forced a smile and proffered his hand. 'I'm very pleased to meet you, Master Bromley. I'm sure that Mr Blackwell has already told you of what has happened in the town. Your aid and advice will be most welcome to me.'

'And you shall have both, Master Potts, and given gladly.' Bromley wrung Tom's hand and fulsomely assured him, 'Of course, you will understand that I must give my primary attention to my business affairs, but any fleeting moments of spare time that I can squeeze from my busy life, I shall lay at your disposal. You may be confident of that, Master Potts.'

'Thomassss? Thomassss? Where are you? I need to speak to you. Thomassss? Where are you, damn you? If ever a poor woman suffered with another such wicked unnatural son as you, then I'd like to meet the poor soul, and share my grief with hers.' Widow Potts' high-pitched screeching echoed from the upper floor.

Tom's heart sank. 'That is my mother calling, Master Bromley. Will you excuse me please?' Tom tried to detach his hand from Bromley's grasp but the man maintained his tenacious, clammy grip.

'You must introduce me to your lady mother, Master Potts. I have heard much about her, and am very anxious to meet her.' Bromley was almost pleading. 'Pray do introduce me.'

'Why not indeed,' Tom thought in a momentary pique of spite; and aloud said, 'Then please do accompany me, Master Bromley. I'm sure that my mother will be delighted to make your acquaintance.'

'And who's this when he's about?' Widow Potts demanded ungraciously, having noted the shabby clothing and crumpled top hat.

'I am, ma'am, a gentleman who admired you from afar when you were the acknowledged belle of the entire needle district.' Charles Bromley advanced and flourishing his hat made a sweeping bow. 'And may I add, ma'am, that it is an honour and a rare privilege to meet you after so many long years. Although, ma'am, I have to say that those years have treated you very lightly. You still look to be the young woman I admired so greatly. In glaring contrast to myself, whom the years have lain upon very heavily.'

Tom almost cringed with embarrassment as his mother fluttered her eyes and preened archly. 'When did you know me, sir?'

'Why, when you and Dr Potts lived on the Fish Hill, ma'am. Your fine son here was just a tiny child then, and you, ma'am, were in the full fresh bloom of your youthful beauty.'

'Oh sir, you flatter me too much,' she simpered, then frowned at Tom and ordered sharply, 'My fan, Thomas. Bring me my fan. And a chair for this gentleman. Forgive me, sir, my oaf of a son has not seen fit to inform me of your name.'

'Bromley, ma'am. Charles Cyrus Bromley, Esquire.'

'It's a pleasure to meet you, sir.' She extended her pudgy hand, and bending low Bromley took it in his and kissed her grubby, stubby fingers.

'Here's your fan, Mother,' Tom said.

She snatched it from him, and began to snap it open and closed, flourishing it with exaggerated gestures and continually holding it momentarily before the lower part of her face so that she could glance coquettishly over its edge into the eyes of Charles Bromley.

Bromley seated himself on the chair that Tom brought for him, and leant closer forwards to Widow Potts, behaving as if enthralled by her grotesque display.

Mortified with embarrassment, Tom excused himself. 'If you'll forgive me, Master Bromley, I have urgent matters to attend to.' And he escaped from the room unnoticed by either of them.

Thirty

It was late afternoon on Saturday. Standing in the cell, staring at the sheet-covered body of Ann Washwood, Tom was struggling to bring order to his troubled, jumbled thoughts. Where had she been between her initial disappearance and her death? Why were both the dead women left in Henry Vincent's slaughter shed, and were had they been killed? Why had they been killed? Had they been known, selected and stalked by their killer, or were they merely random encounters? The deliberate mutilation of the bodies appeared to be the work of a sadistic maniac, but had those mutilations been intended to cover up another, saner motivation for the murders?

Would the body of Siobhan Docherty be the next discovery? Tom had met and talked to her parents many times now, and was satisfied that they had nothing to do with her disappearance. The Docherty family had reluctantly moved on the previous week, her parents clinging to the hope that she had run away with the young pedlar, or to join up with another tinker band, and they might meet up with her on the road.

Tom's thoughts swung to his recent conversation with John Hancox. Could Erasmus Dolton be the killer? He was well known to be a violent man, who mistreated women. He owned horses and carts and so had the means of transport to carry the corpses to the shed in Red Lane. He also had barns and outhouses spread across his extensive land-holdings where he would be able to keep a woman imprisoned.

On impulse Tom pulled off the sheet covering Ann Washwood. The green and purple staining of putrefaction had spread to her limbs and her veins had marbled.

'Why did he clean your body before leaving you in the shed?' he wondered. 'Were there deposits of dirt or dust or anything on it which might indicate where you had been kept?'

He bent and carefully parted her toes, gusting a sigh of satisfaction when he saw the small compressed particles of dried mud trapped between them. 'If I put these under my microscope, they might well tell me something.'

In his candlelit cottage in Brecon, Jonathan Johnson, nurseryman and seedsman, palm-maker, shoe-maker and vendor of quack medicines, squinted closely at the tiny objects in the palm of his large, calloused hand, and pursed his lips judiciously.

'Now let's see, Master Potts. These be biggish seeds. Flat and orbicular in shape. Greyish-brown colour. Oily lustre.' He carefully rubbed the seeds between his palms and then squinted closely at them once more. 'These be hemp seeds, Master Potts. That's for definite, that is. Hemp seeds, these be.'

'Hemp?' Tom frowned in puzzlement. 'I'm no farmer, Master Johnson, how would I recognize it growing?'

'Oh, you'd know it all right. It grows as tall as hops, so it do. It aren't planted a deal in these parts, but one or two of the farmers raises the occasional crop of it. It's a good payer, do you see, but it weakens the land.'

Tom experienced a quickening of excited anticipation, but said casually, 'I'd be interested to see some when it got that tall. Is anybody hereabouts growing any this year?'

'Oh yes. I sold a few bushels of seed to Squire Guest at Bordesley Lodge, and some to Erasmus Dolton, and three bushels to Daniel Smout up in Bentley there. He's just going to sow the single acre, do you see, just to try it. But meself, I don't think his soil is suited to it. Where did you find these few seeds?'

'Oh, I bought a couple of old sacks from a carter who was passing the lock-up, and these seeds fell out of them. I was just curious to know what they were. Many thanks to you.'

Tom parted from the man, and his excitement was bubbling. The seeds had been embedded in the trapped mud between Ann Washwood's toes.

'So, Erasmus Dolton bought some bushels of hemp seed earlier this year. I've got to find out where he stored it, because that's where he might have kept Ann Washwood locked up.

'Now don't get too fired up,' he warned himself. 'A few seeds are no proof that he killed her. And don't forget that Squire Guest and Daniel Smout also bought hemp seeds.'

Tom suddenly recalled some talk he had overheard some months since, concerning Squire Guest. The man was considered to be something of a mystery. He had come to Redditch a few years previously and bought the Bordesley Park estate some two miles to the north of the town. No one knew his antecedents, and he did not socialize with any of the local gentry or masters, but lived a reclusive life in his grand house, Bordesley Lodge, with his small staff of Indian servants.

Daniel Smout was of blameless character: a staunch Methodist, who lived with his wife and large brood of children. 'I think that I can discard him from my list of suspects,' Tom mused. 'But if Dolton proves guiltless, then it might be worth my while to investigate Squire Guest more thoroughly.'

Full night had fallen while Tom had been in Johnson's cottage, and the moon had not risen fully. The thought of going back to his room in the lock-up to sit for weary hours listening to his mother's nagging and complaints depressed him. He was passing the King's Arms, which stood at the top of the Holloway where it joined Brecon, and could hear the sounds of song and laughter coming from its tap room. Suddenly the need to be among lively company and good fellowship overwhelmed him, and on impulse he went inside.

The low-beamed room was fuggy with tobacco smoke and the smells of sweat and beer breath emanating from the throng of drinkers. In one corner men sat playing dominos, slamming down the counters on the table top, jocularly ribbing and cursing each other. In another corner young men and girls sat flirting and giggling. At the bar counter a group of men were singing a lugubrious lament.

'From morning till night, from early light,
God help the poor of Redditch Town
Throughout each weary dayyyyy . . .'

The jovial-mannered landlord, Billy Bray, came to Tom, asking, 'Am you here on official business, Master Potts?'

'No, I'm not, Master Bray. You'll see I haven't brought my staff with me.'

'Then in that case, you're more than welcome. What's your pleasure?'

'I'll take a quart of ale and a pipe, if you please.'

The landlord brought him a large foaming pewter tankard and a long-stemmed clay churchwarden pipe, and placed a stone jar filled with fragrant-smelling tobacco on the counter.

'Take a fill o' this at no extra cost, Master Potts, it's me own special blend. The finest Eyegiptian and Turkish. It's too good for the likes o' this bloody lot, but a gennulmen like yourself 'ull appreciate it properly.'

'Many thanks.' Tom willingly accepted the offer, and was shortly puffing out clouds of smoke and supping his ale with great relish.

Bray served a couple of other customers then came back to where Tom was standing at the bar counter, and leaned across. 'How near am you to collaring the bastard who killed them poor wenches?'

'I'm making some progress, I think,' Tom replied guardedly.

'Well, I hope it won't be too long afore you does, because most of the women in this town am too fritted to step foot on their own outside their houses of a night-time for fear they'll be slaughtered.'

'My missus is one of them,' Dick Millington, a burly pointer, scowled, face brick-red and sweaty with drink. 'Them fuckin' nancy-boys of yeomanry aren't doing anybody any good parading round the town.'

'They're keeping the streets safe,' Tom pointed out. 'No one is going to risk attacking any woman while they're about.'

'Does you really think that the yeomanry am there to protect our womenfolk?' Millington jeered angrily. 'If you does then you'm as daft as you'm ugly. The yeomanry am there to be ready to ride all over us if we kicks up about having our pay cut. They aren't here for us, they're here to keep the fuckin' masters safe while they steals the bread out of honest people's mouths! The same as you fuckin' wankers who gets appointed as constables.'

There was a chorus of growled agreement from those who had heard Millington's angry words, and many surly glowers were directed at Tom.

He sensed that the mood in the tap room was threatening to turn violent. Deciding that discretion was the better part of valour, he put some coins on the counter to pay for his ale and pipe, and left to a chorus of jeers and insults.

Outside in the cool moonlight he walked on towards the Big Pool, his mood soured and depressed by what had happened. Yet he could not in all honesty blame Dick Millington and the other people in the tavern for being so suspicious and resentful of the yeomanry and the constables. 'We are, after all, the visible guardians and enforcers of the corrupt oligarchy that rules this country by virtue of the mere accident of birth. We are the instruments of their political power.'

When Tom reached the Big Pool he could hear the lilting notes of a fiddle and see that there were people dancing on the flat ground next to the Horse and Jockey. Feeling the need for distraction from his own sombre thoughts he went closer to stand at the rear of the small crowd of onlookers. Almost immediately he recognized one particular young couple waltzing gracefully together, smiling happily as they gazed into each other's eyes, and his already depressed spirits sank even lower. Amy Danks and Davy Rowley circled to pass before him, seemingly oblivious to anything around them, intent solely on each other.

Tom turned and walked away. 'She is really lost to me now, isn't she,' he told himself, and poignant sadness whelmed over him, coupled with the bleak sensation of utter loneliness and despair.

Thirty-One

Tom groaned and stirred as the brass ferrule of the walking stick gouged painfully into his ribs.

'Wake up, you drunken wretch! Wake up, damn you! How dare you be like this on the Sabbath day? The good Lord should strike you dead, you worthless wretch! If ever such another pitiful creature as me was ever cursed with such a wicked unnatural beast of a son, then I'd like to meet her, and mingle my tears and sorrows with hers. Wake up, you worthless drunken hound!'

His mother's grating voice penetrated his sleep-fuddled senses, forcing him to reluctant wakefulness.

'Ohhh God help me!' Realizing that he was still fully clothed and booted, he groaned and dragged himself upright to sit on the side of his narrow bed. Dull pains pulsing through his head, mouth tasting foul and sticky, stomach queasily rumbling, Tom was bitterly regretting the fact that he had drunk himself into oblivion on gin to try and blot out the memory of Amy smiling so happily in the arms of her young beau.

'All that I've achieved is to make myself feel like death warmed up, and still feel not a jot better about losing her. Bloody pathetic fool that I am!' he castigated himself furiously.

Sounds of talk and laughter came from the floor below, and Tom struggled to clear his still-fuddled senses.

'Who is that downstairs?'

'It's Charles, and his visitors,' his mother scowled.

'Charles? Visitors? What do you mean, Mother?'

'I mean exactly what I say, you drunken oaf!'

'Charles who?'

'Charles Bromley, of course! You bone-headed dolt!'

Tom's head was beginning to clear. 'Who are these visitors? And who are they visiting? Have they come to see John Hancox?'

'Why would a fine gentleman like Sir Francis Goodericke visit a slum rat? Have some sense, you fool!' Widow Potts' thin lips twisted sneeringly. 'Charles is doing what you should have been doing. He's earning some money for us all.'

'Earning some money? Sir Francis Goodericke?' Tom repeated thoughtfully. Then realization burst upon him, and with that realization came fierce anger. Jumping up from the bed he hurled himself down the stairs.

The passageway outside the cell where Ann Washwood lay was crowded with expensively tailored men and fashionably clad women.

The loud clattering of Tom's hob-nailed boots and his headlong onset caused heads to turn and eyes to stare curiously.

'Who the devil might you be?' a young dandy drawled.

Tom strode to confront him. 'I don't care who you might be, sir. You are leaving here this instant!' His angry glare went from face to face. 'And the same goes for the rest of you. So get out now!' He pushed through them to enter the cell, and his anger rose to white-heat.

Ann Washwood lay naked and Charles Bromley was using a short cane to probe into the terrible cavity of her wound.

'The child's head was there, Sir Francis, grinning out at the world as if it were a mad thing.'

Tom physically shoved the tall, aquiline Sir Francis to one side, and ripped the cane from Charles Bromley's hand.

'If you don't get out of my sight this instant, Bromley, I'll ram this up your arse until it comes out of your mouth!' Tom said, shaking with fury.

Bromley's face blanched. Tom grabbed him by the collar and swung him so violently that he stumbled against the door post and almost fell out of the cell.

'What the hell do you think you are doing?' Goodericke's expression was a study of incredulity.

'I'm doing my lawful duty,' Tom fronted him, 'and if you don't leave immediately, and take these others with you, then I'll pitch all of you out of here on your arses!'

'I'll have you arrested for your damned insolence,' Goodericke spluttered.

'Oh no!' Tom shook his head emphatically. 'I'm the appointed headborough of the constables of this parish. It's me that will be doing any arresting that needs to be done. So you'd best leave now.'

'Do you know who I am?' Goodericke demanded forcefully.

'Oh yes. You're Sir Francis Goodericke of Studley Castle. Which makes your present behaviour even more shameful!'

'Shameful? How dare you speak to a nobleman in such an insolent manner!'

'Noble? You think it noble to treat this poor woman as a tuppenny freak show? Hasn't she been wronged more than enough already? Yes, your behaviour is shameful.'

Tom's initial unthinking fury was fast cooling now, metamorphosing into a dogged determination to see this confrontation through to the end, no matter what that might be. He continued, gritting out his words now in a lower hard-edged tone, 'This is the last time that I shall tell you to leave. In law this cell is a prohibited area, and any entry into it must be authorized by the magistrates of Worcestershire. I am ordering you to leave in the King's name, or I shall take you into custody for unauthorized trespass onto crown property.'

He tensed for the other man's reaction.

Goodericke stood silent, face red and twitching. The silence lengthened for what seemed to Tom to be an endless, almost unbearable passage of time. His fists clenched with tension, and he could feel the violent thumping of his heart. He was desperately fighting the urge to flee himself, when his adversary spat out viciously, 'You shall pay for this! And it will be a heavy price! That I guarantee!' Then he turned and stamped out of the cell and through the arched entrance of the lock-up.

The party of men and women followed, whispering excitedly together, some casting looks of amusement, some almost of awe, at Tom; and the whole of them got back into the three open carriages and left in procession, with Sir Francis Goodericke at the head.

'What have you done, you stupid great oaf?' his mother shrieked from the far end of the passage. 'You fool! You cretin! You've ruined us! I shall end my days in the poorhouse, and it's all your fault. You great stupid moron, you!'

The enormity of what he had just done was beginning to thrust itself into the forefront of Tom's mind, and his anger ebbed away to be replaced by ever-increasing apprehension.

Sir Francis Goodericke was the most powerful man in the Studley parish. He was the largest landowner, a justice of the peace, and reputed to have influential friends in the government in London. He also frequently rode to hounds with the Earl of Plymouth.

Tom swallowed hard and resigned himself to ruin.

Thirty-Two

It was midday when Joseph Blackwell's manservant came to the lock-up to summon Tom to his master's office.

'My master says that you're to come straight away, and to bring your staff wi' you.'

'That's it, then,' Tom thought resignedly. 'He wants the staff back. I'm to be discharged from my post, and then charged with whatever Goodericke has decided.'

As he walked towards the Chapel Green he found to his own surprise that he was feeling a definite sense of chagrin at losing his post.

'I enjoy being a constable, don't I? Even though I'm not very successful at tracking down murderers. But at least it gives me the opportunity to do some good at times. And God only knows, I've not been much use at anything else I've ever tried.'

By the time he was standing in front of Blackwell's desk his spirits were at a low ebb.

Blackwell laid aside his quill pen and steepling his fingers in front of his chin sat staring at Tom with an enigmatic expression on his deeply lined face. Tom had to struggle to stop himself fidgeting like a truant schoolboy as the intent stare continued.

'Well, Master Potts?' Blackwell finally broke the lengthening silence. 'What have you to say for yourself?'

'About what, sir?'

'About the threats of violence you made against Sir Francis Goodericke, and his party, which of course can be construed as assault: also the actual physical assault that you made on Charles Bromley. For either or both of these offences you can be brought before the bench.'

Although inwardly quailing, Tom was doggedly determined that he would not humiliate himself by trying to lie his way out of this predicament.

'I did indeed physically eject Bromley from the cell, sir; and

I also threatened Sir Francis and his party with physical ejection.' He fought to keep his voice level and firm, and with a flash of wry humour added, 'Whether or no I would have succeeded in physically ejecting them all, is debateable.'

He fell silent, waiting for the other man to reply, but Blackwell only nodded for him to continue.

'There's nothing much that I can add to that, sir. Except to say that should that same circumstance arise, I would act in exactly the same way.'

A bleak smile momentarily touched Blackwell's thin lips. 'Would you now, Master Potts?'

'I would, sir.'

'Why?'

'Because I feel that it is the right thing to do, sir.'

'Come now, what harm is there in Bromley earning a few shillings for displaying a dead body? As you must know yourself, it is an accepted practice among the poor to allow people to view their dead relatives in exchange for a few pence as a gratuity.'

'That's as may be, sir, but Ann Washwood is in my care, and while she remains so I will not permit her to be made into a tuppenny freak show. She suffered too much degradation in her life as it is, and it is wrong that she should be further degraded in death . . .' Tom paused and laid his staff on the desk, before going on: 'I'll save you the trouble of discharging me from my post by resigning from it now. The only request that I would make of you, sir, is that you permit me to arrange a decent Christian burial for Ann Washwood, for which I will pay.'

He was shocked by Blackwell's reaction, which was to emit a throaty chuckle and tell him, 'Pick that damned staff up, Master Potts. You are most certainly not going to be discharged from your post, and I will not permit you to resign from it. As for the complaints made to me by Goodericke and Bromley, well be damned to them both! You will not have to answer to the bench. I shall make sure of that because I happen to be in full agreement with your sentiments regarding the unfortunate woman . . . Now tell me, what progress are you making in discovering who killed her?'

Tom's spirits lifted instantly with his relief at having escaped prosecution, but he could only answer, 'Sadly, sir, I'm making little positive progress. At this stage I only have strong suspicions about certain individuals.'

'Who might they be?' Blackwell pressed.

'Erasmus Dolton and Gareth Jenkins, and another possible is a young pedlar named Ricardo Pozo.'

'Why those three?'

'Pozo was seen with the tinker girl Siobhan Docherty before her disappearance. Both Dolton and Jenkins have a reputation for sexually abusing and ill-treating women, and Dolton in particular has every facility needed to enable him to transport a dead body, and to keep a woman captive . . . .' Tom went on to tell Blackwell about his discovery of the hemp seed, concluding, 'Tonight I intend to search Dolton's farmstead and try to find where he stored the seed. It may well be that he kept Ann Washwood a captive there. If so, I may discover some trace of it.'

'Take great care that you are not discovered yourself, Master Potts,' Blackwell warned, 'because I cannot officially authorize you to take this course of action. Erasmus Dolton has considerable influence with the vestry, and is a sergeant of the yeomanry held in high regard by Richard Hemming and Captain Emmot. He is also in great favour with the Earl.'

'In great favour with the Earl?' Tom found that hard to believe.

'Oh yes,' the other man confirmed gravely. 'When they were both younger men, Dolton was instrumental in saving the Earl's life when a mad bull trapped him in a barn. At risk of his own life Dolton interposed himself and drew the bull away. Unpleasant brute though Dolton is, it cannot be gainsaid that he is a very brave man. He is also very ready to shoot at intruders upon his land. So be careful.'

Tom took a long deep breath. 'Oh, I will be, sir. You may be very sure of that.'

Thirty-Three

It was past midnight when Tom quietly left the lock-up and set out for Dolton's farm. He carried a leather satchel over his shoulder which held a bulls-eye lantern, flint, steel and tinderbox, a short crowbar, a small parcel of raw meat and a homemade slingshot. The sky was heavy with cloud and it took some time for his eyes to accustom to the darkness. He moved slowly and warily, not wanting to encounter any lurking yeomanry patrol, and only quickened his pace when he had left the town behind him.

When he came near the farmstead he left the track and went into the fields, circling the buildings until the fitful breeze was blowing against his face, then moving cautiously towards them. He was nervous and tense, yet at the same time strangely exhilarated. The buildings formed three sides of a square around a cobbled courtyard, with the farmhouse at one end and the double wings of outhouses and stables running out from it at right angles.

'The guard dogs? Where are the guard dogs?' He halted at the end of one wing and pressed close to the wall, peering cautiously around it. No lights shone from the house windows, and he could distinguish nothing but the black-shadowed bulk of the buildings around the courtyard. He stayed motionless for long minutes, straining eyes and ears in a fruitless effort to discover where the dogs were.

The clouds rifted and a shaft of moonlight briefly illuminated the courtyard. Tom spotted that one of the outhouse doors near to the house was opened outwards. 'Is that where they are?'

Stooping, he found a large stone and sent it noisily skittering across the cobbles, striking sparks and finally thumping against the wooden door. He heard the faint rattle of chains and hissed with satisfaction as the dark figures of two big bull-mastiffs came growling through the doorway, the long chains fastened to their collars dragging behind them.

Tom quickly took the parcel of raw meat and the slingshot from the satchel, and in rapid succession sent several pieces of meat flying through the air to land around the dogs. The animals sniffed the chunks and gulped them down. Tom waited for the laudanum with which he had impregnated the meat to take effect. 'Where are those German shepherd dogs that ripped up John Hancox?'

The rifts in the clouds became more frequent, the shafts of moonlight lengthening as they widened. Tom's nerves began to jangle.

'I could do without this much moonlight. Someone could look out of a window and spot me moving about.'

One of the dogs went down on its haunches and its head sank to the cobbles. The other moved towards it, whining, staggering drunkenly, then toppling over onto its side to lie motionless.

Tom drew a long breath, summoned his courage, and swiftly crossed to the first outhouse door. Relieved to find it barred but not padlocked, he slipped out the bar, opened the door just wide enough to squeeze through and went inside. He took the bullseye lantern from the satchel, together with the flint, steel and tinderbox, struck showers of sparks to ignite the tinder and lit the lantern with it. Removing the leather cup that shielded the lens he swept the beam of light across the interior, and found it to be empty. He replaced the leather cup, left the outhouse, barred the door behind him and moved to the next door. Inside here he found only rusty tools, so he went on to the next in line, which was a stable. There were three horses stalled inside, and they neighed and stamped restlessly as the beam shone into their eyes.

It took several hours to complete the search of both wings of buildings, and Tom was bitterly disappointed at its end. He had found no sacks of seeds. No trace of recent bloodstains. No discarded clothing other than a ragged, dust-heavy jacket and a riding boot without a sole.

For a few moments he stared at the farmhouse, contemplating whether he should force an entry and make a search there. But he realized that to do so would be courting disaster. He had no knowledge of its interior layout, and no idea who or how many might be inside. Also the two guard dogs were showing signs of recovery, and he had no more drugged meat to quieten them with. Weary and dispirited, he reluctantly walked away from the farmstead.

Halfway back to the town he slowed and halted, to disgustedly chide himself.

'I'm going about this like a damned simpleton, aren't I? If Dolton is my man, then it stands to reason he wouldn't have risked keeping Ann Washwood in a place where there are people coming and going all the time. He'd have kept her in an isolated spot, where no one is ever likely to choose to come. Somewhere like Brockhill Wood. Is there an old shed or cottage inside the wood?'

Fired with fresh determination Tom turned on his heels and immediately headed back in the direction of the wood, but after taking only a few paces slowed and halted once again.

The desultory breeze had freshened to a continual gusting, and the low clouds were being scattered, so that the land was bathed in moonlight bright enough for Tom to be able to read the time on his pocket watch.

'It's turned half-past four o'clock. It'll be dawn soon, and Mother will be screeching her head off if I'm not there when she wakes. And I've got to bring John Hancox before the bench at eight o'clock because the Reverend Timmins likes to make an early start. Damn it! I've not time to make any decent search of the Brockhill. I'll have to leave it for now.'

Once again he turned and headed back for the town at a run.

The man who had been covertly observing Tom ever since he had first entered the farmstead was now hidden in ambush behind the wayside hedgerow. As the lanky, gangly figure loped swiftly past him, he aimed the small flintlock pistol and pulled the trigger.

The lead ball struck Tom before the crack of the discharge reached his ears, and it was the shock of impact which caused him to stumble and fall face forwards. There was no initial pain, only a numbness at the wound site, and blank-minded bemusement as he struggled to comprehend what had happened.

Erasmus Dolton grinned with savage satisfaction. 'That'll teach that long streak o' piss a lesson not to come sneaking around my property.' He pocketed his pistol and stole stealthily away.

The numbness in Tom's left buttock gave way to excruci-
ating throbbing pain, and he winced as his fingers tentatively
explored the punctured hole, and the oozing wetness of warm
blood.

'I've been shot!' Terror flooded through him at the thought
that whoever had fired could even now be reloading to shoot
again and this time kill. 'I've got to get away from here!'

He pushed himself up and scrabbled on hands and knees
across the track seeking the shelter of the black-shadowed
hedgerow, and once in the shadow kept scrabbling along the
line of the hedge in panic-stricken desperation, dreading the
onset of another attack, bruising and scraping the skin of his
palms and knees upon the stony ground.

He covered scores of yards before sheer exhaustion forced
him to a halt, head hanging low, lungs straining to drag in
wheezy gasps of air, his thoughts fatalistically verging on acceptance that his assailant had him at his mercy, that death was
even now hovering over him, to take him into its dark oblivion.

Then, from deep within his being, an impulse to show defiance suddenly flared, and a voice in his mind ordered him, 'If
death has come for you, then face it on your feet like a man,
and not cowering on your knees like a snivelling coward!'

Obeying the voice, Tom grabbed the hedge branches and
dragged himself up onto his feet, biting his lips to stop himself
crying out with the agonizing pain the movement sent lancing
through his wound. Summoning every atom of resolution that
he possessed, he forced himself to turn around and face whoever
or whatever might be there to confront him.

The narrow moonlit track was empty. Nothing moved except
the tallest branches of the hedgerows swaying gently in the
wind. He stood listening intently for long minutes, but heard
only that same soughing wind.

'I've got away!' The realization made him feel weak with
relief. 'Now I've got to get back home and get this ball out of
my arse.'

Cautiously he flexed his left leg, and put weight on it, taking
a few tentative steps, and found that although movement was
very painful, he could hobble upright. Gritting his teeth he
slowly and painfully limped towards the town.

Back in his room Tom gulped several mouthfuls of neat gin,
gasping as the fiery spirit burned its way down his gullet. Then

he opened his father's medical chest and extracted what he needed from its capacious depths. Next, he bit down hard on the strip of leather between his teeth, dropped his breeches and drawers to his ankles and working by blind touch inserted the long slender metal probe into the puncture wound high on his left buttock

'Thank God!' he thought, when the probe's tip scraped against metal only about a quarter of an inch within the flesh. 'It didn't go in too far. The powder charge must have been weak.'

He discarded the probe and took up the forceps, drew several deep breaths and pushed the claws of the tool into the wound. He groaned deep in his throat, clammy sweat beading on his face, his eyes watering as agony pulsed through his torn flesh. After several failed attempts he succeeded in gripping the lead ball and with a sudden jerk drew it from the clinging wound. Bile rose in his throat, waves of giddy, nauseating faintness swept over him, and he fought desperately to keep his senses. He ripped a small piece of clean rag and soaked it with vinegar then rolled it and used it to plug the bleeding puncture wound. He was forced to wait again for the biting pain and threatening waves of giddy faintness to recede, before fashioning a pad of rag and using sticky plaster to secure it over the wound.

Moving very slowly he gingerly lowered himself face downwards onto his narrow bed to rest his aching, weary body, and try to calm his overstrained jangling nerves.

'What a damned mess I've made of things. It's me who's rightfully the town idiot and not King William. Was it Dolton who shot me? Or some Brummagem poacher who took me for a gamekeeper? Or thought he'd try his hand at highway robbery? Judging from the size of the ball it's a pistol that I've been shot with . . . Surely a poacher would be more likely to be carrying an air gun to avoid the noise of a flintlock's discharge . . . But if it was Dolton trying to kill me, then why didn't he finish the job? . . . And if it was him, then I've not a snowball in hell's chance of proving it, have I.'

Tom's weariness gradually overcame him and still struggling to make sense of what had happened he drifted into uneasy shallow sleep.

Thirty-Four

The observance of 'St Monday's Day' was a long-established, deeply engrained custom practised by the most feckless and reckless roisterers and drinkers throughout the needle district. Men and women both would celebrate it as an extra day for carousing following the excesses of Saturday night and Sunday, and would only go back to work on Tuesday morning when their money was all spent and their tavern credit exhausted. The cut in pay imposed by the needle masters had done little to curb this custom, particularly among the pointers, whose earnings were still very high in comparison to their fellow toilers.

One of the favourite 'Saint Monday' mornings pastimes of those pointers who lived in and around Silver Street was to attend the petty sessions at the Fox and Goose, to jeer at whichever enemies and support whichever friends were being brought before the Bench. Knowing this practice only too well, Tom was dreading the reception which would greet him this morning when he escorted John Hancox there. He had already experienced a taste of what might befall him when he had taken his mother's breakfast bowl of onion porridge into her room.

'Why have I had to wait so long to get my breakfast, and shout meself hoarse for it?' she had demanded pettishly. 'And why are you lolloping about like a three-legged rabbit, you great lazy lummox?'

Tom gritted his teeth against the gnawing pains in his buttock and thigh, and told her, 'I slipped on the stairs, Mother, and banged my leg. It's a little stiff and sore, that's all.'

'I should hope that is all, because you're no use to me as a cripple! But then, you're little or no use to me with two good legs, are you!'

For a brief instant Tom was sorely tempted to empty the bowl over her head, but then reproved himself, 'She's only a poor old woman, and you're her only son.'

Aloud he told her quietly, 'Eat your porridge, Mother, it'll do you good.'

'Not if it's like the rest of the muck you feed me with,' she whined. 'If any other poor woman ever suffered by having such a wicked, unnatural son like you, then I'd like to meet her.'

Tom limped from the room as fast as pain permitted.

John Hancox received his bowl of porridge with a good grace. 'I've got to admit, Master Potts, that you'm the best turnkey I've ever had. The grub in here aren't bad at all since you took over. In fact some on it is better than the stuff me mam serves me.'

'Well, I'm pleased to hear you say that, Johnny.' Tom was inordinately gratified by this compliment. 'It's good to know that I'm appreciated for something, at least.'

'What's you walking round like a cripple for?' Hancox enquired.

'I slipped on the stairs and banged my leg.'

'You should put a bit more water in your gin, then,' Hancox chortled.

'Yes, I will in future.' Tom forced a smile, then asked casually, 'Are there any buildings, like old cottages or barns or suchlike, in Brockhill Wood?'

'There's two or three scattered about from the old days when the monks from the abbey owned the woods, but they'm fallen down now. Except for the one where Dolton and his mates keeps their fighting dogs. But I always keeps well clear o' that one. Them dogs'll tear you to pieces if they gets at you.' He grinned broadly. 'Like you and me well knows, don't we.'

'Dolton's mates?' Tom queried.

'That stepson of Old Joe Turner for one. What's 'is name? Jenkins! He's got dogs there. I knows that for a fact because Alfie Payne told me.'

Tom's interest was instantly intensified. 'How does he know?'

'Because he goes there to train the dogs for all of 'em. He's a bloody good dog trainer, Alfie is. It's always worth laying a few bob on any dog that he's trained to fight. More times than not, it wins.'

'I'll remember that in future.' Tom nodded thoughtfully, then deliberately changed the subject. 'Do you want a wash and shave before I take you in front of the bench?'

The young pointer fingered his burgeoning stubble, then

shook his head. 'Fuck it! Let folks see me like this! It makes me look like a real hard-chaw, don't it. It does, don't it? Makes me look a hard-chaw?'

'Yes, it does.' Tom gave the young man the assurance he was desperate for. 'It makes you look as hard as nails.' Then he tried to persuade him. 'But that will do you no good with the magistrates, Johnny. If they think you to be a desperate character, then they'll be tempted to give you a stiffer sentence. It will go easier with you if you appear clean-shaven and fresh-looking.'

'Fuck 'em! Let 'em do their worst! I'm a pointer lad, I am. I aren't feared of any sentence the beaks might give me! Fuck 'em all!'

Tom sighed regretfully and accepted defeat. He had come to like this youngster, who he knew was good at heart, and it saddened him to see youthful vanity rushing headlong into troubles which could be easily avoided.

Tommy Chance and his cronies had breakfasted on gin and cider in the Red Lion and now at eight o'clock were heading towards the Fox and Goose. They came abreast of the lock-up just as Tom and his prisoner were leaving. John Hancox was wearing the mandatory shackles on wrists and ankles, and was feeling proud that his chains denoted what a tough and desperate character he was.

Chance stared at Tom's clumsy hobbling gait, and his broken yellowed teeth bared in a grin of delight. 'Look there, lads! It's "Dot and Carry One" hisself! Come on, let's join the procession!'

Howling with raucous laughter, catcalling, shouting for others to come and see, the group of pointers formed a ragged line and followed behind the pair, all of them aping Tom's limping gait.

As always in the streets of Redditch, when there was noise and tumult people instantly came hurrying to see what was happening, and before the grotesque procession had covered many yards eager onlookers were swarming, laughing, jeering, egging the gang of pointers on to further mockeries.

Tommy Chance began to roar out a measured chant, and a score of voices quickly took up the chanted cadence.

'They calls me Cripple Dick, Cripple Dick.

Yes they calls me Cripple Dick, Cripple Dick.
Because I got no prick, I got no prick.
It's true I got no prick, I got no prick.
That's why I'm Cripple Dick, Cripple Dick . . .'

Tom was inwardly writhing with embarrassment, but managed to keep his expression set in dour disdain. John Hancox's expression, however, was murderous. His appearance before the bench today was meant to demonstrate that he was a true pointer lad, tough, reckless, contemptuous of authority and defiantly fearless in the face of punishment. He had eagerly anticipated this parade in chains to be accompanied by his peers shouting their support and applauding his bravado. Now it had metamorphosed into a spectacle of ridicule. Driven beyond endurance he turned on Tommy Chance and bellowed, 'If you don't fuck off I'll swing for you, you bastard!'

Chance struck an effeminate pose, and trilled in a high falsetto, 'Ohhhh, hark at her? Aren't she grown very bold lately!'

Jerking the lead chain from Tom's grasp, Hancox hurled himself at his tormentor, bringing him down, and the two men grappled furiously, rolling over and over on the ground.

Almost immediately a pushing, jostling circle formed around the combatants, howling encouragement, hungry for blood.

'Stop this! Stop this in the name of the King!' Tom shouted, and hobbling to the circle tried to force his way through, but was simultaneously buffeted violently backwards and tripped so that he fell and landed heavily on his backside. The crushing impact sent an agonizing jolt through his wound, and he cried out in pain. His constable's staff was ripped from his hand and sent flying through the air, and heavy clogs thudded into his ribs, smashing the breath from his lungs. Instinctively he wrapped his arms around his head and rolled away from his assailants, then mingling with the cacophony of shouting there sounded the thudding of horses' hooves and the crack of carbine shots.

Tom lifted his head to see the crowd scattering in all directions, women and children shrieking in fright, men cursing, other men laughing uproariously as they fled before the onslaught of the red-jacketed, black-shakoed yeomanry troopers.

John Hancox and Tommy Chance were still fighting furiously on the ground, oblivious to all around them. Orders were bellowed, and troopers dismounted and used the butts of their carbines to club the two into stunned submission.

Erasmus Dolton, resplendent in sergeant's uniform and silver chevrons, reined in his mount and grinned down at Tom.

'It's a good job that we came along in time to save your bacon, Master Potts.'

Tom blinked in shocked surprise, but indoctrinated with good manners, managed to pant out, 'Thank you very much, Master Dolton. I'm most grateful to you.'

'It's Sergeant Dolton, when I'm wearing His Majesty's uniform, Master Potts.' Dolton's beefy red face was glowing with satisfied pleasure as he pointed towards the crowd now watching at a safe distance, and declared, 'These buggers hereabouts might be brave when they're facing the likes of you constables, but they runs like rabbits when we come against them.'

'They do indeed,' Tom acknowledged ruefully.

He turned onto his hands and knees, and biting his lips against the sharp pains lancing through his buttock managed to clumsily lever himself upright and stand.

'Have you been hurt?' Dolton enquired with apparent solicitousness. 'Only you appear to be moving with a great deal of difficulty. Would you like my men to help you to get to the Fox and Goose?'

'No, thank you. That won't be necessary. I'm perfectly well.'

Inwardly his thoughts were a maelstrom. Was it Dolton who had shot him? Or wasn't it? How could he ever find out for certain?

The troopers had dragged Hancox and Chance to their feet, and Tom limped up to them.

'Get on your way,' he told Tommy Chance. 'If you utter a single word, I'll arrest you for breach of the peace.'

Head bruised and bleeding, still dazed by the hammering of the carbine butts, Tommy Chance was only too willing to stumble away.

'How are you feeling, Johnny?' Tom asked the equally bruised, bleeding and dazed Hancox. 'If you want I'll go and request the magistrates to put back your hearing until the next sessions. I'll tell them that you're too badly knocked about to appear today.'

The pointer shook his head. 'No, let's get it over with now.'

'All right, if that's what you want.' Tom took the chain, and escorted by mounted troopers on each side led his prisoner on.

A few yards from the inn door, Amy Danks came hurrying to meet them.

'Oh, Tom, what's happened to you? Why are you limping so?' Her pretty face radiated anxious concern.

Poignant yearning flooded through him as he met her eyes, and he was forced to remind himself sharply, 'She's lost to you now, you mawkish fool!'

He forced a smile and told her, 'I'm fine, Amy. I slipped on the stairs and banged my leg, that's all. It'll be fine in a couple of days.'

'Why have you been neglecting me so badly?' She displayed a flash of petulance. 'Why haven't you called in to see me these last days?'

A momentary flash of jealousy struck Tom, as in his mind's eye he once more saw Amy and Davy Rowley dancing together, smiling fondly at each other; and he could not stop himself from snapping pettishly, 'I didn't think that I'd be welcome, now that you've found yourself a fine handsome young beau!'

The instant he voiced the words he wished that he had bitten off his tongue instead, and waited in miserable anticipation for a sharp rejoinder. But before she could answer Charles Bromley came bustling self-importantly through the doorway, using his constable's staff to clear his path through the onlookers. 'You are to present your prisoner before the bench immediately, Constable Potts. My lord Aston is most displeased with you to have been kept waiting.'

'Lord Aston?' Tom was very unpleasantly surprised. 'But I thought he was in Worcester today.'

'Well, you thought wrongly, did you not,' Bromley sneered spitefully. 'But then, that's a notable trait of yours, isn't it?'

Tom bit back an angry reply, knowing that any further delay would only redound badly upon John Hancox. 'I must go,' he told Amy, and limped as fast as he was able into the inn.

Tom received yet another unpleasant surprise when he entered the room and came face to face with the magistrates. Lord Aston was ensconced in a large armchair with one leg outstretched and the heavily bandaged foot resting on a low stool.

'He's got the gout again,' Tom realized. 'God help poor Johnny Hancox.'

Aston's drink-purpled features glowered as Joseph Blackwell read out the charge of poaching against the prisoner, and then asked Hancox, who was standing flanked by Tom and Charles Bromley, 'How do you plead, guilty or not guilty?'

'I'm not guilty of fuck-all! How can I be guilty, when I never laid a bloody snare down?' the young pointer questioned defiantly, and grinned when his words were applauded by the spectators crowded around the door.

'Silence, damn you!' Aston roared. 'I'll have the next one who utters a sound brought up before me for contempt of court!'

He waited, glowering threateningly until there was complete silence, and then questioned, 'Are there witnesses to this offence, Mr Blackwell?'

'Two, my lord. Mr Erasmus Dolton and Gareth Jenkins Esquire.'

'Two honourable men whose characters are well known to me,' Aston stated positively. 'I've no need to hear their testimonies, because I know that they would not bear false witness. I find the case proven. John Hancox, you are sentenced to pay a fine of ten guineas.'

'You bloody rotten old cunt, you! That aren't fair, that aren't!' the young pointer protested indignantly. 'I's already told you that I never even laid a snare! So how the fuckin' hell can I be done for poaching? I never took beast nor bird from that fuckin' wood!'

Aston's bloodshot eyes widened, and his jowls quivered violently, as he bellowed furiously, 'You are also guilty of contempt of court! For this offence I sentence you to be publicly whipped. You shall receive twenty-five lashes at the cart tail commencing at two of the clock this very day.'

Hancox blanched.

'Take him away!' Aston roared. 'Take him from my sight this instant, or I'll double the dose!'

'Come on, Johnny, for God's sake!' Tom hissed urgently into the pointer's ear, and half led, half dragged him from the room and out of the inn.

'Do you know the procedure for whipping at the cart's tail, Master Potts?' Joseph Blackwell was sitting in Tom's room in the lock-up.

'No, I don't, sir.' Tom was feeling greatly troubled.

'It's straightforward enough. The man will be stripped to the waist and his arms spreadeagled and secured to the rear of the cart. Firmly secured, mind. I've witnessed occasions when the prisoner has managed to break free and create uproar. You'll need a steady man at the horse's head, there are times when the wilder spirits among the crowd try and make the horse bolt.

'The first five strokes will be administered outside the entrance of the lock-up. The next five at the crossroads. The third five at the junction of the Front and Back Hills outside the Duke of York, the fourth five at the Big Pool and the final five once again outside the entrance of the lock-up.

'Dr Laylor will accompany the cart, as will the Reverend Clayton.'

Blackwell smiled bleakly.

'The one to deal with any medical emergency, the other to commend the prisoner's soul to God should he collapse and die during the punishment.

'You are fortunate enough to have available an escort of yeomanry on this occasion, which is a blessing. There have been many instances where the crowd have used force in an attempt to free a prisoner, and unfortunately our parish constables are not sufficient in number to cope with any such attempt.'

'And from where is the horse and cart to be obtained, sir?'

'From butcher Vincent. His old horse is well used to the blood and shrieks of animals being slaughtered, so with a steady man at its head it will undoubtedly be docile.'

'And the whip?' Tom was becoming increasingly uneasy.

'Get a new one from Thomas Hands, the saddler on Unicorn Hill. Tell him to bill the vestry for it. You will receive the standard payment of ten shillings for administering the punishment. To be paid when your next quarterly accounts for expenses are accredited by the vestry.'

Suddenly Tom felt that he had heard more than enough. He shook his head emphatically. 'I can't do this thing, sir. I can't whip John Hancox!'

Blackwell's eyebrows arched in surprise. 'Why ever not?'

'Because I don't think that he deserves to be so savagely punished. In fact, I don't think that he deserves any further punishment than he has already received. He was badly bitten by the dogs, and he's already been kept in a cell for more than a week. Surely he's paid whatever dues he owes?'

Blackwell appeared to choose his words with care when he answered quietly, 'It is not for you or I to decide whether or

no Hancox deserves his punishment. That is the prerogative of
the bench, and we are obliged by law to uphold their verdict,
and carry out their orders. However, I will not force you to
whip this man by using any threats of unhappy consequences
for yourself if you do not obey the bench's order. You could of
course claim that your whipping arm is injured, and that renders
you unable to do your lawful duty . . .'

He paused and the familiar bleak smile fleetingly curved his
thin lips, as he studied Tom's expression.

'For the sum of ten shillings there are many men in this town
who will be only too eager to volunteer to take your place and
whip John Hancox. Because be in no doubt, Master Potts, the
punishment will most definitely commence at two o'clock, no
matter who is wielding the whip. But before you make any
final decision, I want you now to go and have a word with John
Hancox. I want you to ask him whom he would prefer to administer the whipping. Go now and ask him.'

It was more of an impassioned request than command, and
Tom complied without argument.

'I wants you to do it, Master Potts.' John Hancox was almost
pleading. 'Because there's them in this town who's got scores
to settle against me. I've seen it happen afore. When a chap's
got a score to settle, then he takes the whip and does his best
to tear the poor bugger he's whipping to pieces. Now that me
and him have had a fight, Tommy Chance'll take the whip,
even if he has to pay good money for it hisself. I knows that
for a fact, and then he'll belt me over me kidneys till I'm
pissing blood. I've seen him do it afore. He's bloody handy
with a whip, and knows just how to do the most damage with
it. He can drag and slice like a bloody flogging drummer, so
he can.'

'But I'll be damaging you if I use it, won't I, Johnny,' Tom
protested.

'That's as maybe.' The fresh youthful face was set hard with
resolve. 'But you won't be enjoying it, will you. All you got
to remember is that when you strikes you must aim the lash
for me shoulders and the top o' me back. Don't send it low.
Because when it's low it does harm to the kidneys. And when
it strikes home, then don't straight away drag it back, let it fall
of its own accord.'

'I don't know, Johnny.' Tom shook his head doubtfully. 'I really don't think that I can bring myself to whip you.'

'Does you want me to beg you to do it?' the young man demanded angrily. 'Because I 'ull do, if that's what's needed.'

'Of course I don't!' Tom was appalled.

'Well then, say that you'll do this for me.' Hancox was forcefully demanding now. 'Be a friend to me, and take the whip. Please! I'm begging you!' He snatched Tom's hand and gripped it hard between his own hands. 'Do this for me, Master Potts. Please! I'm begging you!'

'Well, Master Potts?' Joseph Blackwell raised his eyebrows expectantly.

'I shall administer the punishment,' Tom told him unhappily.

'I thought you might see the advantages of doing so.' Blackwell's pallid, deep-lined face showed no emotion, but there was a glimmer of satisfaction in his eyes. 'Now listen carefully, for what I shall say is for the best for the prisoner. You must lay on hard, because even if Lord Aston is not there, he will have his spies in the crowd, and if he hears that Hancox has got off lightly, then he will order a repetition of the sentence. Do you accept that?'

Tom nodded wordlessly.

Blackwell was satisfied, and next asked, 'How did you come by your injury? The complete truth now, Master Potts.'

Tom related the full account of what had happened, and Blackwell listened in silence until the end, then agreed, 'Yes, there is no way of proving that it was Dolton who shot you, Master Potts. How do you intend to continue your investigations?'

'I shall search Brockhill Wood as soon as possible. John Hollis is meant to call on me at around midday to tell me what he has discovered. He's been making enquires about Siobhan Docherty in the Ipsley and Studley parishes. Unfortunately, because he is forced to go on foot, it is taking a considerable time to cover the ground.'

'Forced to go afoot, is he. Well, I've some news for you, Master Potts. I've managed to persuade the vestry to grant funds for horse-hire for both yourself and Master Hollis, for the next month.' Blackwell emitted a throaty chuckle. 'I trust that your wound will not dissuade you from sitting in a saddle.'

Tom smile in delight. 'Indeed it won't, sir. I shall strap a feather pillow to my arse.'

Thirty-Five

When John Hollis came to the lock-up just after noon he was accompanied by another man, whom he introduced as William Shayler, the constable of Studley.

'I've found out nothing about Siobhan Docherty, Tom, but Master Shayler has got something of interest to tell you.'

William Shayler, youngish and burly bodied with a weather-beaten complexion, spoke somewhat diffidently.

'I don't know how this can help you, Master Potts, but about a year ago I had a young wench come to me who said that she'd been raped by Gareth Jenkins in Slough Wood just down the hill from Crabbs Cross. She said that she knew his name because she'd called at his house earlier to look for work, and that he'd arranged to meet her in Slough Wood, and told her he'd give her money if she did a favour for him.'

'And that favour was to let him make free with her, I suppose?'

'Oh no. He said he was training tracker dogs, and all she'd got to do was to run through the wood and he'd be following her with the dogs on leashes. She said she'd bring her mate with her as well, but Jenkins said no, because if there was two of 'em, it'd confuse the dogs. And she must come at nightfall because he wanted to practise the dogs in darkness so they'd have to rely on scent alone. But she wasn't to tell anybody about where she was going or who she was meeting because Jenkins' stepdad, Old Turner, didn't approve of him keeping dogs, and he mustn't find out about 'em.'

'To cut a long story short, she went to the wood and Jenkins was waiting for her with three dogs. She reckoned they looked like wolves. She said that she was deep in the wood when the dogs caught her up, only Jenkins hadn't got 'em on leashes and he wasn't up wi' 'em. She reckoned that they started to bite her legs and pulled her down flat onto her face. She was screaming and skrawking out, and then all of a sudden the dogs left her alone and just kept circling round her. The next thing she knew was that Jenkins come and pulled her over onto her back, and raped her. Then after he was finished, he give her a silver florin and just went off wi' the dogs. She said that while Jenkins was atop of her, she could see another chap hanging about and watching, but he never touched her, and it was too dark for her to see him clear.'

'What action did you take, Master Shayler?' Tom asked eagerly.

'Well, I went to Turner's house down by Brecon there, and I spoke with him and his mam. He said that the wench was lying, because he'd not been anywhere near Slough Wood for months. And his mam said that on the night in question he'd been with her in the house, and hadn't gone out at all. She said that if the wench persisted in her lying, then she'd bring a charge against her for defamation of her son's character.'

'So what happened then? What further action did you take?' Tom could guess the answer.

'None.' Shayler frowned. 'It wasn't that I didn't believe her story. She'd got bite marks on her legs and arms all right, and she showed me bruises on her thighs which looked to be made by fingers. The trouble was that she had no right of settlement in my parish, and was a known bad character as well. She'd birthed two bastards, that had both died while they was still new-born, and she'd been brought up afore the Warwick magistrates for thievery when she was still only a nipper. There wasn't a bench in the land that would take her word against the word of gentry like Jenkins and his mam.'

'Well, I can personally vouch for the fact that Jenkins has got those dogs, and they're trained to hunt down human beings. Can I see this woman and talk to her?' Tom requested.

'No, you can't.' Shayler shook his head regretfully. 'The poor cow took a fever just afore last Christmas, and died from it. I was there when she went, and right up to her last breath she kept on telling me that it was the truth what she'd said about Jenkins.'

'And I'm very much inclined to think that it was the truth,' Tom muttered thoughtfully. 'Thank you very much for taking the trouble to come and tell me this, Master Shayler. If ever I can be of any service to you, then please don't hesitate to ask it of me. Come and take a pot of ale with us, I don't have to do anything until two o'clock.' He quickly explained to them about the whipping, and grimaced uncomfortably. 'I confess, I'm not relishing the prospect of whipping the poor fellow.'

'Pay me half the fee and I'll do it for you,' Shayler offered readily. 'I'm a dab hand with the lash. I used to be a drummer in the army, so I've had a lot of practice at it.'

'Thank you for the offer, but I have to refuse it,' Tom told him regretfully. 'I've given my word to the man that I'll carry out the punishment myself. I'd like you to lead the horse, John.'

'Certainly I will,' Hollis assented.

There was a holiday atmosphere among the crowds waiting outside the lock-up. The news of the whipping had spread like wildfire and caused a mass exodus of the workers from the needle mills and workshops throughout the town. The needle masters were also there in strength, some on horseback, others in carriages, their womenfolk decked out in their most fashionable gowns, twirling silken parasols above their elaborate bonnets and turbans.

The innkeepers and alehouse proprietors were continually hurrying backwards and forwards with trays of foaming tankards, and Timothy Munslow, the town pieman, was doing a roaring trade.

Hugh Laylor and John Clayton were sharing the carriage of Eleri Turner and her son, and when the pieman passed close by Gareth Jenkins called him over and demanded, 'What do you have in those pies, Munslow? The usual gristle and fat, I suppose?'

Timothy Munslow was a grizzled, stocky veteran who had fought at Waterloo and feared neither God nor the gentry. He grinned contemptuously at the plump featured young dandy.

'It's well known hereabouts that I only uses the best beef, mutton and pork for my pies, young man. But surely you aren't been weaned yet, has you. So my pies might be too rich for your blood.'

'Touché, Master Munslow!' Hugh Laylor laughed. 'He's struck home there, Gareth, and had the best of the exchange, has he not?'

Jenkins flushed and glared murderously. 'He'd best take care that I don't strike home to him, and teach him to mind his manners when speaking to his betters.'

The veteran chuckled scornfully. 'I's killed bigger and better men than you afore breakfast, young man, and more than once as well.'

Any further exchange between the two was interrupted by the arrival of butcher Vincent's horse and cart, which was greeted with cheers, and the escort of yeomanry following it with boos, catcalls and jeering.

Inside the lock-up Tom, pale-faced with tension, was watching John Hancox slurping down the large glass of gin that he had bought for him. Standing beside Tom, John Hollis also was nervously tense, but William Shayler appeared to be wholly at ease.

'This is your chance to show everybody that you got guts, Johnny.' He grinned amusedly at the young pointer. 'This is your glory day. If you shows that you can take it like a game 'un, then the crowd'll love you. But if you shows a yellow streak, then they'll turn against you. I've seen it happen afore.'

Hancox drained the last drop from the glass, and belched loudly. 'Ugghhh! That was a drop o' good, that was. Don't you bother about me showing any yellow streak, Master Shayler. I'll show everybody what I'm made of.'

'O' course you will, boy,' Shayler encouraged him. 'I don't doubt it.'

Tom stared at the prisoner, marvelling that the young man was indeed showing no signs of fear, but instead appeared to be elated. 'It must be the gin giving him Dutch courage,' he thought.

John Hollis took out his pocket watch. 'It's two o'clock, Tom. We'd best get started.'

When the group emerged from the arched entrance, a roar of cheering greeted them. Hancox grinned and stripping off his shirt waved it above his head like the winner of a contest.

'You'll be grinning on the other side of your face when you feels the kiss of the drummer's daughter, you piece of dirt!' Erasmus Dolton, who was commanding the escort, shouted contemptuously.

Hancox lifted two fingers to Dolton, and shouted back, 'Up your fat arse, Dolton!'

The crowd applauded this show of defiance uproariously.

Not waiting for Tom to lead him, Hancox strutted to the cart rear and spread his arms wide, shouting boldly, 'Come on, Master Potts, don't keep me waiting. I'm a very busy man!'

His sally brought another roar of applause from the crowd.

'That's it, Johnny, show 'em how a pointer lad can take his gruel,' Ritchie Bint bawled, and the group of pointers surrounding him added their exhortations.

'Show 'em what you's made of, Johnny!'

'Take it like a true pointer!'

'Show this lot why we'm paid our prices!'

John Hollis went to the horse's head and Tom went to the cart rear and used pieces of rope to secure the young man's outspread arms to the outer stanchions.

'Here, you can bite on this, Johnny.' He pushed a thick wedge of leather between the pointer's teeth, then stepped back and to one side.

William Shayler handed him the whip, and advised him, 'After each stroke draw the lash through your fingers and strip the blood and skin from it. If you leaves it on it'll tear him worse.'

Tom swallowed hard, and asked, 'Will you keep the count?'

'I will.'

Tom lifted the whip and slashed it through the air several times, trying to get the feel of it. Also trying to steel himself to make that first stroke.

He measured the distance, and fixed his eyes on Hancox's muscular back, its milky-pale skin contrasting starkly with the young man's sun-darkened forearms and neck.

'Commence on my word, Master Potts,' Shayler shouted.

A clammy sweat burst from Tom's pores, and he could feel his body trembling.

'Begin!' Shayler bawled.

'God forgive me!' Tom prayed beneath his breath, then lifted his arm and brought the lash hissing through the air.

'Agghhh!' Hancox ejaculated, and the horse started and whinnied loudly, and it took the combined strength of John Hollis and Butcher Vincent to hold it steady. From the crowd came a concerted indrawn gasp, and some among them paled and looked away, but others smiled wolfishly, eyes glistening with pleasure.

Hancox's widowed mother, standing in the forefront, shrieked and fell onto her knees, wrapping her shawl around her head, rocking her body backwards and forwards, sobbing and moaning incoherently until kindly neighbours lifted her up and led her away.

'One!' Shayler counted.

A thin streak of reddening skin marred the alabaster whiteness of Hancox's upper back.

Tom drew the lash through his fingers, steadied himself and struck again.

'Two!

'Three!

'Four!'

The fifth stroke drew the first ooze of blood, and Tom's stomach heaved sickeningly as he felt and saw it on his hand. It was not the blood itself which nauseated him, but the fact that he was responsible for shedding it.

'Five! The first set is completed!' Shayler shouted.

Tom stepped close to John Hancox, and asked, 'How is it going with you, Johnny?'

The young man's fresh complexion was grey and sweaty, as he grunted, 'It aren't too bad. It only hurts when I laughs.'

'Listen, just pretend to collapse and faint,' Tom whispered urgently. 'I can call a halt to it then.'

Hancox shook his head. 'No! I'm going to show 'em that I got guts. That I'm a game 'un.'

'Are you ready to move, Tom?' John Hollis called, and Tom reluctantly gave the order to go to the next stopping point at the crossroads.

Here the more enterprising of the householders whose premises overlooked the crossroads had rented out their upper rooms to spectators, and the noise of the excited crowd was deafening.

Tom stared anxiously at Johnny Hancox, and was relieved to see that the walk from the lock-up had appeared to help the young man, whose features had regained some tinges of colour.

'Six!

'Seven!

'Eight!' Shayler's stentorian count echoed over the heads of the crowd.

Now there were more cuts on Hancox's white flesh, trickles of blood were snaking down his sweat-soaked back, and Tom's hands were red, wet and slippery with it.

'Nine!'

'Ten! The second set is completed!' Shayler roared.

Hancox threw back his head and vented a defiant crowing, and the crowd wildly applauded him.

'Good on you, Johnny!'

'That's the way!'

'Go it, Johnny! Go it!'

'You'm a proper pointer lad, you am!'

Erasmus Dolton was scowling disgustedly to see the pointer being feted like a hero. John Clayton's expression mirrored his distaste for the barbaric spectacle. Gareth Jenkins' eyes were gleaming moistly, his tongue continually flicking out to run over his slack lips. Sitting by Eleri Turner's side, Hugh Laylor could feel the repetitive covert enticing pressure of her succulent thigh and rounded hip, and was impatient for the punishment to end so that he and his lover could keep their previously arranged tryst and slake their feverish passions.

'Move on, John,' Tom ordered, and the cart lurched into movement.

'Master Potts,' Ritchie Bint shouted and ducked between two of the escort to pass Tom a bottle. 'Give Johnny this.'

Erasmus Dolton spurred his mount to block Ritchie Bint's passage, but Bint only laughed and spun away.

Tom removed the cork from the bottle and sniffed the contents. It was rum. He bent to tell Hancox, who was striding with his head high, basking in the plaudits being showered upon him by the accompanying spectators, 'As soon as we stop again, I've got some rum for you. It's from Ritchie Bint.'

They mounted the Front Hill and halted in front of the Duke of York inn. The landlord in anticipation of trade had set up a trestle table loaded with kegs of ale and cider, and the clamorous crowd swarmed to quench their thirst.

Tom took the leather wedge from between Hancox's teeth and held the rum bottle to his lips. The man took a huge gulp, and coughed chokingly, spilling the fiery liquid from his mouth, down over his chin and chest.

'Hey, you can't give the bugger anything while he's under punishment,' Erasmus Dolton objected angrily.

Tom met his aggressive glare levelly, and replied quietly, 'Mind your own business, Sergeant Dolton. I'm administering this punishment, and I'll give this man whatever I choose to give him.'

'On whose authority?' Dolton blustered.

Tom signalled to William Shayler to hand him his staff, and lifted its crowned head in front of Dolton's eyes.

'On this authority, Master Dolton. I act here in the King's name. Now just stick to doing what you have been ordered to do, and that is to escort and protect us from any interference.'

Furiously cursing beneath his breath, Dolton wheeled his mount and retreated.

'Give us another drink, Master Potts,' Hancox gasped hoarsely, and Tom carefully dripped more rum into his gaping mouth.

'Is the pain very bad, Johnny?' Tom asked with concern.

The young pointer grimaced. 'It's bloody sore, but the funny thing is, where you been hitting me, it's starting to feel a bit numb. It's like its getting easier to bear, the longer it goes on.'

'And the crowd loves you, Johnny,' William Shayler told him. 'You'm showing what a true fighting-cock you am. You'm showing 'em that you'm a real game 'un!'

'I am that,' Hancox agreed proudly. 'Everybody can see now that I'm a real hard-chaw.'

'That they can, Johnny.' Shayler laughed. 'That they can! Only fifteen more strokes to go now, my buck. They'll feel like bloody feathers tickling you, now that you've got that rum in your belly.'

'Let's gerron on wi' it, Master Potts,' Hancox urged, slurring his words a little as the potent rum took quick effect. 'Shove that fuckin' leather back into me gob.' He opened his mouth wide, and Tom carefully arranged the leather wedge between the strong white teeth.

In Eleri Turner's carriage, John Clayton enquired, 'Should you be checking the man to see if he's fit to continue taking punishment, Hugh?'

'Oh no! Certainly not!' The doctor's handsome face was smiling as he waved his hand in emphatic dismissal of the suggestion. 'Let the rogue enjoy his moments of fame and glory, John. I know these local ruffians only too well. A public whipping like this is their chance to display how tough and fearless they are. It gains them great prestige amongst their fellow roughs and scruffs if they show what game bulldogs they are, and ask for no mercy. It would break that rogue's heart if I were to have this stopped now. He would sooner die first.'

'And I would let the scum die before I'd remit one single lash of his sentence,' Gareth Jenkins spat out sourly. 'These slum rats must be shown that we are their masters, otherwise they'll rise up and slaughter us in our beds, just as they did in France.'

John Clayton's craggy features were cold and hard-set as he regarded Jenkins, and he answered curtly, 'You should bear in mind that it is the ceaseless toil of these same slum rats that maintains you in your life of idle luxury and debauchery, Mr Jenkins.'

'If you were not protected by your clerical cloth, I would seek satisfaction for that insult, Parson,' Jenkins glowered threateningly.

'Don't let my clerical cloth stop you from demanding that satisfaction, sir.' Clayton's craggy features grimaced pugnaciously. 'I can very quickly cast it off and put on other clothes.'

'Stop it, both of you!' Eleri Turner scolded angrily. 'You're behaving like silly squabbling children, and ruining our pleasant little outing!'

'Yes! Shame on both of you! Now do let us be all friends together, and enjoy the show.' Laylor added his urgings.

John Clayton was the first to apologize. 'Forgive me, ma'am. And pray accept my apologies if I have inadvertently offended you, Mr Jenkins. I really had no intention of doing so.'

'I am sorry for upsetting you, Mama. Let us say no more of this matter, Parson Clayton.' Jenkins grudgingly followed suit, and then subsided into a sullen silence.

Fortified by the potent rum, John Hancox took the next five lashes without flinching, and even many of the people in the carriages of the gentry were now adding their voices to the plaudits of the crowd.

The procession passed down the steep Back Hill, the horse's hooves slipping and striking sparks from the stony ground.

Hancox's gait was unsteady as the torments of his flesh coupled with the alcohol increasingly clouded his brain and affected his sense of balance, and his feet slipped and slid until he was stumbling so erratically that Tom and William Shayler were forced to support him from each side.

'Listen, Master Potts,' William Shayler said urgently, 'it would be best if we didn't stop at the Big Pool but went on direct to the lock-up, and give him the last ten strokes there. He's near to collapsing, and if he's dragged dangling behind the cart these buggers might go berserk. They'm all happy as pigs in shit now, but if he falls and gets dragged they can turn nasty in a flash, and we'll have a riot on our hands then. I've seen it happen afore.'

'All right.' Tom accepted the advice without question, and shouted to Hollis, 'John, when we get to the Big Pool don't stop but turn straight up Red Lion Street and go directly to the lock-up.'

Outside the Horse and Jockey, Billy Middleton had also set up a long trestle table laden with kegs of drink and when he say the procession veer away into Red Lion Street he came at a run to overtake the cart and grasp Tom's shoulder.'

'What the fuck's going on?' he demanded furiously. 'You'm meant to stop outside my place!'

Tom had one arm around the staggering John Hancox and could feel the man's blood seeping through his coat sleeve; and the fact that he had shed that blood was tormenting him with self-disgust. He rounded on his angry accuser with an equally angry threat.

'Take your hand off me this instant, Middleton, or I'll arrest you for impeding me in my lawful duty!'

'You'll do what?' Middleton exclaimed incredulously.

'You heard me!' Tom retorted. 'Now just bugger off!'

He broke free of the restraining grip and went on.

The ex-prizefighter stood glaring after him, then became aware that the rotund landlord of the Red Lion, Herbert Willis, was standing outside his premises with some other men, laughing at his discomfiture.

Middleton pushed through the passing crowd until he was face to face with Willis, and gritted out, 'What's you laughing at, Willis?'

'Thought you'd make a pretty penny, did you, Middleton?' The other man chortled. 'Just goes to show you, don't it. You never wants to count your chickens afore they'm hatched. You should of done what I did, and that's get your people out wi' trays o' drink, not wait for folks to come to you. That's why I's made a pretty penny today, and you aren't! Because I got brains.'

Middleton's fist travelled only a few inches, and Herbert Willis went over backwards to thump senseless onto the stone-flagged entrance of his tavern.

'Does any of you others fancy you got more brains than me?' Middleton growled, and the group's smiles instantly metamorphosed into frozen rictuses of apprehension.

'No! I thought not,' Middleton spat out scornfully, and stalked away.

The cart lurched to a halt outside the arched entrance of the lock-up and the yeomanry escort used their horses as battering rams to push the eagerly clustering onlookers back and create a clear space.

Tom was fighting a desperate inner battle. All his instincts were screaming at him to throw down the whip and take John Hancox immediately into the cell and treat his wounds. But he knew that if he did, Lord Aston would order the punishment to be completed, and would almost certainly decide that the twenty-five lashes were repeated in full measure, and thus subject the young pointer to extra torture.

For a few moment Tom toyed with the idea of giving William Shayler the whip and letting him administer the final ten strokes. But then thrust the notion from his mind, castigating himself bitterly, 'That would be a betrayal of my sworn word to Johnny, wouldn't it. A pathetic attempt to salve my own conscience, when I've already done the damage.'

Even as he thought this, John Hancox raised his head and bawled drunkenly, 'Come on, Master Potts! What's you waiting for? Has I worn you out already?'

His sally was greeted with a tumultuous roar of approbation from the crowd.

'Keep the count, if you please, Master Shayler,' Tom gritted through his clenched teeth, and summoning all his fast ebbing resolve, sent the bloody lash whistling through the air.

'Sixteen!
'Seventeen!
'Eighteen!
'Nineteen!'

Tiny droplets of blood sprayed out each time the lash fell across Hancox's torn back and shoulders, and was carried on the breeze to spatter Tom's face and clothing.

'Twenty!

'Twenty-one!

'Twenty-two!'

Hancox raised his grey, sweat-pouring face to the heavens and shrieked, 'Lay it on! I can take it! Lay it on!'

The pointers roared encouragement.

'That's the way, Johnny!'

'Stick it! Stick it!'

'Good on you, mate!'

Ritchie Bint bellowed, 'Three cheers for Johnny Hancox! Hip hip, hurrah!'

The crowd took up the cadence in full-throated unison.

'Hip hip, hurrah! Hip hip, hurrah! Hip hip, hurrah!'

Each cheer was counter-pointed with the soggy impact of the lash.

'Twenty-three!'

'Twenty-four!

'Twenty-five! The sentence has been carried out,' Shayler shouted, and told Tom urgently, 'Get him inside as quick as lightning, Master Potts, or we'll have these buggers trying to carry him off to the nearest pub.' Then Shayler told Erasmus Dolton, 'Be ready, we could have trouble now!'

Dolton issued rapid orders and the troopers lifted and cocked their belt-hung carbines.

Tom and John Hollis quickly released Hancox, and half-led, half dragged him into the lock-up. Once inside Tom bolted the door behind him, and rushed to help Hollis to place the pointer face down on the wooden cell pallet.

'I'm going to wash and dress your back, Johnny, so be a good lad and lie quietly,' Tom said, and then stared in astonishment. John Hancox had instantly lapsed into a coma-like state of unconsciousness.

Tom went upstairs and took a sponge, a flagon of vinegar, some leaves of brown paper and a linen sheet from his room.

His mother shouted from her room, 'Thomas? Thomas, get in here, will you!'

He pushed open the door and was shocked to find his mother and Charles Bromley sitting at the open window overlooking the tumultuous scene below and companionably sharing a bottle of brandy.

'Will you chase these noisy buggers away from here.' Widow

Potts' face was puce with drink, and her words disjointed. 'I need my peace and quiet. Why must you always do things to cause me such trouble and grief? If ever a poor woman suffered by having such a worthless, wicked, unnatural creature for a son, then I'd like to . . .'

Driven beyond endurance, Tom snapped curtly. 'Oh, do shut up, Mother!' and slammed the door closed against her grating voice.

Back in the cell he gently bathed Hancox's bruised and torn flesh with the sponge and vinegar. Then covered the wounds with the vinegar-coated leaves of brown paper, and tearing the sheet in long trips used it as pads and bandages.

Only when his task was completed did he ask his companion, 'Will you be kind enough to watch over him for a short while please, John?'

Hollis assented immediately.

Tom left the cell, walked quickly out to the privy in the back yard, and vomited, heaving and retching until his throat was sore and his stomach aching. Then with his senses spinning, energy spent, he slumped weakly against the wall, and wiped his streaming eyes.

'Dear God, I pray that I'll never again have to flog a man who didn't deserve to be so unjustly punished.'

As his stomach slowly ceased churning he went to the pump in the opposite corner and cranked the handle violently until water spouted, then held his head under the cold gouts until his senses steadied, his overstrained nerves had eased their jangling and the strength returned to his body.

Back in the cell William Shayler had joined John Hollis.

Both men regarded Tom's soaked head and shoulders keenly, and Shayler grinned knowingly. 'I remember how I felt after flogging my first man. I was only a boy still, and hadn't been in the army little more than a couple o' months. There I was learning the flams, paradiddles and stick-clicking one minute, and the next minute I was standing in front of the regiment helping to flog the shit out of some poor benighted bugger who'd tried to desert. I spewed me guts up after it was done. But after that first time, it became just like skinning a rabbit, and never bothered me at all.'

Tom smiled ruefully. 'Then I hope it becomes like that for

me also, Master Shayler, because I've just left last night's supper and today's breakfast in the privy.'

The noise from outside the building was fast lessening as people adjourned to the taverns and alehouses or went home, and in some cases even returned to their work.

'I'd best be getting back to me own parish,' Shayler told them. 'There'll no doubt be devil's work going on there when they find I'm absent.'

Tom rummaged among the few coins in his pocket and brought out two half-crowns which he offered to the Studley constable.

'Here, Master Shayler. This is yours by right, because without your help I don't believe I could have managed this affair successfully. I'm most grateful to you.'

'And I as well, Master Shayler,' John Hollis added. 'And if we can ever do you a service, then we will be very happy to.'

Shayler took the coins and pocketed them. 'I'll take these, because it's Tardebigge parish money.' He chuckled and winked slyly. 'And it's a bloody rare thing that happens I can tell you, for a Studley man to get any money out of Redditch. All we normally comes away from this town with am black eyes and broken bones.'

They parted with handshakes and mutual expressions of good will.

Once Shayler had gone, John Hollis asked, 'What about young Hancox?'

'I'll leave him to rest for now, and take him back to his home later,' Tom answered. 'And in the meantime we carry on with the search for our murderer, John. I won't sleep easy until we lay him by his heels.'

Thirty-Six

The pillow tied across the saddle cushioned Tom's buttocks, but the ride to Brockhill Wood was still a painful experience, and he was relieved to dismount on the edge of the treeline

and tether the horse. It was just after midnight and the moon
was shining in a clear sky, but very little of its light penetrated
the thick foliage and the narrow pathway threading through the
undergrowth was mostly black-shadowed. In the satchel slung
from his shoulder he carried the same equipment that he had
used when searching Dolton's outbuildings, but tonight he had
also brought the pair of loaded pistols, and as he cautiously
moved along the pathway he carried one in each hand, prepared
to fire back if he should be ambushed again.

Deep in the wood the pathway opened out into a long wide
glade, at the far end of which stood a large stone-built building
with a thatched roof. Keeping in the shadows Tom spent long
minutes watching and listening for any sight or sound of occu-
pancy, before going slowly nearer. The moonlight clearly
displayed the barred windows and padlocked door, and Tom
crept towards the nearest window.

Loud barking suddenly erupted. Tom's heart thudded with
shocked alarm, and he levelled his pistols ready to shoot, then
realized that the barking came from inside the building. He
went up to the unglazed window and flattened himself against
the wall by its side. The German shepherd dogs hurled themselves against the bars, snarling savagely, trying to force their
heads through the iron rods to attack him. Tom stayed motionless, waiting to see if anyone was with the animals.

Once satisfied that there was no one inside, he took the
laudanum-treated meat from the satchel and tossed it through
the bars, then retreated around the side of the building. With
him gone from their sight, the dogs turned to the lumps of meat,
wolfing them down voraciously, snapping and fighting with
each other for the last remaining pieces. Within a few minutes
one after the other collapsed senseless.

Tom went to the door and used the crowbar to lever the hasp
and staple from the doorpost, then lit his bulls-eye lantern and
went inside. He found that the interior was partitioned into
small rooms, and began his search in the end room where the
dogs were lying, snorting and twitching. There was nothing
else inside it but the bare walls. He carefully secured the door
so that if any dog recovered it would not be able to get at him.
In the next room he discovered a pile of empty sacks, and felt
like shouting out in excitement when he turned one of them
inside out and found several hemp seeds trapped in its seams.

'Ann Washwood could have picked up the seeds here, couldn't she. She might have been in this very room.'

He continued his search throughout the ground floor and then went up a ladder and through a hatchway onto the upper floor. There were no partitions here, and his boots clumped on the bare boards as he searched from end to end, but found nothing to indicate that anyone had been here recently.

Disappointed, he went slowly back toward the hatchway, sweeping the beam of lamplight across the rafters. He caught his breath sharply when the light shone upon something stuffed between one and the roof thatch.

Carefully he freed what looked to be a bundle of rags, and laid it on the floor to open it out. His excitement fired when he realized that it was in fact a woman's gown, dirty and much torn.

'I need to scrutinize this very thoroughly,' he realized. 'I need to have daylight to see it really clearly.'

He folded the gown carefully and stowed it away in the satchel, then descended the ladder stiffly.

In the rear room there was a pump, with a wooden bucket beside it and a hatch cover set into the stone-flagged floor. He lifted the cover and went down the brick-built steps to an empty cellar. The floor here was also flag-stoned and as the shaft of lantern light moved across it Tom noticed that in one corner the stones were uneven, in contrast to their level neighbours. On impulse he took the crowbar and began to tap it on the floor. The reverberations from the uneven flags sounded differently. He returned upstairs and filled the wooden bucket on the sink, then went back down into the cellar and threw the water across the floor. The water stayed on the even flags but seeped away on the uneven section, draining between the joints.

'Has something been buried under there?' Tom wondered. 'Or someone? I'll have to come back with a pick and shovel.'

He returned upstairs and after listening for any sound that the dogs might be stirring, he reopened the door to their room. Then went outside and carefully refixed the hasp and staple in place, using the crowbar to hammer home the nails.

Still keeping in the shadows at the edge of the glade, he cautiously retraced his steps, sighing with heartfelt relief when he reached his horse. Only then did he deride himself. 'You bloody blockhead! Creeping about trying not to make any noise after you made all that racket hammering the nails back in?'

He grunted as he remounted and gingerly lowered himself onto the pillowed saddle, sending pain lancing through his buttock, then set off on a roundabout route to go back into the town from the opposite side to which he had left.

After stabling the horse in Humphries' stables he returned to the lock-up. Dawn was paling the eastern sky and Tom was impatient to examine the gown, but he decided that it would be better to wait until later, after he had completed another duty, which was to bury Ann Washwood.

Thirty-Seven

There was no cortege of carriages filled with grieving mourners. No sad-faced mutes carrying black banners walking alongside an ornate hearse drawn by black-plumed horses. There was only Tom and John Clayton on foot following behind the coal cart on which Ann Washwood's coffin rested, and Thomas Oakley the coal merchant and his helper at the horse's head, both wearing working smocks thick with coal dust and the leather headdress of their trade with its long neck veil hanging down their backs.

The day was dull and dreary with drizzle, in concert with Tom's sombre mood. Because of the succession of warm days her corpse had rapidly deteriorated, its vile stench filling the lock-up and even escaping beyond the walls so that passers-by held their noses. After numerous complaints from Widow Potts and others the vestry had grudgingly given permission for the woman to be buried, but not in the chapel burial ground. Instead she was allotted a pauper's unmarked plot in the old burial ground attached to the ruins of Bordesley Abbey on the flat land north of the town between the bottom of Fish Hill and the River Arrow.

'Even in death the poor woman has not been permitted any

dignity,' Tom thought sourly as he watched the two coalmen puffing on short clay pipes and laughing and joking together, and he opened his mouth to tell them to behave with more propriety, but closed it again without speaking.

'At least they're willing to help us bury her. Nobody else would come near her, the smell is so bad.'

At the old burial ground all four men took turns at digging the grave, the drizzle turning the red-clayed earth beneath their feet into clinging mud. Tom was shovelling out the last few inches of the six feet. He threw the final shovelful up onto the heap of dug earth and began to lever himself out of the hole, but his hand slipped and he tumbled awkwardly backwards, his buttocks thumping on the mud with a jolt that sent a shaft of agony through his unhealed wound.

The coalmen laughed, and Oakley asked facetiously, 'Does you intend staying down there wi' this wench, then, Master Potts? Because if that's the case, then you'm going to need the hole widening a bit. That's unless you intends to spend all the time on top of her.'

'I used to do that when I was first wed to my missus,' his helper grinned. 'But it's a bloody different story now, I can tell you.'

'Now now, men. Remember we are here to commit this poor soul to God's care. It's not a time for levity,' John Clayton reproved them gently, then displayed his prodigious muscular strength by gripping Tom's hands and lifting him bodily out of the grave.

The four men used ropes to lower the coffin and when that was done John Clayton read the burial service and said a short prayer.

The four again took turns to shovel the dirt back into the grave.

Tom experienced a sense of poignant sadness. 'What a damned shame it is that this poor woman has no one here to weep for her. Will there be anyone to weep over my grave, I wonder?'

When the coalmen left Tom told John Clayton, 'I'm going to gather a few wild flowers and put them on her grave. She may look down and see them from wherever she now is.'

'I'll help you gather them.' The clergyman smiled and patted Tom's shoulder. 'It's a very nice gesture to have thought of making, Tom. To my shame it never occurred to me to do it.'

They went among the turf-covered mounds of the abbey ruins

picking white daisies, yellow buttercups, red campions and blue harebells. Tom heard the thudding of galloping hooves coming from the adjoining field and looked up to see that the rider of the splendid-looking horse was Alfie Payne.

'Where did he get that beast from?' Tom was surprised to see a denizen of Silver Street mounted on such a fine animal.

'It could be one of Erasmus Dolton's,' Clayton told him. 'Payne does odd jobs for him from time to time, I believe.'

They took their armfuls of flowers back to the grave and spread them in a deluge of colour across the mound of raw clayed earth, then walked together back up to the town where they parted at the chapel gate.

Tom heard his name being called, and saw Amy Danks coming towards him. He had not seen her since the day of John Hancox's sentencing, and had tormented himself many times with thoughts of her and Davy Rowley being together. Now, as always when he saw her fresh youthful beauty, he was filled with a poignant yearning and bitter regret for what might have been had he possessed sufficient worldly goods to marry and support her.

'I've got a bone to pick with you, Tom Potts.' She was frowning petulantly.

Tom's heart sank. 'What about, Amy? What have I done to upset you?'

'You haven't come near me for days, have you? Why are you grown so cold towards me?' she demanded.

'But I'm not grown cold towards you!' he protested.

'Well, it seems that way to me, when you're deliberately keeping away from me.'

'I'm not!' He was feeling an increasing dismay. 'It's just that I've been very busy lately.'

'Too busy even to come and pass the time of day with me?' She pouted. 'That's not much to ask of my dearest and closest friend, is it? To call in and say, "Hello, Amy. How are you today, Amy? Is your family well, Amy?" '

'But I do want to come and see you,' he said miserably. 'It's only that now you've got a sweetheart, I don't like to. In case it causes difficulties between you both.'

Her eyes sparkled mischievously. 'Who says I've got a sweetheart?'

'Well, no one. But I saw you dancing with Davy Rowley by the Horse and Jockey, and you looked like sweethearts.'

She giggled. 'Did we now. Well, Davy isn't my sweetheart. He's one of my many admirers, and he's always asking me to be his sweetheart, but so do my other admirers.'

'And what do you tell him when he asks you to be his sweetheart?' Tom was driven to ask, but dreaded what the answer might be.

She giggled again and clapped her hands. 'That's for me to know, and for you to find out. And you won't find out unless you keep coming and seeing me, will you.'

She stepped to him, reached up with both hands to clasp his head and draw it down, then planted a resounding kiss on his nose, and ran off towards the Fox and Goose laughing delightedly.

Tom stood smiling fondly after her, his spirits soaring as hope burgeoned in his heart once more.

Thirty-Eight

Tom spread the dirty greasy brown gown out upon the floor of his room and almost immediately found what he had hoped for. A piece of grey cloth sewn onto the right shoulder which bore two faded, red painted capital letters. T and P. The pauper's badge for the Tardebigge parish, which all the inmates of the poorhouse were forced to wear.

'This has to be Ann Washwood's gown.' He was convinced. 'And the rips in it might have resulted from someone tearing it off her.'

From boyhood Tom had been fascinated by microscopy, and had constantly practised the art. He had amassed an extensive and widely diverse collection of human and animal hairs and blood samples and developed a considerable degree of expertise at distinguishing their varying characteristics.

Using his magnifying glass he carefully studied the cloth.

There were some stains inside and out, which he thought might be blood. He cut out a small piece of the stained cloth, placed it on a glass slide and moistened it with some diluted pure glycerine. Within a short time the liquid became a reddish colour. He next prepared a microscopic slide and examined it under the microscope at a power of three hundred diameters. He held his breath as he distinguished the minute globules within the liquid. They were pale yellowish-red in colour, flattish and disc-like. It was blood! Mammalian blood, and therefore possibly human.

Turning back to make a further examination of the gown, he found a single long hair inside the neck, and also found several short hairs embedded in the rough material of its front and in the sides of the long sleeves. He carefully removed all of them and taking the long hair first studied it under his microscope.

Hair consists of three distinct layers: the medulla, the central core of cells; the cuticle, the outer sheath of overlapping scales; and the cortex, sandwiched between the other two, which is formed of keratin and contains melanin, the pigment granules that determine the hair's natural colour.

Tom's excitement mounted. The medulla was fragmented, and the cuticle was that of a human being.

From a small jar he selected other hairs which he had previously plucked from the head of the dead Ann Washwood and examined them carefully under the microscope. Like the first hair they were circular in structure and had split ends. Their medullas were also fragmented. The pigment granules of their cortexes were identical in colour and distribution.

He experienced a warm glow of satisfaction. The gown was for him now proven to be Ann Washwood's. But he doubted that such evidence would be accepted by any court of law.

He next examined the short hairs, subjecting them to the same long and minute scrutiny and comparison.

'These are horse hairs,' he decided. 'And from their colour they've come from a very light sorrel. Judging from the pattern I found them in, she could have been tied face downwards across the horse's back. But how can I identify which particular horse? There can't be many sorrels of this particular shade in this parish. I'll get John Hollis to make a discreet search. Maybe Will Shayler can check Studley and Ipsley parishes for me as well. But even if I find that Dolton or Jenkins have a sorrel of this shade it still won't prove anything conclusive against them. I'll still need more evidence.' Then he thought grimly, 'Perhaps I'll find it tonight under the floor of the cellar.'

The door bell jangled loudly, and from the next room his mother shouted, 'Will you answer the door, you lazy great lump! How can I get any rest with all this noise going on for hours on end? No wonder I'm in such poor health. If ever another poor woman has suffered like I have, then I'd like to meet her.'

'All right, Mother.' He sighed. 'I'll go directly.'

When the door creaked open he found Mother Readman facing him.

'He's come back,' she announced, 'the one they calls Pretty Dick. He come back early this morning and he's in my house right this minute.'

'Wait a moment, ma'am, while I fetch my staff.'

She shook her head. 'No, I aren't a-going to walk back wi' you, Master Potts. My neighbours'd give me stick if they thought I was helping a bloody constable. You must give me time to get home afore you follows me.'

'But he might have gone by then,' Tom objected.

'No he won't. He's cooking himself some grub, so he'll still be there when you comes.'

When Tom entered the large malodorous room he was met with hostile stares from the dozen men and women sprawling at their ease on the benches and floor.

'I'd like a word with you, young man.' He went across to the fireplace where the handsome pedlar was stirring a mess of meat and vegetables in a small iron cauldron suspended from a chain above the fire.

Ricardo Pozo regarded him warily. 'A word wi' me? What about?'

Conscious that the people around them were listening intently, Tom suggested, 'It might be best for you to come outside where we can be private.'

The pedlar smiled, showing fine white teeth, and shook his head. 'No, I can't leave me grub, or these buggers'll guts it down. We can talk here. I've nothing to hide.'

'Very well,' Tom conceded reluctantly. 'I want to ask you

about a young girl that you were seen with, last time you were here. Her name is Siobhan Docherty.'

'Siobhan? What about her?'

'She seems to have disappeared after being seen with you. So you'd best tell me what happened between you both.'

'She can tell you herself.' The pedlar pointed at the door. 'She's just come in.'

Shocked, Tom swung round to see the pretty red-haired girl who was looking nervously at him.

'What do you want with me?' she asked falteringly. 'I just now took the silver plate back to where I got it from, and give it back to the woman. So I never stole it, did I. I only borrowed it for a bit.'

'Don't be alarmed.' He went to stand face to face with her, and told her reassuringly, 'I'm not here to arrest you for anything. You're not in any trouble as far as I know. In fact I'm very relieved to see you. Does your family know that you're safe and well?'

'Yes.' She nodded. 'We only left them yesterday at Warwick.'

'Why did you run off from them when you were here before?' Tom asked curiously.

'To save meself from getting a leathering off me da.' She relaxed a little and smiled tentatively. 'He'd have took the skin off me. But I knew that if I kept well away from him for a few days, he'd be so pleased to see me when I came back safe that I wouldn't get a leathering.'

'But what if you couldn't find him?' Tom smiled.

'Oh, I knew where he'd be all right.' She was completely at ease now. 'He follows the same tracks all the time.'

'What about the silver plate you mentioned.' Tom pressed her gently, 'You won't get into any trouble, whatever you tell me. I only want to know about it to satisfy my own curiosity.'

After a momentary hesitation she related the story, including her confrontation with Hugh Laylor, the threats he made to her and his failure to meet her outside the Horse and Jockey.

'. . . then when I was walking away from the pub, I saw a man following after me, and I got scared and ran here to tell Dick, and we buggered off from here that same night, and kept away till now.'

'The man who followed you, what did he look like? Was he old? Young? Rough dressed? Well dressed?' Tom felt a surge of excitement, which was replaced by instant deflation when she shook her head.

'It was too dark for me to see his face or his clothes properly. But I don't think he was old, because when I started to run, he did as well, and he could run fast. If I hadn't come in here he'd have caught me, I reckon.'

Tom was very thoughtful when he parted from the young couple and walked slowly down Silver Street, trying to marshal and evaluate what he had gleaned up until now during his investigations.

'It was an athletic man who butchered the ewe and lamb, because he was able to vault the gate.

'Siobhan said that the man chasing her was a fast runner.

'Ann Washwood was a sturdy young woman who may have fought back against her attacker, so it would need a strong man to subdue her single-handedly.

'The bodies were carried into Vincent's shed and lifted and arranged upon the slab. Again, bodily strength is needed to do that.

'There was a horse involved at some stage in both crimes. Which points to the killer having his own beast, or easy access to one.

'William Shayler said that the girl who accused Gareth Jenkins of raping her said that there was another man watching. Could that have been Erasmus Dolton?'

Tom pondered on Erasmus Dolton. He judged the farmer to be in his middle forties, and although appearing to be healthy and strong he was carrying a lot of fat. Tom mentally pictured the heavy belly and broad deep rump of the farmer.

'No! He's not athletic enough to vault a gate, or to overtake a light-running young girl like Siobhan on foot. I don't think that he's the man who killed the sheep, or chased Siobhan. That would take a younger man, someone of Gareth Jenkins' years.'

The image of Jenkins' puffy features and incipient jowls rose up in Tom's mind. 'He doesn't look particularly fit or strong, does he, but appearances can be deceptive. If what Shayler's young woman said is true, then Jenkins was strong enough to rape her single-handedly. However, Jenkins' mother vouched for him, didn't she. And the young woman herself was a bad character and a known liar. She could have agreed to let Jenkins have sex with her, and then when he only gave her a florin for it, she tried to get him into trouble.'

Tom reached the lock-up inwardly seething with frustration. 'Dolton and Jenkins are my prime suspects, but I've no real proof whatsoever. Pray God that I find something when I dig up the cellar tonight!'

He decided he would go and report all these latest developments to Joseph Blackwell.

'. . . I'm convinced that the gown is Ann Washwood's, because of her hair; and what I believe to be the human bloodstains, and when I dig up the cellar I shall find added proof of that.'

'In what form?' The older man's pallid features were frowning slightly, as if he was not yet convinced.

'The remains of the infant, and Washwood's own innards. Also there might be more items of her clothing – her stays, for example – and there might—'

'Spare me the details at present, Master Potts. There will be ample time for description when, or if, you actually discover such items. As for what you have told me about your knowledge of microscopy, I personally accept your claims of expertise, but of course such evidence would not be accepted in a court of law. It smacks too much of wizardry for any hard-headed judge to be seen to countenance it.

'For the moment let us concentrate on these allegations concerning Gareth Jenkins. How much credence do you personally place in the Tinker girl's account of him trying to take indecent liberties with her person?'

Tom didn't hesitate. 'I believe her, because I've had several other accounts given to me concerning his blackguardly behaviour towards young women who are his social inferiors.'

'And her allegations concerning Hugh Laylor?'

This time Tom hesitated, before admitting, 'I find those allegations very hard to believe, sir. I think that at best the girl is stretching the truth considerably.'

'Exactly so.' The older man nodded judiciously. 'You must always bear in mind that tinkers are bred from birth to lie, cheat and steal. I cannot for a moment believe that Hugh Laylor would behave so. However, in the case of Jenkins I am inclined to give her the benefit of the doubt. I've received similar reports of that young man's unseemly conduct several times in the past couple of years.

'This being the case, I would advise you to concentrate your investigations upon Jenkins and Dolton, and disregard Laylor.'

'Very well, sir.'

'I further strictly order that you keep your own counsel while furthering your investigations.' Blackwell frowned. 'You had no warrant to enter the premises or to seize the gown, so have acted unlawfully. Therefore do not speak of what you have already discovered to anyone other than me; and above all else, do not get caught digging up that damned cellar! If you discover something suspicious, then leave it in situ, replace the soil and flags and come immediately to me, at no matter what hour of the day or night.'

A bleak smile fleetingly curved Blackwell's thin lips. 'I'm pleased that you are demonstrating your ability to act upon your own initiative, Master Potts, and now I bid you good day.'

Thirty-Nine

The high scudding clouds were intermittently hiding the moon as Tom tethered his horse in the concealment of a thick clump of bushes, then slung his leather satchel on his shoulder and hefting his mattock and shovel went watchfully through the trees and undergrowth towards the building.

Tonight he had come here earlier to allow more time for his digging, and darkness had only fallen an hour previously. As he neared his target the sounds of voices and laughter reached his ears, and he crouched and, moving with great care to avoid shaking the branches and leaves of the shrubs, crept slowly nearer until he saw lantern light shining from the open doorway. He was able to see that there were three horses being held by a shortish man, who was wearing a wide-brimmed soft hat, short coat and breeches.

Then the voices and laughter sounded louder as three other

men all similarly dressed came out from the doorway. Tom's breath caught in his throat.

The man in front was leading the three leashed German shepherd dogs, and now Tom heard his voice more clearly he recognized him as Gareth Jenkins. The second man was Erasmus Dolton. The third man, tall and broad-shouldered, was laughing uproariously. He turned his head and the lantern light from the doorway shone full on his face.

'It can't be!' Tom could not believe what his eyes were seeing. He took the risk of moving so he could see more clearly through the intervening undergrowth, rubbing his eyes and staring hard to be sure that it was not some trick of his imagination.

'Hugh Laylor! It is him, isn't it!' He was forced into shocked acceptance. 'What the devil is he doing here in this company? Has Jenkins arranged to hunt some other poor girl through the woods, and is Laylor going with him? He can't be! Surely he can't be?'

The men mounted and rode off with the dogs, leaving behind the horse-holder, who went into the building. As the man stepped through the lamplight of the doorway Tom recognized him also. 'Alfie Payne? How are you involved in all this?'

He waited impatiently for Payne to leave, but brief minutes multiplied and stretched to many long hours, and still the lamplight glowed through the glassless windows. Tom's body chilled, his muscles cramped and joints stiffened painfully, but he kept up his vigil until near dawn. Only then did he accept defeat and steal stiffly away. To receive another shock.

'Oh dear God! What's happened here? Where's the bloody horse gone?'

He made a frantically rapid search around the area, but there was no sign of the beast. At first he could only think that something had frightened the animal and it had torn its tethering reins free and bolted. But there was no scatterings of torn leaves and twigs beneath the branch he had tethered it to, and no deep indentations in the rain-softened ground to indicate any scrabbling or stamping of hooves.

Another chilling thought suddenly struck him.

'Was someone following me?' He shook his head in incredulous rebuttal. 'Nonsense! I kept the beast in the back yard, so who would see it there? Who would know when I should leave the lock-up to come here? No, I must have tied the tether insecurely. That must be it. What a bloody mess I've made of it all. Damned useless fool that I am.'

Utterly disheartened, he hid his tools under a bush before setting out to wearily tramp the long roundabout route back to the town.

Forty

'Feather pillow?' Richard Humphries, proprietor of Humphries' Coaches and Livery Stables, exclaimed in disbelief. 'A bloody feather pillow? Tied over the bloody saddle?'

'Come and see for yourself, gaffer,' the stable-hand invited with a broad grin. 'I've left it there on purpose to show you. The roan mare come back here at first crack o' light this morning wi' her reins dangling and a bloody big pillow tied acrorst her saddle. Come and see.'

'The roan mare? That's the one that's hired out to Potts, aren't it? Well, where's he when he's about?'

The stable-hand shrugged. 'Fuck knows! The mare come back by herself first thing this morning wi' her reins dangling. That's all I knows.'

'Is she damaged at all?'

'No. Her's as right as rain. Not a mark on her. But there's no saying what might have happened to him.'

'Bugger him!' Humphries' weather-beaten face displayed only relief. 'It's my mare I'm worried about. I don't give a bugger what's happened to that lanky sod!'

They went into the mare's stall and when Humphries saw the big pillow on the saddle, he burst out laughing. 'Never mind calling that soft weak bugger Cripple Dick. We ought to be calling him Tommy Glass-Arse.'

'Tommy Glass-Arse!' the stable-hand chortled delightedly. 'That's a good 'un, that is, gaffer! I'll have to tell the lads that 'un. Tommy Glass-Arse!'

Forty-One

'Hey up, lads, Tommy Glass-Arse is coming!'
The warning shout reverberated through the wide yard and brought men and boys hurrying out from the stables and coach-houses as Tom limped through the high archway.

Richard Humphries came to the open doorway of his office at the far end of the yard, and stood grinning broadly as the jeering shouts and raucous bursts of laughter erupted.

'Does you use a leather or rags to clean your arse, Master Potts?'

'I'll bet he polishes it till it shines.'

'He has to keep it clean so he can look through it to see when the turds are coming down.'

'Just think, lads, if he stuck a lighted candle up it, he'd be a living lantern!'

'We could bend him over and use him for a carriage lamp!'

'Hide all the stools and chairs, because if he sits down we'll be sweeping up glass for a fuckin' week!'

Tom was quite bemused by this reception, then from the stable door next to the office a man came leading the roan mare, still saddled and pillowed, and understanding came in a rush. With it came mortified embarrassment, intensified by his awareness that he was blushing furiously.

'Pay no mind to them, Master Potts,' Richard Humphries chuckled in greeting. 'They'm only having a bit of fun with you.'

'Then I wish them joy of it,' Tom replied ruefully.

'Have you come for this pillow? It is yours, isn't it?' Humphries enquired with feigned concern. 'Only if you'd asked me, I would have supplied a softer saddle, seeing as how your backside is so delicate.'

Tom stoically accepted the mockery, and merely explained

quietly, 'The horse pulled free of the tether, Master Humphries. Obviously I tied it too loosely. I trust that you'll accept my apology for it. I'll take care that it won't happen again.'

'Don't give it another thought.' Humphries was graciously magnanimous. 'My beasts can all make their own ways home when needful. Will you be wanting the mare again?'

'As soon as it's rested. Shall we say six o'clock this evening?'

'We shall indeed.' The other man grinned. 'The mare and the pillow will be waiting for you, Master Potts.'

Mustering what dignity he could, Tom left the yard, to the sounds of several voices singing in rhythmic accompaniment to his limping gait.

At the lock-up, Tom's mother immediately called him into her room and assailed him furiously.

'Where have you been? What about my breakfast? Are you trying to starve me to death now? I'm famished with hunger! Famished! If ever another poor woman ever had such a wicked, ungrateful brute for a son, then I'd like to meet her.'

'Calm down, Mother, I'll make you something to eat straight away.' He attempted to pacify her, but she was now in full flow.

'Where have you been all night? Sleeping with whores? Lying drunk in some low kennel? It's God's mercy that your poor father is in his grave, because it would break his heart to see how his son has become such an evil rotten blackguard!'

Tom escaped to light the fire in his own room and begin cooking some onion porridge. As he stirred the savoury gruel he pondered on what he had seen at Brockhill Wood.

'Why was Laylor with those other two? Where did they go with the dogs? Why was Alfie Payne spending the night there?'

The questions followed one after the other, but he had no answers to them, only mounting frustration at his own impotence.

He took his mother a bowl of porridge, enduring a further tirade of complaint and abuse, then ate some bread and cheese. He lay on the bed and drifted into an uneasy sleep, only to be roused an hour or two later by the continuous jangling of the door bell, and his mother's angry shouts for him to go and answer it.

He opened the door to find a small, thin, swarthy-featured man glaring at him.

'You were supposed to be with me an hour and a half since, Master Potts. I'm a busy man and can't waste time waiting for you to attend to your duty. Unlike yourself I'm not able to sit on my arse and do nothing day in and day out.'

George Pardoe was the parish customs and excise officer. On one day each week Tom had to accompany him while he went to various shops and checked the weights and measures used by the shopkeepers, and the taverns and inns to check that the customs duties had been paid on the spirits they sold.

Tom had completely forgotten that he was to accompany Pardoe today, and he hastened to apologize.

'I'm very sorry, Master Pardoe, I'm afraid that our appointment had slipped my mind. I'll come with you straight away, just let me get my hat and staff.'

'Humph!' Pardoe grunted disparagingly. 'Cashmore never forgot. But then, he was a proper constable he was. And well respected by everybody for being so. Nobody dared take liberties with him.'

Tom said nothing in reply. He was only too miserably aware that the news of his latest humiliation would already have spread far and wide throughout the parish, a fact which was very quickly confirmed during the rounds of the shops and taverns by the sly whispered asides and sniggers which greeted his entry into the various premises.

The final call of the afternoon was at the King's Arms in Brecon, and Tom was relieved to part company with his surly companion after the checks had been made.

He walked slowly up the long gradual slope of Ipsley Street and turned at the Big Pool to head for the lock-up. He passed the quaint half-timbered cluster of houses that comprised Salters Yard and came to the short cul-de-sac at the bottom of which stood the smithy and stable yard belonging to Davy Rowley.

'Tom Potts?' Davy Rowley called and came out onto the roadway to face him. 'It's strange, isn't it, that though we're now pretty close neighbours I hardly ever set eyes on you.'

The young man was in shirt-sleeves, wearing the fringed leather apron of his calling, and hefting the heavy sledgehammer in his hand as if it were a child's wooden toy. He was the visual epitome of handsome, youthful strength and vigour, and Tom could only ruefully concede that Davy Rowley would make a far more fitting marital partner for a beautiful young girl like Amy than an ungainly ageing failure like himself.

Fighting to control his involuntarily stirrings of jealousy, he managed to smile pleasantly.

'Well, just lately I've been working some odd hours, Master Rowley, and haven't been here about in the town centre a great deal.'

'Oh, haven't you? Where have you been, then? Hanging around Amy Danks?' The young man bared his strong white teeth in a grin which was more a savage snarl. 'Is that why she's turned against me, all of a sudden?'

Puzzled by the hostility glinting in the other man's eyes, Tom shook his head. 'No. I've hardly had a glimpse of Amy.'

'I don't believe you,' Rowley spat out. 'I reckon that you've been poisoning her mind against me. Telling her lies about me.'

'I've done nothing of the sort,' Tom protested. 'I've already told you that I've hardly had a glimpse of her these last days. And why would I want to tell her lies about you when I hardly know you?'

'Because you want her for yourself, don't you? Well, you'll not get her, Potts. I'll make sure of that. I'll make very sure.'

He turned and stalked back down the cul-de-sac, swinging the heavy sledgehammer furiously from side to side as if he were wielding it against an enemy.

'Is he jealous of me?' Tom wondered. 'Is he jealous of my relationship with Amy? It can't be. Can it?'

Tom walked on, debating furiously with himself. 'Amy must have indicated that she's very fond of me, otherwise why would he talk to me in such a manner? Or am I reading too much into this?'

He pulled out his pocket watch and checked the time.

'Dammit, it's coming up for six o'clock, I've not time to go and find Amy now. I have to fetch the mare.'

Forty-Two

'It's nearly six o'clock, I have to go.'

Eleri Turner threw off the bedclothes and started to get up, but Hugh Laylor immediately reached out and pulled her tight against his naked body.

'Not yet,' he whispered urgently. 'Stay a while longer.'

He pushed her onto her back and nuzzled her breasts with his lips, taking the large brown nipples between his teeth, gently nipping and sucking until they grew erect.

'No, Hugh,' she whimpered. 'I really do have to go. Joseph will be home shortly, and he already suspects us.'

'Let him suspect all he wants.' Hugh Laylor's breathing was quick and throaty, his hands moving over her body, stroking, fondling, exploring every intimacy of her flesh.

'No, I must go.' She tried to push him away, but was powerless against his strength. He moved on top of her, forcing her thighs open with his own, thrusting deeply into her hot moistness. She cried out and her fingers dug into his powerful shoulders, her hips jerking upwards to meet his thrusts.

On the landing outside the closed bedroom door, Hugh Laylor's ancient crone of a housekeeper listened avidly to the gasps and moans and the frantic creaking of the bed, and pushed her hand between her toothless gums to stifle her cackles of lewd laughter.

When the creaking stilled and only the sounds of heavy panting could be heard through the door, the ancient crone lifted her skirts and scurried back downstairs with a light-footed speed that belied her advanced years.

In the bedroom Hugh Laylor was smiling contentedly as he watched his mistress dressing.

She saw his smile and snapped irritably, 'It's all very fine for you to lie there grinning like the cat who's drunk the cream, but that miserable old swine will be back at home by now, and when I get there he'll be throwing accusations at my head.'

'And you will tell him to go hang himself, as you always do, my darling.' He chuckled, then added, 'Oh, by the way, would you tell Gareth that I need my last night's bill settling as soon as possible. If it were just him personally I wouldn't press, but I'm damned if I'll let that blackguard Dolton keep me waiting for my cash.'

Eleri Turner's youthfully smooth complexion suddenly looked aged and wrinkled with worry. 'He's getting out of control again! He'll bring us both to ruin! Because if Old Misery Guts finds out, he'll throw both of us out of the house. I know he will! Then what will happen to us?'

'You're worrying unduly,' Laylor soothed her. 'The dogs are well trained, and money keeps mouths well closed.'

Her white teeth showed in a bitter grimace. 'And keeps me in the bed of a man I cannot stand the touch of.'

Laylor shrugged casually. 'Necessity can be a hard master at times, my darling.'

'But it's so easy for you, isn't it!' she flared in sudden temper. 'You only ever make promises, and never keep them!'

His smile hardened, and he chided her, 'Don't be sharp with me! I shall keep all my promises when I'm in a position to do so. Until then, you must be patient. Now give me a kiss, and go back home to your husband.'

'Here you are, Master Potts. The mare has been fed, watered and well rested, and your pillow's been well plumped up for you.' Richard Humphries greeted Tom genially, while in the background some of his workmen sniggered together.

'Thank you.' Tom took the proffered reins and led the horse from the yard, once again to the softly chanted accompaniment.

As he headed for the lock-up a woman came running along Red Lion Street towards him, waving her arms and shouting, 'Hey, I wants a word wi' you, Potts! I wants a word!' As she neared him he recognized the irate features of Nance Harper.

He halted and waited for her to reach him, before asking, 'What can I do for you, Mrs Harper?'

'I wants the bastard locked up! I wants him done proper this time!

'Who?'

'That bastard Alfie Payne, o' course! Who else?'

'What has he done?'

'What's he done?' she screeched furiously, shaking her clenched fists in Tom's face. 'What's he done?'

He took an involuntarily step backwards as her knuckles flailed past his nose.

'I'll tell you what the evil bastard's done. He's gone and got poor Sal near torn to fuckin' bits and pieces, so he has! He oughter be hung! He oughter be swinging on a fuckin' gibbet!'

From the corner of his eye Tom saw that her hysterical screeching was already attracting interested onlookers.

'Look, Mrs Harper, the best thing is for you to come into the lock-up with me, and then tell me all about it. You need to calm down a bit so that I can understand exactly what's happened. Come now, please. Come inside the lock-up.'

She followed him into the building and along the cell passage spouting epithets and threats against Alfie Payne with every step.

In the back yard he let the mare go then said again, 'Now calm down, and explain what it is that Payne's done this time.'

'He rented her out like some wild beast to be hunted by fuckin' dogs!' The woman was so agitated that her breaths were ragged gasps, and she could not restrain from shaking her clenched fists in the air. 'The poor little cow was fritted to death, so her was. And there's dog bites all over her legs and arse. It was them two bastards Dolton and Jenkins who done it, and it was that bad rotten husband of hers that rented her out for it.'

'When did this happen, and where?' Tom demanded.

'Up in Brockhill Wood yesterday. Alfie took her up there first thing yesterday morning, and he brought her back here today. And now the bastard is in the Red Lion swilling the money he got for it down his fuckin' throat. Sal's legs are all bandaged up, because her was so bit and bleeding they had to fetch Dr Laylor. Her can hardly stand, the poor little cow can't. Her's laying on her bed crying with the pain.'

An intense anger was igniting within Tom's mind, but he realized that he must not allow it to impel him into headlong action. He must keep full control over his emotions, and behave coolly and rationally.

'Let me get this clear, Mrs Harper. Jenkins and Dolton gave

money to Alfie Payne, and in return he took his wife to Brockhill Wood to be hunted down by dogs?'

'That's what I's just told you, aren't it?' she screeched indignantly.

'When the dogs ran her down, did either Jenkins or Dolton do anything else to her?'

'How do you mean?'

'Did either of them make sexual overtures towards her?'

Nance Harper's grimy features twisted uncertainly, then understanding slowly dawned. 'Ohhhh, you means did they try and shag her?'

He nodded.

'No. They just slung her across the back of a horse and took her to some house in the wood for the night, and Laylor come and bandaged her up. And then today Alfie slung her on a horse and brought her back home, just like she was a sack o' spuds, the poor little cow.'

Tom's thoughts raced. He knew that Sal Payne would not say that her husband had forced her to become a human quarry, and therefore she would appear as a willing participant in the hunt; and hunting a willing human was not a statutory crime. Yet still his hopes rapidly burgeoned.

'Listen, Mrs Harper, I need your help, if we're to make those three pay for what they've done to Sal! Will you? Will you help me?'

'O' course I 'ull!' she assented instantly.

'I need you to bring me the clothes that Sal was wearing when this happened to her. Just bundle them up and bring them as they are. Don't try to clean them or brush them or anything else. You just bundle them up and bring them as they are. Can you do that right away?'

'I can.'

'Then go now, and be as quick as you can,' he urged her, as he shepherded her to the door.

He could hardly restrain his impatience and paced up and down the cell passage for what seemed to be endless hours, but in reality was only scant minutes, until the hinges squealed and she reappeared carrying a bundle of clothing.

His hands were trembling with tension as he took it from her. Now he needed above all else to be alone.

'Thank you, Mrs Harper. Remember this, you must not

breathe a single word to anyone about talking to me, or giving me these clothes. Not even to your nearest and dearest. Is that understood?'

'All right,' she agreed, and drew her forefinger across her throat. 'I'll slit this afore I breathes a word.'

'Good! Go back and look after Sal, Mrs Harper. You can leave me to deal with this matter now.'

She glared at him challengingly. 'When? When am you going to deal with it?' Lifting her clenched fists she threatened him, 'If you don't deal with it right quick, then I'll take these to them three bastards and chance me head being bust open by 'em!'

Tom gently folded his hands over her fists, and promised quietly, 'I swear to you on all that I hold holy that I'll deal with this matter; and I'll make sure that these men get their just deserts. But you will have to trust me to do it in my own way and my own time.'

She stared searchingly into his eyes for long, long moments, and then slowly nodded and lowered her fists.

'All right, Master Potts. Sarft, lanky, gangly cunt that you may be, I reckon that I can trust you to do what's right by Sal.'

'You can,' he assured her firmly. 'You go back to your friend now, and leave this matter to me.'

When she was gone, he drew long deep breaths to try and slow the excited pounding of his heart and hurried up to his room with the bundle of clothing.

'Thomassss? Thomasss? When are you going to empty my commode? It's stinking my room out, so it is. What did I ever do so bad in my life, to deserve being cursed with such a cruel-hearted monster for a son?'

'God give me strength,' Tom gritted out between clenched teeth, and then consoled himself. 'Never mind, the light will be good for another couple of hours so I'll still have time enough.'

Aloud, he called, 'I'm coming, Mother, try not to upset your-self so. The smell's not nearly so bad as you imagine it to be.'

As soon as he had done the unpleasant chore he laid out the clothing and made a careful examination of it.

There were several hairs embedded in the torn bloodstained cloth of the shabby gown and he subjected them to lengthy study under the microscope. He judged them to be a mixture of dog and horse hairs, and could have crowed aloud with delight when he found that several appeared to match the sand-coloured sorrel hairs he had found on Ann Washwood's gown.

'When I find the horse, then I shall have found the man. Once I've settled Mother for the night, I'll go and see what John has found.'

Forty-Three

'Halt! Who goes there? Stand and be recognized!' The staccato challenge came from the wooded shadows bordering the Mount Pleasant roadway, and Tom reined in and shouted, 'I'm Thomas Potts, headborough constable of Tardebigge parish.'

Three mounted troopers emerged into the bright moonlight and Tom recognized Erasmus Dolton.

'Good evening, Master Potts, and where might you be off to?' Dolton greeted him, politely enough.

'Good evening, Sergeant Dolton. I'm on my way to see John Hollis, my fellow constable. His house is close to Webheath,' Tom answered with equal politeness.

'You might do well to keep a sharp eye for anyone lurking about while you're on your way there and back, Master Potts. Josiah Danks chased off a prowler from his house about half an hour since. That's why we're in ambush here, in case the prowler might still be about. You never know, it might be the maniac who slaughtered Annie Washwood.'

Concern struck through Tom as he heard Dolton's words.

'Thank you for telling me, Sergeant Dolton. I'll go and see Josiah Danks directly.'

He kicked his horse into a canter, and headed for Danks' isolated house.

'The girls was undressing for bed, and Amy come into the room and saw a face looking through the window, didn't you, Amy.' Josiah Danks sought confirmation from his eldest daughter.

'That's right, Dad. I saw it as plain as plain could be. I skrawked out because it give me such a fright.' Amy's pretty face was still strained with nervous tension. 'When I come into the room, I heard a sort of squeal from outside, and I looked at the window and saw the face.'

'I run into the room, and Amy pointed to the window, and strike me if the bugger warn't still a-looking through the glass.' Her father took up the story. 'O' course, I snatched up me gun and run outside then, and he took off like a bat out o' hell. And I give chase, but he run like the wind, he did, and he soon left me standing. I shot at him, but he never faltered. God damn me for a bloody fool for missing the shot, because most times I'd have fetched him down like a flighting partridge! Then Erasmus Dolton and his toy soldiers come riding up and said they'd been patrolling and heard the shot and come to see what was what.'

'Dolton and his men?' Tom queried.

'That's right. The pity was that they come from the opposite direction to where he run, or they might have copped him else.'

'So it seems I can take Dolton off my list of suspects,' Tom told himself, and after brief consideration asked, 'How tall would you say he was?'

The other man shrugged. 'About my height, I would reckon.'

'And what pane was he looking through?'

'That one there.' Amy pointed to the lowest of the rows of leaded panes.

'Then he must have been kneeling or crouching,' Tom mused aloud, then, 'Will you all stay inside for the present, please?'

Going outside he took his bulls-eye lantern from his satchel and lit it. He moved slowly, sweeping the lantern beam over the wall and the ground, then drew a sharp breath and abruptly halted a pace from the window. On the grassy ground beneath its frame lay a small huddled heap of bloody fur and flesh.

Tom remained stock-still for several seconds, evaluating what he could see, then crouched low and with infinite care inserted his hand beneath the limp, still warm body of the dead rabbit and with his fingertips gently felt the bloodied ground beneath, utilizing his delicate sense of touch to find the indented narrow slits that were the mute testimony to the impacts of the stabbing knife-blade.

'He was watching the girls, and stabbing this rabbit while he watched. He's truly a perverted maniac!' Tom felt a shiver of horrified fear. 'Is he targeting Amy? Is it her he's after now?' Fighting to sound calm he tapped the window and called, 'Will you come out here please, Master Danks?'

When the gamekeeper joined him, Tom shone the light onto the dead animal.

'He's a bloody loony, right enough,' Danks spat out angrily.

'You'll need to keep a close guard on your daughters, until I arrest him,' Tom said.

'Have you got an idea about who he might be, then?'

'Oh yes,' Tom nodded, 'I've an idea all right, but proving it is another matter.'

'Never mind the proof,' Danks growled menacingly. 'Just you tell me who you thinks it is, and I'll dispose of him meself. I've took the lives of Frenchies, Spaniards and Yankees, and it'll be a pleasure to take this bugger's.'

'I can't do that, Master Danks,' Tom said, although inwardly he was sorely tempted to give the name of his prime suspect to the gamekeeper. For a few moments he remained undecided as to what to do next. Then, driven by his fears for Amy's safety, he made a decision, and told Danks grimly, 'But rest assured, I'll arrest my suspect this very night. I'll be much easier in my mind, though, if I know that you'll be here at home with your family.'

'Oh, you can be sure o' that, Master Potts. I'll be here, with my guns primed and loaded. If that bloody loony dares to come back, then he'll not leave here alive, that I can guarantee you.'

Tom rode directly to John Hollis' cottage and when his colleague answered the door, told him without preamble, 'I want you to come and help me to make an arrest, John.'

'Who is it?'

'Gareth Jenkins. Joseph Turner's stepson.'

Hollis' lean features creased in a smile. 'Did he steal it, then?'

'Steal what?' Tom was bemused by the question.

'That sand-coloured sorrel you asked me to look for. I've found three of them so far, and one of them was in Joe Turner's stables. I was coming to report to you tomorrow, after I'd checked what sand-coloureds Will Shayler might have found.'

Hearing this, any remaining doubts as to the wisdom of what he intended to do were swept away from Tom's mind.

'Fetch your staff, John, and saddle up. I'm not arresting him for horse-stealing, but for murder.'

'Murder?' Hollis' long jaw dropped open with shock.

'That's right,' Tom confirmed, and a grim elation suddenly gripped him. 'I'm arresting him for the murder of Ann Washwood, and while I'm at it, I'm going to arrest Alfie Payne as well.'

'What for?' Hollis asked.

'Because I feel like doing so.' Tom grinned. 'And who knows what he might tell us when we get him into the cells.'

As John Hollis turned away to fetch his staff, Tom added, 'Oh, and bring a shovel with you. We've got some digging to do as well.'

Forty-Four

On the ride back into Redditch the prospect of the physical confrontation which he knew that these arrests would entail was causing nervous flutterings in Tom's stomach and a quickening heartbeat.

'Dear God, give me the courage to carry it through,' he prayed silently. 'Give me the strength to tackle both of them.'

As they neared the junction of the Front and Back Hills, Tom was debating with himself whether or not to inform Joseph Blackwell of what he was going to do.

'Shall I take the Front Hill which leads to Blackwell's house, or the Back Hill which leads to Brecon?' A disturbing train of thought intruded upon him. 'What if Blackwell were to tell me to wait before arresting Jenkins? What if he says I need more concrete proof? No! I can't risk leaving Jenkins at liberty, not now that he's stalking Amy!'

He led the way down the steep incline of the Back Hill.

'Is your master at home?' Tom asked the neat little maid-servant who opened the door to his knocking.

'He is.'

'Please tell him that Constables Potts and Hollis must speak with him immediately.

'What about?'

'Never you mind, missy,' Tom admonished her sternly. 'We're here in the King's name. So just go and tell your master that we must speak with him.'

She stuck her tongue out cheekily, and flounced back into the house, only to reappear almost immediately. 'The master'll see you. Follow me.'

She led them to the first door on the right and ushered them in.

Joseph Turner was sitting at his desk, and he frowned at Tom. 'This call had better be for a very good reason, Constable, because I don't like being interrupted at my work.'

Tom swallowed hard, and fought down his nervousness to announce firmly. 'Yes, sir, I have a very good reason for coming here. I intend to arrest your stepson on suspicion of murder.'

'What? Murder? What the hell are you talking about, man?' Joseph Turner rose to his feet, his expression one of total stupe-faction.

'I've reason to believe that your stepson, Gareth Jenkins, murdered Ann Washwood. Where is he now, sir?' Tom demanded.

'I've no idea, but what makes you think he's a murderer?'

'I've good reason to believe that he is.'

'What reason?'

'You will learn it in due course, sir, but this is neither the time or place. Have you any notion where he might be found?' Tom pressed.

Still struggling to come to terms with what he had heard, Joseph Turner muttered, 'He'll be in some tavern or other, worthless drunken wastrel that he is. But I can't believe that he's killed a woman. How can I tell his mother what you are accusing him of?'

'I take no pleasure in bringing you this news, sir,' Tom told him sincerely. 'If you'll excuse us, we must go in search of him.'

They left Turner shaking his head, as if he still couldn't comprehend what had just taken place.

Moving at a gallop, Tom and John Hollis went from inn to inn, and finally saw the sand-coloured sorrel tethered in a line of other horses outside the Unicorn Inn close to the town's central crossroads. They tethered their own horses and Tom went to the sorrel.

Its hide was lathered in sweat as if it had been hard ridden.

'I'll get him to come outside and then arrest him,' Tom decided. 'You wait here, John.'

He pushed open the door and went inside the inn. There were several rooms opening off the entrance lobby and as Tom looked inside the first a waiter came into the lobby carrying a tray of drinks. Tom beckoned him.

'Where is Gareth Jenkins?'

'He's playing cards with some other blokes in the snug. I'm just taking these into 'em.'

'How long has he been here?' Tom asked.

'Only a few minutes.'

'Will you ask him to come out to his horse,' Tom requested. 'Tell him the beast has collapsed.'

'All right.'

Tom stepped back outside and stood waiting at the side of the door. Now that the moment of confrontation had arrived he found to his own surprise that although he was still nervous, at the same time he was excited.

The door slammed open and Gareth Jenkins came out, cursing, 'Bloody horse! I'll put a ball through its bloody head!'

He brushed past Tom and walked along the line, then halted, staring in puzzlement at his horse.

He turned as Tom came up behind him and John Hollis moved in from the side. Looking from one to the other he demanded arrogantly, 'What the bloody hell is going on here? What are you clowns doing?'

'We're arresting you in the King's name, Master Jenkins, and you had better come quietly,' Tom told him.

'What?' Jenkins' eyes bulged with shock. 'Are you mad? You can't arrest me!'

'We can, and you are now under arrest.' Tom was trembling with nervous tension, but inwardly marvelling at how calm and even his voice was.

'You'll come with us now to the lock-up. We've no desire to use force, Master Jenkins, but we will do so if you refuse to accompany us.'

'But why are you arresting me? What am I supposed to have done?' Jenkins looked and sounded so genuinely nonplussed that for a fleeting second doubt as to his guilt flashed across Tom's mind.

'You'll be told everything once you are in the lock-up. So just come along quietly,' Tom repeated and took his arm

For a moment it seemed that Jenkins was going to resist.

John Hollis brandished his staff in front of Jenkins' face and warned him harshly, 'If you don't do what we say, then I'll break your head with this.' He grabbed the young man's other arm and jerked him into motion.

'All right, I'll come quietly.' Jenkins' face was twitching with fury. 'But you fucking clowns will regret this. I'll have your guts for garters. You're going to wish that you'd never been born by the time I've finished with you.'

Relief flooded through Tom as Jenkins allowed himself to be drawn along without a struggle.

As soon as they reached the lock-up they locked Jenkins into a cell and only then did Tom tell him, 'You've been arrested on suspicion of the murder of Ann Washwood.'

'Murder? Me? Are you fucking mad?' Jenkins almost screeched. 'I've not murdered anybody! You are fucking mad! By God you'll pay for this! You'll pay, all right!'

'Come on. We'll go for Payne now.' Tom jerked his head at John Hollis, and they left the lock-up with Jenkins' screeching protests reverberating in their ears.

The tap room of the Red Lion was packed with drinkers and the hubbub of talk and laughter could be heard from a distance.

'I think we should do what we did with Jenkins and get Alfie Payne outside before arresting him,' Tom proposed.

John Hollis' face was flushed with excitement and he chanted aloud:

'Mr Boney, your heart is stony.

If England you invade,

With your ragged crew,

We'll run you through,

And put you to bed with a spade.'

Tom experienced a rush of concern, fearing that his friend was having a relapse into madness.

Hollis saw his expression and laughed. 'Don't worry, Tom. I'm not going off my head again, I'm just enjoying myself. I'm really looking forward to seeing Payne's face when we take him in. I've always hated him, you see.'

Tom grinned with relief, but was uncomfortably conscious of his own mounting trepidation at the prospect of fighting with Payne once more.

Some ragged urchins were playing in the street outside the tavern, and Tom beckoned one of them and gave him a penny. 'Go inside and tell Alfie Payne that a gentleman wants to speak to him, and I'll give you another penny.'

'Ta, mister.' The urchin whooped with glee and went into the tap room. He returned shortly, with Alfie Payne lurching drunkenly behind him.

Tom tossed the boy another penny and then, steeling himself, told Payne, 'I'm arresting you in the King's name.'

Payne blinked owlishly, then mouthed a curse and came at Tom with raised fists.

John Hollis stepped forwards and swung his staff. The heavy leaded crown thumped against the side of Payne's head, and he staggered sideways and fell. Tom and Hollis grabbed his arms and half carried, half dragged him along the street, John Hollis chanting exultantly,

'We think it right with you to fight

For our liberty and laws;

The God we serve will us preserve

All in so good a cause.'

They locked the still half-stunned Payne into the cell furthest from the one occupied by Jenkins.

Tom grinned thankfully, and looked at his colleague with a touch of awe.

'Dear God, John, but you're a man of action right enough!'

'I am, aren't I,' Hollis agreed complacently. 'What shall we do now?'

'We ride to Brockhill Wood and start digging.'

'What are you expecting to dig up?'

'Human remains, John,' Tom told him soberly. 'Ann Washwood's innards, and the body of her unborn child.'

Gareth Jenkins began shouting, but they ignored him and left, locking the outer door behind them.

The barking of the German shepherds slowly lessened and ceased as one by one they were overcome by the laudanum-soaked raw meat. Tom carefully levered the door open and after making sure that the doped dogs were securely fastened into the front room the two men went down to the cellar, and by lantern light began the task of excavation.

When the flagstones had been removed Tom took a long stick and thrust it down into the earth, then pulled it up and sniffed its end.

'Jesus!' He grimaced in disgust. 'There's rotted meat down there all right. About a yard deep.'

As shovel-load after shovel-load came out of the pit, so the nauseatingly foul stench increasingly thickened the air.

John Hollis gagged violently, and he gasped, 'I'll need to go outside for a breath of clean air, Tom, or I'll be spewing my stomach up else.'

'Yes, go on up for a while.' Tom was beginning to feel increasingly queasy himself despite the long years of experience he had had of death and decay, but he was desperate to obtain evidence, and forced himself to continue shovelling out the earth.

When he judged that he was only inches from the remains, he positioned the lantern to cast its beam on the bottom of the hole, and carefully removed the earth with his hands. His fingers dug into corrupted stinking flesh and when he peered at his hands he frowned doubtfully. There appeared to be a mass of short hairs mingled with the putrid mess.

'John?' he shouted urgently. 'There's a pump and bucket in the back room. Bring me a bucket of water down here straight away.'

When Hollis came, Tom told him, 'Hold the light close to my hands.' With infinite care he lowered the mess into the bucket of water and worked it gently with his fingers to cleanse the earth away, then peered closely at what was left.

'This is a piece of skin and hair.' Acute disappointment coursed through him. 'And to me it looks as if it could be a dog's.'

With redoubled urgency Tom scrabbled to uncover more, and found the rotted eyeless head of a large dog.

'Damn and blast it!' he growled in angry frustration.

'Sorry, Tom.' Hollis emitted a half-strangled apology and putting the lantern down ran up the steps and outside, where he fell down onto his knees and retched violently.

Tom wanted with all his heart and soul to follow his friend and escape from this nightmarish task. But he forced himself to continue at his gruesome work, until he was satisfied that the sole contents of the pit were the remains of the dead animal.

Only then did he clamber from the hole, refill it and carefully replace the flagstones.

He reopened the dogs' room and reaffixed the outer door's fastenings.

John Hollis shamefacedly apologized, 'I'm sorry for letting you down like I did, Tom. I've always been somewhat kettle-stomached, I fear.'

'You haven't let me down, John. Quite the contrary, in fact. Without you I'd never have managed to take Jenkins or Payne in.' Tom ruefully examined the sorry state of his hands and clothing by the lantern light. 'I stink as bad as that dog. I can't go home like this.'

'Then come to my place. We can skirt around the woods and get to my house without anyone seeing us. You can clean up there.'

'People might not be able to see us,' Tom replied wryly, 'but I'll bet they can smell me if they come within fifty paces.'

Forty-Five

At John Hollis' cottage Tom stripped off his jacket, breeches, waistcoat and shirt and put them to boil in the wash-copper, then sluiced himself from head to toe in the stream that ran behind the cottage, gasping and shivering in the cold water. He put on John Hollis' spare smock and breeches and as dawn was breaking rode into Redditch and went directly to Joseph Blackwell's house to rouse its occupants from sleep.

'What in Heaven's name did you think you were doing, Master Potts?' Blackwell's pallid features were scowling in disbelief. 'What proof do you have against either Jenkins or Payne that will convince a court of law of their guilt?'

Tom was racked with nervous strain, and gritty-eyed and bone-weary from lack of sleep, but he was grimly determined to pursue his course of action.

'Unfortunately I didn't find the conclusive proof I hoped for last night, sir. It was a dog buried in that cellar. But after the incident of the prowler at Josiah Danks' house, I couldn't risk leaving either Jenkins or Payne at liberty. I'm sure of Jenkins' guilt, and equally sure that Payne knows what Jenkins has done. I believe that Payne will offer to turn King's evidence against Jenkins, when I put pressure on him.'

'You had better pray he does so,' Blackwell snapped, 'because I don't think that horse hairs on women's gowns are going to be sufficient evidence to convict Jenkins of anything.' He paused, steepling his fingers beneath his chin and squinting as if he were trying to discern something that was half-hidden. 'Dolton? Erasmus Dolton? Where do you think he comes into all this, Master Potts?'

'Well, he was definitely involved in the human-hunting of Sal Payne, sir,' Tom said slowly. 'But I don't think that he bears any guilt for the murder of Ann Washwood, or of the first victim. I'm convinced that the killer is an exceptionally athletic younger man. Dolton is too fat and old to run fast or vault gates like the killer can.'

'I agree.' Blackwell nodded.

To Tom's surprise the older man's thin lips quirked momentarily in a bleak smile.

'Well, you have certainly put the cat among the pigeons with this latest exploit, and fully justified my confidence in your personal qualities and capabilities. I don't doubt but that the town will be in uproar before many more hours have elapsed, so I shall order the yeomanry to mount a guard over the lock-up, and inform Lord Aston and the vestry of what has occurred. In the meantime I suggest that you press on with finding some really conclusive evidence. Good day to you, Master Potts.'

'Good day, sir.' Tom experienced simultaneous relief and gratification that Blackwell was displaying such faith in him, and felt his own confidence soaring as he walked from the house and around the Chapel Green.

He suddenly remembered that Jenkins' horse was still tethered outside the Unicorn. 'Dear God! I hope it's not been stolen during the night!'

He broke into an ungainly run, until the sharp pains in his wounded buttock brought him back to a limping shuffle, and sighed thankfully when he came in sight of the inn and saw that the sandy sorrel was still there.

'I'll take it back to the lock-up, give it a thorough grooming, and check the saddlery over. There might be fibres from Ann Washwood's gown on it, or even some of her hairs,' Tom hoped fervently. 'God only knows I need as much proof as I can find.'

There was a man moving up the hill towards the sorrel and Tom recognized the bowed body and bent head of King William, the town simpleton. King William reached the horse and began stroking its neck and patting its flanks.

Tom smiled sympathetically. 'The poor benighted soul has a kind heart despite all his own afflictions,' he thought.

'Hello, William,' he greeted him as he reached the man, and gently patted his shoulder. 'Is this a friend of yours?'

King William nodded his shaggy head, beaming with delight, words tumbling from his distorted mouth accompanied by sprays of saliva.

'Me mate this is. We shares our bed, don't we, Ginger.' He flung his arms around the beast's neck and kissed it fervently. 'Me mate's gone now. Gone somewheres else. I misses him. I misses him. I'm cold in that bed now, I am. I gets cold! I likes ginger-tops, I does. I likes 'em.'

'I know you do, William,' Tom smiled. 'But now I have to take Ginger here back home with me.'

'Back home? Take him back home?'

'That's right,' Tom nodded.

'Ohhhh!' The simpleton crowed with delight, clapping his hand like an excited child. 'Take him back home! Take him back home! Can I come? Can I come?' the simpleton begged. 'Ginger's me mate.'

Tom hadn't got the heart to turn the man away. 'All right, you can come with us, and I'll give you some breakfast as well. Would you like that?'

'Yeah! I'd like some breakfust I 'ud. I'm real clemmed, I am. Real clemmed.'

Tom let King William lead the horse, and all the way to the lock-up the simpleton was babbling into the beast's ear. Tom paid little attention; his mind was too engrossed with how to prove the case against Jenkins and Payne.

They reached the lock-up and Tom halted and reached for the reins.

'Here we are then, William. You can come in with me, and I'll give you some breakfast.'

'Noooo! Noooo!' the simpleton cried out in protest. 'Ginger go back home now! Ginger go back home!'

He tried to tug the reins from Tom's hand repeating constantly, 'Ginger go back home! Ginger go back home! The chap likes Ginger, he does. He likes pretty little ginger-tops, he does. He likes ginger-tops. Ginger go back home now.'

'He likes pretty little ginger-tops!' The words brought a flash of memory into Tom's mind. A memory of the simpleton babbling about the hidden man watching the pretty little ginger-top down by the Big Pool.

Sudden ideas clamoured for attention, causing Tom to catch his breath. Could the pretty little ginger-top have been Siobhan Docherty? And could the hidden man watching her have been the same man who chased her? Could this be more proof of Jenkins guilt?

'Let's see if he takes the beast to Joseph Turner's stables,' Tom decided, and relinquished the reins. 'Take Ginger back home then, William.'

As Tom expected, King William headed down Alcester Street, but then just before they reached Salters Yard, William veered sharply into the cul-de-sac leading to Davy Rowley's smithy and stables.

'Whoa, William! Whoa!' Tom grabbed the reins and halted the horse. 'You're going the wrong way. Ginger's home is down in Brecon.'

'Noooo! Ginger lives down here! Ginger lives here!' William pointed towards Rowley's yard. He became very agitated and tried to snatch the reins back, shouting plaintively, 'Nooo! Nooo! Ginger go back home! Ginger go back home! The chap likes Ginger! The chap likes Ginger! Ginger go back home!'

An early passer-by stopped to shout at them. 'What's all the bloody rattle about?'

Confused thoughts were once more creating a maelstrom in Tom's mind, and his overwhelming instinct was to get away and back to the lock-up. He turned to the curious passer-by. 'Give me a hand here, will you? I need to get this beast to the lock-up, and poor King William is getting all moithered about it, but he means no harm. Just hold him still while I get the beast away.'

'Ahr, all right.' The passer-by came and held William back while Tom quickly led the horse away, his ears ringing with the simpleton's pathetic wailings.

'Noooo! Noooo! Ginger go back home! Ginger go back home! The chap likes ginger-tops, he does!'

The loud rattling of the horseshoes upon the stone flags of the cell passage roused both Gareth Jenkins and Alfie Payne, their loud shouts in turn roused Widow Potts, and her harsh screeching echoed down from the upper floor.

Tom doggedly endured the bedlam and led the horse through into the rear yard, removed its harness, saddle and blanket, and gave it water from the pump. He carried all the accoutrements up to his room and then went in to his mother.

'You're killing me, you bad, wicked hound from hell! This noise is all your fault!' she screeched at the top of her voice, her hanging jowls shaking, her face almost purple. 'And where's my breakfast? And when are you going to empty my commode? It stinks worse than a midden.'

Tom felt light-headed and weak from lack of sleep and food. He lusted only to lie down on his bed and close his eyes. The shouting voices were dinning into his eras, drumming into his brain, driving him almost mad. His control abruptly snapped, and he roared, 'Shut up, Mother! Or I swear to God, I'll gag and bury you six feet deep!'

She was stunned into silence, and stared open-jawed at him, her watery eyes blinking rapidly.

Tom rushed down the stone steps and hammered on both cell doors in turn, roaring angrily, 'Keep quiet, or I'll have you kicked to pieces as soon as my friends get here!'

The threat silenced both men.

Tom went wearily back upstairs. He re-entered his mother's

room and scowling, ordered her brusquely, 'Wake me up in three hours. Not a minute less, and not a minute more; and if anyone comes ringing the bell, then poke your head out of the window and tell them to come back in three and a half hours.'

Then he went to his own room to throw himself upon his narrow cot, and marvelling at how this particular worm had at last turned, was asleep within scant moments.

Forty-Six

The dream was nightmarishly vivid. His assailant was concealed by thick grey fog, but the spear point was plunging into Tom's body over and over again.

Tom came awake with a jerk, as the ferrule of his mother's walking stick jabbed painfully into his ribs once more.

'It's three hours, you vile bully! Not a minute more and not a minute less,' she screeched.

He wielded off another jab and rose instantly to hurry down into the yard and sluice his head beneath the pump. The cold water roused him to full wakefulness, and he became aware of a hubbub emanating from the road outside. He went to the front entrance and unlocking the door stepped outside, to be taken aback in bewildered amazement as a roar of cheering greeted him.

The crowd numbered hundreds, and the dismounted line of red-coated yeomanry troopers were hard pressed to hold them back as they surged forwards, yelling plaudits, hands reaching to touch Tom.

'Well now, Constable Potts, how does it feel to be the hero of the town?' The mahogany-complexioned Captain Emmot saluted Tom with his drawn sabre. 'Allow me to offer you my own congratulations for bringing these villains to justice. I'm looking forward immensely to seeing them hung.'

Erasmus Dolton came to Tom with an outstretched arm. 'Let me shake your hand, Constable Potts. By God, you're a shrewd

man and no mistake. Those two murdering bastards had me
fooled good and proper. I admits that to me own shame. They
had me fooled good and proper, so they did.' Dolton grasped
Tom's hand and pumped it vigorously up and down.

Joseph Blackwell's manservant forced his way through the
crowd and shouted to Tom, 'My master says that you are to
attend at the Fox and Goose at two o'clock sharp, Master Potts.'

Still bewildered by this mass demonstration, Tom could only
nod abstractedly. Needing desperately to collect his thoughts,
he excused himself to the two troopers and returned back inside
the lock-up, barring the door behind him.

'Master Potts, I must speak with you.' Jenkins' voice was
muffled and muted by the thick cell door, and Tom opened the
small viewing hatch and saw that the young man appeared to
be very frightened.

'What do you want, Master Jenkins?'

'Is that a lynch mob outside? Is it? You have to protect me!
It's your duty! I'm innocent of any crime whatsoever! Totally
innocent!'

'No, it's not a lynch mob, and yes, I know that it's my duty
to protect you. So be calm. I'll bring you some food and water
in a while.'

Tom closed the hatch and deep in thought went slowly back
upstairs to his room. He couldn't shake the memory of King
William's agitation from his mind.

'Why was he so insistent that the horse was stabled at
Rowley's yard? Why did he say again and again "the chap likes
ginger-tops"? Why?'

The questions dominated Tom while he prepared bread,
cheese and onion for himself, his mother and the two prisoners.

When he returned to the cells with the food and water, he
opened Alfie Payne's hatch first, and totally ignoring the man's
angry, foul-mouthed protestations of innocence, merely thrust
the food and jug of water through the hatch and slammed it
shut.

When he opened the hatch of Jenkins' cell, however, he felt
driven to ask, 'Do you have any connection with Davy Rowley,
the farrier? Any business dealings with him, perhaps?'

'Yes, he's broken in a horse for me, Master Potts.' Jenkins'
previous bravado had completely deserted him, and now he
seemed near to tears, and pathetically eager to cooperate.

'I see.' This answer created a flicker of disturbance in Tom's mind, but he only nodded and asked casually, 'Is Rowley a good horse-breaker? I've a mind to buy a horse myself, and need to buy cheaply, so it will have to be an unbroken beast.'

'Yes, he's very good. He broke in my new sorrel. The one I was riding when you arrested me.'

'How long have you had the sorrel?'

'I bought it some weeks since, but only took it into my stables the day before yesterday after Rowley had finished with it.'

The flicker of disturbance in Tom's mind abruptly burgeoned into a fully fledged storm, and it took all his self control to merely nod curtly. 'Eat your food, Master Jenkins.'

He closed the hatch as Jenkins was begging plaintively, 'Please ask me anything you wish, Master Potts. I'm innocent of any crime, I do assure you. I swear on my dear mother's life that I'm an innocent man.'

Tom went back to his room and sat on his cot, fighting desperately to calm the maelstrom in his mind.

'Have I got the wrong man?' he asked himself over and over and over again. 'Have I got the wrong man?'

An hour before he was to attend the meeting at the Fox and Goose, Tom led his horse out from the lock-up and spurred it through the still sizeable crowd of eager onlookers, who once again cheered and applauded him.

He went directly to the home of Josiah Danks, and here as well the man, woman and their children rushed out to meet him and to offer their plaudits and congratulations.

He restrained himself until their initial excitement had quietened, and then asked Josiah Danks, 'May I please speak to Amy in private?'

Man and wife exchanged meaningful glances, and Josiah Danks grinned. 'You most certainly can, Master Potts.' He winked broadly. 'Or should I start getting used to calling you simply, Tom? We don't use formalities wi' members of the family.'

'You may call me whatever you will.' Tom could feel his face reddening with embarrassment as he realized that they were placing the wrong connotations on his request. 'Dear God! They think that I've come to ask her to marry me!' he thought with dismay.

She also was blushing, but her eyes were sparkling and she was smiling delightedly.

'Let us walk for a little while, Amy,' he invited her and she giggled and eagerly grasped his hand as they went off side by side, leaving the family grinning and nodding behind them.

As soon as they were out of eyeshot Tom stopped. 'Amy, I don't wish to pry into your affairs, but I must ask you something.'

She smiled radiantly. 'You can ask me anything you want, Tom dear.'

'I need to know what has happened between you and Davy Rowley, to cause him to speak so angrily to me, and accuse me of coming between the two of you.'

She frowned, disconcerted by this unexpected question, and muttered, 'I don't know if that's any of your business.'

'Perhaps not,' he conceded, 'but believe me, Amy, I am only asking you about this because it is very important that I know.'

After a moment's hesitation she said, 'All right, I'll tell you. The reason that I've fallen out with Rowley is because he tried to make free with me when we went for a walk in Pitcheroak Woods, and when I wouldn't let him have his way he went mad, and tried to force me. He said he'd slit my throat and bury me there if I didn't let him. I only managed to get away because a couple of foresters came to see why I was screaming, and Rowley ran off.' She paused, cupped Tom's face with her hands and pleaded fervently, 'You must promise that you won't say a word to my dad about this. Because if he found out, he'd kill Davy Rowley, and I don't want my dad to hang for killing anybody, even that animal.'

As he listened to her story a fierce desire to kill Davy Rowley himself swept over Tom, and it was with considerable difficulty that he acceded to her plea, then told her, 'Listen, Amy, I have to go now. I've been summoned to appear before the vestry at two o'clock. Will you be working at the Fox and Goose today?'

'Yes, I'm starting at four o'clock.'

'Perhaps I'll see you later, then.' He turned and walked quickly away from her, yet again asking himself, 'Have I arrested the wrong man? Could it be Davy Rowley who murdered Ann Washwood and the other woman? Rowley has his own transport, and he goes to different farms to do blacksmithing and farriery work. He's strong and athletic, and can easily run very fast or vault a gate.'

After hearing Amy's account of what had happened to her he was now convinced that Rowley was the prowler who had left the dead rabbit beneath her bedroom window, and he was desperately anxious about her safety.

His mind so busily weighing the connotations of what he had just been told that he didn't even notice Amy's disappointed frown, or hear her indignant protest, 'But I thought you wanted to ask me something else, Tom!'

Forty-Seven

'The bloody yeomanry won't let me near the lock-up! I can't even get near enough to call through those damned arrow slits! Everyone is calling my son a murderer! You surely can't believe that my Gareth is capable of such a crime?' Eleri Turner's tone was pleading, her face drained of all colour and wrinkled with agonizing anxiety.

'I don't know what to believe.' Hugh Laylor shrugged his shoulders uneasily.

The woman flared into angry remonstrance. 'I thought you at least would stand up for him. I knew that that swine I'm wed to would be only too happy to think the worst of my son, but I expected better from you!'

'But you've said to me before that you feared that Gareth was again getting out of control,' Laylor reminded her, with an impatient edge in his tone. 'What did you mean by that? What is it that he's done before when he's been out of control?'

'I only meant that there was an unfortunate incident when he was younger. It could have happened to anyone who was young and unaccustomed to strong drink. It was his companions who got him drunk and egged him on, when he didn't know what he was doing,' she flustered desperately. 'It wasn't his fault!'

'Tell me what he did!' Laylor's handsome features were set and hard. 'And tell me the truth! Don't try to shield him further!'

'He gave a thrashing to a trollop who tried to pick his pocket, that's all,' she muttered resentfully.

'And?' Laylor pressed.

'And later she tried to claim he had thrown acid in her face and blinded her. But of course it was all lies. All Gareth had done was to give her the thrashing she deserved. It was one of the other men with him who threw the acid over her, and he fled the country afterwards. It wasn't Gareth. All Gareth did was to thrash her for picking his pocket.'

Laylor was unconvinced by her account, but he merely replied, 'I have to go to the meeting at the Fox and Goose. I'll let you know what happens there as soon as possible.'

Forty-Eight

The increasing conviction that Rowley could be the killer tormented Tom as he rode back into the town, and the people he passed were going out of their way to call his name and shout praise for him having caught the murderers.

His entrance into the bar parlour of the Fox and Goose was greeted with more handclapping and shouts of applause.

'Bring this gentleman whatever he desires, landlord. I trust that you'll allow me to drink to your health, Constable Potts, and to offer you my sincerest congratulations.' Lord Aston smiled, enthroned in the centre of the vestrymen like a monarch surrounded by his courtiers.

'Gladly, my lord.' Tommy Fowkes, red-faced and sweating profusely, bowed low and obsequiously enquired of Tom, 'What's your pleasure, Constable Potts? If I might make bold to suggest, I've just broached a keg of the very finest French brandy. Might that be to your taste?'

'Yes, indeed it will be, thank you,' Tom assented, knowing that at this particular moment he was in desperate need of a strong drink to give him the courage for what he was about to do.

'Now then, Constable, will you tell us what it was that put you on to them two murdering bastards?' Jason Holyoake asked.

Tom was saved from replying by Tommy Fowkes bringing him a large tumbler filled with brandy. He raised the glass to Lord Aston.

'Your very good health, my lord.'

'And yours also, Constable Potts.' Lord Aston raised his own glass, and a chorus of good wishes towards Tom echoed around the room.

'I shall summon a grand jury this very day,' Aston announced, 'and the moment that a true bill is declared against those villains you can transport them both to Worcester Gaol to await their trial.'

Tom drew a deep breath and summoned all his courage. 'My lord, may I speak with you and Mr Blackwell in private?'

Aston frowned in surprise. 'In private, Constable? What is it that you have to say that cannot be heard by the rest of these gentlemen?'

'Matters pertaining to the two accused, my lord, which I believe you may wish to keep your own counsel on,' Tom said.

His words were greeted with an outburst of resentful exclamations from the vestrymen.

'You'm acting very high and mighty all of a sudden, Potts,' Jason Holyoake scowled. 'We'm all men of honour and probity here, and let me tell you that we can be trusted to keep our own counsels as well as any high-born gentlemen in this land.'

'I mean no offence to you, Master Holyoake, or to any other gentleman present,' Tom assured him. 'But you must understand that in these matters there needs to be pre-trial secrecy at times. We are dealing with the life and death of two men here.'

It was Joseph Blackwell who smoothly intervened.

'Quite so, Constable Potts. Legal proprieties must be observed very strictly in such serious crimes as we are dealing with here. I'm sure that every honourable gentleman in this room appreciates the need for us to observe the very letter of the law. Is that not so, gentlemen?'

There was a grudging murmur of acquiescence, and the vestrymen filed reluctantly out of the room.

'Well?' Aston frowned.

Tom's mouth was dry, his heart was pounding and for an instant he quailed.

'Well? I'm waiting,' Aston demanded impatiently.

'It's about the men I've arrested, my lord,' Tom stammered nervously. 'I'm no longer sure they are guilty of these crimes.'

'You're not sure?' Aston's face turned puce as he barked angrily. 'Not sure? Then why in hell's name did you arrest them? Not sure?' He swung on Joseph Blackwell. 'Haven't I always said that this lanky gangly bugger is a buffoon? Here's the proof of it!'

Blackwell's pallid features remained impassive, and he asked Tom calmly, 'What is the reason for your doubt, Master Potts?'

'There is another strong suspect in this case, sir.' Tom was grateful for Blackwell's calm reaction. 'But I need to keep the other two in custody until I can obtain proof of this new suspect's guilt. So for the time being it is necessary that the town continues to believe in Jenkins' and Payne's guilt, so as not to put this new suspect on his guard.'

'Why the devil should we place any further trust in your judgement, you damned clown,' Aston sneered, 'when on your own admittance you have arrested two innocent men?'

'With all respect, my lord, his admittance that he may have made a mistake is the very reason why we should place trust in his judgement,' Blackwell stated firmly. 'Just think how easy it would have been for him to continue basking in this universal admiration, instead of being honest with us to his own detriment.'

Blackwell's words gave Aston pause for thought, and after a brief reflection he nodded. 'You have a point there, Master Blackwell.' Then he scowled at Tom. 'Very well, Potts, I shall allow you further time to bring the killer to book. But hear me well, if you fail I shall ensure your life will no longer be worth the living. Now get out of my sight!'

Tom went disconsolately back to the lock-up. The yeomanry troopers were still there, under the command of Erasmus Dolton, who was greatly relishing the role of guarding the murderers.

He greeted Tom genially. 'Hullo there, Constable. You've no

need to hurry back here, you know. Not while I'm commanding the guard. Wild bulls couldn't get past me, I can tell you.'

'I'm sure they couldn't, Sergeant Dolton,' Tom replied civilly, and on impulse enquired, 'Does young Rowley the blacksmith ever do any work for you at your farm? Is he good at his work?'

'Yes, he does a bit for me. He fitted some new grilles on a couple of windows at my kennel house in Brockhill Wood a while back, and made a good job of it.' He grinned savagely. 'Why do you ask? Are you thinking of giving him the work of making Jenkins' and Payne's gibbet suits?'

'I was thinking of mentioning Rowley's name to Mr Blackwell, Sergeant.' Tom forced a grin. 'I was thinking I might well get a few shillings out of him for making the recommendation.'

'Ahr, you might indeed.' The other man laughed.

Tom went inside, telling himself, 'So, Rowley's definitely had access to that place. He could well have hidden Ann Washwood's gown there, couldn't he?'

Forty-Nine

Tom spent the remaining hours of the afternoon curry-combing the sorrel and carefully examining the resultant loose hairs, but found nothing that resembled a human hair. Next he turned to the harness, saddlery and blanket, but again drew a blank.

'I need to search Rowley's property, but how can I entice and keep him away from there?'

He went to stand at his window, staring blankly down at the road beneath, racking his brains for an inspiration.

But none came.

The door bell jangled loudly, and from the next room his mother shouted angrily, 'Thomasss? Thomasss? Will you answer that bloody bell? It's no wonder that I'm so sick and poorly, is it! I can't get a moment's peace and quiet in this vile place. If

ever another poor woman has suffered like I have, then I'd like
to meet her.'

'All right, Mother! All right!' Tom hurried downstairs and
unbarred the door. To find John Hollis smiling at him.

'Well, Tom, how does it feel to be the toast of the district?'

'It feels damned uncomfortable, John. Because I'm likely to
be burnt toast very soon. Come, let's walk and talk.'

He locked the door and led his friend towards the Chapel
Green, urgently relating all that had happened since their last
meeting.

Hollis listened in silence until Tom at last fell silent, and
then asked, 'What do you want me to do?'

'I need you to get Rowley away from his yard, and to keep
him away long enough for me to make a thorough search.'

The other man chuckled. 'There's no need to trick him
away. He's away off to Bromsgrove to do some shoeing. He
reckons he'll be staying there tonight and coming back late
tomorrow.'

'Are you sure?' Tom demanded eagerly.

'Yes, I saw him on the road when I was coming here. We
passed the time of day, and I asked him where he was off to
with his travelling workshop.'

'And you're definite about this? That it was him?' Tom
pressed.

'Of course I am. I've known him for years.'

'Thank you, God! Thank you a million times!' Tom prayed
in fervent gratitude, and clapped Hollis on the shoulder. 'Come
on, my friend. We've work to be doing.'

Fifty

'**W**hy can't we get an ass?' Siobhan Docherty petulantly
demanded for the twentieth time that day, and for the
twentieth time Ricardo Pozo wearily answered her, 'Because
we haven't got enough money to buy one.'

'Well, I'm sick and tired o' humpin' this bloody great pack. It's near on breaking me back, so it is. And now I'm carrying a babby inside me as well, as if this bloody pack weren't bad enough,' she complained bitterly

'Oh, come now, sweetheart, it's not that heavy. You've only a few ribbons in it, and your own clothes. I'm carrying all the heavy stuff, aren't I?' he riposted good-naturedly.

'When I was with me da and ma I didn't have to carry anything. We had our asses to do that for us. We lived like proper travellers, so we did.'

'Look, honey, as soon as we get enough money put by, then I swear I'll buy you a fine ass, and you can ride everywhere, like a lady.'

'And pigs might fly!' she muttered sulkily.

'Well, we've not far to go now.' He was trying his best to cajole her. 'Come tonight we'll be sitting at our ease in Mother Readman's kitchen, drinking good ale and eating a fine thick beefsteak. How does that sound to you?'

'Like all the rest of your fuckin' promises!' she spat irately into his smiling face. 'I'll only believe it when I'm there wi' me mouth full o' grub and drink.'

He gusted a sigh of resignation, and the couple trudged on along the dusty road leading from Worcester to Redditch in dour silence.

The hours lengthened and by the time they had passed through its long High Street and left the town of Bromsgrove behind them the skies were darkening with night.

Siobhan's heels had blistered and she was limping, so Ricardo was now carrying both of their packs.

'We've only about five miles to go now, sweetheart,' the young man tried to encourage her.

'I need to sit down and rest for a bit,' she snapped pettishly. 'Me feet are burning like lumps o' fire and near killing me, and there's you rushing along like a fuckin' racehorse, and dragging me along with you like I was a dog.'

'All right, darling.' He readily acceded and they halted and sat down on the roadside bank.

The wind was rising, and spatters of rain fell randomly upon the woodlands and stretches of open heath, the falls increasing in density, threatening to turn into a downpour.

'If it's coming on to storm maybe we should find shelter for the night?' Ricardo stared anxiously at her. 'I don't want you getting soaked to the skin, it might hurt the babby.'

'"It might hurt the babby",' she mimicked irritably. 'And what about me, you rotten hound? Never mind the babby.'

He stood and stared about him, but could not see far through the intervening gloom. 'If I remember rightly, there's a cottage over there somewhere. We could try and find shelter there.'

'I'm not traipsing around looking for a cottage that you don't even know for rights is there, you bloody idjit you! You go and find it, and then come back for me. Me feet are so sore I can't go another step.'

He stood undecided, his expression troubled.

Another chill flurry of rain swept over them, and she shouted, 'Go off now, will you? Don't stand there like a bloody mawkin while I catches me death o' cold!'

'I'll be as quick as I can, honey,' he assured her and hurried away into the darkness.

Siobhan pulled her shawl closer around her head and shoulders, and sat miserably waiting.

Time passed slowly and her impatience for Ricardo's return mounted. Under her breath she was cursing his lengthening absence when she sighted the twin glows of cart lamps approaching from the direction of Bromsgrove.

'Thank God for that. With any luck we'll get a lift.'

She got to her feet and went towards the lights, calling eagerly, 'Please, are you going in the way of Redditch?'

The driver halted the vehicle, and got down to meet her.

As she entered the light of the lamps he drew breath sharply, and told himself with a surge of excitement, 'She'll do! She'll do very well!'

'Ahr, very well, young man, you and your missus can shelter here for the night. But I've only the floor to offer you, wi' a bit o' sacking to soften it,' the elderly cottager told Ricardo.

'My thanks to you. I'm really grateful. We both are. I'll be back very shortly.'

'Take care you don't fall into a ditch. Some on 'em are overgrown and hard to see it when it's dark and rainy like tonight.'

'I know, I nearly fell into one on my way here. I'll see you shortly, and thank you again.' Ricardo hurried away from the cottage, anxious to get back to Siobhan. 'She'll be bloody angry at me taking so long to find the cottage. But I can't help how dark it is, can I?'

Peering ahead he could vaguely see a pair of glowing lights. Then a terrified shrieking reached his ears.

'Siobhan?' Propelled by fear he broke into a run, and the next instant his leading foot met empty air and he went headlong into the deep ditch, crashing his temple against the further edge, knocking himself senseless.

It was the heavy rain drumming upon his face that brought him slowly back to skull-pounding, nauseous consciousness.

Not knowing how long he had lain senseless, panic whelmed over him, and dragging himself upright he stumbled on towards the road, screaming at the top of his voice, 'Siobhan? Siobhan? Where are you? Where are you, honey? Siobhaaannn?'

Fifty-One

'We have to get out of here. Rowley might be back at any moment. He said he'd return tonight, didn't he?' John Hollis had left his post of lookout at the cul-de-sac entrance to come into the upper bedroom of the small house and warn Tom.

'Not yet.' Tom shook his head. Despite not having slept or eaten for many hours, his energy was fuelled by what he had already discovered during the previous night and the course of this day. 'I'm absolutely sure that he's our man, John!' he declared confidently. 'All I need to find now is something that will convince a jury beyond all doubt.'

The beam of light from his bulls-eye lantern flickered and died.

'God damn it!' he cursed. 'The bloody candle's gone. It's a good job I brought another with me.'

The darkness hid the doubt on John Hollis' face, but Tom

could still detect the doubt in his friend's voice. 'But how can you be so sure that he's our man?'

While Tom replaced the candle and struck sparks with flint and steel against tinder, he reiterated his reasons.

'The high beam hook in the shed next to the stable, John, and the ground beneath it. Didn't I demonstrate to you in my room this morning that the dirt was saturated with mammalian blood, and show you the maggot pupae that I'd dug up? That hook was where he hung Ann Washwood when he eviscerated her. And that bundle of women's clothing that I found buried in the midden heap – why would he have shoved it in there, if not to hide it? And there were human hairs on those clothes, weren't there? Pubic hairs which looked like the pubic hair I took off the headless body before we buried it. And what about the other hair I found on the clothes? The different coloured hair? That must be Rowley's!'

'But old rags rot down into manure, don't they, Tom? We all chuck our rags onto midden heaps. And truth to tell, all I could see when I looked through your microscope was tiny tubes that could have been any sort of colour,' Hollis argued. 'And the high hook and the blood in the shed doesn't mean it was Washwood that was hung there to be slaughtered. It could have been a sheep or a dog, or even a damned cat! And what else have you found? Nothing! And you've searched every inch of this place now, haven't you?'

'No!' Tom shook his head and shone the beam of light onto the trapdoor set between the low ceiling beams. 'I haven't looked up there yet.'

'Oh leave it for now, Tom,' Hollis urged anxiously. 'If he comes back and catches us in his house, he could charge us with breaking and entering with intent to rob. We could end up in jail, or even bloody well transported for seven years.'

Tom ignored his friend, and dragging the bed under the trapdoor, stood on it and pushed the trap open. His great height enabled him to lever his shoulders through the narrow hatch and he shone the lantern beam around the steep-pitched rafters and the wooden floor of the loft. The light shone on a row of wooden buckets at the far end. He pulled himself fully through the hatch, and on hands and knees crawled to them.

'Well?' Hollis' strained nerves were making his voice sound

unnaturally high-pitched. 'Is there anything? Do be quick, Tom, for pity's sake! Rowley could be back here at any moment!'

'There are buckets. And they're full of vinegar, by the stink of it.' Tom's voice throbbed with excitement.

'Vinegar?' Hollis ejaculated. 'Then they're probably full of pickled onions! For God's sake, let's get out of here!'

He heard the splashing of liquid, and a cry of shock, followed almost immediately by Tom's triumphant shouting.

'They're pickles right enough, John! But not onions! There's a pickled human head in this one! We've got Rowley now! We've got the bastard!'

Tom lowered himself back through the hatch and closed it, then moved the bed back to its original position. He was smiling with elation.

'What shall we do?' Hollis wanted to know.

Tom pulled out his pocket watch and squinted at its dial. 'It's just turned midnight. Time for some supper I think, John.'

'Supper?' Hollis stared at Tom as if he feared for his sanity. 'Time for supper?'

Buoyed up by success, Tom was feeling amazingly clear-headed, charged with energy and above all else, totally elated.

'Yes, it's time for supper. We'll leave this place as we found it. Then we'll go to the lock-up, and while you keep a lookout for Rowley to appear, I'll get us something to eat. I don't know about you, but I'm starving!'

John Hollis shook his head bemusedly. 'My God, Tom, and people say that I'm a lunatic.'

The rain clouds had passed over, the misty murk had dissipated and now the moon shone clearly and all was quiet and still in the town's streets, alleys and courts. The only sounds to occasionally break the silence around the lock-up was an occasional cough, or shuffled footsteps from the succession of yeomanry sentries standing their stint of the night guard.

Tom and Hollis sat companionably munching bread and ham at the small upstairs window overlooking Alcester Street and the entrance to the cul-de-sac lane.

'Rowley must have decided to stay another night in Bromsgrove,' Hollis remarked.

'No matter if he has.' Tom smiled grimly. 'We can take turns to get some sleep, and keep watch until he appears.'

'But wouldn't it be better if we told what we've found, at least to Blackwell? He might well say that we should raise an immediate hue and cry for Rowley.'

'No!' Tom shook his head in emphatic rejection. 'If there's one thing that I've learned about this town, John, is that if a sparrow farts in Brecon at crack of light, it's known all through the town before the sun shows its face. If we were to even whisper to anyone about what we've found tonight, then it would be being shouted from the rooftops before we could even close our mouths again.'

'True enough,' Hollis admitted ruefully.

A shouted challenge sounded from the front of the lock-up, followed by voices raised in noisy altercation.

'What's happening?' Tom wondered aloud. 'Stay and keep watch, John. I'll go down.'

Outside he found the two sentries forcibly restraining a third man.

'What's going on here?'

'It's this young bugger, Constable. He's fuckin' drunk, or mad, or both,' one sentry growled.

In the clear moonlight Tom could recognize the dishevelled young man's sweat-streaming face, and see how distraught he looked.

'You're Ricardo Pozo, the pedlar, aren't you? What's the problem here?'

'She's been snatched from me! She's been took! And I can't find her. You've got to help me! You've got to send out search parties!' Pozo was half mad with desperation. 'You've got to help me look for her! You've got to!'

Premonition struck into Tom's mind. 'Who's she? Your sweetheart, is it? Siobhan Docherty?'

'Yes, yes, she's my Siobhan! She's been snatched. Took from the side o' the bloody road!'

'Let him go,' Tom ordered, and taking Pozo's arm led him into the lock-up. 'Now calm down, and try to tell me exactly what's happened.'

Pozo, half sobbing, hiccupping, gasping for breath, tumbled out his story of what he had heard and seen. Tom made him repeat his account several times and as he listened his initial sensation of premonition inexorably strengthened, dread tightening his throat and chest so that it became almost a struggle to draw air into his lungs. But his mind was grappling with the problem and trying to formulate a course of action.

Speed was absolutely essential, because Pozo could only give the vaguest estimate of the time elapsed since the girl's abduction. The thought drilled sickeningly through Tom's head, 'It may well be already too late to save her.'

'Which way did you come back here?'

'Through Headless Cross and down the Mount Pleasant,' Pozo told him, and then shouted in frustration, 'We'm wasting time! Why won't you go and get search parties looking for her, instead o' standing here asking me the same things over and over again?'

Before Tom could make a move to prevent him, the young man slammed back out of the front door and ran out into the night screaming frantically at the top of his voice, 'Siobahaannn? Siobhaaannn? Where are you? Where are you? Siobhaaann? Siobhaaannn?'

Tom went upstairs to Hollis and quickly related what had happened, finishing grimly, 'I think it's Rowley who's abducted her. In fact, I'm bloody sure of it.'

'Well? Shall we call out the people and form search parties?'

Tom shook his head. 'There's no time for that now, John. In fact I fear that it may already be too late to save the girl.' He paused briefly, turning over possible courses of action in his mind, then decided, 'You remain here and keep watch for Rowley's return, John. I've an idea where he might have taken her; and I need to get there as quickly as I can.'

'Where?'

'Vincent's old slaughter shed, down the Red Lane.' Tom went to his room, and snatched up his satchel. With trembling hands he primed and loaded the brace of pistols, then returned downstairs and led his hired horse through the cell passage and out to the road. He fixed its bridle and bit in place, mounted bareback and kicked it into a gallop.

The yeomanry sentries stared after him with puzzled faces.

'What the fuck does he think he is? A cavalry rough-rider?' One of them grinned, and the other chuckled.

'I'll lay odds that he comes off and breaks that long scrawny neck of his afore he gets to the crossroads.'

'Taken, at two pints to one!'

Tom didn't come off the horse, but he had great trouble in

controlling its wild gallop, and it took all his strength to bring it to a halt at the entrance to the narrow lane where the slaughter shed was situated. He tethered his mount to the remnants of a picket fence, and for a few moments stood listening hard for any sounds that might be human. Then driven by his terrible fear for the girl he took the pistols from the satchel and moved cautiously on with one in each hand, struggling to control his heavy loud breathing and to steady his shaking hands and legs.

At the entrance to the gravelled yard of the slaughter shed, Tom's heart thudded violently as he saw the open doors and the glow of lantern light within.

'He's here! The bastard is here!'

Nervous tremors fluttered through him as he watched and waited, straining his ears for any sounds, trying desperately to gather his courage.

After what was only brief moments, but what seemed to him to be endless hours, he summoned enough resolve to move towards the shed, shuddering inwardly as his heavy boots crunched loudly upon the gravel.

He reached the open door with his pistols levelled before him, and emitted a strangled gasp of horror when he saw the naked body of the girl spreadeagled across the huge chopping block.

'I'm too late!' the thought dinned into his mind. 'I'm too late!'

The cudgel exploded against the back of his head. His fingers involuntarily tightened on the triggers, and the pistols exploded, sending their lead balls into the opposite wall.

'Welcome back, Master Potts.' Davy Rowley smiled down into Tom's face. 'You've been so long asleep that I feared I'd killed you. Of course, I am going to kill you, but first I want you to witness what I do to this whore.'

Absolute terror whelmed over Tom as he realized that he was trussed and gagged, and completely helpless. With an ease that demonstrated his immense physical strength, Rowley lifted Tom and dragged him across the floor to prop him up against the wall.

'There now, Master Potts, from here you'll be able to see exactly what I'm going to do to the whore.' Rowley smiled, and patted Tom's cheek. 'And then I shall do the same to you.

Send you to your Maker, minus a few parts of your anatomy.' He shook his head, smiling deprecatingly. 'You'll be much more likely to be allowed to enter the Kingdom of Heaven if you're minus those great clod-hopping feet of yours. They made so much noise that I heard you coming a mile off.'

Tom's eyes focused on Siobhan Docherty, and horror flooded through him as he realized that she was conscious, and helplessly bound and gagged like himself.

Rowley's eyes glistened with an unholy joy as he went to stand over the huge chopping block and stare avidly down at her squirming body.

'What a waste of such beautiful flesh, Master Potts.' He shook his head regretfully. 'But I might as well enjoy it before I dismember it.'

He unbuttoned the flap of his breeches.

Tom tried to hurl himself forwards, but only crashed face down onto the ground. Blood spouted from his smashed nose, and the agony of his physical pain was matched by the mental agony of his failing to save the girl.

A momentary roar filled his ears, and he twisted his head and saw Rowley slowly sinking down onto his knees, jets of blood gouting from a hole in the centre of his forehead.

A black shadowed bulk loomed, and the voice of Josiah Danks sounded in Tom's ears.

'I was looking for them Brummagem poachers, Tom, and I heared the shots going off. So I come down here and listened for a while.' He fondly stroked the barrel of his Brown Bess musket. 'She's taught him a lesson, aren't she. She's taught him that he can't frighten my kids, and walk away with it!'

Tom heard little or nothing of the words, because he had fainted with relief.

Fifty-Two

Tom groaned in pain as Hugh Laylor carefully kneaded and straightened his broken nose, then applied plaster and bandage.

'There now, Master Potts, don't touch it, or blow it, and it should be working as good as new within a couple of weeks or so, albeit a trifle crooked perhaps.' Laylor chuckled amusedly and held the looking glass for Tom to see into. 'But then, you were not by any stretch of imagination ever an Adonis, were you?'

Tom stared at the reflection of his two swollen blackening eyes peeping over the great splodge of plaster and bandage bisecting his face and muttered in rueful agreement, 'No, Doctor, nor never will be now, I fear.'

It was an hour after dawn and the two men were in Tom's room in the lock-up. From the street outside the humming noise of many voices penetrated the leaded windowpanes and Laylor clapped Tom's shoulder.

'There's hundreds waiting to give you a cheer, Master Potts. You're the hero of the hour. Let me offer you my own sincere congratulations in catching that murderous bastard, Rowley. My God! You proved yourself to be too artful for him, did you not! That's what the people are calling you now, you know. Tommy Artful.'

'The girl? Siobhan Docherty? Is she truly all right?' Tom enquired anxiously.

'Oh yes,' Laylor assured him. 'She's suffered a few bruises and abrasions, and obviously had a bad fright. But she'll get over it. But never mind her now, Master Potts. Mr Blackwell and the gentlemen of the vestry are already gathering at the Fox and Goose to do you honour, and Lord Aston is on his way there also. So I suggest you attend upon them post-haste.'

Waves of absolute weariness were shuddering through Tom,

and his head was throbbing painfully. The very last thing he wanted at this moment was to be lionized by anyone, and least of all by Lord Aston and his sycophants.

'John Hollis, Doctor? Where is he?'

'Where I've been this last hour, Tom.' The door opened and John Hollis' smiling face appeared around its edge. 'Waiting out here for the doctor to finish ministering to you.'

'Come on in, John, please.' Tom beckoned and his friend came to him exclaiming enthusiastically.

'Congratulations, Tom. You've exceeded all my expectations.' He took Tom's hand and wrung it up and down. 'I hope they give you the reward you thoroughly deserve.'

'Any reward I might receive will be shared equally with you, and with Josiah Danks, John. Where is he, by the way?'

'He's in the Fox, being bought rum by all and sundry, and by now he'll be well on the way to getting drunk, I shouldn't wonder,' Hollis told him.

'I doubt that,' Tom murmured dryly. 'He's an ex-marine and is very well drilled in taking strong grog.'

Hollis became serious. 'All the buckets have now been emptied, Tom. There was that female's head, of course, and in the others there was the baby's body and what looks to be different bits of entrails and innards.'

'Probably poor Ann Washwood's,' Tom sighed. 'I can't help but wonder how many other poor souls that maniac may have butchered.'

'Oh, there are all sorts of wild rumours flying about concerning that, Tom. Every unsolved murder throughout the country for these last ten years is being blamed on Rowley. But we'll never know the truth of it.' Hollis shook his head. 'Speaking for myself, I think he's only begun this killing spree very recently, starting with the headless woman.'

'I hope to God you're right,' Tom said quietly.

Hugh Laylor had replaced his implements back into his medical chest, and now he stared quizzically at Tom.

'I take it that you'll be releasing Mr Jenkins and Mr Payne immediately, Master Potts? With all due apologies, of course.'

'They'll receive no apology from me!' Tom stated vehemently. 'I loathe the pair of them, worthless evil scum that they are!'

Laylor chuckled, and admitted wryly, 'Well, there is some

justification for your description of them, I agree. But they are innocent of these crimes, and you must now release them.'

'Oh no he mustn't! He mustn't let them bastards go free at all.'

The three men stared in shock at the strident-voiced woman who had so suddenly appeared in the doorway.

Grinning with fierce triumph, Nance Harper strode into the room and with hands on hips confronted Laylor face to face.

'My sarft little mate, Sal Payne, has come to her bloody senses at last. She's going to swear charges against 'em both, for setting them dogs on her to tear her to bloody shreds. And for battering her when she tried to get away from 'em. And you ought to be bloody well ashamed o' yourself for not reporting the bad evil sods yourself, Laylor, when you was called in to patch the poor little bugger up.'

Laylor's handsome features were a kaleidoscope of changing emotions – shock, indignation, chagrin and dismay.

Tom experienced a rapidly energizing elation, and demanded, 'Is she really going to swear charges, Mrs Harper, or will she change her mind when the time comes?'

'Oh no!' Nance Harper shook her tousled head vigorously. 'She won't change her mind. I've seen to that.'

Tom rose from his chair, forcing himself to ignore the nauseous giddiness which struck through his head and body.

'Then I shall come with you this instant to speak with her, and Master Hollis will come also, to bear witness to what she tells me.'

Laylor lifted his hand as if to bar Tom's way, and protested weakly, 'But what about Lord Aston and the vestry, Master Potts? They are all waiting to do you honour.'

Tom stepped forwards, compelling the other man to stand aside.

'I trust that you will explain to Lord Aston and the gentlemen of the vestry, Doctor, the reason why I am unavoidably detained from attending upon them.' He couldn't help but smile with grim amusement. 'After all, having forced me to become a very reluctant parish constable, they surely cannot complain if I am now trying my best to carry out my imperative lawful duties, and put those duties before the pleasure of their company.'

He bowed to Nance Harper, and invited her delightedly, 'Lead on, ma'am, I beg you. Lead on to Silver Street.'